# THE

### *Four years old and better than ever!*

We're celebrating our fourth anniversary...and thanks to you, our loyal readers, "The Avon Romance" is stronger and more exciting than ever! You've been telling us what you're looking for in top-quality historical romance—and we've been delivering it, month after wonderful month.

Since 1982, Avon has been launching new writers of exceptional promise—writers to follow in the matchless tradition of such Avon superstars as Kathleen E. Woodiwiss, Johanna Lindsey, Shirlee Busbee and Laurie McBain. Distinguished by a ribbon motif on the front cover, these books were quickly discovered by romance readers everywhere and dubbed "the ribbon books."

Every month "The Avon Romance" has continued to deliver the best in historical romance. Sensual, fast-paced stories by new writers (and some favorite repeats like Linda Ladd!) guarantee reading *without* the predictable characters and plots of formula romances.

"The Avon Romance"—our promise of superior, unforgettable historical romance. Thanks for making us such a dazzling success!

# HOSTAGE HEART

## EILEEN NAUMAN

**AVON**
PUBLISHERS OF BARD, CAMELOT, DISCUS AND FLARE BOOKS

HOSTAGE HEART is an original publication of Avon Books. This work has never before appeared in book form. This work is a novel. Any similarity to actual persons or events is purely coincidental.

AVON BOOKS
A division of
The Hearst Corporation
105 Madison Avenue
New York, New York 10016

Copyright © 1987 by Eileen Nauman
Published by arrangement with the author
Library of Congress Catalog Card Number: 87-91600
ISBN: 0-380-75420-7

First Avon Printing: December 1987

AVON TRADEMARK REG. U.S. PAT. OFF. AND IN OTHER COUNTRIES, MARCA REGISTRADA, HECHO EN U.S.A.

Printed in the U.S.A.

K-R 10 9 8 7 6 5 4 3 2 1

To
Oh Shinnah,
Tineh medicine woman and crystal healer,
and
Richard Graves,
Cherokee medicine man,
and
Rene Anderson,
medicine woman.


Thank you for showing me
the way of The People.
Chichin Chia.

# Chapter 1

Dark, swollen cumulus clouds rose over the barren Arizona foothills, casting shadows across scraggly oaks and twisted pinyon pines. Matt Kincaid hunched his shoulders as his gunmetal-gray gelding traversed the raw cinnabar-colored land. He kept his eyes down and narrowed on the rocky, cactus-strewn escarpment as the lethargic gelding stolidly continued the upward climb.

The hoofprints of several shod horses were barely discernible on the pebble-hard ground; evidence that the red dust had been disturbed, the break of a twig on a low-lying mesquite bush, or the flattened stalks of hardy buffalo grass were all he had to follow the Apache murderers of his wife, Katie, and his six-year-old daughter, Susan. Kincaid's mouth tightened and sweat ran in glistening rivulets down the uncompromising length of his solid, unshaven jaw. His bloodshot gray eyes burned with an inner hatred that hadn't left him during the four weeks he had relentlessly tracked Ga'n and his renegade cohorts.

The sun set early, snuffed out by the encroaching thunderclouds rolling in from the Hualapai Mountains in the west. A pregnant lull settled around Kincaid. His horse plodded on, head hanging, feet stumbling every few strides. That was how Matt felt—bone-weary. Every time he remembered returning home to his small, successful ranch outside Tucson and finding his family dead, his exhaustion was torn away by anger.

He had returned home unexpectedly from Tucson and found Ga'n and his band in the midst of raiding his ranch. While his house burned to the ground, he'd tried to save his wife and child—to no avail. Two crosses now stood near where his home and his dreams lay in ruins.

Matt would never go back to that land. He'd sold everything except the cemetery plot. He had nothing to live for now except revenge. Ga'n was going to pay with his life.

The gray picked his way delicately across a rocky slope, avoiding larger rocks that could cause him a stone bruise on the sensitive soles of his shod hooves.

Matt glanced up briefly, glaring at the vanguard of storms ready to break around him at any moment. Dusk was closing in on him like a shadowy predator. A bitter pang shot through him: the rain would wipe out any trace of Ga'n.

Matt's gaze moved methodically as he urged his horse to a faster pace. The wind whipped around him in frenzied patterns, a harbinger of the storm following on its heels. Matt's eyes wrinkled at the corners as he squinted, trying to separate shadow from substance on a small bluff covered with pine trees. His mouth compressed into a single line as he studied one particular rock formation. Or was it a rock? His brows dipped. Was it Ga'n on his rangy buckskin sitting up there on the promontory or just dusk light playing tricks on his vision? Matt wiped his watering eyes with the back of his gloved hand and blinked, studying the formation more closely.

Forks of lightning lanced out like a rattler's tongue as the first storm raced down the slopes. Damn. Out of habit, he ran his fingers down the neck of his horse to calm the gelding. It was a nervous gesture he'd acquired during his Civil War days when he had led his men on cavalry charges into the mouths of enemy cannon.

Tension knotted in Matt's hard belly. He sensed danger. The hair stood up on the back of his darkly sunburned neck. But was the danger real or imagined? He knew from experience that chasing Ga'n for thirty-six to forty-eight hours at a time without sleep could play tricks on his mind and eyesight. It made shadows resemble the Apache and sent screaming tension through him, leaving him with a pounding heart and a shaky weakness. Kincaid wiped his mouth and pulled the horse to a stop. The gelding, exhausted from the two-day marathon, stumbled badly, his mouth opening to escape the curb bit.

The wind was picking up, chasing away the squalid stillness. The buffalo grass and grama grass, long and green from recent rains, bent their thick, graceful stalks to the will of the surging gusts. The gray horse snorted, shaking his head, his ears pricked. The chaps that hung over the back of the saddle slapped against the animal's rear legs. The horse whinnied plaintively, fighting his rider's hand.

Without thinking, Matt tightened his grip around the horse's barrel, hesitating. He stared hard up toward the rocks, waiting for the next streak of lightning to illuminate the murky crest of the bluff. Matt's mouth went dry and his throat constricted as he waited those heart-pounding moments. What the hell was he doing? By remaining out in the open, he was an easy target for Ga'n to spot. Dazed with exhaustion, Matt realized his normally sharp senses were dulled. Cursing beneath his breath, he felt a sensation of helplessness uncoiling in his gut. That same feeling had descended on him when he had ridden into the yard and discovered Katie and Susan lying in a pool of blood in front of the burning ranch house. Anguish filled his gray eyes as the tortured past roared upon him, making him vulnerable for one split second.

Just as lightning cracked with frightening closeness, the roar of a Henry repeating rifle was muffled by the storm's descending fury. The white-hot piece of lead slammed into Matt's left thigh, settling deep in the corded muscle and lodging next to the bone. The impact nearly knocked him off his startled mount. He automatically set his spurs to the flanks of his horse. The gelding sent a spray of dirt and rock behind him as they headed toward the closest arroyo for protection. Clamping one hand over his heavily bleeding leg, Matt stayed low against the gray's neck, urging him to put every last ounce of strength into getting away.

Hot, scalding tears streamed down Lark's cheeks, curving into the drawn corners of her mouth. She blinked twice to clear her vision and stared down at the freshly dug red Arizona earth. With the back of her calico sleeve, she wiped her eyes. It was no use; tears continued to fall unchecked. Her gaze shifted to a wooden cross over her mother's grave. Four seasons had passed since Mourning Dove had gone to the Big Sleep. Now . . . Lark forced her eyes to focus on the newly made Christian cross set forlornly over a second mound of earth next to her mother's grave.

A sob tore from her as she sank to her knees at the end of the burial mound, her work-worn fingers outstretched, as if to touch her father, Roarke Gallagher, one last time. He had been a loving and understanding father who had allowed her and her mother to keep the ways of the Tineh, the Apache. Lark hadn't totally understood the tenets of her father's complex religion; the Catholic priest who had brought her father's body back from town had muttered over the grave in an unintelligible language.

Her father, with his dark, auburn hair and eyes the color of the sky she loved so much, had been murdered yesterday outside Prescott. Lark's anguish warred with a violent anger that threatened to consume her. The priest, Father Mulcahy, had said her father had been found on the right fork of Denton Road. He'd been shot in the back.

Every month, Roarke took the buckboard to Prescott to pay the mortgage on their ranch and buy supplies. After visiting the Prescott Bank, owned by Jud Cameron, he would go over to the saloon for a couple of Irish whiskeys before buying supplies and returning home. Always, he would bring Lark some small gift, perhaps a piece of bright calico, which she loved to make into shirts, or a new pair of jeans.

This time her father had bought her a ready-made dress of the finest cotton that matched her blue eyes. Now it hung in the bedroom closet, untouched. The rest of the supplies her father had bought had been destroyed. The wallet containing the monthly wages for the wranglers was missing. The only other items that remained intact were the bankbooks Lark had found in her father's pocket.

Digging her fingers into the soft earth, Lark bowed her head, her waist-length black hair sliding across her shaking shoulders, forming a curtain to hide her tears and grief. Who had killed her father? He'd been a successful horse rancher, the animals he raised highly respected by the Prescott community. And then she wondered if the people's prejudice against Roarke for marrying an Apache woman nineteen years ago and siring a half-breed daughter had finally spilled over in the guise of a bullet in his back.

Why had they hated her and Mourning Dove? What had she and her mother ever done to harm the people of Prescott? Roarke Gallagher had bought ten thousand acres of land near Prescott and then gone east. He'd brought back the Kentucky Stud and settled down with Mourning Dove at his side. More tears fled down Lark's cheeks as she recalled how her father had spun story after story of how they had come to Prescott and established the Gallagher Ranch.

Both her parents were gone now. Tuberculosis had claimed her mother, as it had so many Apaches before her. A bullet had stripped her massive father from her.

Sniffing, Lark raised her head. Below her, concealed by blue spruce and fine-needled tamarack and evergreens, lay the Gallagher homestead, a sprawling building of logs and mortar. Now it was nothing more than a silent, empty shell. Suddenly the ranch—the vast network of mustang holding pens and outbuildings that held the mowed hay and grain—looked very large and unmanageable to Lark. At eighteen years old, she must now run Gallagher Ranch just as her parents had before her.

Trying to push away the heaviness in her heart, Lark realized she could no longer mourn her father's passing. The Apache way would be for her to darken her face, cut off her hair, and rub ashes into her scalp as a show of grief. She felt a wild need to wail like a wounded animal caught in a trap, her hot Apache blood clamoring to be expressed.

But she had a ranch to run, Lark sternly reminded herself. Soon, thirty mustang broodmares would begin foaling the Kentucky Stud's offspring. The foals would ensure the ranch's survival; money on the hoof to pay the mortgage so that she could keep the homestead. Resolve threaded through her hurt and anger and forced Lark to her booted feet. Roarke had always tried to temper her wild Apache ways with love and understanding. He counseled love of the enemy and turning the other cheek. Lark's blue eyes hardened as she stared fixedly down at the ranch. She could not understand or accept her father's strange beliefs. Among her people, the Chiricahua Apache, murder was always avenged by a member of the victim's family.

Her foreman, Paco Hernandez, slowly guided his jugheaded bay gelding up the hill to where she stood beneath the spreading bough of a pine tree. A weathered sombrero shaded his forty-year-old features. Lark brushed the red dirt off the knees of her Levi's. Lifting her chin, she wondered if her father's hired hands would stay on. The fifteen wranglers had held her father in high esteem, almost awe, but would they leave or stay?

Paco and his family had lived on the ranch for seventeen years. Miguel and five other hands had been with the ranch between five and fifteen years. Would they drift away now that her powerful father had left for the Big

Sleep? Would they leave and the ranch be gulped up by Cameron's evil bank? Lark's lips tightened as she walked toward Paco. *I'll die before Cameron gets our ranch. That snake of a man will never claim it. Never!*

"Señorita Lark?" Paco took off his sombrero as she approached. His round, tobacco-colored faced mirrored his own grief, his brown eyes permanently squinted from years of fighting the powerful rays of the sun. "The piebald mare . . . she paces her stall."

Lark halted. Already ranch responsibilities were pressing down on her shoulders. But with a sense of relief she realized that Paco was showing his allegiance by asking her to make the decision regarding the piebald.

"Is she waxing up?" A mare close to foaling time always swelled heavily with milk, the two teats forming a waxy substance on the end of each nipple.

Paco shook his head. "No, *patrona*. She merely paces the stall."

*Patrona.* Lark's shoulders sagged in relief. Paco had called her father *patrón*, or boss. Now he was acknowledging her as his leader.

"It will be a while yet, Paco. This is her first foal, and she's probably nervous about the forthcoming labor."

*"Sí, patrona."*

"Paco?"

*"Sí?"*

"The other hands . . ." Lark swallowed hard, a lump forming in her throat. Her hands knotted at her sides. Pushing past her fear, she forced out the words. "Who's staying and who's leaving?"

Paco's eyes widened. *"Qué, patrona?"*

"The other hands. Is anyone leaving because my father is dead?"

His white teeth showed from beneath the heavy black mustache. "You need not concern yourself, *patrona*. We all stay."

"Are you sure?" Her throat ached with unshed tears. Two years ago, Jud Cameron had called her father a collector of human garbage because he employed Mexicans, Negroes, and people of other races, who were considered by some to be little more than animals. Cameron, one of the most powerful men in Prescott, had been trying to buy their ranch for as long as Lark could remember. He was a man who hated any color except his own white skin. The fact that his thirty-thousand-acre ranch butted up against their property hadn't been lost on Lark. Cameron wanted their ranch. He'd *never* get it.

Chewing on her lower lip, Lark wondered if she could earn the wranglers' respect as her father had before her. She was a woman, not a man, yet the Apache way was to encourage a woman to be physically fit, to ride, shoot, and emulate the men.

Paco's grin deepened, and he wiped sweat off his furrowed brow. "You are his blood, *patrona*. No one knows horses better than you. The *patrón* said that you have the gift of working with horses. The Kentucky Stud favors you over your father and he admitted as much."

It was true. Her father's words came back to her. "Colleen, it's got to be the blend of your mother's and my blood that gave you a double dose of horse sense. The Apaches are the best horsemen in the southwest, and the Irish know good horseflesh. Between the two, you've got the best of both worlds." Lark had bowed her head. Such praise always made her feel good about herself, especially when the *pindah-lickoyee*, the white-eyes shunned her as a "half-breed squaw."

"It might not be enough, Paco."

"*Qué?*"

"Father handled the finances, I didn't." Frustration curdled deep within her. "I left school before I learned math. I don't know if I can handle the account books my father kept."

"*Patrona*, you will do it."

Despair and doubt filled Lark. She forced a feeble smile. The hired hands trusted her, believed in her. She couldn't let them down. "Yes."

"The *patrón* wanted us to round up the twenty-five mares in the western pasture in order to breed them to Huelga and Kentucky. We'll have to gather them from the nearby hills into a herd and then bring them here, to the corrals. This is the time of year that the mares come into season and are easy to breed. Do you want us to bring them in?"

Absently Lark nodded, already thinking ahead. She touched the yellow and red calico shirt where her heart lay. The pain of loss was almost tangible. *Oh, father, I love you so much. Why did Ihidnan, Supreme Being, have to take you? You said your god was a kind and loving god. I don't understand why he had you murdered.*

Lark forced herself back to the present. "Yes, take the hands, Paco, and bring in the mares."

"It may take up to a week to chase them out of the hills and bring them to the ranch, *patrona*. You will be left here alone with our families and the Old Ones, the elderly Apaches." It was more of a question than a statement.

Lark would run the ranch while the wranglers went to find the mares. "The only thing I must defend us against is Cameron's greed in wanting the mortgage money every month." Cameron was *hako* in Lark's opinion, a man who always took and never gave in return.

Paco's laughter was like the yip of a coyote. "Aiyee, *patrona*, I think you are right. Still . . . I could leave Rufus behind to protect you and the families."

Rufus was their Negro grub cook. He and his chuck wagon would be needed to feed the hardworking wranglers out on the trail.

"No, take Rufus along. We'll be fine." Lark realized that Paco needed to be persuaded that she was in charge. Squaring her shoulders and walking briskly down the hill, she gave the appearance of a leader, not a follower.

The rest of the day she spent in the office with the

account books, trying to understand the pages of numbers that stared back at her.

In her seventh year Lark had been told not to return to school. The prim teacher, Miss Somerset, had said she was incapable of learning, so she had been educated at home, along with the children of the hired hands, by her father until she was old enough to seek formal education in Prescott. There, Lark had stayed with Abe and Millie Harris, owners of the dry goods store, while she attended school. It was there in Prescott, during those painful four weeks, that Lark had realized all the whites except the Harrises hated her. And it was there that Lark had learned to hate Jud Cameron and his hired gun, Bo Shanks. She quickly pushed aside that painful period in her life when Shanks had embarrassed her in public. Unable to stand the ostracism, the prejudice, and Shanks shadowing her like a salivating wolf cornering a helpless victim, Lark had left Prescott, vowing never to return.

Lark buried her face in her hands, feeling the warmth of tears flooding her eyes again. The ranch house was so quiet, almost eerie. Where was her father's booming voice or the deep laugh that rolled like thunder from his chest? Raising her head, Lark turned to other pressing matters. The mortgage had just been paid. That meant that she had another month in which to gather the necessary monies for the next payment. She might not know much about math, but uppermost in her father's mind had always been payment of the mortgage—even if they starved, it would always be paid.

Roarke Gallagher had watched his parents' home stolen out from under them in Ireland. His parents had been poor potato farmers. And because they were Catholic, the English didn't renew the twelve-year lease on the soil they tilled. His parents had died early, broken in spirit and penniless. When he left to make America his new home, he swore he'd never allow that to happen to him.

Lark's mother, Mourning Dove, had been a fearless Chiricahua chief, a blood relative to Cochise. She had

fought valiantly against a band of marauding Comancheros and would have been taken captive if not for the
unexpected help of Roarke Gallagher, who was seriously
wounded during the melee. Mourning Dove had nursed
Roarke back to health, and they had fallen in love.
Roarke had convinced Mourning Dove to come with him
to the Prescott area, marry him, and help build a horse
ranch. Her parents had been brave people with generous
hearts. Lark missed them terribly.

Darkness fell, almost to Lark's relief. She stood at the
office window and looked up at the stars in the sky. The
ranch was still, all the wranglers having left earlier. She
was alone.

The urge to go for a walk won out over the need to
work on the account books, and she blew out the flame
in the hurricane lamp. Her footfalls were noiseless. She
wore the Apache kabuns, or moccasins, which had tough
leather soles that turned up in a distinctive tip. The rest
of the comfortable boot was made of soft calf leather that
was rolled up and cuffed just below her knees. As she
shut the door, the cool May air stirred her sluggish
senses. Lark lifted her chin and stared at the hill where
both her parents were buried. Quickly she turned away,
wanting to find solace against the pain in her heart, but
not knowing how.

Just as Lark stepped off the porch, she heard horses'
hooves. Frowning, she went back inside for the loaded
Winchester rifle. By the light of the full moon rising over
the mountains that circled the ranch, she could see the
silhouettes of two riders. Both were Apache.

Lark set the lantern on the porch swing, keeping the
rifle in a state of readiness. It wasn't uncommon for the
Tonto clan of the Apache to come for a trading visit. Or,
sometimes, one of Mourning Dove's relatives from the
Chiricahua band farther south would visit.

The lead rider was tall and lean, like a starving
mountain lion. As they slowed their ponies to a walk, a

hiss escaped Lark. In one motion, she tripped the lever action of the Winchester repeating rifle and held it against her shoulder, aiming it at the leader.

*"E-chi-ca-say!"*

Lark tensed as the lead rider came to a halt fewer than five feet from where she stood. "Ga'n! There is no greeting here for you!" she shouted. Ga'n, which meant Devil in Apache, was a renegade wanted by both the *pindah* and his own Apache people, who were also her people, the Chiricahua. Many years ago, Roarke Gallagher had come upon Ga'n alone and starving in the desert. Ga'n was fourteen at the time and had become conscious long enough to tell Roarke that his sister, Small Deer, had been raped and carried off by the band of whites who had attacked them. The rest of Ga'n's family had been brutally murdered. Lark's father had tended Ga'n's wounds and brought him back to the ranch to recover.

Since that time, Ga'n had sworn allegiance to Roarke and his family. That included Lark, whether she wanted Ga'n's protection or not.

Ga'n had spent years since then trying to find his sister. Small Deer had been sexually enslaved by a cattle baron near Phoenix named Jason Colburn. When Small Deer saw her chance to escape, she took it. She sought safety in Geronimo's rancheria, which was composed of over two hundred families, thinking she would be welcomed. But Small Deer had been stoned to death by the women who had accused her of willingly sleeping with a *pindah*. Ga'n had already declared war upon the whites and Mexicans for murdering his family. Once he learned of Small Deer's death, he attacked and killed his own people with the same reckless abandon.

Ga'n's face was broad, his black hair worn long and loose over his red cotton shirt and leather vest. "Is that any way for my sister to greet me?" he teased. He placed his rifle across his trousered thighs, studying her with amusement. He knew Lark felt uncomfortable in his presence, but that didn't bother him. Lark reminded him greatly of his lost sister. She had Small Deer's beauty, kindness, and generosity. And because Lark had played a key role in his recovery at the ranch, he would remain forever loyal to her.

Her heart beating like a sledgehammer, Lark stood her ground. She knew only too well of Ga'n's infamous exploits: he was a rebel who had left the peace talks that Cochise was trying to hold with representatives of the government. Ga'n had then set about terrorizing people on both sides of the border, angering whites, Apaches, and Mexicans alike. Wherever he went, he left a trail of rape, kidnapping, and brutal murder in his wake.

She sharply recalled Ga'n stealing her father's small supply of Irish whiskey while he convalesced at the ranch. The fire spirit of the *pindahs* held Ga'n in its ugly clutches to this day. Ga'n had once told her that whiskey was the only thing that dulled the pain of his family's death. Lark always feared Ga'n when he was drunk because he was *heyoke,* crazy. Her father had explained that the Apache warrior was filled with a hate that was eating him up. Later, after Ga'n had started his reign of terror, Roarke had commented sadly that he was sorry he'd saved the Apache's life. Now Lark quaked inwardly, watching Ga'n's large brown eyes.

"I am no sister to you, *hako!*" She deliberately hurled the insult at him; Ga'n was, indeed, a selfish person.

"*Hako* or not, I want to talk with Voice of Thunder."

Lark flinched. That was the name the Apache had given her father. "He's gone to the Big Sleep," she forced out.

Ga'n's brows slanted up. "Ho! Tell me no lies!"

Lark lowered the rifle, pointing toward the hill. "Then go to the pines. He sleeps beside my mother."

Rubbing his square jaw, Ga'n eyed her uneasily. "Who has done this? No doubt *pindah!* I will avenge his death."

"I don't know who killed him," Lark said wearily. "Now, what do you want?"

"Information."

"What kind?"

"There is a *pindah-lickoyee* hunting me."

"Geronimo has sent out a squad to hunt you down also, Ga'n. Why do you seem so surprised? Don't tell me the yellow legs are closing in on you."

Anger darkened Ga'n's features. "This is one *pindah!* He has followed us for one moon and we've not lost him. Three days ago, I wounded him. We lost his track after a storm. I know he is nearby, and I want his death!"

"We've seen no *pindah-lickoyee* through here for the past three weeks, Ga'n."

With a growl, Ga'n nudged his mustang closer, glaring down at her. *"Itna-iltc-'he!"*

Lark cocked the trigger and took a step back. "I tell you no lies, Ga'n! The day I stoop to a dog's underbelly as you have, then I will lie. There is no *pindah* here! You know they shun us as if we were ghosts."

Mirthlessly, Ga'n sawed on the mouth of his mustang. The horse backed up. "This *pindah* is dangerous to you, too, Lark Who Sings. He hates The People. He's wounded, and like a bear, he is angry and will strike out at anyone. Even you! If you are wise, you will tell me where he hides."

"He's not here! No one has seen him, Ga'n."

"Very well. We leave now. I will go toward Prescott to hunt him. If you do see him, send a rider."

Lark shook her head. "On this ranch, anyone can seek protection, Ga'n. You know that. If he comes here, he will remain in our protection."

"He's dangerous!"

"Probably because you've done something to him to make him hunt you down. You're like the Evil Owl, Ga'n; you stir up trouble in your flight. *Ugashi!* Go!"

Ga'n shrugged, curtly issuing orders to his partner, whom Lark recognized as Alchise. He stared down at her hard. "Did Voice of Thunder give you to a warrior before he died?" he taunted.

Lark blushed furiously. "No. I will choose my own warrior, Ga'n."

"Who would have a sharp-tongued shrew such as you?" And then amusement momentarily erased the darkness in his eyes. "I would have you, little sister."

"*Ugashi,* Ga'n! Waste no more of my time. You are not welcome here."

His smile was slight, reminding her of a weasel grinning. "I will be back."

Lark slowly lowered the rifle as the two Apache riders trotted away, heading up and over the hill, disappearing into the tree line. Shakily she touched her perspiring brow. Picking up the lantern, Lark went inside and barred the door. As she went through the motions of washing up for the night and donning her floor-length white cotton nightgown, exhaustion played havoc with her senses. Slipping into the brass bed, Lark was asleep in minutes. In her dreams, she saw a huge, wounded bear making his way down to her ranch. . . .

# Chapter 2

Matt watched as Ga'n and his war partner rode out of sight. His vision was deteriorating, sweat running down into his eyes, making them smart. He had brought his weary horse to a halt just inside the timberline that overlooked a large, sprawling ranch. Shivering from loss of blood and a three-day fever, he waited another hour before leaving the protection of the forest and moving down toward the ranch.

Had his vision deceived him? Had Ga'n stopped and actually *talked* to someone holding a rifle? Ga'n talk? Impossible. He must be delirious. No rancher would give the renegade safe passage. Clutching the horse's thick black mane, Matt was too weak to fight off another wave of dizziness. With a muffled groan he leaned forward, his brow pressed against the animal's neck in an effort not to fall off again.

Matt clung to the horse, knowing this was the beginning of another siege of delirium from the high fever. His left thigh was so swollen that the material around it had stretched to its limits. The heavy, throbbing ache was continual, and he knew somehow in his feverish state that lead poisoning had set in. He could die. At that thought, he called on his almost nonexistent reserve of strength. He would not die before Katie's and Susan's lives were avenged. Clenching his teeth, he felt another tidal wave of pain move through him. He felt light-headed. *No . . . can't fall off again . . . can't . . .*

The gelding stumbled to a halt next to the larger of two barns located side by side. At the nicker of horses nearby, Matt slowly raised his head, reorienting himself. Everything was dark, and there was no light or movement from the main ranch house or the two bunkhouses. No guards were posted, and he wondered why. At this time of night, it would be safer not to approach the house and possibly scare the owners, getting himself killed before he could explain who he was or that he needed help. No, it would be wiser to seek shelter in the barn and wait it out until daylight. Then he could ask for help without being shot first and asked questions later. Dismounting with difficulty, Matt pushed the horizontal bar off the two main doors.

The haymow was barely illuminated by the partly open door. Matt made his way toward it. If he could just lie down and sleep and know that he was safe from Ga'n. If only . . .

The sudden cry of a stallion jerked Matt momentarily out of his stupor. He leaned heavily against a roughly hewn oak timber. Damn. The ranch owners would be awakened by that squealing stud who was apparently stalled in the other barn and was busy kicking down the walls. Matt could hear the thunk of wood being struck by the angry animal. Dammit. Too weak to move, he rested against the beam.

The stallion's screams made Lark sit bolt upright in bed, her heart pounding hard in her breast. Her black hair, brushed until it shone like ebony, fell around her shoulders and breasts.

Had Ga'n returned? It would be typical of the renegade to lie and sneak back! He was probably in need of better mounts, having driven his own horses to exhaustion. Again she heard the Kentucky's shrill scream, muted through the log and mortar wall of the bedroom.

Kicking the sheet and quilt aside, Lark leaped out of bed. She groped for the Winchester rifle in the gun rack

near the dresser. Hands shaking, she quickly lit a lantern
to show her the way to the barn. Her black hair flew
behind her as she quietly opened the front door and sped
lightly across the dry earth toward the stud barn, the
loaded rifle at her side.

Above her, the stars hung close, cold, and silent. The
nearly freezing air seeped through her light cotton gown,
making her shiver.

Before she came to a halt, Lark saw the barn doors
were partially opened. Tension tightened her throat, and
her eyes grew wide. Was Ga'n back to "borrow" two
new horses and leave his own animals here instead?
Fighting down her anger, Lark wished mightily that she
had listened to Paco and kept at least one wrangler at the
ranch. It was a lesson hard learned. She would never
again leave the women, children, and herself open to
attack without a man around to lend his protection.

The high, trembling whinny of a broodmare greeted
Lark as she stood tensely in the doorway. The inside of
the barn was dim, and Lark couldn't see or hear anything.
Pindah made noise; Apaches did not. Ga'n must be
playing a trick on her, to humiliate her because she'd
spoken so sharply to him earlier. Yet in the back of her
mind, Lark knew that if Ga'n had wanted to wreak havoc,
he would have already raided the ranch. She knew she
was safe from his murdering ways. Instead, he was
playing a game with her. He wanted to teach her a lesson
for the way she, a woman, had spoken to him, an Apache
warrior. She didn't appreciate either his timing or his
joke.

In Apache, she called into the barn. "Come out of
there, Ga'n. I know you're in there. The time for games
is over! Come out. Now!"

Several of the twelve mares that were near foaling
whickered urgently in response, recognizing her voice.
Lark sensed their trepidation. Whoever was in there was
making them nervous. Her Irish temper overcame her
normally patient Apache blood. "Ga'n! How dare you

scare my mares. They're almost ready to foal! Come out of there right now, or I swear I'll shoot you! If you cause one mare to abort, I'll cut off your right ear. I swear it!''

No answer came, except for the movement of the mares in their stalls. Then an unfamiliar whinny greeted her ears. Lark knew each of her mare's neighs; each was as distinctive as a human voice. Raising the lantern, Lark began to enter the barn. Ga'n's childish game had gone far enough! She wished mightily for her trusted bowie knife, which she always wore. Her mother and old Ny-Oden had taught her how to use it for hunting as well as for defense. Right now, she would have preferred a knife instead of an unwieldy rifle.

"I'm coming in, Ga'n! You had best show yourself. I have a loaded rifle, and I'll shoot if you don't give up your game!" Taking a deep breath, Lark rounded the barn door and walked determinedly into the hay mow.

Matt froze when he heard the guttural Apache come from outside the door. Ga'n had found him! He broke into a heavy sweat, shaking badly in the grip of the fever. Leaning behind the solid oak beam, he turned sideways so he couldn't be spotted by the Apache. Drawing his Colt, he found he could barely hold the heavy pistol. Hate mixed with anger. All right, if Ga'n wanted him, he'd have to come after him. He had the advantage of being hidden deep in the barn. Apaches might be the world's best hunters and trackers, but they didn't have eyes in the backs of their heads. He squinted, forcing what little attention was left in his fevered mind on the opened doors. The Apache commands were becoming higher and more strident. Attack was imminent. Matt raised the pistol and positioned it against his other arm to steady it. He'd only have one chance. Savage satisfaction soared through him. One way or another, Katie and Susan would be avenged.

In the next instant, he saw a tall woman in a white

nightgown move cautiously around the opened door. He froze. A myriad of impressions assailed him. Her midnight hair swirled like a glorious cape around her shoulders and high breasts. Her slender body was silhouetted against the thin cotton of the simple gown. The glitter in her narrowed eyes as she slipped silently between the doors reminded him of a cornered cougar. He shook his head. What was going on? He could swear he had heard Apache. Was he delirious again? Was she a figment of his imagination?

As the woman drew closer, Matt could see the fear and determination on her face. He wasn't dreaming. She was real—a beautiful, wild animal. She placed the lantern on the peg of another beam, still holding the rifle with both hands. Confused and disoriented by the chain of events, Matt felt his left leg giving out. He lowered the pistol and slid it into the holster. The woman meant business with that Winchester. The trigger was cocked, and he knew that if he spoke, she'd shoot first and ask questions later. Luck turned in his favor. She had halted no more than five feet away, backing slowly toward him, looking toward the stalls.

Suppressing a momentary twinge of guilt, Matt lunged out from behind the beam. He threw one arm around her slender waist and grabbed the rifle with the other.

Lark gasped as an arm like steel jerked her backward off her feet. The rifle was torn out of her grasp and sailed harmlessly away from her. A scream clawed up her throat, her hair flying wildly as she struggled to free herself. A rough, callused hand clamped hard against her mouth, crushing her lips against her teeth. Her nostrils flared, and she drank in the sweet stench of blood and the smell of a white man. Fear ate away her previous anger. It wasn't Ga'n! Lark twisted, biting his fingers. He groaned and jerked away his hand.

She made a half turn, twisting to catch a glimpse of her captor. He towered over her. Though tall, she felt like a mere child against his powerful chest and broad shoul-

ders. The harsh planes of his face were frozen with—
what? A small cry escaped her and Lark tried to push
away from him. They both tilted off balance. She saw the
man tense and he gave a cry, his left leg suddenly
collapsing out from beneath him. They toppled to the
straw.

The air was knocked out of Lark as the man landed
heavily on top of her. She lay for several seconds,
stunned and gasping for breath, unable to move. The
sensation of a man's body touching hers was shocking.
No Apache man ever touched an Apache maiden. It was
forbidden before marriage. His hips ground into hers and
another electric sensation uncurled through her. Panicked
by the sudden turn of events, Lark began to struggle,
trying to pull her hands free.

Matt cursed, clamping one hand across her mouth and
capturing her wrists above her head. He lay on top of her,
both of them breathing heavily. Despite his fever and
weakness, he was wildly aware of her firm, young breasts
pressing into his chest. The soft yielding of her hips
beneath his sparked a primal animal urge in him. He
looked down, able to study her closely for the first time.
His voice came harsh and rasping.

"Quit struggling, I won't hurt you. I need your help."
Her huge blue-violet eyes widened. Slowly he removed
his hand. That mouth . . . He stared down at it: a full,
expressive mouth with corners that turned softly upward;
lips that were wildly sensual and begged to be tamed.

Lark ceased struggling. Terror mixed with confusion as
she heard the pain lacing his words. "What?"

He liked her slightly breathless voice, which reminded
him of mellow whiskey. "I need help. My name is Matt
Kincaid. I've been shot and I need a doctor." He saw the
fear dissolve in her luminous eyes; eyes in which a man
could lose his soul forever. She must be someone's wife.
The lucky bastard. Matt slowly loosened his hold on her
slender wrists. "If I let you go, will you stay? I've got
to have help."

Gulping unsteadily, Lark nodded once. Fire licked through her straining body as she felt each point of contact with him. The sensation wasn't unpleasant, and she was shamefully aware that her nipples were hardening beneath his chest. "Y-yes. I won't leave," she managed to say.

Matt rolled off her, releasing her completely. Too weak to move, he gave in momentarily to the pain and fever, rolling over on his back. Another wave of light-headedness assaulted him. He didn't fight it this time. Through half-closed eyes he watched the woman get slowly to her knees. He knew she would help him. Maybe it was her heart-shaped face, those eyes now fraught with concern and kindness, that told him so. Or was it the soothing touch of her cool hand upon his sweaty brow after she gently removed his hat? Matt didn't know. Closing his eyes, he gave in to his weakness.

"Wake up!" Lark begged, shaking his broad, powerful shoulders. In the dim light, she could see blood covering his left leg. The putrid smell of torn flesh stung her sensitive nostrils. The stench of blood and sweat mingled with the sour odor of his unwashed body and almost made her retch. Lark gripped his dirty cotton shirt and gave him another sharp shake. "Wake up! I can't help you unless I can get you to the house. You've got to get up!"

Lark struggled to her feet. He was a *pindah-lickoyee,* a white eyes . . . someone who hated her kind. But there was something about his broad, generous face, the curve of his mouth, and the look in his pain-filled gray eyes that pushed her defensiveness aside. She tried to analyze why this man had touched her heart as effortlessly as Holos, the Sun, caressed the meadow flowers with his warming rays. He tried a taut, one-cornered smile to reward her, and Lark's heart beat once in response to his unspoken thanks.

Lark gasped for breath as she tugged and pulled Matt Kincaid to his unsteady feet. She sagged beneath his weight. His arm went around her shoulders, and he leaned heavily on her, his head against her hair. She felt him shudder with each step they took.

"You can make it," she insisted, her arm wrapped tightly around his waist. "It's just a little way to the ranch house. Please, try . . ." She groaned as he leaned more heavily against her. If only one of the wranglers was present to help. None of the other women was as tall or as strong as she was, so there was no sense in waking them to get their help.

Matt bit back a groan, his head swimming, making it impossible for him to limp in a straight line. Despite his semiconscious state, he was aware of the woman's surprising strength. She reminded him of a lithe cougar. His six-foot, three-inch frame weighed nearly two hundred pounds yet she was supporting him. As he rested his face against her head, he inhaled the natural feminine sweetness of her hair. Beautiful hair, he thought disjointedly. Not coarse like a horse's mane, but just as thick. He buried his face in the strands.

Lark staggered up the three steps of the porch with the cowboy in tow. How she managed to push open the front door and get him inside she didn't know. She remembered her father describing how his god would perform miracles for his people every now and then. Did this cowboy believe in the same god?

Lark got the stranger to the brass bed and let him fall backward onto it. She watched as he sank into the feather mattress, already unconscious.

Rubbing her aching shoulder, she looked down to see rust-colored blood smeared across the pristine whiteness of her gown. It struck Lark that, despite the racial gulf between them, they both shared red blood. Was her father right? Was there truly little difference between the races, as he had always preached? She cast a backward glance at Matt Kincaid, who lay half on the bed and half off it. Ga'n's words haunted her as she quickly pulled off the gown and donned her usual workday clothes. Was this the bear he had spoken of? Was this the man who had been hunting Ga'n?

Shivering, Lark tugged and pulled until she got the dusty cowboy boots off the man's feet. After getting Kincaid situated on the bed and covered, she ran lightly across the yard. The eastern horizon was lightening from gray to a pale pink, announcing that within another hour Holos would rise.

There were two bunkhouses, one for the single wranglers and the other for the old Apache men and women who had been left behind by their clans to die. Small homes set farther back in the forest housed the families of the married wranglers.

As Lark neared the second bunkhouse, she thanked Us'an and her father for his generosity of spirit. It had become widely known over the years that Roarke Gallagher would take in the Old Ones who could no longer move with their rancherias.

Nomads, the Apache clans moved around the desert and mountains with the seasons. When the elderly could no longer keep up, they voluntarily stayed behind to starve to death. Roarke had taken in twelve such Apaches over the years and, in return for one hour of work a day, they got free room and board. A soft smile touched Lark's mouth as she mounted the steps and quietly opened the wooden door.

"I was expecting you, daughter."

Old Ny-Oden, his white hair hanging long across his shoulders, sat on his bunk. Once he had been the shaman, or medicine man, for the Jicarilla Apache. Roarke Gallagher had made it known years ago that when Ny-Oden wanted to step down as shaman and pass his knowledge on to a younger man, he would be welcomed at the ranch. Lark remembered the small, wiry Apache with sparkling obsidian eyes who had come to the ranch when she was five years old. Ny-Oden had taught her the ways of a shaman, and she loved him like a grandfather.

"There isn't much time, grandfather. A man is hurt. A bullet wound in his leg. He's asked for our help."

Ny-Oden placed his clawlike hand in hers, allowing her to help him stand. His hands, once supple, were now frozen into the talonlike positions of an eagle hunting prey. The knuckles were permanently swollen, and over the years he had lost all of his manual mobility.

When that had happened, Ny-Oden had gone to Roarke and told him he was no longer of use and would leave the ranch to die alone. Roarke had told him that if he would teach Lark the ways of shaman and guide her in nursing the people as well as the animals, he could stay. The bargain had been struck to the happiness of all concerned.

"You were waiting for me," Lark said, noticing that the old man was already dressed. "Why?"

"Daughter of mine, Us'an awakened me moments ago and told me to wait for your arrival."

Lark patiently led Ny-Oden out to the porch. "I wish Us'an talked to me the way he talks with you. Ga'n was here shortly after sunset," she said.

Ny-Oden tilted his white head, studying her intently. "There were words between you?"

"Aren't there always? At one time, he wasn't evil. Now, he is. I think he's under the wicked spell of Owl-Man Monster."

The Apache believed that the monster took on the guise of a man with the face of an owl and stalked the night, hunting for victims to kill. Roarke had told her that Owl-Man Monster was akin to the bogeyman that white people believed existed in the dark of night. She placed her arm around the frail, ninety-year-old Apache. "I'm frightened, grandfather. I think this is the man for whom Ga'n was hunting. He's badly wounded."

"My *di-yin* told me that a *pindah* would come," Ny-Oden agreed in his reedlike voice.

"I wish you had told me." But Lark knew that a shaman's *di-yin*, or power from the unseen world, often told him many things. Whether Ny-Oden passed them on to her was up to him. Many times, Ny-Oden would get a vague feeling of something about to happen, but be unable to describe it in detail. Still, Lark would have settled for even an inkling of this night's unending surprises.

When they had climbed the porch steps, Ny-Oden halted to catch his breath. "My *di-yin* has told me much of this stranger's arrival, daughter."

Worriedly Lark looked down at the old man, who was stooped over with age. "Grandfather, tell me that no more sadness or violence will befall us. I'm young, but my heart is torn and bleeding. I cannot take much more. I have forty people to clothe and feed. I must make money for the bank so that we can keep our beautiful home. I cannot disappoint those who have created this ranch." She gestured toward the bedroom, and they walked toward it at a snail's pace. "My own feelings tell me this is no ordinary *pindah*. I sense much trouble and anger in him, grandfather."

Several seconds passed before Ny-Oden spoke. "You come from the strongest of Apache blood, my daughter. Those in your family were all chiefs and leaders. You are no less than them. Take heart and remember that. The stranger must be cared for. No *pindah* doctor will come from Prescott to save his life. He is in our hands, as it should be."

Shoving aside her own personal disappointment in Ny-Oden's riddlelike answer, Lark led him through the door.

Ny-Oden lowered himself slowly into a maple rocking chair near the bed. Lark took a multicolored blanket and placed it across the old Apache's lap to keep him warm in the chill of the early morning.

"Daughter, you will need your shaman's supplies," Ny-Oden directed. "But first, examine the extent of his wound."

Lark gazed down at the ugly, festering wound that

could be seen through the slit in Kincaid's dirty Levi's.
"It appears to be a single bullet, grandfather."

"How many days old? Your nose will tell you."

With a grimace, Lark straightened. She lit three
kerosene lamps, setting two on stands on either side of
the brass bed and a third on the mantel of the fireplace.
"It festers badly. I would guess three, perhaps four
days."

Ny-Oden nodded sagely. "Does it seep with a straw
color or blood?"

Lark would have to slit open the Levi's in order to
ascertain that. "I don't know."

"Undress him completely, daughter."

Lark stared at the shaman. "Grandfather?"

"Undress him. His clothes are of filth and more than
likely filled with lice or other vermin. Place many
blankets beneath him to soak up his fever sweat."

"But . . ." She had never seen a man completely
undressed except for the young male children who played
naked in the summer. It was not permissible for any
maiden to look on a man's body until after she was
married.

"I would do it myself were it not for my frozen hands
and failing eyesight," Ny-Oden said. "All I can do is sit
here and guide you. Hear me, daughter. Us'an has placed
this man's life in your hands. A shaman, whether man or
woman, must minister to both without blushing like a red
field poppy."

Lark nodded, ashamed of her reaction to his request.
Ny-Oden had not been able to treat anyone for the last
five years. Instead, he had led her verbally, step-by-step,
through whatever needed to be done; whether it was to
mend a child, a woman, or a man, or to heal an animal's
wound. The situation had never arisen in which she had
to doctor a naked man. Lark woodenly began to strip Matt
Kincaid of his clothes. Her fingers trembled as she unbuttoned the dark blue cotton shirt, pulling it apart to expose
his darkly haired barrel chest. Eyes widening, Lark

hesitated. Among Apaches, a hairless body was desirable and considered a pleasing mark of beauty. No Apache had hair such as this man! He looked like a black bear in her mind. Yet, as Lark stared at him, she acknowledged that he had a primal male beauty about him. His shoulders were clean and broad, silently attesting to the hidden strength lying in wait in them. Like the Apaches, his chest was well rounded, the muscles taut and firm beneath that mat of unsightly hair. A sheen of sweat glistened beneath that curly abundance, and it forced Lark back to work.

"He's sweating heavily, grandfather." She removed the shirt and dropped it on the oak floor beside the bed.

"Fever is eating him up. We must hurry, daughter."

Ny-Oden rarely sounded so urgent, and Lark quickly pulled open the belt. Her mouth grew dry as she unsnapped the six buttons to the Levi's. Apache men wore a breechclout beneath their trousers. He wore something similar, although Lark thought the garment looked strange as she peeled the Levi's down his narrow hips. Her bowie knife was beneath the other pillow and she retrieved it, then positioned the tip over the wounded thigh. The steel blade glinted in the predawn light as she snagged a torn slit of the Levi's, ripping it cleanly open.

"Ugh." Lark groaned, watching with mounting fear as a straw-colored ooze pearled across his swollen and discolored leg.

Ny-Oden leaned forward, watching her intently. "Quickly, daughter. The wound is crying to be cleaned and eased of its fevered state."

Matt Kincaid was beautiful, Lark realized as she finished removing his trousers. His thighs were hard, and as powerfully built as the finest of stallions. Despite the hair on his legs, Lark admitted he was well proportioned as few men could be. He was a giant, even taller and larger than her father. He possessed walnut-brown hair that held strands of gold beneath the lamplight.

Girding herself to follow Ny-Oden's orders, Lark pulled

off the strange-looking breechclout. Heat burned in her cheeks, and she avoided Ny-Oden's gaze. She scolded herself: he looked no different from the Kentucky Stud before he was going to breed a mare in heat.

"Cover him with many blankets except around the wound," Ny-Oden urged more gently. "Later he will need to be bathed."

Lark nodded, tucking several blankets around him. His name is Matt Kincaid, she reminded herself sourly. Ny-Oden had said Us'an had chosen her to care for him. Humbly she must accept his dictate. Didn't Us'an realize how unsure she was around pindahs? Would Matt Kincaid wake to curse her as the children at the school in Prescott had done when she rode in with her father? Biting down on her lower lip, Lark went to the kitchen to start a fire in the iron stove and set several kettles of water on to boil.

For the next half hour, while the water heated, Lark set out the supplies she would need. After determining that a single bullet was lodged deep in Matt's thigh, she concentrated on how to get it out. She mixed yerba santos mer, an herb that coagulated the blood, into a thick pulp. Taking some moldy tortillas from the kitchen, Lark crumbled them up with the herb and added hodenten, made from ground poppies and made sacred by Ny-Oden's incantations. A bit of water finished the preparation and she set aside the large bowl. After passing the tip of her smaller hunting knife through the flame of one of the kerosene lamps, Lark was ready.

She prayed to Us'an that he would keep Matt Kincaid unconscious so that he would not feel the pain. Her hand shook briefly as she held the knife over the wound.

"I am afraid, grandfather."

"Us'an will guide your hand, my daughter."

Taking a deep breath, she twisted the knife once and dug deftly. Dark black blood flowed out of the wound, spilling across her fingers as she held his leg steady. And then fresh red blood followed as she retrieved the flattened piece of lead from his body.

Kincaid groaned, and Lark froze. He moved slightly, muttering unintelligibly, but remained unconscious. Grateful, Lark quickly took hot, soapy water and a cloth and cleansed the wound. Around the ranch, she was called upon to minister to animal wounds all the time. She tried to imagine that Matt was an animal in need of her gentle hand.

After packing the wound with the poultice, Lark wrapped his thigh. Wiping the perspiration from her brow, she glanced over at Ny-Oden, whose black eyes were shiny with silent praise.

She set to work cleaning Matt Kincaid's filthy body next. By the time she got to his hips, Lark began to feel shaky inside. She tried not to stare at his large male symbol, pretending he was the stallion instead. Nevertheless, her heart quickened as a cauldron of new and undefined emotions swirled and eddied deep within her. She gently held him captive in her fingers, cleaning him. Was this the source of mysterious joy that a newly married woman described in whispers only to her married friends? Was this the source of delight she had heard them talk about in words of awe and trembling beauty?

Keeping her thoughts to herself, she looked up and saw a gleam in Ny-Oden's eyes. The shaman was reading her mind! Lark turned crimson, the heat prickling her cheeks as never before. No Apache maid should be thinking such thoughts.

"It is done," she said some time later, her voice scratchy with strain. Matt Kincaid was sleeping soundly, wrapped warmly from head to toe in several blankets. Lark had always thought that the brass bed had been built for a giant and not for her, but Kincaid's feet touched the bottom of the footboard. Again, she was in awe of his height. Truly he was like a bear.

"You've done well, daughter," said Ny-Oden. "I will sit with him and chant to my *di-yin*. His fever is high and needs to be broken. Prepare lobelia tea for when he awakes. We must chase the fever from his body or it may claim his life.''

Terror wrenched at her heart and Lark stood very still. *He is too beautiful to die!* she wanted to cry out. Hadn't Us'an taken enough from her? Wasn't he satisfied with the lives he'd already claimed? Moistening her lips, Lark stared down at the man. Some of the tension had drained from his gaunt, whiskered face. His mouth was slightly parted, and she liked the shape of it. Lark saw so much in his now-peaceful features. She saw kindness there and, yes, even sensitivity. What drew her so powerfully to this stranger? Confused and exhausted, Lark turned away.

''Daughter?''

She halted in the doorway. ''Yes?''

''Us'an may leave the decision as to whether or not he goes to the Big Sleep in your hands.''

''How can that be? No one's life lies in another's. Us'an gives and takes. That's what you've always said.''

''Sometimes,'' Ny-Oden said softly, ''Us'an bids us to give more than what we think we have to give, daughter. But he also provides us with the courage to carry that extra load.''

''I'm so tired of death, grandfather.'' She choked on a sob, fighting the tears that wanted to come. ''I would never let any person or animal die that came to me. I would do whatever I could to save that life.''

''You have the wisdom and generosity of The People, daughter. Right now, you carry many responsibilities on your shoulders. Why not awaken Maria and have her help you this morning? You are tired and need to rest here where I now sit.''

Later, Holos, the Sun, rose brilliant and powerful, the rays flooding the east bedroom where Lark sat dozing off and on. Maria moved quietly about the house. For the last fifteen years she had kept house for the Gallagher family. Paco, her husband, was the ranch foreman. Wrinkling her dark brow, Maria pushed aside a stray gray hair that had escaped from the carefully fashioned knot at the back of her head. She had made Lark hot porridge, but the girl had refused it, too exhausted by the chain of events of the last twenty-four hours to eat it. Maria had given her a sad nod of understanding, leaving the bedroom door ajar after she had left.

Once an hour, Lark would leave her rocking chair and sponge down Matt Kincaid, trying to cool his hot, feverish body. She mixed lobelia into cool spring water in an effort to moderate the fever that ate away at his beautiful male form. At first, Lark avoided the massive chest with all that hair on it. And then, out of feminine curiosity, she hesitantly touched the dark, curling strands. To her surprise and delight, his chest hair was soft and springy. After that, she bathed his chest without further consternation, secretly delighting in her newfound discovery.

Twice that first day, Lark had to change the blankets beneath his male symbol after he urinated. Ny-Oden had taught her to examine the color of urine for evidence of internal bleeding. To her relief, as she studied the damp blanket each time, there was no sign of further injury to Matt.

Despite her promise to Ny-Oden to tend to Matt Kincaid, the ranch demands pulled at her, too. Lark found herself giving orders that usually her father would have given to some of the older Mexican boys in their teens, whose job it was to care for the broodmares. It was a strange feeling to be taking her father's place, one that made her uncomfortable. But if anyone noticed her uneasiness, they said nothing and willingly carried out their duties. Lark took it upon herself to check on the broodmares. The medicine-hat-marked mare paced endlessly and Lark felt sorry for the young, nervous horse. As she scratched the mare's ears, Lark wondered if she would feel similarly nervous about the arrival of her first baby.

That thought rooted her to the spot. She had never

before contemplated marriage or babies. Had the handling of Matt's male symbol turned her mind in a completely new direction? Disturbed and yet sensing a sweet anticipation she'd never felt before, Lark continued to check on each one of the mares. An hour later, exhausted, she closed the last stall door.

Standing at the opening to the barn, Lark wiped the sweat from her brow. Dizziness made her shut her eyes for a moment, and she leaned tiredly against the door. Her father's image wavered in her mind's eye. "Colleen, you can never give up. You must always go on. There's nothing in this life you can't overcome with a good heart and courage." Lark remembered those words, remembered that day when her father had crouched at her side as her favorite pony, Storm, lay dying from old age. Roarke had gathered her into his arms and carried her inside the barn.

Storm's breathing had been labored and raspy. Roarke had placed his arm around his daughter's thin shoulder, watching as tears squeezed from her eyes. "Death isn't to be feared, colleen," he told her gently. "Your mother's people have the right idea about it: death is a bridge to a new and better life on the other side."

Lark looked up into her father's kind blue eyes. "W-will Storm go to a new life, too?" Her heart ached with so much pain.

Though his hands were huge, the fingers thick and callused, Roarke delicately picked a stray strand of hair off Lark's damp cheek. He placed it behind her ear and then cupped her small face. "Storm will go over the Rainbow Bridge," he told her gruffly.

The Apache believed that a rainbow led to an open door into a different, invisible world. Those who were going to the Big Sleep walked across that multicolored bridge on their way to a happy new life. With a sob, Lark threw her arms around her father's neck, relieved to know that Storm would live on in a new, unseen form. She remembered holding the horse until he died some hours later, his head resting on her lap. And all that time, her father had been there at her side.

Sighing, Lark opened her eyes and stared blindly at the blue sky, bright with sunshine. "I miss you so much, father, so much . . ."

# Chapter 3

"*Patrona*, it is Señor Kincaid. He cries out and fights the blankets. I'm afraid he will cause more injury to his wound," Maria called urgently from the porch where she was standing.

Lark's heart was pounding from the four-mile run she'd taken down the valley on the stud. As she noiselessly rounded the corner of the house in her kabuns, her heart began a different, more apprehensive beat.

Matt Kincaid lay sprawled in a tangle of blankets, a sheen of perspiration covering his body. His lips moved in an unintelligible garble. Maria hesitated at the door, awaiting Lark's orders.

It was natural for Lark to lay her hand on his bare shoulder, as if to banish the nightmares that plagued his sleep. She placed her other hand on his wrinkled brow. Almost immediately, he quieted.

"Maria," Lark called softly, "bring me another bowl of cool spring water and the lobelia."

"*Sí, patrona.*"

Lark had no explanation for the thrill that raced through her as she used her palm to wipe the sweat away from Matt Kincaid's brow and temple. And then, in a gesture that wrenched her completely, he pressed his cheek into her open hand. Lips parting, Lark sat at his side, stunned. She had seen children bury their tiny heads in their mothers' bosoms, seeking protection in moments of trauma. She searched his pained expression, seeing only his vulnerability, and not the frightening, bearlike power she had glimpsed before. He was weak, sick, and needed the solace she offered.

Maria placed the bowl on the stand near Lark. The instant she removed her hand from Matt Kincaid's stubbled cheek, he called out names that were unfamiliar to her.

Maria nodded, watching the cowboy worriedly. "Aiyee, *patrona,* the fever stalks him."

After quickly bathing Matt's upper body, Lark placed the cloth aside. "Yes, the fever is rising. After I get him in position, I want you to hand me a spoon filled with the lobelia, Maria."

Lark wasn't sure she had the necessary strength to bring Matt upright enough to spoon the fever herb into the slack line of his mouth. Slipping her arm beneath his shoulders, she positioned herself against the headboard to give her leverage. A strange, fluttering feeling fled from her heart down to her lower body as his head sagged against her jaw, his cheek coming to rest near her breast. Struggling to tip his head back, Lark finally got him into a favorable position. Maria handed her the wooden spoon filled with the dark green herb that had been ground up and mixed with a few drops of whiskey.

"Drink this, Matt Kincaid," she crooned in his own language. "It will bring your fever down and fight for you." She slid the thin spoon between his lips and watched the liquid disappear.

Afterward, Lark tucked Matt back under the blankets. Six spoons of lobelia would be enough to combat the raging fever he was fighting. Maria left, and Lark took her place in the rocking chair near his side of the bed. A pleasant exhaustion overcame her.

She studied Matt Kincaid's square face through half-closed eyes. What was it about this man that possessed almost a magical hold over her? She longed to ask Ny-Oden. As she slowly began to rock the chair, Lark's lashes drooped closed, the strain of the last twenty-four hours catching up with her. In that in-between state that lies at the border between sleep and wakefulness, she remembered her mother's wise words of counsel.

"Mother?" she had asked one time as a fourteen-year-old. "How does a warrior know when he loves a maiden?"

Mourning Dove smiled at her tall, gangly daughter. She had been busy making the favorite food of her people, ash cakes. She set aside the bowl of ground mesquite flour and beef tallow. "Both will feel a certain undeniable pull toward one another, Lark."

Lark sat down at her mother's feet. "A pull? Like the cord attached from the foal to its mother after birth?"

Mourning Dove laughed softly. "You will feel it here," she said, touching the place over her heart. "And, yes, it is like the cord that binds the foal to its mother. But it's invisible and the feelings are much more than I can explain."

"Did you and father feel it?"

Mourning Dove's face melted into a fond look. "Oh, yes. We felt it very strongly from the moment he rescued me from the Comancheros."

"But he was a *pindah*, mother. I didn't know heartstrings could be tugged by white men."

"Daughter, love recognizes no color, no country, and no tribe. Love between two people is theirs alone, no matter how many others may want them to deny it."

"Because you feel this invisible string binding the two of you to one another's hearts?"

"Yes, for exactly that reason, my daughter."

Lark sat there for long minutes, contemplating the perplexing answer. "Will it happen to me, mother?"

"I'm sure it will."

"Soon? For Juanita is only fifteen and she is getting married in another month to Esteban."

With a chuckle, Mourning Dove added a pinch of salt to the ash cake mixture. "Only Us'an knows when your heart will be touched, my curious daughter. He chooses the warrior and the time it will happen.''

"But what if I don't know that my heartstring is being pulled? Is it possible that I will miss the man I'm to marry?''

A gentle smile curved Mourning Dove's full mouth. "You are of my blood, Lark. And you have the same strength and intensity of feeling that I carry. If anything, you will be smitten so completely when the right warrior walks into your life that you will not be able to think about anything else. That was the way it was for your father and me. No matter what I did or how I tried to ignore the magic that throbbed between us, I could not. This feeling,'' she said, lightly touching Lark's breastbone, "will become so powerful that you will feel helpless beneath it. Only the warrior who has chosen you will be able to quell those wild, restless feelings deep within you. His touch will be branding and you will react without reason. Once this happens, daughter, do not become afraid of the power he unleashes within you. Trust the warrior to whom you are drawn, for only he will give you the inner peace and fulfillment that you as a woman blindly seek. He will be like a flower heavy with the promise of nectar, and you the starved bee in search of it. Once you have met, you will know a bliss like no other. The bee and the flower become one. . . .''

Lark's chin sagged toward her chest, her mother's softly murmured words, rich with emotion, whispering across time. Unconsciously Lark pressed a hand to her breast. The strange, sweet, unfulfilled ache continued. It ceased only when Matt Kincaid was in her arms.

With a start, Lark jerked out of her cramped position in the rocker. Blinking, she realized Maria had lit a kerosene lamp to chase away the darkness. Rubbing her neck ruefully, Lark rose and went over to Matt. The covers were still in place and he was sleeping deeply. Pleasure suffused her as she pushed several strands of hair

off his brow. The fever was down, but not gone. Saying
a prayer of thanks to her *di-yin* of healing, Lark knew the
lobelia was responsible for his improvement.

Matt was aware that a cool hand had left his brow.

"Katie? Katie, is that you?" He saw his dark-haired
wife walking out of their ranch house as he rode up, a
tired but welcoming smile on her mouth. She was so
fragile, so like their daughter, Susan. He dismounted,
allowing the reins to drop to the ground. He saw his
pigtailed daughter laughing, her gray eyes dancing with
delight as she ran from behind her mother's skirts and
threw her arms around his neck. She smelled of the spring
wildflowers her mother held. Matt laughed as Susan
covered his unshaven, dusty face with kisses. Holding her
in his right arm, he walked over to Katie. She was petite
against his side, still holding that small bouquet of flowers
in her red, work-worn hands. Her clean, unmarred
features were radiant in silent welcome. He'd just spent
five days in Tucson, selling their first herd of cattle, and
had missed them terribly. Katie whispered his name, her
voice tremulous as she slid an arm around his waist.
When she laid her head on his chest, an overwhelming
joy shot through him. He stood there in the dusty yard,
holding the two women he loved most in the world. Life
couldn't get any better. "Katie," he murmured.

Lark hesitated. Who was Katie? His wife? She noted
that he wore a wedding ring on his left hand.

Matt moved restlessly, a frown puckering his forehead.
"Katie? No!"

The strained cry tore at Lark. She reached out, gently
massaging his temples and bearded cheek. Her breath
caught as his hand came up, capturing hers. Strong, warm
fingers swallowed up her hand and he buried his sand-
papery cheek against her palm, a sob tearing from deep
within his powerful chest.

"Katie! God, please . . . no. It can't be. No . . ."

Lark's eyes widened as she saw tears flow from beneath
Matt's tightly shut eyes. He was crying! She sat stunned,

her heart tearing as he sobbed out Katie's name over and over again, pressing Lark's hand hard to his cheek. The walls Lark had erected to protect herself from white men lowered. She had no defense against him, she discovered in that poignant moment. She watched the tears wind down his pale cheeks and tangle in the bristly growth until they slid along the strong line of his rock-hard jaw.

Scalding tears rushed to her own eyes and Lark automatically leaned forward. "Hush. You are safe. Safe. Do not cry, for I'll be here with you throughout the night. I'll not let the evil spirits plague your dreams, my bear. Hush, you are safe in my arms. . . ."

Her husky voice seemed to have a miraculous effect on him. The tears ceased and the anguished line of his mouth eased. Slowly, as she ran her other hand in a caressing motion, through his thick, rich, walnut-colored hair, he calmed.

Wearily, Lark rested her head where his heart lay. A rush of peace spiraled through her and she closed her eyes. The frantic, drumlike beat of his heart slowed. And Lark, whose own heart had been stricken with grief, felt the first tentative healing begin to bind her wounds.

*Somehow,* she thought drowsily, *he is good for me. I quiet his tortured dreams, but he also gives me peace from my tortured days.* Her lips moved slightly. *Thank you, Us'an. Perhaps we can heal one another. . . .*

The raucous crow of a rooster brought Lark awake. The first rays of Holos moved like silent fingers through the lace curtains at the window, stealing across the oak floor and the brass bed where she lay. A wonderful sense of fulfillment infused her. It was only as full awareness gradually came to her that she became aware of the slow, drumlike beat of Matt's heart beneath her ear. Shock shot through her and Lark sat up, gasping. Her hands flew to her opened mouth as realization struck. She had fallen asleep on Matt Kincaid's chest and slept there the entire night!

"Us'an," she murmured, "forgive me! I know it is not right for a maid to lie with a man to whom she's not married." Dread filled her as the shock of what she had done brought her completely awake. And yet, as she looked down at Matt, she saw the peace in his serene features. Her back ached, as did her neck, from the contorted position in which she had lain all night. Her right leg, which had been tucked beneath her, was asleep. Grumbling at her stupidity, Lark carefully placed her booted feet on the floor.

Stealing a look at Matt, she felt heat rush up her neck and into her cheeks. Thank Us'an he hadn't awakened to find her sleeping like a kitten on his chest! What would he think? What would anyone who had seen them think of her? She had broken a strict Apache law. Rubbing her face, Lark slowly stood up. She covered Matt with a wool blanket and checked his brow for fever, satisfied to find that it was lower. Gathering a bar of soap, a towel, and a robe, she left the room.

Ny-Oden was standing at the bottom of the porch steps waiting for her when she opened the front door. Her eyes widened and she halted abruptly.

"Us'an greets us strongly this morning," he said, moving forward, using the cane that Paco had carved for him.

Gathering her scattered wits, Lark nodded. "My grandfather, why are you here so early? I was going to have Maria come for you later when I was ready to change the dressing on Matt's leg."

A merry twinkle shone in Ny-Oden's black eyes as he allowed Lark to help him up the steps. "Ah, you call him by name. That is good. And did he pass the night in peace, daughter?"

Nervously Lark touched her hair, which was in dire need of washing and combing. "He slept peacefully, grandfather." That wasn't a lie, but it wasn't the complete truth, either. Lark bit down on her lips, realizing

she could not fool Ny-Oden. In a rush of words, she told
him what she had done.

The shaman hitched one shoulder upward in a shrug.
"Healing comes in many forms, daughter. You were tired
and meant only to soothe his agitated state. You did not
lie with him out of lust, but rather out of care. Do not
trouble yourself. Us'an understands."

Relief flooded her and Lark gave him a shaky smile.
"So much is happening so quickly, grandfather. I feel as
if I've been swept up in a column of spinning wind and
have lost my direction. My world narrows only to Matt
Kincaid and I do not understand why."

Ny-Oden gave her a grizzled smile. "Who can explain
how Holos makes the heads of flowers follow his path?
Or why rain makes the plants grow tall and strong? Some
things are not to be questioned, daughter, only accepted."

"I know you speak words of wisdom, grandfather, but
I am wrestling with so many new emotions. Will these
feelings smooth out after a time? Will I know my direction once more?"

Ny-Oden nodded his silver head and made himself
comfortable on the porch swing. "You will, my daughter.
Go, attend to your personal needs. I shall stay here and
guard your patient."

Lark thanked the shaman and went to the creek behind
the ranch house. There, in a secluded spot formed by the
ranch house and high cranberry bushes, she had the
necessary privacy in which to bathe.

Matt frowned. Whether it was the throbbing pain in his
leg that awoke him or another noise, he wasn't sure.
Slowly his vision cleared. He felt hot and his thoughts
came sluggishly. Pain and heat were all that he was aware
of until his gaze moved to the left toward a slight noise.
His mouth parted as he stared at the woman standing
naked with her back to him.

He must be delirious. He must be dying. Floating in
and out of consciousness, he stared at her lithe, golden

form. It was she, he thought groggily, his golden cougar
. . . the woman in the white nightgown. Only this time
there were no clothes to mar the tall, sensual lines of her
form. The sun brought a golden splendor to her skin. He
watched, mesmerized, as the blue-black waterfall of her
hair flowed back and forth like a living being across her
back as she moved. His gaze followed the swanlike curve
of her throat as she raised her head and partly turned
toward him. Her small, perfectly formed breasts were
high and pink-tipped. It was her legs, Matt thought
torridly, that were her best feature, the long, rounded
thighs made firm by riding, he guessed.

He must be dying. She was too beautiful, an apparition
from heaven. An angel . . . He had no strength left and
closed his eyes. But not before her profile was branded
into his feverish memory. Her hair was parted in the
center of her scalp, her brow broad and smooth. Her nose
flared into delicate nostrils that reminded him of a fine,
blooded racing horse. He had felt heat stir in his loins as
he savored that mouth of hers: full, cherry-colored lips,
ripe with vulnerability, begging to be worshipped by the
right man. Her chin was stubborn, filling out her heart-
shaped face. She must be an angel, Matt thought deliri-
ously, one of God's finest handiworks. No woman he'd
seen in his twenty-six years of life could compete with
her sculpted beauty. A slight smile tugged at his mouth,
as he drifted toward unconsciousness. He recalled his
mother reading aloud tales about Helen of Troy, whose
beauty had launched a thousand ships. Well, he had just
seen her.

After fastening her Levi's, Lark shrugged into a long-
sleeved blue calico shirt that reached below her hips, then
captured the shirt with a wide leather belt. A cotton
headband would keep her long hair out of her face. She
sat down on the rocker and pulled on her leather knee-
high kabun boots, absently stuffing the pant legs down
into them.

Feeling refreshed and clean, Lark glanced over at Matt

as she rose. Following an urge, she leaned down, barely touching his brow. "Sleep in peace, my bear," she whispered, then went to fetch Ny-Oden.

She helped the aged shaman into the house and settled him in the rocking chair, then went to the kitchen to make up a new batch of the special poultice. Humming softly, she returned with a bowl and a fresh dressing for Matt's leg.

"He looks better this morning," Ny-Oden commented approvingly.

Lark set the bowl on the stand and removed the blanket from Matt's wounded leg. "Thank you, grandfather. Look, the flesh is not as angry."

Ny-Oden studied the wound intently. "There is no more blood. That is good. He has also slept soundly and the fever is lower."

Taking her slender knife, Lark cut through the bandages. "I feel more rested myself, as if a great load has been taken off my shoulders," she admitted. Matt groaned as she worked to remove the dressing. "He awakens," she whispered to the shaman.

"It is time," he agreed.

Lark sat facing Matt as she continued to soak the dressing until she was sure it could be peeled back with a minimum of pain to him. She saw his lashes flutter, and her heart beat a little faster. What would he do when he found out that he was with Apaches and not his own kind? Trying to steel herself for any eventuality, she lifted the knife to carefully cut away the dressing from the wound.

Fire jagged up Matt's thigh into his hip and gut. A harsh sound worked its way up his throat, jerking him out of his delirious state. His eyes flew open and he automatically recoiled. No! He was seeing things again! That face. It was she. But why the hell was she wearing Apache clothes? Confused, he stared at her for several taut seconds, fevered memories of his family's murder mixing with the present. Reacting instinctively, he knocked the knife out of her hand. The blade sailed harmlessly through the air, landing on the floor. Matt tried to pull away and defend himself. He was back at the burning ranch house, turning Katie over, watching the blood stain her lavender dress where an arrow had penetrated her abdomen.

"Get away from me, you filthy Apache squaw!" he cried.

Lark leaped to her feet with a cry of shock. She watched his well-shaped mouth curl back, exposing even, white teeth. Terror and confusion flashed from his hawklike gray eyes, eyes that burned with an icy fury. She held out her hands in a soothing gesture and opened her mouth to calm him, but he spoke first.

"Stay away!" More memories assailed Matt. He remembered the agony of lifting his six-year-old daughter gently into his arms. An arrow had struck her through the heart.

Lark flinched from his anguished cry. Why had she expected any reaction other than hatred from him? Why had her blind and foolish heart allowed her to believe that Matt Kincaid was any different from other whites? Swallowing against her constricted throat, Lark raised her chin and fearlessly met his glare.

"I am Lark Gallagher and you're here at our ranch, near Prescott. You're safe here, Mr. Kincaid."

Matt struggled to sit up, only to find he lacked the strength to do so. His helplessness enraged him. His gaze flicked to the wrinkled, silver-haired Apache in the rocker. "This isn't making sense," he rasped. "No Injun owns a ranch. You're lying. You're all supposed to be on reservations." Looking down, Matt realized he was naked except for the blankets drawn over him. Where the hell was his gun?

"Please, calm yourself. We mean you no harm," Lark begged. "You've been unconscious over a day since finding your way to my father's ranch."

"Who's your father?"

"His name was Roarke Gallagher."

Matt heard the pain in her voice and saw the sudden luminosity in her eyes. His head was spinning with pain and fever. "I don't understand. This is a house. Injuns live in wickiups."

Wrestling with her grief, Lark stood uncertainly, holding his wild-looking glare. The fever still had him in its grip; he wasn't coherent. Keeping her voice low and soothing, she said, "My father was from Ireland, Mr. Kincaid. My mother was Apache. They owned this ranch until— Well, they're dead now and I'm the owner. You rode in yesterday, remember? You leaped from behind a beam in the barn and wrestled me to the ground."

No, dammit, he didn't remember! Gasping for breath, Matt lay back, staring up at the wood ceiling. Sweat popped out on his brow and trickled in tiny rivulets down the sides of his face, making his skin itch. "I don't believe you," he snarled, closing his eyes. It couldn't be! Apaches couldn't have found him! Was she part of Ga'n's bloodthirsty gang?

Lark twisted around, looking to Ny-Oden for counsel. The shaman shook his head. "Repack his wound, daughter," he told her in Apache. "He is a man possessed of devils. We must give him yarrow to drive the fever spirits from him."

When he heard them speaking in Apache, Matt jerked his eyes open. As she reached forward to touch his leg, he mustered all of his draining strength and lunged toward her outstretched hand. He gripped her wrist cruelly, feeling her soft flesh grind against her slender bones.

"Don't touch me," he ordered through clenched teeth.

A cry erupted from Lark. His bruising strength made her wince. She tensed and held still, not resisting him. His breath was coming in ragged gasps, and she felt the hotness of his flesh against her skin. In her heart, she forgave his violence and cruel words because he was out of his mind with fever. But he must gain control of himself. "You're hurting me," she whispered in a strained voice. "I've done nothing to deserve this from you. I'm only trying to save your life."

His fingers tingled against her cool, silken flesh. Matt saw tears gather in her eyes and immediately felt contrite, having never raised a hand against any woman in his life. Still, her Apache garb aroused his hatred. With disgust, he shoved her hand away and sank back down on the bed. Making a monumental effort, he gathered what was left of his strength and demanded, "Get out of here and never touch me again. I hate your kind. I hate all of you. You cold-blooded, killing bastards."

A shaft of anguish lanced Lark's heart as his hate-filled words smashed against her. She watched as Matt Kincaid lost consciousness, breathing hard, his chest rising and falling sharply with exertion. Her wrist throbbed with pain and already bluish-purple bruises were forming where he had held her. He had meant to hurt her. Bowing her head, Lark fought against the raw disappointment.

"I—I thought he would be different, grandfather," she said softly.

"Does a cougar run every time she sees a bear?"

Lark swallowed her pain, determined to put on a brave face for the shaman. "I am the cougar and he is the bear?"

"Yes."

She managed a short, nervous laugh. "No cougar would be foolhardy enough to engage a bear in a fight."

Ny-Oden smiled slyly. "In my years, I've seen a cougar steal meat from a bear. It can be done, daughter."

"Then you have more faith in me than I do, grandfather. You heard the hate in his voice." She held up her wrist. "He hates us so badly that he would punish us physically. I'm sorry, I do not have the emotional strength that the cougar has to challenge that bear."

"Play the patient cougar, my daughter, and you will perhaps learn why Matt Kincaid hates The People so much. He is possessed by fever. He may not be so filled with hatred once you drain the poison from his body. Have patience.''

An hour later, Sheriff Cole from Prescott arrived. He was a lanky man of thirty-five with a prematurely gray mustache that drooped across the corners of his thin mouth. Lark met him out in the dusty yard of the ranch. His watery blue eyes narrowed as he drew his bay gelding to a stop.

"You Gallagher's young'un?" he demanded in a gruff voice.

Stiffening at his poor manners, Lark nodded. "I'm his daughter."

Cole hitched one arm up on the saddle horn and gave her a lazy look. "Came out to tell ya about yore pa's death."

Swallowing against the sudden deluge of emotions, Lark tried to keep her voice steady. "What did you find out, sheriff? Who killed my father?"

"Pure and simple, girl. That thievin' renegade Ga'n nailed yore pa in the back."

Lark's eyes went wide. "Ga'n killed my father?"

"Yep."

"That's impossible!"

Cole scowled, twisting one end of his mustache. "That's what my report will read."

"But Ga'n would never harm my father or anyone in my family."

Cole straightened in the saddle. "Ga'n kills anything that moves on two legs. Of course, you being a breed, he might respect that," he added with a sneer. "But that left yore pa wide open to a bushwack by that bastard."

Lark tried to calm herself. She explained why Ga'n would never harm Roarke Gallagher. Cole shrugged. "Look, girl, I did my job. I came out here, told ya what I figured out happened. The case is closed." He reined his horse around, ready to leave.

"Wait!" Lark grabbed the reins, jerking the horse to a

halt. She was breathing hard, unable to control her grief and anger. "You can't do this! Ga'n didn't kill my father! I know he didn't!" Her anger spilled over. "Bo Shanks would do something like this! He's Jud Cameron's hired gun. Everyone knows that. You must find out who really did it."

With a hiss, Cole jerked the reins out of her hand. "Mind yore business, girl. You ain't the sheriff here, I am. Now, I've done all the investigatin' I'm gonna do."

"But—"

"No buts, breed. Mind yore manners and know yore place." His eyes drilled into her distraught features. "My report stands. And that's how it's gonna be filed. You want justice, you go to those Injuns you prefer over us and have them hunt down that renegade."

Fighting back her tears, Lark remained standing in the yard while Cole's slouched figure rode out of the yard and disappeared over the hill. Ga'n hadn't killed her father. So who was Cole covering up for? She rubbed her aching brow, simmering with rage.

The rest of the morning rushed by for Lark. Before her father's death, her duties had included overseeing the broodmares and two stallions and helping with the mustang hunts. Now, she also had to deal with the ranch families, who came to her for job assignments, or with grievances and problems, or who just needed someone to confide in. That morning a broodmare foaled a spindly-legged carbon copy of Kentucky and some of the depression lifted from Lark's shoulders. The fuzzy chestnut foal had four white stockings and a flaxen mane and tail. In about three years he would make a showy gelding for the cavalry.

Two emissaries from Fort Whipple, located ten miles north of Prescott, came to the ranch late that afternoon. Lark recognized Captain Frank Herter, but not the younger officer with him. Frank had been a friend of the family for the last ten years, ever since he'd been assigned to the army post which had been established to protect Prescott and the silver-rich country around it. Herter was in his early thirties, with closely cropped black hair, and there was always a twinkle in his brown eyes. Small and wiry, he reminded Lark of a feisty badger. Fortunately his personality was far more pleasant. She recalled the times when she was a little girl and Frank had brought her small gifts of peppermint candy and a stuffed doll that she had loved with all her heart. As she had blossomed into a woman, he had gifted her with flowery words of praise for her beauty, making her feel wonderful.

Lark raised her hand in greeting as Frank neared, and his dark, sunburned features crinkled into a smile. There was a lean quality to his face, with its high cheekbones and intense gaze. Although he had always been friendly to her, Lark also knew of his high reputation among the Apache, who respected his courage and integrity. The Apache gave a wide berth to any soldiers Herter commanded. He was like a badger in a fight to the finish: dangerous and competent.

Herter tipped his dusty white hat to Lark and pulled his tired mount to a halt. "Miss Lark, I just heard about your father's death. I'm sorry as hell it happened. Is there anything I can do?"

"No, thank you, Frank." She managed a slight smile, watching as he and the officer with him dismounted.

Climbing up on the porch to get out of the bright sunlight, Frank regarded her intently for a long moment. "You're lookin' peaked, purty lady. What'd that sidewinder of a sheriff have to say about Roarke's murder?"

"He said Ga'n killed him," she replied, unable to keep the anger out of her voice. "And I know Cole is lying. Oh, Frank, do you have any idea who would want to kill my father?"

He grimaced and looked toward the corrals full of horseflesh. "Yeah, I do." He turned to the other officer, who had also dismounted and stepped up onto the porch.

"First, I'd like to introduce you to Lieutenant Barry Wilson. From now on he'll be acting as purchasing agent for your fine stock. He's just come out of West Point Military Academy and I'm sure he'll be a big help to us."

Lark glanced up at the clean-shaven young man, who stood at stiff attention in his blue uniform, his eyes fixed on her with obvious curiosity. She grew uncomfortable under his steady gaze. She tried to forgive his white man's stare—after all, how many half-white, half-Apache women had he seen in his life back east?—and offered her hand to him. "It's a pleasure to meet you, Lieutenant Wilson."

Wilson colored fiercely as he took her hand and shook it limply. "Miss Gallagher."

Herter grinned from beneath his gray and black mustache, the white cavalry hat perched at a rakish angle on his head. His uniform was dusty and the throat of his dark blue vest was open to reveal a red kerchief tied around his neck. "Call her Lark," Herter said. "Beautiful name, isn't it? Like her." He winked at Lark, enjoying Wilson's embarrassment.

"Er, yes, sir," Wilson acknowledged, reluctantly releasing Lark's hand. "Mighty pretty, sir."

Herter returned his attention to Lark. "How many three-year-olds have you got ready for us to look at, Lark?"

With the change of subject, she relaxed. Over the years, Frank had urged her to take a larger role in the horse breeding and the choosing of future foals that the army could buy to replace their worn-out animals. He had been pleased to note her growing confidence in business discussions.

"Twenty, Frank. But you decide. There isn't a bad leg among them. A few blemishes, but nothing that will stop any of them from being good mounts."

"Are they all the Kentucky Stud's offspring?" he asked.

"Five are Huelga's, the medicine-hat-marked mustang.

They're slightly smaller, and what they don't have in height, they more than make up in spirit and muscle. They're more heavily built.''

Frank glanced over at Lieutenant Wilson. ''Why don't you start the inspection, Barry? I'll be along shortly.''

''Yes, sir.''

Lark felt the tension in Herter's lean body. She waited until Wilson was out of earshot before speaking. ''You still haven't answered my question, Frank. Do you know who killed my father?''

With a grimace, Frank rubbed his jaw. ''Got a sneakin' suspicion it was the Ring.''

Frowning, Lark searched her memory. Yes, her father had spoken of the Ring once, over a year ago, in vague terms to her mother. It was some mysterious group that was supposed to be causing havoc between whites and Indians alike. ''What do you mean?'' she asked.

Frank sat down in the porch swing and motioned her to join him. Lowering his voice, he said, ''I suspect the Ring exists, but I don't have firm proof, Lark. Your father and I talked on this subject long and hard over the past couple of years.'' His eyes narrowed on her upturned face. ''The Ring is a group of men in powerful positions. I think some of them are even in the army, though I can't be sure.''

''Who are they?'' she whispered.

''Greedy men who want money,'' he explained. ''Your father thought that Cameron and his bunch of hired guns, who work out at his ranch, were part of the Ring. Also Colonel Morgan, my boss. You see, men like Cameron stand to make a heap of money if the U.S. Army keeps funneling men into the Arizona Territory. The troops have to spend their paychecks somewhere. Why not in the towns where Ring members own saloons, brothels, and other establishments designed to take the soldiers' money?

''But the only way to ensure that the troops keep coming to this area is to keep the Indians on the warpath, attacking the folks who are trying to settle the land. Your father and I both figured, but couldn't prove, that the Ring was hiring gunslingers to raid and kill Indians, and paying renegade Apaches, Yavapai, or other tribes, to attack white settlers. That way, they were keeping things stirred up on both sides, and the government was being forced to send more troops."

Lark thoughtfully considered Herter's explanation. Finally she looked up into his compassionate brown eyes. Her voice trembled. "Do you think Cameron killed my father because he'd figured out about the Ring?"

"No, we never spoke to anyone about our theory. I'd seen too much evidence that suggested law enforcement officers were also in cahoots with Cameron and the Ring. There was nothing we could do, Lark, so we kept our thoughts to ourselves. And you should too. As to why your father might have been killed, I'm not sure. But I do think Cameron had a hand in it."

She took a deep breath, trying to steady her roiling emotions. "What did he want, then?"

Frank gently patted her shoulder. "The water rights to this ranch, Lark. For years he's known that the water on his own big spread next to yours would eventually dry up. Now it has, and his cattle are going to be in desperate need of water as soon as the spring snow runoff melts. Your land has natural artesian wells.

"I know for a fact that your father refused to sell Cameron water rights. As big as your ranch is, you have just enough to feed your stock, and that's it. I don't think Cameron realized that. Or maybe he didn't want to."

Lark couldn't believe all that she was hearing. Although her father had been preparing her to take over the ranch someday, he'd never spoken about Cameron wanting water rights. She searched Frank's weathered face. "Sheriff Cole lied to me, then."

"In all probability. It'd do him no good to investigate and find out that that oily snake Shanks drilled a hole through your father's back. No, I think Cameron is payin' Cole to look the other way."

She gave him a worried glance. "And you said your commanding officer might be involved in this Ring?"

Frank nodded sadly. "Which is why I'm leavin' the army this summer. I won't be a party to such corruption. Yet I can't fight superior officers in a court of law and win, Lark. I just can't lay my hands on the kind of evidence that would be needed. Colonel Morgan ordered me and my column to go out and raid a Tonto Apache rancheria yesterday, but I refused." He held up his thumb and index finger. "I came this close to getting court-martialed."

"Why exactly did you refuse to go, Frank?"

"Because he wanted my men to kill that band of Indians as payment for the murder of a ranch family by the name of Kincaid, whose bodies were found down near Tucson last month. I'm not goin' to go out and slaughter a bunch of Indians just to get even, especially without proof of their guilt. I told Morgan that the officers down at Fort Apache should be investigating this matter, that we shouldn't be killin' possibly innocent people up here for it."

Lark gasped. "Kincaid?"

"Yeah, a man by the name of Matt Kincaid lost his wife and daughter to an Apache raid."

Bowing her head, Lark felt renewed pain for the man recuperating in her bedroom. Matt had called for Katie. That must have been his wife. No wonder he'd reacted so violently when he'd awakened and seen her dressed in Apache garb.

"Lark?" Frank placed a finger beneath her chin and forced her to meet his concerned gaze. "What's wrong?"

She swallowed hard and told him about Matt Kincaid's unexpected arrival at the ranch. When she was done, Frank got up.

"In the telegraph from Fort Apache, they said Kincaid was trailin' Ga'n. Looks like that devil damn near did him in. Does Ga'n know he's here?"

"No, and he's not going too, either."

Frank nodded soberly. "Maybe, when he's up to it, Kincaid should drop over to the fort and talk to me. I'm interested in gettin' Ga'n, too. We might be able to collaborate and figure out where's he's hidin'."

Miserably, Lark told him of Ga'n's late-night visit to the ranch. As she spoke, Frank's jaw tightened, and she knew that spelled trouble for Ga'n.

"Did he say where he was going?"

"He was heading toward Prescott, Frank."

Pacing the porch, Herter muttered, "Ga'n probably won't show up here again for six months or more. As far as you're concerned, I'm more worried about Cameron and his gang."

Lark tried to keep the bitterness out of her voice. "You're one of the few whites who bears us no grudge, Frank. There are many people in town who were jealous of my father's success selling horses to the army. I'm sure Cameron is rubbing his hands with joy over his death."

Frank gave a snort of disgust but didn't disagree. "If Cameron thinks he's going to steal this ranch from you just because Roarke's dead, he's in for a big surprise. You're a cougar when you're cornered. In fact, I've told him as much." His brown eyes sparkled with amusement as he held her gaze. "Talk's goin' around town that you're sellin' out because of what happened. Any truth to it?"

Her cheeks flushed with anger. "I'd never sell our ranch!"

"Bo Shanks, Cameron's hired gun, is goin' around tellin' everyone you're sellin' out since your father's not around to manage it anymore."

Lark's chin lifted. "The Gallagher Ranch is staying in the family, Frank," she said tightly. "As long as I can make those monthly mortgage payments to Cameron's bank, it's safe."

He laughed, tucking his dusty white gloves into his black belt. "Well, since I'm here today to sign a contract for at least twenty sound young horses, I think you'll be able to make the next couple of payments, don't you?''

Twenty colts! Lark had expected Frank to pick ten colts, no more than that, for the army's use. This was an unexpected monetary windfall. She didn't try to disguise her broad smile.

By early evening, all the transactions were complete. Lark signed the army documents that would give her fifty dollars a head for the twenty three-year-olds.

Despite the hectic day, Lark's thoughts were never far from Matt Kincaid. Twice she had stolen a few minutes while the officers were inspecting each horse individually to check up on him. Maria had also dutifully peeked in on him every hour, checking to see if he had gained consciousness. To Lark's relief, he slept like a baby, his fever still high but the wound no longer infected.

Frank Herter wrote out a voucher and signed it. ''Well, there you go, young lady. One thousand dollars. Enough money to pay the bills and buy yourself a purty new dress.''

Fingering the crisp green voucher, Lark forced a smile as she sat behind the massive oak desk. ''Is that what young ladies do with money they earn? Buy dresses?''

Frank grinned. ''Absolutely.'' He motioned to her clothes. ''You're the prettiest Apache maid I've seen in warrior's clothes, but I'll bet you'd look twice as good in one of those fancy dresses from Madam Bouchard's in Prescott.'' His expression grew serious and he glanced over at the lieutenant. ''Lieutenant Wilson, why don't you bring our mounts around? I'll meet you outside in a moment.''

Wilson snapped to attention. ''Yes, sir!'' He inclined his head toward Lark. ''It was a great pleasure meeting you, Miss Gallagher. Perhaps, ah, we can see one another soon?''

''If you want to come and look at our weanlings in September, you're welcome to stop by, lieutenant,'' Lark parried, trying tactfully to avoid Wilson's amorous invitation.

His face filled with disappointment. "I see, ma'am. Very well, you can expect me September first. Since Captain Herter will be retiring early this year, I'll consider it my duty to come and see the new crop of fine youngsters that red stallion of yours is siring. Good night."

"Good night, lieutenant."

Frank slouched against the wall, his arms crossed over his chest. "You know," he began hesitantly, "running a ranch this size was hard enough on your father, Lark. It's an awful big responsibility to heap on a young woman's shoulders. You're getting to a good marryin' age and maybe you ought to think about tying the knot."

Lark toyed with the voucher, avoiding Frank's penetrating gaze. "The blood of my father runs in my veins, Frank. I have his strength as well as that of my mother. I'll manage."

"You have to do more than scrape by, Lark." He began to pace slowly back and forth in front of the desk. "Cameron's already claiming how he's gonna take this ranch away from you. Now, I knew your father for years. He was an honest man who never cheated anyone out of a nickel. A lot of town folk respected him even though they felt it was wrong for him to marry your mother. Roarke earned their respect the hard way, after years of honest and fair dealing with them. But that's all changed now."

He placed his hands flat on the desk, looking down at her. "What I'm trying to say, Lark, is that you're a woman. Cameron doesn't respect any woman, but especially not an Indian. You're the one who's going to have to ride into town and do business with that carpetbagger. Are you prepared to handle the sneers of men, women's gossip, and children calling you names when you ride in? I'm sorry to bring this up, but I've been hearing this kind of nasty talk for too many years. And with the Yavapai and Tonto Apaches causing havoc all over the area, there's no love lost right now between the citizens of Prescott and the Indians.''

Taking a deep breath, Lark steeled herself to face the painful truth he spoke. ''My father sometimes mentioned how some townspeople would hurl insults at him.''

''There were a few, Lark, but not many. If I recall rightly, they were unmercifully cruel to you when you tried to go to that white school when you were a little girl. They spit on you, called you names, and the boys beat you up a couple of times. It wasn't right that they tormented a defenseless twelve-year-old girl just because she was half Apache.''

She frowned. ''I've not forgotten it, Frank.'' She clasped her hands and met his worried eyes. ''But I don't have a choice, do I? I'm my father's daughter. If I don't ride into Prescott and do the banking and buy new supplies, who can?''

Frank grimaced. ''I'm just trying to prepare you, Lark, that's all. The people are nervous because of recent Apache attacks. They're looking to take out their frustration and anger on someone. If you come into town, I don't know what will happen.''

''All Apaches revere the wisdom and courage of their women, and it isn't uncommon for a woman to be a warrior beside her man or to be chosen as a leader. My mother was a woman chief for her tribe, Frank. I'll pray for her courage.''

With a slight frown he asked, ''Would you like a small army escort? I'd be happy to provide it.''

Warmth flowed through Lark and she rose. ''Your kindness won't be forgotten, but no, I'll ride in alone. You won't be able to bring in a detachment from the fort each time I come to Prescott. That would cause problems with your Colonel Morgan.'' She strove to smile for Frank's benefit, seeing that he wasn't convinced she would be safe without his help. ''I don't want to give him another reason to court-martial you.''

Frank sighed. ''I suppose you're right, purty Apache

maiden." He picked up his hat from the desk. "Walk me to the door?"

"Yes," she responded shyly.

He grinned, setting the hat at a rakish angle on his head and placing his hand on her elbow. "Are you about ready for that marriage proposal I keep threatening you with? I'm not such a bad *hombre*, Lark. With my pension, I'll be a rich man. I'm a hard worker and I like half-Apache maidens with big blue-violet eyes. How about it?"

Lark avoided his half-teasing, half-serious gaze. For years Frank had claimed he would someday make her his wife—she had only to choose the time and place. The only problem was, he didn't pull her heartstrings. Frank liked her just the way she was, but she couldn't return the feeling, while the man who hated her because she had Apache blood running through her veins was the one who filled her with yearning.

# Chapter 4

The next time Matt awoke his mind was clear. Although still weak, he no longer felt feverish. Barely opening his eyes, he saw the woman who had been dressed as an Apache sleeping in a high-backed rocker beside his bed. Matt's eyes widened at her breathtaking beauty as apricot-colored dawn light spilled over her from the east window.

She sat with a lavender shawl draped over her shoulders, hands on the lap of her familiar long white cotton gown. He couldn't ignore an inner hunger as his gaze moved from her slender, work-worn hands. The thin gown lovingly silhouetted her high breasts, the neckline opened to reveal her delicate collarbones and graceful neck. But it was her face that held Matt captive. Thick, ebony lashes lay against her golden skin. Her ripe, red lips and their soft, parted vulnerability created heat that began to uncoil in his loins. She had the face of a madonna, he thought raggedly. How could she be so beautiful and yet be half Apache?

The sequence of events after he'd been shot by Ga'n flooded back to Matt. He flexed his fists tentatively, and found he was appallingly weak. His brows furrowed as he vaguely recalled speaking to the woman. Speaking? He'd practically ripped her head off with his anger and hatred. He squinted, looking at the woman hard and long as she slept deeply. That black waterfall of hair across

63

her shoulders and arms was the only indication that she was Apache.

Strenuously, Matt fought against the idea that she was one of *them,* the murderers of his family. And then he remembered her low, husky voice telling him her father was Irish. She was a half-breed. She had the coloring of a woman who spent much time in the sun without the protection of a bonnet. Her features were clean and delicate. And her eyes—sweet God in heaven, her blue eyes were wide and childlike with trust every time she looked at him. Guilt shot through Matt as he recalled the shock and then the hurt that had registered in those eyes when he had reviled her.

Matt squeezed his own eyes shut, as if to deny what he had done. His hatred for all Apaches warred with his respect for common courtesy. She had Indian blood in her, and that made her different. She could be just like that cutthroat, Ga'n. *But,* his heart said, *if that's so, why didn't she just slit your white throat and get it over with?*

There was a bitter taste in his mouth as Matt lay there, torn between his anguish over the loss of his wife and child and the fact that this woman had saved his life. How could he be grateful and yet hate her at the same time? He released a long sigh. There was no room in his battered heart for anything but grief, hate, and revenge right now.

Matt heard her stir, watching through barely open eyes. Was he a prisoner here? Would she turn him over to Ga'n once he had healed sufficiently? Maybe, if he pretended to be asleep, he could find out more.

A Mexican woman tiptoed into the room. She went over to Lark and gently shook her shoulder. *"Patrona? Patrona?"*

Lark jerked awake. "Maria?" Disoriented, she looked toward Matt. "What's wrong? Is he worse?"

Maria shook her head. "No, no, *patrona.* Remember? You wanted me to awaken you in case you overslept this morning. I have breakfast waiting for you."

With a relieved sigh, Lark got up. "Will you start a fire, Maria? As soon as I make sure Matt is all right, I'll go eat."

Heartened by her mistress's words, Maria bobbed her head. "*Sí, patrona,* I'll get the wood and make a fire that will warm the room quickly." She hurried out of the room.

Rubbing her eyes tiredly, Lark moved over to Matt and sat down on the bed, facing him. This morning some of the dark shadows beneath his eyes had disappeared. A soft smile touched her mouth as she pressed the palm of her hand against his brow. His skin was cool and dry.

"Thank you, Us'an," she murmured in Apache, relief washing through her. And to her healing *di-yin,* she prayed, "Speed his recovery so that he may once again feel his bearlike strength."

Lark no longer questioned her need of Matt Kincaid; she simply accepted the strings that tugged at her heart each time she touched him.

She pushed several strands of his brown hair, which now gleamed with gold highlights, off his brow. A tremor of yearning fluttered through her as she moved her hand through those wonderfully thick locks.

Maria returned with a rustle of skirts. "*Patrona,* I have heard the Old Ones talking," she said. "They do not think you should risk this trip to Prescott today. Can you not wait until my husband, Paco, returns? They think it is dangerous for you to go into the white people's town alone."

Lark slipped into her newest pair of Levi's and pulled a red long-sleeved shirt over her head, smoothing it out across her tall, slender form. "I know the wranglers will be back soon, but I've waited too long as it is, Maria. I can't let it go one more day. I have that army voucher, which means I can buy food and deposit money for the mortgage. If there was a fire or I lost the voucher, then we would lose the ranch." She shook her head, her hair a silken curtain around her shoulders. Standing in front of the mirror, she wrapped a red headband securely around her hair to keep it in place.

"But, *patrona*, it is dangerous! I heard Captain Herter tell Lieutenant Wilson as they rode out that you were doing a foolish thing by going alone." Maria wrung her hands. "Please, *patrona*, we all love you. We have already lost your mother and now your father. We cannot lose you, too."

Impulsively, Lark hugged the small, plump woman. "Thank you for your concern, Maria, but I have to go. Danger or no danger." Silently Lark added, *I am doing this for my father. He wouldn't want me to act like a weakling at this time.* Besides, the Apache respected courage and a show of strength, not cowardice in the face of danger. Today Lark must be an Apache. In some small part of her heart, she knew she was frightened. But pride in her Indian heritage would get her through this day. She buckled on a hand-tooled leather belt inlaid with silver and turquoise, a gift from one of the Tonto Apache chiefs. It would hold her eighteen-inch bowie knife.

Poignantly Lark recalled her father taking her aside when she was twelve years old, just before she went to live weekdays in Prescott with the Harrises. "Remember, colleen, people only respect someone who shows strength and courage. Go there with your head held high and be proud of who and what you are." She allowed the grief to move through her, missing her father even more.

Still unconvinced of Lark's safety, Maria pleaded once more. "One day, *patrona*! Perhaps two. Surely you can wait that long?"

"My father was supposed to bring back a month's worth of supplies a week ago, Maria," she said tightly, moving to the bed. "We have no more flour for your tortillas and we're low on salt. Not only that, but Opata is in need of nails with which to shoe our horses. And you know how rough the country is on their hooves without proper protection." She wrung out a cloth, scrubbing the soap until it lathered against it. "More impor-

tantly, that voucher must be safely placed in the bank."
She looked up at Maria, who stood by the fireplace. Her
voice grew strained. "Father always went to Prescott the
day after receiving such a paper from the army. He knew
the urgency in getting it to safety." She shook her head
stubbornly. "I'll hear no more of your worry, Maria. We
have enough problems; please don't make me feel any
worse than I do already."

Contrite, Maria moved to the other side of the bed, her
round features solemn. "Aren't you afraid to go into
Prescott alone?"

Lark gently washed Matt's face, neck, and shoulders.
"I would be lying if I said I wasn't afraid." Her nostrils
flared as she scrubbed his long, well-muscled limbs. "My
mother was a woman chief. She had courage that they still
sing about at each gathering of the Chiricahua tribe. How
can I shame her by putting my tail between my legs like
a beaten dog? No, I'll pray to my *di-yin* to protect me.
I will have my knife and my rifle; I need nothing more."

"Then take me with you! I will drive the buckboard
and you can ride Kentucky."

With a sigh, Lark looked over at the Mexican woman.
"*A-co-d.* Thank you." She used the word rarely because
it meant so much to the Apache people. Maria bowed her
head, her lower lip trembling.

"Will you watch over Señor Kincaid while I am
gone?" Lark asked. "Change his dressing tonight? I
won't arrive back in time to do it."

With a sniff, Maria nodded. "*Sí, patrona,* I will care
for him."

"If anything happens and you need help, bring Ny-
Oden to the room. He will instruct you."

Maria moved dejectedly to the door. "*Sí,* I will ask
him, *patrona.* I won't be able to care for Señor Kincaid
as well as you do, but I promise I'll do my best."

A slight smile came to Lark's lips as she settled her
gaze on Maria. It moved her deeply that Maria was
worried for her safety. She had no idea how much the

people who had worked for her father also cared for her. "I see," she said lightly. "You will make me worry that he'll be a snarling bear in pain so that I will return more quickly. Is that it?"

A hesitant smile fled across Maria's bowlike mouth. "You see too easily through my plan, *patrona*." She giggled, her hands pressed to her lips, her eyes dancing. "I see you care deeply for this *hombre*."

Heat prickled Lark's cheeks as she washed Matt's broad chest and hard, flat belly. "I would care the same for any injured human or animal," she told Maria defensively. By Us'an, were her feelings for Matt *that* transparent? Lark nearly choked on the discovery.

Another giggle escaped Maria as she stood poised in the doorway. "Aiyee, *patrona,* do not blush so! You look like a red poppy in a green field. Indeed, if I did not love my Paco and our four *niños,* I would gladly make it known that I liked Señor Kincaid."

With a soft snort, Lark rinsed out the cloth before wiping Matt's chest and belly free of soap. "Bring me the freshly ground poultice. I'll change his dressing. And have Rafael hitch up the two mules to the buckboard and bring them up to the house."

"Right away, *patrona*." Maria turned on her bare feet and disappeared down the hall. As soon as she returned with the new poultice, she went about her morning household duties.

Lark pulled the blanket away from Matt's wound. She set to work slitting the bandage and then gently sponging the dressing free from the leg. As she tried to carefully lift the yellowish-pink dressing, she heard him draw in a swift breath. Hands frozen over his leg, her head snapped up. Her widened blue eyes met his dark gray ones.

Lark went hot as his eyes probed her like a hawk preparing to devour his prey. But she saw something else in the dark, pain-filled depths of his gaze, an emotion that she couldn't readily identify. Automatically she felt her

breasts tighten, her nipples growing hard against the rough
cotton of her shirt. He was so blatantly male.

Shakily, as if in a daze, Lark lifted away the dressing.
"I do not mean to hurt you," she said, "but the packing
must be changed."

Matt stared at her, unable to stop the hardening of his
male member. Sweet God in heaven, her touch on his
body was like wildfire consuming dry prairie grass. He
had tried valiantly to ignore it. The conversation between
the two women was too important to give away the fact
that he had been awake. Later, he would think about what
they had said. Right now, he couldn't think, could only
feel the licking flames in the wake of her cool, gentle
touch upon his flesh.

Struggling to control his powerful desire, Matt tried to
use his hatred and anger to consume those flames burning
deep within him. He tried to resurrect his hatred of Ga'n
and direct it against Lark instead. But it was impossible.
The red shirt she wore only emphasized the dusky gold
of her young, glowing skin and heightened the blush over
her high, smooth cheekbones. When she nervously licked
her lower lip, he almost groaned. The thought of feeling
that full mouth blossom beneath his own almost unstrung
him and his heart hammered away in his chest.

Her face was young and innocent. It was not a perfect
face, but somehow it was maddeningly arresting, to the
point that he couldn't tear away his fascinated gaze. Guilt
consumed him. Katie had just died, yet he was responding
to Lark like a ram in rutting season. What the hell was
happening to him?

Matt had seen the same confusion in Lark's clear,
widening eyes. Whatever it was, they both felt it equally.
He tried to concentrate on the imperfection of her face.
Her cheekbones were too high, giving her eyes almost a
catlike tilt. But they only made her look like the golden
cougar he had imagined her in his fevered dreams. There
was a bump on her nose, indicating she had broken it
once. Her eyebrows were slender and winged, framing her

flawless eyes. Grudgingly, Matt had to admit he could find no further imperfections.

Lark blinked, as if in a dream. "I . . . I must change the poultice." Did her voice sound breathy, like a wisp of fog stealing through a pine?

"Do it," he growled.

The coldness in his voice snapped her out of her daze. Lark frowned, feeling his icy eyes slash straight through and scar her wildly beating heart. But, despite his anger, her nipples continued to pucker against her shirt. The strange, aching feeling in her breasts continued.

What could she do? The peaks of her nipples were clearly outlined by the fabric. It was taboo for her to react this way. As she got up to retrieve the poultice, she inadvertently bumped the water bowl, sending it smashing to the floor. Stumbling back, a hand across her mouth to stifle her cry, she felt the tenuous, throbbing cord that bound them to one another break.

Maria came rushing into the room, her skirts flying around her ankles. She halted upon seeing the broken crockery. "I'll clean it up, *patrona*," she reassured Lark, and left for towels to sop up the water spreading quickly across the oak floor.

Humiliated, Lark bowed her head, feeling her cheeks burn as never before, feeling Matt's eyes scalding her. Her fingers trembled as she picked up a cloth, preparing to cleanse the wound.

"For being half white, you sure as hell act like a shy Apache woman."

Lark lifted her chin, furious at his grating comment, prepared to do verbal battle with him. When she realized there was no condemnation in his gray eyes, she was momentarily at a loss.

"I'm half Apache."

"You're also half white, if I recall."

Bristling, Lark gingerly washed around the wound with warm, soapy water. She felt him stiffen and took almost savage pleasure in giving back some of the pain he had caused her. Almost . . .

Matt saw the anger burn in her eyes like blue cobalt. He tensed, locking his hands into fists as she gently dug the old poultice out of the wound. Sweat beaded his drawn brow and a curse hissed from between his clenched teeth. "You have a hell of a way of getting even," he rasped, sweat dribbling down his temples.

"I'm not getting even! Your wound must be cleaned before I can put on a fresh poultice."

"Why the hell didn't you get me a doctor from Prescott like I asked?"

Stung by his ungrateful attitude, Lark stubbornly set her lips and replaced the poultice. "No doctor would come out here, that's why."

"You can't be more than forty miles from Prescott. Or didn't you even try, thinking you could kill me with your chants and that smelly green stuff you're jamming into my leg."

The man was insufferable! Lark washed her fingers and gently laid a new dressing over his leg. "We're twenty miles from town, Mr. Kincaid. Very few whites ever come to the Gallagher Ranch."

The throbbing pain began to recede and Matt slowly let his muscles relax, feeling suddenly shaky in the aftermath. In all fairness, Lark's touch was anything but painful. She was expert and quick about changing the dressings. With maddening ease, he found himself perversely enjoying prodding and poking at her. The anger in her eyes only made her appear that much more desirable.

"Why don't whites come here?" he goaded.

"Because the whites of Prescott hate us. We are the wrong mix of color and belief for them." She flashed an angry look toward him. There was a contemptuous smile on his unshaven face and Lark wanted to slap it off his features. He was a rude and obnoxious guest. But what else did she expect? He was a *pindah*.

Maria came in and silently began picking up the pieces of broken pottery and mopping up the water.

"Don't they respect your white half?" he drawled.

"Not any more than I respect them," she replied between set lips. Carefully Lark rolled clean strips of white cloth around his thigh, covering the poultice.

"Maybe if you'd dress like a normal white woman, someone might take you seriously and quit treating you like an Injun."

That did it! Lark sucked in a swift breath, her hands stilling on his leg. Her eyes narrowed in blue fury. "And if I tended you in a dress instead of in these clothes, would you treat me any differently?"

"Might."

Her nostrils flared. "Then you're as blind and insensitive as all the other *pindahs* I know! Clothes do not make a person. At least the Apache judge one another on far more important considerations than that!"

Matt grinned lopsidedly, thinking how fiery and untamed she appeared in that molten moment. He longed to reach out, slide his fingers through that ebony cascade, and find out how just how soft and silken it was. "What do Apache judge another person by?"

She forced herself to finish the bandaging, her temper stealing her ability to think clearly. "Apaches celebrate the good in another person, their wisdom, physical strength, industriousness, and, most importantly, their generosity with food and gifts to those who are less fortunate than themselves." She nailed him with a glare, knotting the cotton savagely and then standing up. "Clothes mean nothing to us. They are practical, that's all. Which just shows me how shallow you *pindahs* are. Why should I claim my white half when I'm ashamed of how they act?"

Matt scowled, watching as she stood stiffly before him. "So where are you going all dressed up?" he asked sarcastically.

Bending down, Lark helped Maria retrieve the last

shards of the bowl. "I'm going into Prescott. Not that it's any of your business."

"Then bring a real doctor back with you. I don't want my leg to fall off."

Fury boiled through her. Her hands clenched into fists at her sides. "If I could, I would. If I was allowed, I'd dump you into *pindah* hands and have peace once more on the ranch."

At that moment, she looked to Matt like an Apache war chief. Her head was high, her chin thrust out, her shoulders proudly thrown back with her booted legs slightly spread for good balance. She was part woman, part savage, and part beautiful animal. Her long, black hair hung almost to her waist, cloaking her in an ebony sheet that enhanced her natural Apache wildness.

"Then take me along with you," he said. "Anything's better than staying here."

Maria glanced apprehensively at Lark, then at Kincaid, and then excused herself.

Lark wrestled with her temper. She placed her hands on her hips, a distinct Apache gesture that meant to warn the other person that she was in a joking or teasing mood. She had done it unconsciously. "If you want to risk bleeding to death over a bumpy road for five hours, I don't care. If dying is suddenly more important to you than living, that is your choice. I have no men here to help carry you to the buckboard, so if you want to go with me, then get up!"

Matt didn't believe he would bleed to death. He tried to sit up—three times he tried. Sweat stood out on his brow as he struggled. Glaring at her, he saw amusement etched clearly in Lark's narrowed blue eyes. She was laughing at him. Damn her! He wanted to strangle her. As he lay back, breathing hard, Matt knew that wasn't true. No, he wanted to take her down beneath him and feel her body move sensuously below his, like a big, golden cat being stroked by her master. A flash of desire snuffed out his anger.

"Looks like you win this round," he gritted out. "I'm still your prisoner."

"You are a guest here, not a prisoner." Lark allowed her hands to slip from her slim hips, suddenly feeling drained by their confrontation. She walked around the bed to the dresser and pulled out the honed steel blade of her bowie knife. It was a beautifully balanced weapon, one that Cochise had gifted her with many years before. Slipping it into the scabbard she carried low on her left hip, Lark turned back to Matt. He was watching her with a strange expression on his face. Was it admiration or disgust? She was too exhausted to care.

"Wait," he called as she walked toward the door.

Lark barely turned toward him. "I want no more words with you, Mr. Kincaid. I am not your enemy. I never have been. If you hate me and my people, so be it. While I'm gone, I ask that you treat Maria and Ny-Oden, the old shaman, with respect. If you hate Apaches, then take it out on me when I return, not on them. They only want you to get better and live. They don't deserve your rudeness."

His mouth softened as he heard the infinite weariness in her low voice. The change in Lark was startling; one moment she was a fiery hellion, the next a woman who carried too many heavy responsibilities on her young, inexperienced shoulders. He vividly recalled the conversation earlier between Lark and Maria about the dangers of going into Prescott alone.

"Look, I didn't mean to get carried away," he muttered, coming as close to an apology as she was ever going to get from him. His heart wrenched as he saw the corners of her once tense mouth relax into a vague smile. It changed her entire face, and a keen need for her swept through him with unexpected force.

"You've been gravely ill. I didn't mean to get angry or short with you, either. It's just that I . . . well, I've had many burdens to carry of late."

Moved by her halting apology, Matt felt the last of his

anger dissolve. She was right; she didn't deserve his hatred. He liked her strength and her vulnerability. In that poignant moment, as she met and held his gaze, he wanted to reach out and protect her. He cleared his throat. "When will you be back?"

Lark noted the change in Matt and was warmed by his sudden concern. "It is a five-hour ride to Prescott. I will try to get a doctor to come out, but I cannot promise you anything. There is other business I must also attend to. Perhaps by moonrise I'll return."

"I see."

"Before you sleep tonight, Maria will change the poultice once more."

"You won't be back in time?"

Lark shook her head. "Tomorrow morning I will tend you."

Matt stared after her as she left the room, excruciatingly aware of the loss of her vibrant presence. Was Lark really in danger by going into Prescott alone? Dressed like a damned Apache, she was certainly going to draw plenty of attention to herself. He strained to hear the voices of Lark and Maria outside the room, but it was impossible. When the two burly brown mules drawing the wagon walked by, Matt was able to get one last glimpse of Lark as she sat on the seat of the buckboard. Frustrated, he lay back down, filled with guilt and anger.

# Chapter 5

Lark tried to ignore the malevolent stares of the people of Prescott as she drove the buckboard down the dusty main street. Two years ago, her father had begged her to come to town with him so she could try again to adapt to the white world. Since her humiliation by the school children when she was twelve, she had never wanted to return to the place that held only painful memories for her. At sixteen, she had reluctantly joined her father on his monthly trips. He had wanted to show her "his people" and had tried to tell her that there were kind white people, not just bad ones like Cameron and Shanks. She remembered with mortification that the trip had only multiplied her pain. Although she had worn a dress like a white woman, the children had taunted her when she walked down the wooden sidewalk from the bank to the dry goods store, calling her a breed and throwing rocks and clods of dirt at her. Finding safety in Abe Harris's store, Lark had thought she was finally safe, but she had been wrong. Bo Shanks had ambled in and caused her the worst embarrassment of her life. Lark slammed the door shut on those memories, concentrating instead on the present.

The children were in school now, so she was saved from their revilement. Fleetingly she saw the white women in all their finery and remembered Matt Kincaid's words about dressing as they did. Wearing a white woman's dress did not guarantee her acceptance by them, as Lark had already discovered.

She passed Madam Bouchard's Dress Shop and saw in the window a dress made of blue silk with a violet sheen to it. The cloth took her breath away as she stared at the confection. But her momentary awe was squelched when an obviously wealthy patron emerged and spotted her. The woman raised her nose daintily into the air and pressed a lacy handkerchief to her face, disdain evident in every line of her aristocratic features. Her lips set, Lark forced herself not to react to the woman's rude behavior.

Why Matt would want her to acknowledge her white heritage was beyond her. Did white men want their women merely as pretty baubles? The Apache were the opposite; they applauded a woman's strength, intelligence, and ability to fight at her husband's side.

The three-story brick building owned by Jud Cameron loomed ahead. Lark's fingers tightened around the worn leather trace reins. Nervousness rose like stinging bile in her throat as she pulled the buckboard to a halt. Tying the nearest mule to the hitching rail, Lark girded herself for the confrontation with Cameron.

She had no more than pulled open the glass and brass door and stepped inside when two women who were doing business with tellers turned and ogled her. Lark froze, staring back at them. It was noon and the bank was filled to capacity with customers; at least ten people were present. Her mouth went dry as she saw two men automatically scowl in her direction. A third man whispered, "Apache squaw." Everyone in the bank fell silent, their eyes focused on Lark.

Squaring her shoulders, she walked to the first teller. "I'm Lark Gallagher and I wish to see Mr. Cameron. I have business with him."

The clerk, who was no more than seventeen, with a hint of acne on his pale face, gave a jerky nod to the left, as if seeking approval for her request.

A shiver of warning rippled up Lark's spine. She barely

turned her head. Standing in the background was Bo
Shanks, his tall, lean body slouched against the wall, his
guns worn low on his narrow hips. His eyes focused
intensely upon her. They were the eyes of a coyote. All
her senses shrilled in warning, but she refused to react to
the twisted smile on his full mouth. He chewed on a
toothpick like a cow chewing on its cud, his arms across
his chest. Silence built to a brittle crescendo as they
locked stares.

Bo Shanks eased from his position, spitting out the
toothpick on the highly waxed tile floor. He grinned as
he walked with the ease of a predator who knew he was
master of his territory. As he approached Lark, his smile
reflected barely veiled insolence.

"Roarke Gallagher's breed daughter, eh?" he said in a
soft, sinister voice. "Well, what do ya know . . ."

Lark stood her ground. She was as tall as the gunfighter
and refused to look away from his amber eyes. Her heart
beat hard in her breast as his scalding gaze traveled
upward from her booted feet, lingered hotly at the apex
of her thighs, then moved on to where her breasts were
thrust against the shirt she wore, the soft cotton emphasizing their fullness. Finally his gaze swept up her neck
to her face. Her nostrils flared as she registered his sour,
unwashed smell. His sandy hair was parted to one side
and slicked down with grease, emphasizing the long lines
of his face. He was in his early twenties, yet his face
looked unduly aged due to bouts of hard drinking. Lark
doubted the lines in his face had come from an honest
day's labor. Everyone knew Shanks was Jud Cameron's
hired gun even though he was supposed to work as a
drover on the banker's ranch.

"What's it been, Lark? Two years since I last saw
ya?" He grinned, his uneven teeth exposed as if in a
snarl. "You've changed," he added with more than
passing interest.

"And you haven't, Shanks." Her voice vibrated with

hatred. "Now let me pass. I have business with Mr. Cameron."

"And if I don't, breed?"

Lark remembered with humiliating clarity how Shanks had once grabbed her in Abe's store and mauled her playfully, unmercifully. His long, skinny hands had roved across her breasts and she had frozen in shock and pain. Then, gathering her wits, she had fought back. The proof of her attack, four long scars, lay like dull pink slashes along Shanks's left cheek where she had raked him. As he had backed off, he'd sworn he'd have her someday—his way. At the time she had been too young to realize what he meant by his threat. Now she understood completely.

Lark checked her anger, feeling all eyes upon her. Automatically she placed the palm of her left hand over the butt of the knife that rested in the scabbard. "I'm taking care of my father's banking business now. Let me pass, Shanks," she said in low tones.

Shanks snickered and took a step back. "Yeah, I heard yore old man took a bullet in the back. Ya oughta be careful that yore not next." He threw a look at the nervous young teller. "Willy, tell Mr. Cameron he's got a visitor. A *Miss* Gallagher," he emphasized, grinning.

Jud Cameron had just raised his shot glass full of mellow sipping whiskey in a toast to Colonel Parker Morgan, commanding officer of Fort Whipple, when the knock interrupted him. With a scowl, he ordered, "Come in." Damn, he didn't want to be disturbed, and Shanks knew that. What the hell was going on?

Willy doffed the green visor he wore over his eyes. "Sir, Mr. Shanks says to tell you a Miss Gallagher is here to talk business with you."

Morgan shot a wry glance at Cameron. "That Apache half-breed daughter of Roarke Gallagher's?"

Jud smiled as he rose, tossing the whiskey down his throat. It burned pleasantly all the way down. "The *late*

Roarke Gallagher." He turned back to his clerk. "Take her to my other office, Willy. I'll be there in a minute."

"Yes, sir. Right away, sir."

Jud waited until the door closed before speaking. "This is the beginning of the end for the Gallagher Ranch," he announced. "And don't say I didn't tell you so."

Morgan shrugged his broad shoulders and poured himself another whiskey. "I didn't think you could get Gallagher, but I was wrong. What's next in your campaign to get the water rights to that ranch?"

Jud rebuttoned his paisley, velvet vest and shrugged into his gray business coat. "I've told Sheriff Cole to tell Lark Gallagher that an Apache shot her father outside of town. Of course, he'll blame it on Ga'n since he's been keeping the area a hotbed of problems for the U.S. Army. Now she's by herself. No woman can run a ranch on her own. I plan to offer her cash to sell it. In her present position, I'm sure she'll accept."

Morgan's fleshy features broke into a smile and he lifted his glass in another toast. "I've got to give you credit, Jud. You and the Ring have certainly brought more government funds to the Arizona Territory, more than I ever dreamed possible. Your idea to keep the damned Apaches stirred up and force the government to bring in more troops has been a brilliant success."

Jud checked the time on his gold watch before placing it back in the side pocket. The Tucson Indian Ring had been created ten years earlier by some very astute businessmen in the Arizona Territory who saw a way to make huge profits. Jud was in charge of the northern area. He bribed men like Morgan, Cole, and Shanks to bend or ignore the law completely. Yes, he liked greedy men; they were easy to control. The Ring's power and influence was building yearly, their coffers filling with more money than he'd ever dreamed existed. Now the Ring's influence reached clear back to Washington, D.C. Cameron felt the keen edge of power, and he savored the sensation. It was simple arithmetic: keep the whites and

Indians at war with one another and the government
would keep sending more money and troops.

Jud looked over at Morgan. "You're building a nice
little nest egg, too, don't forget. Just keep turning your
head the other way when I send Shanks and my boys out
to raid an Apache rancheria, and when Ga'n and his
renegades attack the settlers."

"We need to talk about tactical raids along that line,
Jud."

He raised a well-manicured hand. "This won't take
long. I'll be back in fifteen minutes to discuss the Ring's
next series of raids. In the meantime, enjoy this good
whiskey."

Lark looked up as the door to the office opened and
closed. She held the voucher tightly in her hand, along
with the bankbook to her father's savings account.

Jud Cameron reminded her of a snake. Although he
wore only the finest clothes, although his black hair was
neatly cut and his thick mustache trimmed, he was the
most poisonous kind of *pindah*. Again she had to endure
from him the kind of torrid inspection she had come to
expect from white men. As Cameron stripped her naked
with his cool green gaze all her muscles tightened with
wariness. She stood without speaking, her eyes blazing
with distrust.

Finally Cameron came forward and sat down at the
massive maple desk. With a flourish he gestured toward
a leather wing chair. "Sit down, Lark. How long has it
been? Almost two years since I last had the pleasure of
seeing you?" He smiled to himself: she was a breathtaking creature, a wild, untamed golden savage. Just her
proud, silent stance fired his blood. By the age of thirty,
he'd sampled just about every kind of female there was,
but he'd never had a half-breed Apache woman, and he
savored the thought of having her.

Lark sat down on the edge of the chair, the voucher

clutched in her hands. "I've come to take over my father's business with the Prescott Bank, Mr. Cameron."

Jud steepled his long, slender fingers in front of him and leaned back in his chair. "Yes . . . I heard about your father's untimely death. My condolences to you, Lark. It was a shame. He was a respected man here in Prescott." Respected for the quality of horses he raised, Jud amended silently, and endlessly gossiped about because of his squaw wife and breed daughter, plus that menagerie of coloreds, greasers, and God knew what other half animals he had working for him at his ranch.

Lark inclined her head. "I bring an army voucher to place in our account, Mr. Cameron." She stood and laid the voucher and book in front of him. Swallowing her pride, she admitted, "I'm not familiar with how to bank. If you will show me . . ."

"Of course, Lark." He studied the army voucher, some of his smile slipping. That damned Frank Herter was giving her top dollar for the offspring of that red Kentucky Stud! The U.S. Army had commissioned Herter directly as supply officer in charge of buying horses for the forts in the northern Arizona Territory. Because of that, Colonel Morgan couldn't control Herter's dealings or what he paid for a particular ranch's animals. Jud had wanted Herter to buy his own stock at top price, but Herter had claimed the Gallagher stallion sired better foals. Clearly, he needed that red stallion. Well, it was just a matter of time and he'd have him.

Cameron fingered the thick, heavy paper with Herter's signature on it. Herter was due to retire shortly. Soon they'd be rid of that bastard, who had stood like a wall between the Ring and Gallagher's Ranch.

"Before I can take this," Cameron said, "you must sign it. Can you write your name?"

Lark held his gaze. "Yes, I can. I also speak three languages fluently." Lark couldn't read or write well, but she relied on her memory, which had never failed her.

Jud placed a pen and ink pot in front of her. "I'm

impressed," he complimented her smoothly. "After I heard you quit school, I lost track of your education."

She signed her full name across the back of the voucher. "My father became my teacher," she explained tersely.

Studying her neat penmanship, Jud smiled. "And quite a good one judging from the flourish of your handwriting."

Praise coming from a snake was still venom in disguise as far as Lark was concerned. She ignored his compliment. "I want six hundred dollars put in this," she said, pointing to the green bankbook, "and I want four hundred dollars in cash."

"First you've got to pay up on this month's mortgage, Lark," he said, shaking his head.

Lark's mouth fell open. "What? My father paid this month's mortgage already!"

"Do you have any proof that he did? My teller always gives him a payment slip confirming that the mortgage was paid on time. Do you have it?"

Her head swam in confusion. When Father Mulcahy had brought her father's body back in the buckboard, all his money and his gold watch had been missing. There had been no payment slip in the bankbook she had retrieved from his shirt pocket. "But he was killed *after* leaving Prescott. That means he stopped here at your bank and paid the money we owed, then got supplies and had a drink over at the saloon before he left."

With a lift of his shoulders, Jud said, "I'm sorry, Lark, but there's no evidence he paid the one hundred dollars he owes the bank this month."

She sat down, dazed. If only she understood math and banking! If only she wasn't so poor at reading and numbers. Anguished, Lark knew her father had already paid this month's mortgage. She looked up at Cameron's smiling features and hated him even more, knowing she would have to pay two months' mortgage. Education was power, she was discovering.

Jud smiled paternally once the transactions were complete. "Are you going to be selling your ranch soon?"

Lark stuffed the books in her pocket. "No."

With a light laugh, he stood. "Now, now, Lark. No woman can handle a ranch by herself. Surely you know that."

Her jaw tightened. "I'm half Apache, Mr. Cameron. Apaches know their women can do anything a warrior can do. I'll run the ranch."

Jud scowled. Damn her, anyway! She had her father's obstinancy. Trying to soothe her ruffled feathers, he took another tack. "Since you're going to manage your ranch, then I need to discuss buying water rights from you, Lark."

Slowly she rose to her feet. "I have only enough water for my livestock, Mr. Cameron."

"Come now! You've got artesian wells on your property. Surely you can see your way clear to selling me some water over the summer months. I've got ten thousand head of cattle that will die if I don't get them water."

Lark stood her ground, her jaw set. "I don't have enough for both my stock and yours! I'm not interested in selling water rights."

"Goddammit, I'm not going to have my herd die just because you're being a stubborn redskin!"

Lark gasped, anger exploding within her. She lunged toward Cameron, poking her finger into his chest. "You cowardly dog! You shot my father over this very issue! I know you did!" Her nostrils quivered, and she held his shocked stare. "My father wouldn't sell the rights to you and I won't either," she whispered tightly.

With a curse, Jud strode to the door and jerked it open. "Get the hell out of here! You're as crazy as those drunken Injuns! Going around accusing me of killing your father—that's ridiculous! Get out!"

She stood where she was, trembling with fury. The

silence became suffocating, both of them breathing hard. Her voice was a rasp when she spoke. "I'll leave, Cameron. But I'm going to track down my father's killer. I *know* you had something to do with it. I *know* it had something to do with the water rights to our ranch. And I won't let you get away with cold-blooded murder. I swear it . . ."

"You little idiot." He jerked a thumb toward the doorway. "Get out of here. I could have you arrested for making these ridiculous accusations. You're grieving, so I'll let it pass—this time."

Lark walked up to Cameron, her fists clenched at her sides. "My father's killers will be brought to justice."

Jud watched her walk down the hall. The arrogant bitch! As he returned to his desk, a plan formed in his mind. First he'd get hold of Shanks. Then he'd drive out to the Bar T, his ranch, and call a meeting of the Ring. He needed the water rights to Gallagher's property, and if he had to use a little of the Ring's influence to get it, so much the worse for Lark Gallagher.

Abe Harris greeted Lark warmly as she entered his dry goods store. His other lady customers were not so inclined and muttered darkly under their breaths before quickly leaving the premises. Within a minute, the store stood empty and silent. Abe scratched his balding head and pushed his square spectacles up on his large nose.

"Looks like they all had someplace to go in a hurry," he noted wryly. He came around a bin containing bolts of colorful cotton and extended a hand to Lark. "We were terribly shocked and saddened to hear of your father's death, Lark. Both Millie and I were shaken. Father Mulcahy said you buried him out at the ranch. We'll be coming by shortly to pay our respects."

Lark gripped his firm, dry hand. "Your words touch my heart, Abe. Thank you."

He patted her hand and then released it. "Is there anything we can do for you, Lark? You're there at that ranch all alone now.'' Before she could reply, the door opened and closed. Abe's face went blank.

Lark turned, perplexed, and her eyes narrowed on Bo Shanks as he ambled into the store.

''Afternoon, Mr. Harris,'' he drawled. He lifted his boot, and the match he held exploded into flaming life as he struck it against the hardened leather. He sucked on a thin brown cheroot pressed between his full lips. The smoke drifted upward, making him squint. Negligently, he tossed the dead match aside.

''Afternoon, Mr. Shanks. What can I do for you?'' Abe asked in a tense tone.

''Oh . . . nothing. Nothing. Just lookin' around is all. Go ahead, wait on the little lady.''

Stifling an urge to scream at him, to tell him to quit following her, Lark tried to keep her mind on the business at hand. ''The supplies my father bought from you earlier were destroyed after he was murdered—''

''Way I hear it, Ga'n killed him,'' Shanks volunteered, moving around a bin. He lifted a bolt of red cotton. ''You'd look good in this. Would bring out that wild Injun blood.''

Lark turned her back on Shanks. ''Abe, can you fill this order?'' She handed him a long list. ''I have the wagon outside.''

Abe studied the paper. ''Sure can, Lark. It's identical to the last order. Let me get my boy, Hastings, to help load it—''

''She gets no help, old man.''

Anger congealed into hatred and Lark turned toward the gunslinger. ''You have no right to bother me, Shanks. Get out of here and leave Mr. Harris and me alone.''

''Look, Mr. Shanks,'' Abe added, ''those flour sacks weigh a hundred pounds apiece. No woman ought to tussle with that kind of weight.''

Shanks drew deeply on his cheroot and released another cloud of white smoke from his mouth and nostrils. His eyes glittered. ''She won't mind. Apaches are bred to be like mules—they're nothing but beasts of burden. Ain't that right, breed?''

Fully aware of how dangerous Shanks could be when riled, Lark realized with sinking finality that if she bucked his order, Abe might be roughed up. No one crossed Shanks's path. If someone did, he was apt to find his home or business mysteriously destroyed by fire. She loved Abe and Millie too much to subject them to Shanks's brand of revenge.

"I'll pack my own supplies, Abe," she whispered tautly. "If you'll just credit—"

"No credit for you," Shanks said softly, giving Harris a look that spoke volumes.

"You stay out of this!" Lark cried.

Shanks looked steadily at Harris, a silent warning in his green eyes. "She gets no credit."

"My father had credit with Mr. Harris for years! You can't just decide that I can't have it."

Sliding his fingers over the curve of his Colt, Shanks smiled. "Sure I can. Ya may be queen of that ranch of yores, but here in Prescott, yore nothin' more than a breed. And Injuns and breeds ain't wanted here. Understand? Next time I suggest ya send some of those greasy Mexes in to do yore business for ya. No tellin' what the town folk might do if ya show yore face here again. They're in a scalp-huntin' mood." He smiled slightly. "Why, a scalp like yores would fetch a twenty-dollar gold piece over at Fort Whipple . . ."

Lark's nostrils quivered. "Why are you doing this?"

"Let's just say I'm doin' ya a real big favor by warnin' ya."

"You work for Jud Cameron. Has he put you up to harassing me?"

"A squaw that thinks. I'll be damned." Abruptly his smile disappeared. "Get yore supplies and get out of here. I'm runnin' out of patience."

Fearful for Lark, Abe tugged on her sleeve. "Come on, Lark, do as he says. Please?"

Resigned, she nodded.

After the supplies were loaded, she reluctantly paid the one hundred dollars. That meant only three hundred was left with which to pay each of her wranglers fifteen dollars per month until they earned the next army voucher. Tucking the money into the left breast pocket of her shirt, she glared one last time at Shanks, who was leaning lazily against the hitching post outside, finishing off his third cheroot. As she slapped the reins to the backs of the mules, she reassured herself with the thought that, as soon as she talked to the sheriff, her business in Prescott would be finished and she could go home.

Sheriff Dan Cole didn't even move his feet off the desk when she entered his office. He looked up from the handful of wanted posters he held and sized her up like the other white men had. Lark swallowed against her disgust.

"What are ya doing here?" he drawled, smoothing his long, blond handlebar mustache with tobacco-stained fingers.

Lark looked around the empty office, noting that several cells contained prisoners. Wanted posters filled one wall. Cole's watery blue eyes missed nothing. Lark didn't like his thin-lipped mouth, his hooded eyes, or the deceptive ease with which he examined her.

"I want you to continue to investigate my father's murder, sheriff."

Cole stopped stroking the end of his carefully manicured mustache. "I tole ya, the case is closed, girl."

"Ga'n knew and respected my father, sheriff. He'd never kill him."

With a shrug, Cole eyed her carelessly. "The report I filed said he was shot in the back by an Injun. Pure and simple."

Rage twisted through Lark and she took a step forward. "You liar! You haven't even investigated who might have done it, have you?" She fought to control her anger, clenching her hands. "He was a good man, sheriff! How can you justify ignoring his killer?"

"Watch yore mouth, breed. I'm tryin' to keep my patience with ya precisely because yore father was respected in this community. But I won't take that kind of talk from anyone. Certainly not from a woman and especially not from a breed. Now get out of here. I've got work to do."

She stood wavering, torn between anguish and frustration. "Did you even go out to Denton Road where he was killed? Did you check for hoofprints to see if the horses were shod or not? What about the bullet? Did you have my father's body examined? What kind of gun or rifle did it come from? He was killed with one shot between the shoulder blades. Only a gunslinger kills from behind and with that kind of accuracy. Have you questioned Bo Shanks? He's a known killer!"

Slowly, his every movement full of menace, Cole pulled his boots off the desk and rose to his feet. "Nobody tells me how to do my job," he said with soft harshness. "I rode out and gave you a copy of the report. That's the extent of my responsibility."

In her heart, Lark knew Cole was covering up for someone. But who? Acid burned in her mouth. "I won't let you get away with this, Sheriff Cole. I'll ask Ga'n about this myself the next time I see him."

Cole snorted. "Then yore gonna be in a heap o' trouble, girl. Ga'n's wanted by every U.S. agency in this territory. If yore caught consortin' with him, yore gonna be hauled up on charges too. Just remember that. An accessory after the fact."

"My own people are trying to hunt him down just like yours are," she said. "He's killed Mexicans, Apaches, and whites alike."

"Just proves my case: yore father was a white and Ga'n hates us worse than any other race. Git out of here. I've wasted enough time on you."

Without another word, Lark left. Before she climbed

into the buckboard she checked the wagonload of supplies. She couldn't afford to have them stolen from under her nose. How quickly the money from the voucher was running through her fingers. As she urged the mules into a brisk walk, anxiety ate at her. Was this how her father had felt when his hard-earned money had trickled away like fog before Holos? Her mind spun with thoughts of how many mortgage payments could be made over the next year, how much money would be left for monthly supplies and the wranglers' wages.

She was so engrossed trying to sort out the numbers that she didn't notice the glares of the townspeople as she left main street and headed home. Holos had slipped from the zenith two hours ago. When Lark finally pushed aside her troubling thoughts, it was time to turn off the main thoroughfare and take the poorly maintained Denton Road that would eventually lead to the ranch.

She brought the mules to a temporary halt and took a long drink of the warm water in the canteen. Some of it spilled from the corner of her mouth, winding down her slender throat and soaking into her shirt. Capping the canteen, she studied the pine-covered mountains that rose around her. Was this where her father had been bushwacked? Certainly the silent hills could hide an attacker. She wrestled with a surge of grief as she wondered who had killed her father. He hadn't stood a chance, the bullet striking him with deadly accuracy in the back, straight through to his warm and generous heart.

Suddenly Lark tensed, her attention drawn to the mules, whose ears had abruptly pricked up. She sniffed to catch any unusual scent she might have missed and tilted her head, listening intently. A violent shiver worked its way up her spine, her father's killing branded too freshly in her memory.

As she reached down to retrieve the loaded Winchester, the mules veered suddenly to the right and five riders, men with bandannas drawn across their sweaty faces, swooped down at a gallop from behind a towering cliff.

Lark was jerked backward by the unexpected movement of the buckboard, and the mules came to a sudden halt as one man yanked the reins out of her hands. Red dust billowed around them as the horses milled restlessly around her buckboard.

Lark's eyes widened as she recognized Shanks's lean form, despite the black, broad-brimmed hat drawn down across his yellow eyes.

"Heeyyy, what have we here?" crowed a hulking cowboy in a black shirt. He pulled his sweaty bay gelding up to where Lark sat stiffly. When he reached out to touch her, she shrank away from him.

"Leave me alone!" she shrieked, striking him with her fist and rising to her feet. The men on their nervous mounts guffawed and pressed closer to the buckboard, making it impossible for Lark to keep her eye on all of them.

"Nah, we can't do that, breed," another shouted, his laughter high and off pitch.

The hulking cowboy behind Lark stretched up in his stirrups and wrapped his hand in her hair. With a vicious yank, he pulled her off the wagon.

She struck the dry, dusty earth with jarring force, her head slamming backward. Momentarily stunned, she saw the hooves of several horses dancing close to where she lay. Gasping for breath, she struggled to rise to her feet, but from another direction a boot caught her in a glancing blow to the shoulder, sending her sprawling forward on her belly.

"Get those supplies out of there."

Lark recognized Shanks's soft voice. Spitting dirt out of her mouth and ignoring her aching shoulder, she lunged swiftly to her feet while two men dismounted, clambered onto the bed of the buckboard, and began throwing the supplies out onto the trail. There were yips of approval and bursts of laughter as one of them used his knife to slit open a hundred-pound sack of flour. The stone-ground meal spread in all directions, lost to the wind and dust.

With a cry of rage, Lark charged them. A horse blocked her path. Blindly she tried to push past the animal, but the rider only laughed, forcing her away with the sheer bulk of the lathered animal.

"No!" she shrieked, pounding at his chapped leg, then dropped to her knees and rolled beneath the horse's legs. Breathing hard, she pulled her knife from the scabbard and leaped with startling ease into the back of the wagon. With a scream of pure fury, she slashed the bowie knife first in one direction, then the other, at the two men who were destroying the supplies.

Was this how they had treated her father? Had they taken his supplies first and then shot him? She struck out again, watching as the cowboys scrambled to evade the blade. She caught one across the belly, watching with satisfaction as the tip tore through the leather vest and cotton shirt he wore. The man cried out, tripping and falling out of the wagon. Lark spun around and faced her second foe. The man's eyes bulged and he went for his gun, but Lark's blade was quicker than his hand and she slashed forward, catching him in mid-reach. Blood spurted as the point sank into his wrist. The man howled, staggering and then pitching to the ground, holding his injured hand.

Shanks watched Lark through slitted eyes. He smiled, thinking how graceful she was in action. Pity she was a breed. Then, abruptly annoyed because his men weren't doing what Cameron had ordered, he shouted, "All of ya, stand back. And keep yore guns holstered." He glared at Oley, who was whining that his hand was permanently maimed. "Tie yore neckerchief around it, ya braying jackass."

Shanks watched as Lark slowly straightened, the bloody bowie held tightly in her white-knuckled hand. Damned if she didn't look beautiful—defiant like a wild mustang with her eyes wide, and nostrils flared like a stallion ready to fight for his territory. His eyes gleamed as he approached her.

"Get out of the wagon, breed."

"I'm not moving, Shanks. No one's taking any more of my supplies."

Cameron had said he wanted no rough play with Lark. He'd almost bet his boss wanted the girl for himself. He had seen an interest in Cameron's eyes, all right. "Don't hurt the merchandise," was how he had put it to Shanks. Well, a few bruises wouldn't hurt, would they? Besides, his men wouldn't squeal on him if he roughed her up a little. Someone needed to bring her down a peg or two—teach her a lesson. No squaw challenged him or his men and got away with it.

Trembling with anger and fear, Lark watched as Shanks pulled his horse to a halt beside the buckboard, his yellow eyes narrowed. "You'll have to kill me before I let you take any more of my supplies," she stated.

"Make a deal with ya, breed," he drawled.

"What kind?" Lark turned warily, watching as the men gathered at the heads of the spooked mules.

"I'll fight ya fair and square with a knife. If I win, ya lose your supplies and go home empty-handed."

Dread fear wound through her like a venomous snake. Shanks was evil, one of the fastest hired guns in the Arizona Territory. "Why can't you just let me go? I've done you no harm. I came to Prescott in peace and I left in peace. Why must you follow me?"

Shanks dismounted and untied his bedroll from behind the cantle of his saddle. "Because," he said with a contemptuous smile, "ya need to be taught a lesson. Now climb down out of there. We'll fight over there," he said, gesturing toward a flatter piece of ground.

She saw his face was set. There was no way out. Lark remembered Maria's pleading words to wait for the wranglers to escort her into town. Bitterly, as she climbed from the buckboard, she acknowledged her mistake. She saw Shanks wrap a wool blanket around his left forearm and draw a bowie knife from the saddlebag. Her throat ached with unrelieved tension. He would be fast. Faster than she. *No*, she reprimanded herself, *do not defeat yourself. Us'an will lend you strength and cunning if you are deserving of them.*

Shanks removed the bandanna covering his face and threw aside his black felt hat. He looked over his shoulder at his men. "This is between her and me. Understand? No one draws a gun."

"But, boss, what if she sticks ya?" Oley asked.

Slowly Shanks began to circle the girl. "She won't." He grinned at Lark. "First one who takes the other down, flat on their back, wins."

"If that's what you want," she flung back, crouching and warily watching his languid moves. Boa Juan had taught her to hold out her left hand to ward off the attacker, keeping her knife near her body so it couldn't be ripped from her hand.

Shanks pointed to his left cheek. "Remember these? I ain't ever forgot ya gave 'em to me, breed. I plan to carve ya up just like ya did me. Then we'll be even."

Lark's eyes widened momentarily. Shanks meant it. Licking her dry lips, she said nothing as they continued to circle one another. She moved on the balls of her feet, the sun beating down overhead. A sheen of perspiration covered her dirt-smeared face. Shanks feinted, his blade whistling inches from her face. Lark jerked back, stunned. She hadn't even seen him make the attack, he was so quick. Panic began to eat away her confidence. Lark gripped her own knife harder as sweat trickled down her temples.

"Yore slow," Shanks taunted with a chuckle. He threw up the arm padded with the blanket, but Lark stood her ground, not in the least distracted. Her blade sank deep into the blanket and Shanks jumped back.

"Bitch," he snarled, glancing down at the slashed material. But the blade hadn't completely penetrated all the layers to his arm.

Lark forced her gaze to Shanks's hips—they would move first—her breath coming in sharp gasps. He moved. She whipped to the left just as he lunged. He missed, but as he passed by her, he swung his left arm.

The blow caught Lark in the side of the head. Caught off balance, she staggered. Shanks pivoted and came back to finish her off. Her eyes widened in terror as she saw the blade coming directly toward her throat. She threw herself to the ground, rolling out of reach of his attack.

"Goddamn ya," he snarled, whipping around, embarrassed in front of his men. He tried to get to her before she could scramble to her feet. The bitch was faster than he was! Anger destroyed his detached coolness. Just as she turned to face him, he leaned down and, with a hiss, threw a handful of loose sand into her face.

Her cry echoed as the sand blinded her. The instant she raised her hand to protect her eyes, Shanks tackled her. She was thrown several feet backward, slammed to the ground by the force of his assault. Lark felt his weight crush the air from her. With a scream, she struck out blindly with her knife.

Shanks grabbed her right wrist, wringing the bowie from her hand. With a triumphant cry, he captured both her hands and jerked them up over her head. He laughed between panting gasps as he straddled her wriggling, bucking body.

"Got ya now, breed. Yore flat on yore back! I win. Hey, boys! Don't she look like a wild horse?"

Tears of rage washed the sand from her eyes. Lark fought on for almost three minutes before she finally succumbed to Shanks's superior strength. She opened her eyes, glaring up at him, breathing hard. Humiliation roared through her as the other men surrounded them, laughing and nudging her insolently with their boots, bruising her flesh. Each kick became a little sharper until her entire body ached.

"Ya lose," Shanks ground out, sweat making his face

gleam. "Yore on yore back first. Like it should be. That's where all women belong."

"Never! You cheated! You *pindah yudastein!*" she shrilled, trying to fight again.

Shanks gave a wicked chuckle. "Listen to her, boys. She's cursing me out in Apache. Harley, hold her hands above her head," he snapped.

With a gasp, Lark watched as Shanks picked up his Bowie and ran his thumb along the glinting edge.

"Hey, boss! How about if we all hump her? I got a real itch in my crotch. I could use a piece like her. What ya say?" Harley pleaded.

Shanks looked down at her with the beginnings of a smile as he saw fear replace her hatred. "Wish I could let ya, Harley, but orders is orders. Maybe some other time when the boss gets tired of her and throws her away." He settled the tip of the blade on the cloth near her waist and slowly slit her shirt, ripping the material with a sickening sound, then pressed the tip against the glistening softness of her throat. A pulse leaped at the base of her neck. Grinning, he set the knife aside and peeled back the damp cotton shirt. "But he never said nothing about us gettin' a look at the goods." He ground his hips over the apex of her thighs, watching terror leap to her eyes. She felt pliant and womanly firm beneath him and he rubbed himself a little harder on her, enjoying the rush of turgid blood to his loins that made him hard and ready.

Humiliation swept through Lark. She uttered a small cry, trying to jerk free. It was impossible! The guttural, animal sounds of the men pummeled her ears and she squeezed her eyes shut, unable to bear the lust burning in their stares.

Shanks watched, almost hypnotized as her pink-tipped breasts rose and fell with every panting breath she took. Now he could see why Cameron wanted the breed. He'd stake his life that she was still a virgin. "Take a good look, boys. She's got the makings of a first-class whore. Bet she'd go for a pretty penny over at the Spur Saloon.''

Lark cringed, her heart pounding like a snared rabbit's as she felt Shanks's cool, soft fingers roughly explore first one breast and then the other. His touch was brutal as he massaged and squeezed her, examining her like a horse to be bought. With a cry of pure rage she jerked one hand free and smashed her fist squarely on Shanks's jaw. His head snapped to one side and, momentarily stunned, he nearly fell off her. She was almost free! But before she could squirm out of his grasp, he shook his head to clear it and repositioned himself on top of her. Lark's mouth opened in a silent scream as he balled up his right fist and drew it back. The side of her head exploded in a flash of light and pain.

It was dark when Lark awoke, the metallic taste of blood in her mouth. She was lying sprawled out, face down in the dirt. Throbbing pain lanced through her temple and right cheek. With a groan, she slowly rolled over and sat up. It took her long minutes to realize that the mules and buckboard were nearby. All around her lay the torn and scattered remains of the supplies, already half covered with the red Arizona earth. Tears filled her eyes as she surveyed the carnage. One hundred dollars worth of food had been wasted, money she could ill afford to lose.

With trembling fingers, Lark realized her cheekbone was badly cut, her right eye swollen almost shut. Sticky blood covered her left temple. Her once beautiful red shirt hung open, testimony to the bowie's sharpness and Shanks's hatred. She ran her hands slowly up each leg, gingerly testing for broken bones. To her relief, there were none, just bruises and scarring memories. Groggily she remembered Shanks saying something about not hurting her on orders. Whose orders? Cameron's?

Moving with unaccustomed slowness, Lark staggered to her feet. She found her knife tossed up on the buckboard seat. The Winchester was gone. Otherwise, the animals and the wagon were unharmed. Leaning weakly against one of the mules, Lark fought off a wave of faintness. It was late; Maria would be worried because she hadn't arrived home before now. Suddenly Lark remembered the cash she had placed in the inside pocket of her shirt. Her heart sank. They had taken the money. Three hundred dollars gone . . .

Hot, scalding tears fell from her eyes as she rested her head against the mule. *No. Us'an, no. Why? Oh, why didn't I listen to the Old Ones and Maria? I should have waited until the wranglers were able to escort me into town.* She knotted her fist, overwhelmed by the realization that her own stubborn pride had contributed to the disaster.

Shakily pulling the ripped shirt closed, Lark picked up the reins and managed to climb into the wagon. Shame flooded her as she thought of what Ny-Oden and the Old Ones would think when she rode into the ranch. And then, from some dim corner of her mind, came an image of Matt Kincaid. To face him, a *pindah,* would be even more humiliating.

Clucking to the mules, Lark headed numbly for home.

# Chapter 6

"Aiyee . . ."

Maria's piercing cry jerked Matt awake. The blankets fell away from his bare chest as he forced himself into a sitting position. Kerosene lamps cast deep shadows across the bedroom as Matt twisted to see out the door. Something was wrong. Very wrong. Lark . . .

More excited voices rose in the yard. Maria was sobbing. Someone else was shouting orders in an urgent tone. He tried to tell himself he didn't care. Scowling, Matt wrapped his fist into the blankets and shoved himself up against the headboard, waiting. It was impossible to help in his present condition anyway.

His eyes widened as Consuelo, a heavyset Mexican woman, and Maria half carried, half dragged Lark into the bedroom. Shock riveted Matt as he stared at Lark's torn shirt and blood-encrusted face. She was barely conscious, her chin sunk against her chest.

Maria cast a frightened glance at him as they maneuvered Lark to the bed. "*Señor*, Patrona Lark is hurt. Forgive us, but we must bring her in here."

Matt watched as they gently laid Lark down, nausea rising in his throat as Lark's hair fell away, exposing her battered face and neck.

"My God," he whispered hoarsely, and automatically leaned forward to place a hand on her shoulder.

"*Sí*, it's terrible," Maria cried, quickly retrieving a

101

bowl of water and a cloth. "Consuelo! Awaken Ny-Oden. Bring him *pronto!*"

Fingers closed gently over her shoulder, and Lark barely moved her head in that direction. She was desperately thirsty, but had no strength to ask for water.

"Lie very still," Matt commanded.

Maria began to cleanse away the dirt and blood on her face. "What the hell happened to her?" Matt demanded.

With haunting clarity he remembered Katie's body lying sprawled face down in the dirt. Lark looked exactly like Katie had, her face bruised and swollen, covered with blood and dirt. Nausea assailed him again and he turned away, fighting to regain control of his spinning senses.

Huge tears rolled down Maria's taut, copper-colored cheeks. "Those gringos! That's who has done this. Aiyee, I told her not to go to Prescott alone. I knew they would attack her. Oh, my poor Lark, my poor *niña*. Look what they have done to you."

Matt swallowed hard and his gaze traveled from Lark's face down her slender neck. A puncture wound that could only have been made with the blade of a knife marred her flawless skin, the dried blood a crimson banner against her ashen flesh. Cold anger uncoiled in Matt's gut at the sight of the discoloring bruises on the soft mounds of her breasts. The right side of her rib cage was swollen, where he knew someone had kicked her hard. He turned away, struggling to control his seething anger. After a long, torturous silence he demanded hoarsely, "Who did this, Maria?"

"I don't know," she wailed. "Oh, look, look—they've hurt her so badly, Señor Matt. Why? She has done nothing! My Lark is innocent. All she has ever done is to help those who are less fortunate than herself. She heals animals and people alike. Never has she lifted her hand in anger. Aiyee, this is a terrible tragedy . . . terrible . . .

"When I ran out to meet the *patrona* in the yard, she was barely conscious. She would have fallen off the

wagon had I not caught her. Before she fainted, she told
me she had no broken bones. Thank the Virgin Mother
for that much.'' Maria sniffed again, wiping one cheek
dry of tears.

How anyone could physically abuse Lark—or any
woman—was beyond Matt. Then, remembering his
original treatment of her, guilt assailed him. Though he
hadn't physically harmed her, his verbal assault had been
just as violent, and just as inexcusable. She'd offered him
sanctuary and hospitality—he'd have died without her
care—yet he had repaid her with hate and anger.

"Are you sure this was done by a white man?'' he
asked.

"*Sí*,'' Maria answered. "No Apache would hurt Lark.
Not one! Not even that devil, Ga'n. No, *señor*, gringos
did this. When she awakes, she will name those who are
responsible.''

"Has . . . has she been raped?''

"I do not think so. Aiyee, I pray that it's not so!
Apache maids never know the touch of man until after
they are married, *señor*. Lark is chaste . . .'' At last
Maria broke down, weeping loudly as she continued to
clean Lark's battered body. When she was finally
finished, she drew up several blankets to Lark's shoulder.
"I will be right back, *señor*. Consuelo must need help
with Ny-Oden. Sometimes, he is in such pain that he
cannot move and must be carried. *Por favor,* will you
watch over the *patrona?*''

Matt nodded, his hand never leaving Lark's shoulder.
"I'll take care of her,'' he promised thickly.

The warm afternoon air lifted the lace curtains away
from the window, bringing in the sweet scent of
wildflowers from the valley, but Matt's eyes burned with
anger as he sat next to Lark's bed. Earlier, Maria had
helped him dress in some borrowed clothes and, after
tightly binding his wound, had assisted him into the chair.

The Mexican woman hadn't questioned his desire to be at Lark's side.

Ny-Oden sat stoically in a rocking chair on the opposite side of the bed. Matt saw sadness in the shaman's old eyes, but Ny-Oden had uttered not a word since instructing the women to place healing poultices on Lark's face and shoulder.

With a sigh, Matt shifted restlessly in the chair. He had questions, and plenty of them, to ask Lark when she awoke. Then he caught himself. Why should he care what had happened to her? His conscience needled him as he sourly considered the answer. He owed Lark Gallagher his life. The least he could do was stick around for a while to repay the debt. Besides, he couldn't track Ga'n in his present condition. Maybe there was some less physically demanding work Lark might find for him while his leg healed.

When Lark groaned, Matt's eyes sharpened. Lark had curled up in a tight ball as she slept, only inches from where Matt sat, the white cotton gown she wore accentuating her paleness. A new and unfamiliar ache began in Matt's chest. He longed to heal her as she had healed him. As much as he had wanted to hate her because Apache blood ran in her veins, he could not. She was a woman, and like Katie in some respects. Both had been vulnerable against a man's superior strength. Both had paid a price for that weakness. Katie was dead, but Lark survived.

Matt flicked a glance over at the shaman before he reached out to touch Lark, to help her reorient to the world as she awakened. His hand settled gently on her right shoulder.

Lark frowned, feeling the weight and warmth of a hand on her. She heard Matt's deep-timbred voice move through her like a balm.

"Lark? Don't try to move. You've been hurt. Just lie still and come awake. It's all right, you're home and with friends."

Home . . . she was home. Slowly, as she became more cognizant of her surroundings, she opened her eyes. With a jolt, she realized she was lying in Matt Kincaid's bed. A swift intake of breath followed and Lark jerked away from him. Instantly she regretted the movement as blinding pain lanced through her.

"Make no quick movements, daughter," Ny-Oden counseled in English. "You are safe. Lie there and allow the memory of the past day to slowly come back to you."

Lark cleared her throat. She was thirsty, but her sensual awareness of Matt Kincaid sliced through her grogginess. She lay on her back and stared up at the rough timbers of the ceiling. Silence settled back into the room as she tried to organize her scattered thoughts.

Finally she looked over at Matt. Unprepared for the anxious flame burning in his eyes, she swallowed convulsively. Unable to bear his pity for her condition, Lark slowly turned her head and met Ny-Oden's dark stare. She fought the rush of guilt that consumed her. "Grandfather," she began hoarsely, her voice hardly more than a croak, "I have failed."

"How, my daughter?"

She forced the words through puffy lips. "I did not listen to you or Maria. I allowed my pride and stubbornness to guide me. I shouldn't have gone to Prescott alone. Now the supplies are destroyed and the three hundred dollars I was bringing home to pay the wranglers is gone." She steeled herself for Ny-Oden's response. Whatever he said in admonishment would be justified.

"Far worse," Ny-Oden said gently, "was that you were gravely injured, daughter of my heart. Supplies can be bought once again. Money can be remade. But you cannot be replaced."

A shudder ran through her. "But, I failed you, grandfather. I failed everyone. We needed the food, and the money is gone."

"There is no failure in making a decision and trying to carry it through," Ny-Oden said. "You learned that pride is at best a poor companion. Do not reprimand yourself further. You have learned your lesson.''

Miserably, Lark nodded. ''You've always taught me to be humble, grandfather, but my anger over my father's death and my foolish pride won out.'' Moving with extreme slowness, she tried to pull herself into a sitting position, ignoring Matt's presence.

''Hold it,'' he said, gripping her arm. ''Where do you think you're going?''

It hurt to move quickly, but Lark jerked her head. Her eyes flared with hatred. He was white. He was a man. And his kind had hurt her. ''Let me go,'' she demanded.

Matt held her angry blue gaze, feeling a tremor pass through her. ''You're in no shape to be up and about,'' he said in a level tone. ''If it bothers you that I'm in the same room, I'll leave. It's too soon for you to get up, Lark.''

His voice was calming, and when he called her so tenderly by name, all the hatred within her dissolved. She sat very still, thankful that her long hair hid her expression, which she was sure would reveal all too clearly just how strongly he affected her.

''Let go of me . . . please . . .'' she gritted out.

Shaken by the raw ache in her voice, Matt released Lark's wrist, wincing inwardly when he realized it was the same wrist he'd bruised previously. How much hatred Lark had endured from him since he'd come to the ranch. His mind reeled at the revelation of her father's death. No wonder he had seen such sadness in Lark's features. He would ask her more about the loss of her parents. But now was not the time.

''Who did this to you?'' he demanded.

Her lower lip trembled with emotion, but she refused to cry. ''I'm sure it will give you great satisfaction to know that it was your kind who did it, Mr. Kincaid.''

Matt forced himself to hold her bleak stare. ''My kind is your kind. You're half white,'' he reminded her.

Lark reacted as if she had been slapped. ''No! I'll

never admit that I'm half white! *Your kind* did this to me! They stopped my wagon, destroyed the supplies, and then beat me senseless."

Ny-Oden stirred, getting to his feet with painful slowness. "Daughter," he coaxed, "calm yourself. He seeks only to help you, not anger you."

Whirling toward the shaman, her hair flying around her shoulders, Lark cried out in Apache, "How can you defend him?"

"The truth needs no defense, Lark Who Sings," he answered in the same language. "You live with each foot in a different, opposing world. If you study his eyes, you will not see revenge in them. Instead, you will find care and concern. Do not burden him with your rage."

Stung by Ny-Oden's rebuke, Lark retreated within herself, laying her back against the brass headboard and wrapping her arms around her drawn-up knees. "He has burdened *me* with his hatred and anger before," she flung back, refusing to meet the shaman's eyes.

"And now he is trying to atone for his error by helping you."

Lark set her lips. "I want no help from any *pindah,* grandfather. Not ever. I've learned my lesson."

Hobbling slowly to the entrance, Ny-Oden said, "And I have warned you before: don't judge all *pindahs* by the actions of only a few men. I will tell Maria you are awake. You must eat."

Barely able to contain her simmering anger, Lark forced her feet to the floor, gripping the sides of the bed for support. Her head swam with dizziness, but she fought it off.

"I'm sorry you were beaten up, for whatever it's worth, Lark."

She tried to steel herself against Matt's softly spoken apology. She had to get away from him! "I'd rather have your hatred and anger than your pity," she spat back.

Matt grimaced. "You have my compassion and understanding. Never my pity."

Making a harsh sound in her throat, Lark said, "I'd rather deal with your hate. That's something I can understand."

"You're hurt and angry, Lark. I know what you're going through."

She twisted toward him, glaring. "Do you? How long has it been since five men took you down, hit you, kicked you, and held a knife to your throat?"

"I want to hear what happened to you," he replied quietly.

Lark gauged him in silence. "Why?"

"Because it's important for me to know."

"So you can tell your friends that the beating of a half-breed woman was just payment for your family's death?" Lark forced herself to stand, wavering unsteadily. "You can go to your white man's hell before I tell you anything!"

Matt recoiled at the raw hatred in her hoarse voice. Lark swayed, and he watched as she forced herself to walk with faltering steps across the room to the dresser.

Bending down with great difficulty, she pulled a pair of Levi's and a black cotton shirt from a drawer. She glowered at Kincaid as she walked with halting steps past the bed, out the door, and down the hall.

"Dammit," he snarled under his breath. But he couldn't blame her for her behavior.

Defying Maria's orders, Lark got dressed. Her own discomfort didn't matter. The ranch was more important than her small aches and pains. More important, Lark had to convince her people that she was still in charge.

The sun was an hour away from its zenith, the late May morning warm and fragrant. Lark tried to keep her face impassive as she headed toward the Old Ones' bunkhouse. She knew from experience that if the Old Ones understood, then they would help dispel the shock of the event to the rest of the people who worked and lived on the ranch.

Sitting on the wooden porch was Lame Deer, an aged

but still spry Apache woman. In her arms was Sancho, the five-year-old son of Primo, one of her best wranglers.

Sancho's squeal of laughter was cut short at Lark's approach. His huge brown eyes widened with fear and he scrambled to hide behind Lame Deer's cotton skirt.

Shocked, Lark halted. Of course, she probably looked almost unrecognizable. Swallowing hard, she mounted the steps to where Lame Deer sat in silence.

"Granddaughter," the Old One greeted her in Apache, "you have frightened young Sancho." She reached around, patting the boy's shiny black hair. "He thinks you are Owl-Man Monster."

Lark forced a smile to her lips and sat down on the steps. "You must help me, Lame Deer."

"How, granddaughter?"

"I was beaten by *pindahs* near Prescott." Wryly she added, "I may look like a ghost of my former self, but I am alive, not dead. Will you tell the other Old Ones that I am still able to run the ranch?"

"I shall tell them," Lame Deer promised.

Sancho peeked from behind her skirt, his chin coming to rest on Lame Deer's ample lap. He blinked twice, his small voice shaking with fear. "Señorita Lark?"

She held her hand out to the boy. "Yes, it's Lark, Sancho. Come to me?"

Hesitating, Sancho looked up at Lame Deer's darkly browned, wrinkled face.

"Go, Sancho. Patrona Lark is not Owl-Man Monster. She merely hurt herself. Does not your knee or elbow swell up and look angry when you fall on it? Well, she fell on her face. Go to her. She is the same Lark Who Sings you knew before her accident."

Grateful for Lame Deer's explanation, and for her help, Lark opened her arms. Sancho stood up and came around the Apache woman. Like the other small children, he wore few clothes. His trousers were thin and worn, his feet bare. Shyly, he stepped forward.

Without a word, Lark folded the child into her arms as

she had done so many times in the past. The children of
the ranch were special to her . . . as children were to all
Apache people.

"There," she murmured to the boy, setting him on her
lap and allowing him to snuggle deep into her arms.
"Even though I look like Owl-Man Monster, do I act like
him?"

Sancho shook his head. "No, Señorita Lark. Did you
bring back a surprise for all of us?"

Lark kissed his wrinkled brow. Her father always
brought candy for the children. They had crowded around
his buckboard, dancing about and begging for the sweets
they knew he was hiding in his pockets. Lark gently
tucked away the memory, remembering her father's
generosity with deep affection. "No, I didn't bring any
candy, Sancho. But I promise that the next time I go into
town, I'll bring you a very special surprise."

Satisfied with her promise, Sancho allowed her to place
him back in the elderly woman's arms. She ruffled his
hair.

"Thank you for your help, grandmother."

"You need not even ask, my child. I will tell the
others."

Relieved that Lame Deer understood, Lark left the
porch. Her next task was to visit the small homes of the
wranglers, located in a small grove of fir trees opposite
the main house.

At the end of her rounds, Lark felt confident that the
people of the ranch would accept what had happened to
her with less concern because she was up and around.
With a grimace, she returned to the ranch house. Next
she would have to tackle the account books.

Rubbing her aching brow, Lark slowly climbed the
porch stairs and went inside. Maria gave her a worried
look, but was wise enough not to say anything. Lark went
to the office, in too much pain to be pleasant to anyone
right now.

At noon Maria brought Matt his meal, flashing him a shy smile of welcome as she set down a tray filled with fried venison steak, potatoes, and warm bread. "Will you at least be a good patient and eat, Señor Matt?"

He nodded, his mouth watering. Since the fever had broken, his appetite had returned with a vengeance. He tied a cotton cloth around his neck to protect his bare chest. "I'm hungry enough to eat a bear," he assured her.

Tittering, Maria sat down in the rocker and picked up her mending. "You *are* like a bear, *señor.*"

He managed a smile between bites. "What about Lark? How's she doing?" he asked.

"Aiyee, Señor Matt, she should be in her bedroom, resting." Maria folded her plump hands on the mending. "Instead she wrestles with numbers in the office."

"Numbers?"

"*Sí.* Her father kept books, but she doesn't know how to read them. I think the *patrona* is trying to teach herself so she can find out if there is any money left to pay the wranglers."

Matt nodded. "I see."

Sadly, Maria shook her head. "No, *señor*, you do not. When the *patrona* was in the seventh grade, they told her never to come back to school. She sees words and numbers backward sometimes. The teacher said it was her Apache blood that made her stupid. The teacher refused to allow Lark to continue schooling. Instead, the *patrón* tried to teach Lark to read, write, and understand sums." With a vague shrug, Maria added mournfully, "He could not help her. The *patrona* has the hardest time with numbers. They scare her, I think."

"Because she sees them backward?" Lark should never have been denied schooling. Any fool with an ounce of brains could see the intelligence in her lupine eyes.

"*Sí.* I do not understand it, *señor*. No one does. The teacher embarrassed Lark in front of the gringo class. She took much teasing from everyone for so long that she began to believe she was as stupid as they accused her of being.''

Matt's mouth drew into a straight line. He set the empty tray aside. ''Maria, get me my clothes.''

''*Señor?*''

''Just do as I ask. It's important.''

''But your leg . . .''

He smiled grimly. ''Some things are more important than a little pain. Help me wrap the wound tightly so it won't bleed.''

Lark's cheek throbbed with pain. She rested her wrinkled brow against one palm, watching as the numbers swam before her watering eyes. Nothing made any sense. Certainly not the two account logs her father had kept. Beside her lay the savings and the mortgage payment books. Where was she going to find an extra three hundred dollars to pay her wranglers? And another hundred for more supplies?

A noise at the office door drew her attention. There in the doorway, looking as if he was too large for it, stood Matt Kincaid.

''You shouldn't be out of bed,'' she exclaimed.

Matt gave her a shrug, barely succeeding in hiding his pain. ''Neither should you, but you are.''

Lark's eyes rounded as he limped to the desk and sat down in the chair next to it. She wasn't sure who looked worse right then. Dark stubble shadowed Matt's gaunt cheeks, and a fierce light burned in his gray eyes. His flesh was waxen from exertion, brow beaded with perspiration.

''I have good reason to be up and around,'' she snapped, closing the account books and resting her hands protectively on top of them. ''I own this ranch and it's my responsibility to keep it running.''

Straightening his wounded leg, Matt nodded. ''Commendable loyalty,'' he commented.

"Then why are you here? If you want to exercise, you could have chosen any other part of the house."

Lark looked incredibly fragile in that moment. Matt had to stop himself from reaching out and touching her. He cleared his throat. "I was bored."

"Bored?" Lark repeated, taken off guard by his casual response.

"I'm tired of sitting in that bed staring out the windows. I need something to do. Anything."

Lark gave him a look of disbelief. She gestured toward the shelves lined with leather-bound books. "Then read. Take one of them back with you to bed. You shouldn't be up so soon."

"I don't feel like reading," he muttered, studying the shelves. "I need something more challenging."

Lark's patience thinned as she surveyed him, trying to ignore the powerful force drawing her to him. "I don't have time to keep you entertained by sitting with you."

"Maria did."

"I'm not Maria! I have a ranch to run."

Matt slowly turned his attention from the library shelves back to her. He eyed the green books. "Are those ledgers?"

"Ledgers?"

"Another word for bookkeeping."

Grudgingly she nodded. She'd never heard the term before. "How do you know what these are?"

Matt disguised his interest and continued to study the office. "No reason. My father owns a bank back in Harrisburg, Pennsylvania. While I was going to school, I studied accounting, budgets, and banking."

"I see . . ."

"For some reason, numbers never bored me," he went on in a conversational tone. "I always found them interesting."

Lark had to force herself to relax her grip on the account books. "Y-you like numbers?" She tried to disguise the hope in her voice. If only he would answer a few of her questions, perhaps even show her how to read the books . . .

Matt proffered a hint of a smile. "Prefer them. Say, that's a good idea. I'll go back to bed, providing you let me work with some numbers. I'm pretty handy at balancing budgets."

"Well, I don't know . . ."

"Look, I've got to repay you in some way for saving my life. At least let me earn my keep while I'm here. Fair enough?" Matt offered his hand to seal the deal.

Lark stared. It was a large hand with powerful fingers and a palm thickly callused from years of hard, outdoor labor. Hesitantly she slipped her hand into his, immediately aware of the warmth and gentleness of his grip. Drowning in the dove-gray warmth of Matt's eyes, Lark became aware of good, cleansing feelings washing through her. She quickly pulled her hand free, and stood nervously.

"Will you be able to tell me what I need to know through those numbers?"

Matt retrieved the two ledgers from the desk, plus the banking books, and tucked them under one arm. "Sure. Let me take a look at them, and if you want, drop by in a couple of hours with your questions." As Lark shifted restlessly from one foot to another, he was surprised to realize he wanted to simply open his arms and tell her to come into them. As badly beaten as she was, he didn't see how she could be up and about, much less trying to tackle something as difficult as accounting. Had Ny-Oden's poultices and chants made the difference?

With a faint smile, he held Lark's unsure gaze. "Better yet, how about sharing dinner with me this evening? That will give me plenty of time to prepare for your questions."

Lark was about to answer when the pounding of horses' hooves drew her to the window. There, coming down the valley, rode her wranglers leading the herd of mustang broodmares. Hope stirred in her breast, and she turned abruptly, catching a look of longing on Matt's face. Uncertain what it meant, she ignored his expression and skirted the desk.

"My wranglers are back. I'll be very busy for the next few hours. If I can join you for dinner, I will. If not, later tonight."

Before he could protest, Lark was gone. From the window Matt watched the approach of men and horses. He saw Lark head for the stock pens near the barns. Her shoulders were proudly squared, her chin up, and her walk confident. With a shake of his head, Matt made his way back to the smaller bedroom. Only Maria knew the cost of his effort. As she removed the tight bandage that was now bright red with fresh blood, he began to assess the ranch's financial situation.

Paco's eyes widened in shock as he dismounted in the yard and caught sight of Lark coming toward him. The whinnies of horses filled the air and dust rolled across the ranch in huge, billowing clouds. The yips and yells of his wranglers as they manuevered the herd into holding pens drowned out his first words.

Lark held up her hand, seeing the disbelief in Paco's eyes. "It's all right, Paco."

He dropped the reins to his tired, sweaty horse. "*Patrona,* what happened? *Dios,* did you—"

As briefly as she could, Lark told her foreman what had happened. She saw anger replace Paco's shock as she ended the brief explanation.

"Those gringo bastards!" he exclaimed. "I will ride there and call Shanks out! It will do no good to go to Sheriff Cole. He's as crooked as Cameron." He grabbed the reins of his horse, prepared to remount.

"No!" Lark clutched the Mexican's arm. "Paco! Don't go!"

He stared levelly at her. "*Patrona,* no one is going to get away with hurting you like that." He jabbed his gloved finger toward Prescott. "I will even the score. That is a promise!"

Lark held her ground. "Look, Paco, I need you alive, not dead. My father ran this ranch, I didn't. I know the horse business, but you have more knowledge about general ranch duties. I need you. Please . . . don't go."

The foreman slowly relaxed, then took off his dusty hat to wipe his sweaty brow. "You should be avenged, *patrona*," he told her firmly.

Trying to control her own feelings, Lark nodded. "Yes, Paco, but not right now and not in that way. If you go gunning for Shanks, you'll be acting no better than he has."

"Shanks deserves nothing better than a bullet in his back. That's what he's famed for, *patrona*, for sneaking up behind a man and drilling him."

Relief spread through Lark when she realized Paco would obey her order. She released his sleeve. "Shanks is a coward. We both agree on that. But right now we have to devote all our attention to the ranch. Later, when things are in order, I'll pursue Shanks's attack on me."

Paco's face hardened. "If I see him, I will draw on him."

Lark's mouth tightened. "You won't do anything, Paco, unless I tell you to. Is that clear?"

Grudgingly, he nodded. "*Sí, patrona.* Excuse me, I must help the men settle the mares."

She watched Paco mount and trot off toward the corrals. She wished mightily that her father was there. He had the authority to force the men, including Paco, to obey his commands. Fleetingly she wondered if she could ask Matt for help. The wranglers would respect him because he was a natural leader.

It was near midnight when all the ranch activity finally ceased. The throbbing in Lark's head had worsened, and she knew she had pushed beyond even her own considerable powers of endurance. From the porch steps, she perused the silent yard, then turned and walked into the house, her heart beginning to pound. She tried to tell herself that Matt's offer to work off his debt meant nothing to her, but it did. The Apache way was to repay an obligation. Lark fought the attraction that held her every time she thought of him. The physical pull that bound her to him left her feeling vulnerable in a way she'd never experienced.

She stopped in the kitchen to make a fresh poultice for Matt's leg, then, girding herself for the possible bad news he might have concerning the ledgers, she went to his room. Lamplight spilled into the hallway from the opened door, indicating he was still awake.

A soft knock on the door made Matt look up. He saw Lark standing uncertainly in the entrance. In the dim light, her golden flesh looked taut with fatigue. Hoping to ease the anxiety in her expression, he offered a slight smile.

"Come on in. That was quite a herd your men brought in," he complimented, wanting to establish some neutral ground with her.

"My foreman brought in twenty-five mares. They'll be bred to either the Kentucky Stud or to Huelga." She sat on the edge of the mattress, avoiding his intense gaze. There was something so powerful about his broad chest, about the fistful of dark, curling hair exposed above the unfastened top button of his red full-length long johns. He was so male. Trying to ignore him, she set about cleaning his wound.

Matt reached out before she could cut the bandage over the dressing. He cradled her hand. "Maria did that earlier, and you're barely awake. Why don't you go to bed?"

Lark's flesh tingled hotly in his grip; her hand felt small against his massive, hairy one. His fingers were warm and gentle. Shanks's had been cold and damp. A frisson of panic sped through her and she remained frozen, combating her own internal fear.

Matt released her hand. "I didn't mean to scare you."

She closed her eyes, the knife blade trembling in her hand. "I—I shouldn't be so jumpy," she admitted in a strained voice.

Matt watched her fight the haunting memory of her beating. She sat there, head bowed, face curtained by that thick black hair, through which he ached to run his fingers. "How can I help you, Lark?"

His question was like spring sunlight after winter snows. She forced a lopsided smile to her lips. "Tell me that you've found three hundred dollars in my father's accounting books."

He met her tenuous smile with one of his own. "I did. You can rest easy. How about if I explain it tomorrow morning?"

Relief swept through her, and Lark felt the weight on her shoulders miraculously lift. Her expression took on new hope. "Truly? There is money?"

"Enough," Matt cautioned, melting beneath her suddenly joyous gaze. Her cobalt eyes had turned lighter, a flame of gold flickering in their depths. "Why don't you put those things away and call it a night?"

Wearily, Lark agreed. "I will," she told him, rising. Suddenly dizziness swept through her. She gave a small cry of distress, her hand moving instantly to her brow. Blinding pain stabbed through her head, and she lost her balance.

Matt had seen Lark's face drain of color. When she wavered, her knees buckling, he threw out his hand to break her fall, and she landed on the bed instead of on the floor.

Lark drew in desperate gasps of air, wildly aware of Matt's hand on her shoulder steadying her spinning world.

"You've done too much," he muttered. "You've pushed too hard, Lark."

The pain was worse than Matt's censure. Lark could do nothing but lie there, trying to live with the stabbing ache in her temples.

"I'll be all right," she whispered tightly between thinned lips.

"You will if you just lie still and rest a minute," he said gently. He removed his hand from her shoulder and sat quietly beside her, inches separating them.

Matt was right. As she lay on the bed, eyes closed, the pain began to recede. Was it because of his closeness? Somehow, Matt was giving her strength when she had none left herself.

"How's the head?" he asked her quietly a few minutes later.

"Better."

"You've had a rough week."

She barely opened her eyes. "How do you know that?"

"You said earlier today that your father recently died. I'm sorry."

Fresh anguish washed over her. The tone of his voice told her his sympathy was sincere. "He was murdered." The words came out clipped and angry.

Matt held her gaze. "So was my family. My wife, Katie, and my six-year-old daughter, Susan, were murdered by Ga'n and his renegades a month ago. I've been on their trail ever since. Ga'n is the one who shot me." Irony tinged his voice. "We're a hell of a pair, aren't we? We've both suffered great losses."

Lark drew in a deep, ragged breath. "Captain Frank Herter from Fort Whipple was here the other day. That's when I learned you had lost your family. I'm sorry." She ached for him as well as for herself.

"Look," Matt muttered, "you don't need to hear my troubles. You've got enough of your own, right now."

"I understand why you acted so angrily toward me when you became conscious," she said softly.

"I was wrong to blame you for my family's death, Lark. You don't deserve my hate for what other Apaches did." He gestured toward her wrist, which still bore the marks of his fingers. "I've never before raised my hand against a woman of any race or color. You were the first, and you'll be the last. I'm going to try and undo the damage I've done around here. I don't hate you, Lark. I was out of my head at the time.''

''I realize that now,'' she answered, her words slurred from tiredness.

''We have a lot to talk about,'' he said as her dark lashes caressed her cheeks. Exhaustion claimed her, and she fell asleep.

Silence fell as Matt lay beside Lark. He knew Maria had already left the house for the night and that alone he hadn't the strength to move Lark to her own bed. Reaching down, he pulled a quilt over her. Unthinkingly he grazed her hair with his hand in an effort to soothe away the tension on her sleeping features. Disgruntled, Matt realized that when it came to Lark he was acting on instinct, with very little conscious thought. He'd just lost Katie. How could he respond so soon to another woman? Their attraction was dangerous for both of them.

Somehow, he told himself, sliding back down on the bed, he'd have to ignore Lark's presence tonight. He didn't have the heart to awaken her. No, let her sleep. God knew, she needed some peace and rest. It was the least he could give her.

# Chapter 7

Matt couldn't sleep. Lark's feminine scent filled his nostrils. Unconsciously, he inhaled it deeply. Until a month ago, he had slept with Katie. True, she hadn't curled up against him so he could wrap his arms around her, but she had shared his bed. Now that was gone. A hunger ate at him, a feeling so intense and startling that he scowled.

Lark lay curled like a kitten in sleep, lips slightly parted, breasts rising and falling beneath the crinkled cotton shirt she wore. Guilt over his attraction toward her serrated him. He tried to diffuse his powerful, hungry passion.

The moon shone through the window, the long, unbroken streamers penetrating the lacy curtains. Matt stirred restlessly, obsessed with grief over his family's death. Yet when his gaze moved to Lark, the pain lessened. Her black hair outlined the curves and hollows of her sleeping form. What was it about her that produced this ache in his chest and loins, holding him in a relentless grip? Angry with himself because he could feel anything beyond his loss of Katie, Matt cursed himself softly.

Lark stirred, a whimper slipping from her lips. She moved restlessly, as if trying to escape a nightmare.

Matt rolled to his side, facing her, watching as the terror grasped her. Lark threw the covers off, kicking violently. Matt reached out, sliding his hand down her back.

"Easy, Lark, easy," he crooned. The simple act of rubbing large, soothing circles across her shoulders began to calm her, but he was totally unprepared when she moved the last few inches separating them and pressed her soft length against his steely frame.

His eyes darkened as her head nuzzled beneath his jaw. She was trembling. Automatically he wrapped his arms around her, whispering softly. *You shouldn't be doing this,* his conscience screamed at him. *You shouldn't be holding her. What about Katie? Remember Katie.*

With a sigh, Matt struggled to suppress his errant emotions, tried to stifle his awakening senses. But she was warm and yielding against him. He could feel her moist breath against his chest, her steady heartbeat in synchrony with his own. Tentatively he laid a hand on her hair. Sweet Mother of God, but it was soft and thick. Trying to convince himself that he was only calming her, he ran the ebony strands of her hair through his fingers.

Gradually Lark stopped trembling and her breathing evened out, indicating that she had once more found refuge in sleep. But Matt lay wide awake and wracked with guilt, certain of only one thing. He would never allow Lark to know how fiercely he wanted her.

A scolding magpie eased Lark from her deep, healing slumber. The slow beat of a heart against her ear made a smile lift the corners of her mouth. A pervasive feeling of warmth and safety soothed her aches and calmed her anxiety. Gradually, as the magpie's guttural song trilled into silence, she opened her eyes. The discovery that she was lying on Matt's shoulder, his arms draped loosely around her, came as an abrupt shock.

For an instant Lark froze, her breath caught in her throat, her heart pounding wildly in her breast. She had slept all night in Matt's bed!

A hot flush stung her neck while other sensations, other

longings, clamored for attention and she remained frozen in her embarrassing position, one arm across Matt's flat belly, the other tucked at her side, her legs intimately entwined with his. Oh, the shame of being found in his bed!

Lark quickly untangled herself and retreated to the far side of the bed, pressing her back against the headboard. She must have fallen asleep in Matt's bed last night, and since Maria hadn't been available, he'd been forced to let Lark stay there all night. What must he think of her now?

She stared over at his sleeping form, her gaze settling hotly on his full mouth. Her lower body tightened with some unknown sensation that sent waves of pleasure through her.

Quietly rising, she went to her own bedroom and retrieved a towel and soap, then took her morning bath in the stream. She dried herself in the bedroom. Looking in the mirror, she muttered an oath in Apache. Indeed, she looked more like an abused animal than a woman. No wonder Sancho had hidden from her. Ny-Oden's poultice had done its work, however, and the swelling on both her eye and her cheek were greatly reduced. Wrinkling her nose, she ignored the assortment of colorful bruises that covered her.

Sitting in the rocker, she pulled on her kabun boots, purposely ignoring the ribbon of happiness that flowed through her. It didn't have anything to do with sleeping in Matt's arms last night. Instead, she anchored that inexplicable happiness to the fact that he had said there was enough money left in the bank to replace the stolen three hundred dollars. Rising, Lark went to the kitchen to make herself breakfast. She had a long, grueling day ahead of her.

Matt awoke with a jerk, his first instinct to tighten his arms around Lark. But she was gone, and the bed was cold to his touch. He opened his eyes. Sunlight poured through the east window, and he rolled onto his back.

Last night . . . The aching memory of holding Lark in his arms drowned him in sweet, throbbing longing. Rubbing his face savagely, as if to purge those memories and feelings, Matt sat up.

"Good morning, *señor*." Maria smiled shyly as she entered carrying a tray with eggs, cured ham, and hot bread.

Disgruntled, Matt pulled the blankets across his lap. Was Maria aware that Lark had inadvertently slept with him? He didn't think so, judging from her reaction to him. Relieved more for Lark's sake than his own, he accepted the tray.

"I guess it is a good morning. What time is it?"

"Nearly ten, *señor*. You slept long. That is good. Your eyes look clearer."

He felt like the proverbial bear that Lark had accused him of being. "Maria, can you get my clothes and boots for me?"

She frowned. *"Señor?"*

"And a razor and some soap." He rubbed the bristles on his chin. "I want to shave and clean up. I'm not staying in this bed any longer."

"But—"

"Please?"

With a shrug, Maria said, "I'll tell the *patrona* of your wishes. She must change your leg dressing anyway."

"No!"

Stunned by his growled rejoinder, Maria halted. *"Señor,* she is the *patrona.* I must follow her orders."

Digging in to the hot, tasty food, Matt shot her an irritated look. "What orders?"

"She asked to be told when you awakened."

Damn. "Then at least wait to tell her until after I get dressed."

*"Sí, señor.* I will find the razor that the *patrón* used to shave his face."

Matt's mood improved with each task he accomplished. The food was delicious, and he ate enough for a couple of starved wranglers. Maria brought him a fresh set of clothes from his saddlebags and set them on the dresser. Provided with a small bowl of warm water and a blade, he began to soap down his face.

A few minutes later, Maria returned. "I've told the *patrona* that you are awake and want the dressing changed as quickly as possible, *señor*."

"Good. Thank you." Matt was intent on scraping away a week's worth of bristles when Lark entered soundlessly. Glancing up as she rounded the foot of the brass bed, he muttered, "Good morning."

Shyly Lark inclined her head, gripping the poultice bowl more firmly. A sharp twinge settled in her breasts at the sight of his naked chest. "About last night—"

He looked up, holding her anxious stare. "I didn't have the heart to wake you, Lark. You were exhausted."

Grimacing, she murmured, "I shouldn't have fallen asleep on your bed."

"Does Maria know?"

"No. No one does."

"No one will," he promised her.

Lark felt a weight slip from her shoulders. "Among The People, a maid is not allowed to sleep with a man until she marries him."

"It's the same for white folks," Matt said, wanting to dispel her guilt over the incident. "Don't be hard on yourself. We both understand what happened and why."

Trying to change subject, Lark said, "Watching you shave reminds me of my father."

Matt tried to ignore her nearness. He looked up, the razor suspended over his throat. "Oh?"

"When I was little, I used to watch him." There was a wistful tone in her voice.

Matt tried to ignore the grace of her hands as she worked over his leg wound. The razor scraped across his flesh and he washed off the residue in the bowl. Taking a mirror, he gave another grunt. "Well, at least I'm not going to look like a savage anymore." He saw the beginning of a small smile on Lark's tempting mouth. "What's so funny?"

She flushed and concentrated on the dressing. "Nothing. By shaving, you brought back warm memories for me, that's all."

Matt studied Lark's reddening cheeks. "Tell me what happened to your father. Do you know who murdered him and why?"

"Captain Frank Herter, who is a good friend of our family, said that Jud Cameron wants the water rights to the ranch. Cameron's ranch is located next to ours, and he doesn't have enough water to feed his growing herd of cattle. We've got artesian wells on our property." She stilled her hands for a moment, staring hard at the dressing, fighting her anger. "I think Cameron ordered Bo Shanks, a gunslinger, to kill my father. I can't prove it yet, but I will. With my father out of the way, Cameron probably thinks he can scare me off the ranch. But he's wrong. I'll die before I give up my parents' home."

Matt wiped his face free of lather with a damp cloth. "Is that why you went into Prescott?"

"I went to Sheriff Cole, but he isn't going to do any more investigation." Lark couldn't stand the compassion in Matt's eyes. "You've lost your family, too. At first, when you called out for Katie, I didn't know who you meant."

"Katie was my wife," he began, a catch in his tone. "Susan, my daughter, was six. She had her mother's brown hair and my eyes."

Lark bowed her head, unable to ignore the anguish in his husky tone. "You said Ga'n killed them."

"I saw him," Matt said harshly. "And I'm not going to stop chasing the bastard until I catch him."

Feeling uncomfortable, Lark completed bandaging the wound and got up. If Matt knew that Ga'n knew her and had sworn to protect her, he would undoubtedly be upset. They'd both gone through a living hell and she didn't want to contribute any further to Matt's obvious grief. She forced a slight smile for his benefit.

"Now you no longer look like a bear," she teased, pointing to his shaven face.

Matt rubbed his clean jaw. He realized how depressing the conversation had gotten and rallied for Lark's benefit. "A bear, eh?"

"Yes. The bear is greatly feared and respected by the Apache."

He grinned. "Because of his hair?" he asked, teasing her.

Lark laughed, a clear, musical sound that delighted Matt. In that instant, he understood why her parents had named her Lark.

"Of course not," Lark chuckled. "Because the bear is strong and can overpower a warrior, that's why." She shook her head, more laughter spilling from her. "If The People feared hair, then they would fear the white man, and they do not." She lifted her chin, feeling relaxed because of their small shared joke. Confused by the kaleidoscope of feelings he unleashed with his nearness, she finished bandaging his leg and accepted the towel he handed her. As he shrugged into his dark blue cotton shirt, she shifted nervously from one booted foot to another, feeling on unfamiliar territory with him once again. Somehow, Matt made everything they shared seem intimate, and that frightened her.

Matt slowly shifted until his legs were dangling over the edge of the mattress. The wooden floor felt cold on his feet as he pulled on his Levi's. Not wanting to destroy the tenuous thread of trust between them, he said, "I'll make another deal with you." Standing, he buttoned his pants.

Lark met his sober gray eyes. This morning, Matt was not threatening her in any way. Instead, he was warm and engaging and she could barely think straight, much less talk coherently. "You're always making deals with me," she parried. "And who told you you could get out of bed? Your leg is barely starting to heal."

Matt grinned, hoping to tease the edge off her voice. He reached for the ledgers on the stand. "Deals can be good." *Besides*, he thought, *I want to prove to you that whites can be fair with you.* "Ask me what the deal is. I think you'll like it."

Refusing to be baited, Lark asked with all seriousness, "What is your deal?"

Matt limped to the end of the bed, using the brass footboard for support. "If you'll let me stay out of bed while I'm healing, I'll teach you the basics of accounting. How does that sound?"

She couldn't believe his offer. "Numbers? You'd teach me how to read the numbers?" Did he know how bad she was at sums? Had Maria told him of her inability to be educated? The offer sounded too good to be true.

"Sure." Matt gave a lazy shrug. "My mother's a schoolteacher and I consider myself to be fairly good at teaching people."

Lark lowered her lashes. "Your mother's a teacher?" Would Matt poke fun at her inability to grasp numbers just as her own teacher had?

"A very good one," Matt stressed gently, seeing fear war with indecision in her eyes. "She had a lot of patience and I'd like to think she passed that trait on to me."

Lark moved restlessly toward the door. She halted, staring blindly out into the hall. In a choked voice she admitted, "I have great trouble with words and numbers."

Matt heard the hopelessness in her voice. Even her once proud posture now shouted of rejection. "What kind of trouble, Lark?"

"I, uh, was asked to leave the seventh grade because I couldn't read or write properly. My father tried to teach me instead. He couldn't, but I tried to make up for it by using my good memory. I know history and geography well." Lark made a weak gesture with her hands and stared at the wooden floor between her feet. "I see numbers and letters backward, sometimes. I think Miss Somerset was right, I'm too stupid to learn."

Matt's mouth became a grim line. He limped around the bed and halted within a foot of where she stood uncertainly. "My mother taught children who had the same problem you have, Lark."

She looked up, drowning in his understanding gray eyes. "*Pindah* children have that problem, too?"

"Yes. You're not stupid, Lark," he told her quietly. "If Miss Somerset said that, she ought to be kicked out of the teaching profession."

"Others see numbers and letters backward?" she whispered, hope flaring.

His heart lifted as her expression filled with hope and joy. "My mother discovered that children who have that problem are often brighter and more creative in other ways. I'd say you're a very intelligent young woman. I can see it in your eyes and hear it in your words."

Her heart pounded with a fierce euphoria, so that words failed her. It was only when she felt his hand settle on her shoulder that she finally responded.

"You have a deal, Matt Kincaid," she said hoarsely.

He removed his hand. "All right. How about if I finish studying your present financial situation now, and late this afternoon, I'll begin teaching you sums. By the time I'm healed up, you should have a good grasp of numbers and how to set up a budget."

"Yes, I'd like that."

Late that afternoon, Lark waited while Matt placed both ledgers and bankbooks in front of her. She was wildly aware of him when he sat down next to her at the large desk, but her hunger to know of the ranch's solvency outweighed her uneasiness at sharing such close quarters with him.

"First of all," he told her, opening the first book,

"you've made a double mortgage payment for the month of May."

She scowled, studying the numbers and the initials where he pointed. "Then Cameron was lying to me! He owns the bank in Prescott and said my father did not pay this month's mortgage. I told him he did, but I had no way to prove it."

Anger simmered in Matt, but he kept it out of his voice. "There's a procedure at most banks, Lark. When you pay money toward the mortgage, you not only get a payment slip, but also, the clerk will initial the bankbook and put in the amount you've given him. See here? There's the initials W.B. and one hundred dollars after it."

"W.B. stands for Willy Bradford. He's the young clerk in the bank."

"Yes, and your father put that mortgage money in on this date." Matt traced his finger down one line. "And here you've given the bank another hundred less than two weeks later."

Angry, she muttered, "Cameron lied to me. The snake!" She turned to Matt, hands spread. "But how can I make Cameron give me my extra hundred dollars back? I can use that money to help pay for supplies I have to get again."

Matt sat quietly, mulling over several options. For the next couple of months, he wouldn't be able to ride a horse, but now he saw an important chance to start helping to repay her for saving his life. "While I'm healing up, let me help you in any way I can. Next time, I'll go into Prescott with you."

Her eyes widened. "You will?"

"Why not? I also happen to be the son of a bank owner. I used to be a clerk before the war. There's no one better to talk to this Cameron fella than me."

Worry wrinkled her brow as she considered his proposal. "He's evil, Matt. And dangerous . . ."

"Let's not worry about that right now. I want to show

you how to get that three hundred dollars back.'' Without meaning to, he responded to Lark's tremulous voice. She'd called him by his first name for the first time. God help him, but he had to try and stay his distance.

Lark hunched over the books and ledgers, barely able to contain her eagerness. She wanted to throw her arms around Matt Kincaid and thank him for finding that one bank error. She stole a look at him out of the corner of her eyes.

Matt pointed to the second ledger. ''Your father was a good businessman, Lark. He's got fifteen yearlings out there, according to this account, that he knew could be broken and sold off to the cavalry in case there was ever a need for emergency funds.''

Fifteen two-year-olds. She scowled and sat back. ''That's true but . . .''

''What?''

Lark got up, crossing her arms over her breasts. ''They aren't broken. I can't get twenty dollars a head unless they are.''

''So?''

She sighed, her happiness dissolving. ''I have fifteen wranglers and they're all busy finding our mustang mares out there,'' she motioned toward the mountains that surrounded the grassy valley. ''For the next three months this ranch will devote twelve hours a day to locating the mares, foaling them, and then rebreeding them to one of our two stallions.'' She chewed on her lip. ''After they're bred, we'll turn them loose to graze the valley and mountains for the rest of the year until it's time to foal again.''

Matt leaned back in the chair, looking thoughtful. ''You're saying you don't have an extra hand who can break out those fifteen colts?''

''I'd do it myself, but I'll be busy either wrangling or helping in the broodmare barn. Finding those mares now is the most important thing to the survival of our ranch. We need forty to fifty foals each year to ensure us enough operating money for the next year. I just can't spare a wrangler to break those colts.''

He nodded, understanding Lark's problem. The extra hundred dollars that had been paid on the mortgage would be needed for supplies. It couldn't be used to pay more wranglers.

"Cameron would gloat like a wolf if he heard us talking like this," Lark muttered.

"Why?"

"Because he wants me to lose this ranch. He said no woman could run one by herself."

Matt toyed with the fountain pen. "You've got a good foreman?"

"Yes. Paco. But"—she rubbed her brow—"I'm afraid he doesn't always listen to me. I know so little of the ranching operation. My father put me in charge of taking care of the broodmares and foals, that was all."

Matt saw trouble ahead for Lark. A lot of it. He gently deflected her other concerns and returned to the present problem. "Cameron isn't the type to accept defeat."

Lark gave him a quizzical look. "You sound as if you know Cameron."

"I know his kind," Matt amended. It galled him to see Lark defeated. Her eyes were now dark with worry. "Look, let's take this one step at a time," he soothed. "In another couple of days, after my leg is better, hitch up the buckboard and I'll go into Prescott and solve this mortgage problem for you. I can pick up the supplies then, too."

Fear gripped Lark. "Bo Shanks will be there."

"What's he got to do with this?"

"He's the one who beat me up. He'll stalk me again."

"I don't think so."

Matt studied her for a long moment. "Given that new piece of information, I think *you* should stay here."

Lark compressed her lips, staring down at him. "I'm going with you."

"No, you're not."

"I am, too!" Lark jabbed her finger down at the books. "This is my problem and my responsibility, Matt. I'm not going to stay away from Prescott like a cowering dog." She paced the length of the office, her eyes burning with anger. "This time, I'll go in armed. This time Shanks won't dare—"

"You'll do nothing of the sort," Matt warned her. He saw Lark draw herself up, shoulders thrown back, a feral glimmer in her eyes. Softening his voice, he said, "It would be better if you stayed behind."

"I will not. This is my ranch—"

"I know, your responsibility." He eyed her in the gathering silence. "Do you have a dress?"

Lark gawked. "A what?"

"A dress," Matt repeated patiently.

Heat stung her cheeks and Lark stared down at her feet. "Yes. Why?"

"If you're going to insist on coming with me, I want you to wear one."

Her eyes blazed and she lifted her chin. "So I can look like a white woman?"

She was so damned petulant. A child one moment, a woman the next. "No. So you won't draw so much attention to yourself like you did last time."

Gasping, Lark stormed up to the desk and laid her hands flatly against it. "Two years ago, I wore a white woman's dress into Prescott and it did no good at all! The children threw stones and called me names. Shanks mauled me. I'm Apache. And among my people, I don't have to wear a skirt or blouse if I don't want to. They accept me as I am. You whites—"

"Whoa, Lark," he warned, holding up a hand. "Marching into Prescott looking like an Apache warrior will annoy the hell out of those townspeople. They're scared of the Indians, you know that. And by riding in there dressed like one, you stirred up a hornet's nest."

Dark, consuming anger filled Lark. With a cry, she turned her back on him. "It wouldn't have mattered if I'd worn the prettiest dress from Madam Bouchard's Dress Shop, they would still have attacked me this last time!''

Matt ignored the pain in his leg as he walked to within inches of where Lark stood. ''Children can be irresponsible, Lark. Shanks is another matter. I think if you try to fit in, you'll get less of a reaction from the townspeople.''

''No.''

''Did anyone else treat you badly?''

Stubbornly, she admitted, ''No.''

He sighed. ''Listen to me, Lark. Don't confuse the pranks of a few schoolchildren, or the despicable behavior of Bo Shanks, with the attitudes of the general populace. Give them a chance.''

She pouted, hotly aware of his body so close to her own. ''You don't want to believe their hatred of me!''

''I believe there are good people and bad people of all races, Lark.''

''Wait until you meet Cameron and Shanks. You'll change your mind then,'' she muttered.

''Turn around and look at me.''

Her back stiffened.

Matt sighed. ''Lark, you're going to have to trust me.''

She whirled around. ''Trust? How can you ask me to trust you?''

He gazed down at her anguished features, feeling her pain. Without thinking, he placed his hands on her proud shoulders. ''Listen to me, Lark. Your parents are gone and so is the protection they gave you. Your father shielded you from his world. I don't know why he didn't encourage you in his ways.''

''Because he saw the pain I endured at *pindah* hands when I went to school in Prescott, that's why,'' she whispered rawly.

Matt winced. He wanted to caress Lark's uninjured cheek and whisper that everything would be all right.

His touch sent a spiraling ache through her. She wanted

simply to lean her throbbing head against his massive chest and once again feel his arms about her.

He forced a slight smile. "You can deal from a position of strength with those people in Prescott. Remember, they knew your father, not you. If you give them a reason to respect instead of fear you, then part of the battle will be won."

"H-how do I get *pindahs* to respect me?"

Matt looked deeply into her eyes. "Trust me enough to do as I ask this one time?"

Hesitating, torn by old hurts, Lark moved away. Several seconds passed before she answered, "Give me one reason why I should trust you."

"Because I owe you my life," Matt returned huskily. "And I want to set things right between us, Lark. I wouldn't repay a debt by hurting the person who saved my hide."

She considered his reason, feeling nakedly alone in a situation far beyond her experience. "All right," she uttered tiredly, "I'll do as you ask."

"Good. Today's Tuesday. Come next Monday, you, me, and your foreman Paco will ride into Prescott. And I want you to wear a dress."

*A dress.* Lark darkly pondered Matt's request for the rest of the day. She was busy out in the broodmare barn, and then later took the red sorrel stallion, Kentucky, for his daily ride. In the afternoon, she saw Matt Kincaid out by the breaking corral, looking over the sturdy two-year-olds that would have to be broken in order to earn back the lost three hundred dollars. Putting all her worries out of her mind, she allowed Kentucky to stretch his long legs as she raced on his bare back, lost to the joy of the wind tearing past her.

Returning to the yard, Lark slid off Kentucky and gave him a well-deserved pat of praise. The stallion snorted and nipped playfully at her outstretched hand. Paco's eldest son, Ramone, ran up and took the reins. He would walk the stud to cool him down before restabling him. Brushing her hands against her thighs, Lark felt reborn by the ride. As she crossed the yard dotted with scattered chickens, she saw Matt sitting on the front porch.

Her heart pounded briefly as she endured his intense inspection. Maria was sitting nearby, mending clothes and rocking contentedly.

"That's a fine animal," Matt complimented, watching as Lark slowly mounted the steps, unable to tear his gaze from her tall, lithe form. Despite the male clothes she wore, there was a smoldering sensuality about her that simmered just beneath the surface. Her eyes danced with an inner joy. Her mouth, usually compressed with worry, was full and inviting.

Lark melted beneath Matt's burning gaze. "Thank you. You should see some of Kentucky's foals out in the broodmare barn. They're exact images of him."

Matt nodded. "I was out there while you were riding. I can see why the cavalry would pay top dollar for your stock. He's a fine breeding animal."

Pleasantly exhausted by the ride, Lark sat down on the last step, resting her elbows against her knees. Why was she hungry for Matt's closeness? And why did his praise mean so much to her?

"Jud Cameron has been itching to claim Kentucky for years," she continued. "My father would never allow that snake to breed any of his mares to Kentucky."

"If you've got a powerful stud like that, you want to control what he breeds to," Matt agreed.

Lark twisted her head in his direction. "You understand!"

Grinning, he said, "Sure, why shouldn't I?"

"Well, I mean, you aren't Irish like my father, are you?"

Matt laughed. "No, stubborn Scot mixed with my mother's French blood. See? I'm a half-breed, too."

She colored fiercely and turned away. "It's not the same."

"No?" he teased gently.

"No!"

"What's the difference? My father came from a country called Scotland and my mother from a country known as France. You couldn't get two more opposite types together. My father is a stubborn cuss who is as shrewd as the day is long."

Fascinated, Lark turned, resting her back up against the rail of the porch. "And your mother?"

He smiled. "Fiery and hot-tempered. They came from different continents, met here in America, and got married."

"Did they fight all the time?"

He grinned rakishly. "No. My father would lay down the law and my mother would blithely go about subtly changing his mind." Matt laughed. "Her name's Desiree, which means desire."

Lark stared up at him, digesting this new and fascinating information. "So you really are half and half. Are French women the same color as Scot men?"

Matt chuckled. He liked the way her mind worked. Lark had been protected here on a ranch ringed by mountains. Her father had not allowed her to integrate with the white world, for whatever reasons. Matt longed to teach her of a far larger, broader world, instinctively realizing that Lark would welcome the knowledge. "Scots are a very fair-skinned people." He pointed to his face. "I have my mother's darker skin. She was born very close to Italy, and some of her descendants came from there."

"And do you have many brothers and sisters?"

"Two younger brothers who were both killed in the war," Matt said, sobering. "I also have three younger sisters. All hellions."

"Because they have your mother's fiery blood and not your father's?"

"Precisely," Matt said, laughing.

Lark pondered their conversation, resting her chin on

her drawn-up knees. "And did others hate you because you are half Scot and half French?"

"A few did."

"And what did you do about it?"

"Ignored them." He gently held Lark's luminous eyes. "My mother always told us children that it didn't matter what our lineage was. What counted was what was inside our hearts. She said not to judge a person by his color or the country he came from."

"Your mother is a wise woman," Lark said softly, closing her eyes. "The People believe the same thing."

"Most people do, Lark."

She lifted her lashes, feeling a stir of anger. "Not the people of Prescott."

"I'll bet if you started asking the citizens of Prescott where they came from, you'd find most of them are half-breeds, too."

That was a provocative thought. And one that shook Lark's assumptions. "Can this be so?"

"Most of the people coming to America today are what we call immigrants, Lark. They come from many countries overseas."

Heartened, she lifted her head and smiled over at Maria. "Did you know of this?"

"No, *patrona*. In Mexico our blood is mixed with the Spanish people." Maria wrinkled her nose. "Unless those Comancheros come and rape our women, and they give birth to babies of other blood."

Lark returned her attention to Matt, a warmth settling around her. "I think I'm beginning to understand why different colors of skin doesn't bother you like it does some *pindahs*."

"I think you are," Matt told her, a slow smile pulling at his mouth.

Trying to ignore the heat sweeping up her neck and into her face, Lark stood up. "Well, next week we'll see if you're right about the people of Prescott," she murmured.

Matt nodded, holding her gaze. "Yes, we will. Next Monday will begin a new chapter in your life, Lark."

"Perhaps," she murmured. Already her stomach was knotting at the prospect of leaving the safety of the ranch and returning to Prescott.

# Chapter 8

Anxiously Lark stared at herself in the mirror, studying the violet calico dress sprigged with tiny white flowers.

"*Patrona*, you look beautiful!" Maria exclaimed.

Did she? Lark studied the simple white collar and tiny shell buttons that went from her neck to her narrow waist. She fingered the violet sash that Maria had tied prettily into a bow.

Her nervous gaze shifted to the new hairstyle Maria had devised. Instead of parting her hair in the center and allowing it to hang free, she had brushed back the sides and tied them with a violet ribbon, letting the rest fall in soft folds down her back.

"I look different."

"*Sí, patrona*, but so beautiful! I think Señor Matt was right: you look very pretty in a dress."

Matt . . . His name echoed through her mind . . . and heart.

She touched her warm cheeks. How she had looked forward all week to those hours at night when they met in the office and he patiently taught her all about numbers. How she struggled to keep from staring at him and his strong, male mouth. Never had she been so entranced by a man! And yet he did not touch her or make her think he desired her.

Matt was grieving too, Lark reminded herself. They didn't share happiness; there was only sorrow and pain between them. That thought sent her spirits spiraling

downward. Fighting the feeling, Lark heard Matt pull the
buckboard up to the front door. She gave Maria a quick
hug.

"We'll be back," she promised the Mexican woman.

Maria wrung her thin hands. "Ah, *patrona*, I don't
know. I worry so much . . ." She followed Lark through
the quiet house bathed in early morning sunlight.

"Paco is going with us and we'll be safe," Lark
reassured her. Girding herself, she opened the door and
stepped onto the porch.

Unexpected heat throbbed through Matt at the sight of
her. During the week, the swelling and most of the
bruises had left her face. She looked heartachingly
beautiful standing there, shifting from one foot to another,
unsure of herself. Maria stood at her side, beaming. He
smiled and swept his hat from his head.

"You look like a spring flower, Lark."

Heat stung her cheeks and she looked away from him.
The naked hunger on his face had torn the breath from
her. She'd never experienced a man's longing before, and
it deeply unsettled her. "Thank you." Irritably, she
added, "How am I supposed to get into the buckboard in
this thing?"

A slow smile spread across Matt's face. "Pick up the
sides of the skirt and climb up."

Muttering in Apache, Lark hiked the voluminous skirt
awkwardly up to her knees, revealing the kabun boots she
still wore and struggling to maintain her balance. Finally
she had to reach out and grasp Matt's hand in order to
climb on board. Plopping down next to him, she
muttered, "Now I see why men prefer trousers. This is
awful. I feel like a trussed-up steer in this dress."

Quelling a smile, Matt murmured, "You'll get used to
it."

"I will not!" Lark compressed her lips, shooting him
a mutinous look. "I hate this dress! I can hardly walk in
it. I tripped twice getting out here."

The dress was the color of her wide, searching eyes.

For a week, Matt had fought the urge to drown in those eyes. He yearned to reach out and caress the crown of black hair that shone with blue highlights. The dress outlined her tall, willowy form from her small, uptilted breasts to her flat stomach and slender hips. She reminded him of a golden cougar all over again and he tried to ignore the heat building in his loins.

"Ladies don't wear boots," he rebuked her mildly.

Her mouth dropped open. "What? How can they walk anywhere then?"

"They wear slippers on their feet."

She snorted. "This has gone too far, Matt Kincaid! First you hitch me up like a horse in a harness with this thing you call a dress. Now you want to leave me unshod so that I'll limp around like a horse who's thrown a shoe!"

Matt chuckled. "Slow down, wild filly. You're behaving like a bronc with a saddle on his back for the first time, bucking and kicking."

Lark avoided the amusement in his eyes and folded both hands tightly in her lap. She pouted. "I *hate* this dress!"

"*Patrona*, you look beautiful!" Paco greeted her, riding up on his horse and tipping his sombrero. His copper face broke into a wide smile, revealing crooked teeth. "Better watch out or you'll turn the heads of all the men."

She shot Paco an irritated look. "You, too? Did Matt tell you to say that?"

Paco glanced over at Matt and winked. "No, *patrona*. Believe me, the men in Prescott will turn to stare at you."

"Yes, just like last time. And they'll hurl insults, and the children will throw sticks and stones at me. It won't be any different."

Matt picked up the trace reins and slapped them against the backs of the two mules. "No one will say a thing," he promised her.

"I don't know why," Lark retorted, feeling it strange

to be sitting instead of driving the pair of mules. The buckboard creaked and groaned. She waved goodbye to Maria, who stood on the bottom porch step looking worried.

"Because you're dressed like the woman you are and not a man, no one will insult you," Matt explained.

"This I will have to see."

He caught her gaze and smiled slightly. "Just stick at my side when we reach town."

She nodded, trying to lose herself in the beauty of the May morning. A pair of black-headed jays flew past on their way to another pine tree. The thick buffalo and grama grass shone with dew. The sky was cloudless, the rays of Holos striking the crowns of the trees that bordered the rutted dirt road leading up and out of the valley.

It was impossible to ignore Matt's powerful body next to hers. The buckboard's motion kept throwing them together, making their arms and thighs touch. Lark kept scooting back to her side of the seat. She saw the Colt Peacekeeper that Matt wore and fear stirred deep inside her.

Matt himself looked surprisingly healthy, his leg wound having healed rapidly until he suffered just a slight limp. Ny-Oden's medicine was powerful, as always, Lark thought gratefully. Indeed, in the last week Matt's gaunt cheeks had filled out and he'd begun to regain the weight he'd lost. Despite his height and the incredible power that radiated from him, Lark had found him to be a gentle man with her and the rest of the people on the ranch. He rarely raised his voice, and then only to laugh.

Five miles down the road, Paco decided to ride ahead to town. Left alone with Matt, Lark said, "Tell me of your wife, Katie. Did she love the land as much as you do?"

Matt glanced over at her. "No, she didn't really want to come west, if the truth be known."

"No?" It was on the tip of Lark's tongue to say: how could you *not* love this land?

"We married back in Pennsylvania seven years ago. Susie had just been born when I got the idea to head out here." Matt grimaced, remembering all too well Katie's angry objections to his plan.

"Why did you come?"

"Because I had my heart set on using some of my father's money to start up a ranch, raise beef, and somehow get it back east to the markets. We talked long and hard on it, but Katie still didn't want to come."

Lark tilted her head. "I don't understand. This land is beautiful. It's rich and fertile for all animals."

With a sigh, Matt stared straight ahead. Somehow, speaking of Katie eased the burden he carried in his heart. Lark's voice was so gentle, like a soft wind whispering through the branches of a pine tree. He scowled. "Katie had friends in Pennsylvania, and her family was there, Lark. She didn't want to leave them."

"And she was unhappy?"

"Yes, for a long time," he admitted. "My insistence that we move out here harmed our marriage in a lot of ways, Lark."

She stared down at her work-worn hands. "Marriage among the Apache is forever. The woman is an equal partner with her husband, but she always goes where he wants them to go."

"That's true for many white people, too," Matt said. "But Katie was the daughter of a very rich family and she was used to having things her way." He glanced over at Lark. "You might say she was headstrong. A little like you."

Lark wasn't sure if he was insulting or complimenting her. Her brows drew together. "White men don't like women who think on their own, do they?"

"A lot of them don't," he agreed. "But I don't mind it. Part of what drew me to Katie in the first place was her spirit. She was a first-class hellion, despite her refined upbringing, and classically beautiful.''

Inwardly, Lark cringed. She couldn't help but compare herself to Matt's wife. Unlike Katie, she was neither rich nor well schooled. Her heart sank a little lower. "You said it harmed your marriage by moving out here. How?"

He considered her question thoughtfully, realizing she was asking out of a sincere desire to understand and not from idle curiosity. He searched for the right words. "Did you ever see your parents hold hands or kiss?" he asked.

Lark nodded. "My father was like Holos. He would smile often and embrace my mother, often kissing her hand or cheek.''

"They were happy," Matt concluded, a tinge of wishfulness in his voice.

"We all were . . .''

"After we moved out here, Katie didn't want that kind of touching anymore. She found pioneer life too difficult. The hot sun sapped her strength, and she was constantly catching a chill.'' Matt compressed his lips and muttered, "When she lost the second baby four years ago, things became worse. I don't think she ever recovered from the loss.''

"She must have been terribly sad.''

Matt held Lark's questioning gaze. "Katie blamed me for the loss of the baby. She'd wanted to go back east to have it and I said no. In a roundabout way, I killed our son by not letting her return to Pennsylvania.'' Bitterly he added, "Just a few days before Katie and Susie were murdered, I decided to take them to a coach so they could return east.'' He closed his eyes for a moment. "They never made it.''

Lark placed her fingers on Matt's arm, trying in some way to assuage his pain. "How could you have known?''

Matt gently shook off her touch. "I should have paid attention to the warning posted by the army fort in that area, Lark. There had been a recent increase in Apache raids, and if I hadn't been so damned bullheaded and cocksure of myself about defending them, I'd have taken them to the fort for safety. I never dreamed we'd be attacked. Never . . .''

Lark searched for words to heal his grief and guilt, but she found none. His voice gently intruded into her thoughts.

"Katie was very unhappy, Lark. We both decided it would be best if she went back east to live. Besides, she wanted Susan to get a good education and grow up with children her own age. There wasn't much left of our marriage anyway, and I felt responsible for making her life hell. In the end, I just wanted to see her smile again. That's all that mattered. If that meant letting her live back east, I was willing to do it.''

Tightening her fingers on his arm, Lark felt his pain as if it were her own. Finally she whispered, "I'm sorry, Matt. I can see how much your family meant to you.''

He shrugged, putting aside the pain. Somehow Lark's simple touch lessened his guilt and anguish. "That's all right, Lark. Don't waste your feelings on me. I thought I knew what I was doing, but I made some poor decisions.''

"But surely you hoped that Katie would grow to love this land as you do.''

Matt smiled sadly. "Yes . . . I'd hoped that would happen, but it never did. Back east, there were parties to attend, places to see and be seen.''

Lark shook her head. "The east sounds like a strange place.''

Lark's naivete made him smile. "I belong out here, Lark. I always have.''

"So you will stay?''

"Right after my family was murdered, I sold all my land. There were too many sad memories. I didn't have the heart to rebuild my ranch. All I want to do now is hunt down Ga'n. If I survive that, then I might think about starting over.''

Lark removed her hand, her emotions in turmoil.

Seeking a way to take his mind off his sadness, Lark pointed to the Colt he wore at his side. "You wear your gun low like Shanks. Are you a gunslinger, too?"

Matt shook his head. "No, but I learned to wear it low for a fast draw during the Civil War. I was a captain in the cavalry and my men and I did a lot of riding behind enemy territory. I was a good shot, but I got a reputation during the war for being quicker than most."

"I have heard about this war. Which side did you fight for?"

"The North."

"Then you were a yellow legs."

He smiled at her use of the Indian slang for cavalry. "Yes, for the duration of the war, I was."

She scowled. "I'm glad you aren't a soldier now."

"I am, too. I'd rather raise beef and farm than kill people. It's a lot safer."

"When we get to Prescott," Lark muttered darkly, "you will have to be a soldier again."

"I hope not, Lark. I think our visit can be made peacefully. First, we'll stop by your bank and talk to this Jud Cameron."

Her heartbeat quickened and Lark gripped her hands tightly. "I'm so angry at him for cheating me!"

Matt covered her clenched fingers with his own. "Take it easy, golden cougar. The man may have made an honest mistake. It won't do any good to go in there accusing him of cheating you. That would only lead to more problems."

Cameron frowned when Willy came running into his office. "What do you want, Willy?" he demanded irritably. It was almost noon and he was due to go down to the Belle Hotel for lunch with Colonel Morgan.

"Sir . . . you just won't believe this," he exclaimed. "Miss Gallagher's here. Again! And she's come back with a gunslinger in tow. I swear, he stands seven feet high! And he's mean-lookin', too."

Scowling, Jud rose and straightened his black velvet vest. Today he wore the newest style from New Orleans— a dark gray waistcoat and trousers with a white silk shirt and black tie. "Where's Shanks?" Damn him, Cameron cursed silently, the man was never around when he needed him.

"Uh, I don't know, Mr. Cameron."

Waving the clerk toward the door, Cameron snapped, "Get one of the boys to fetch him. Tell him I want him over here on the double!"

Willy hurried out the door. After fitting a small derringer into the pocket of his vest, Cameron followed at a more leisurely pace. Now he was prepared to deal with that breed hellion. The little bitch had guts coming back so soon after the beating she took last time.

Cameron hesitated at the bottom of the marble stairs, unprepared for what he saw. Lark Gallagher was wearing a dress. His narrowed eyes moved to the man standing almost protectively next to her. Willy hadn't exaggerated by much: the gunslinger was built like a damned grizzly bear. Cameron noticed that the cowboy's hands hung loosely at his sides, another sign that the man was handy with a gun. Dammit, anyway!

"Howdy, Miss Gallagher," Cameron greeted with feigned joviality, walking over to them. "What brings you here today?" He could see the faint traces of bruises on her set features. Cameron simmered. He'd told Shanks to rough her up, not beat the hell out of her.

"Mr. Cameron," Lark said, her voice wobbly with nervous tension, "I've come to point out a banking error you made." She thrust the mortgage book at him.

Cameron eyed the gunslinger. He didn't like the look in the man's icy gray eyes. And Lark hadn't even bothered to introduce him, the bitch. He took the book. "Oh? What seems to be the problem?"

Trying to suppress her anger, Lark said, "You said my father hadn't paid the mortgage for May, but he did. It's in there, initialed by Willy Bradford. See for yourself."

Jud slowly opened the book, pretending not to be the least bit ruffled. He took his time, noticing that Lark moved restlessly but that the gunslinger stood quietly at her side.

"Well, well," he murmured, smiling, "you're right."

Lark's eyes bored into Cameron's narrow face. "You knew it all along," she accused, "and yet you tried to fool me into thinking I owed more."

Matt gently took her arm. "If you'll get Miss Gallagher another slip showing she's paid the mortgage, that will be sufficient, Mr. Cameron. She wants the extra hundred dollars she paid returned to her in cash today."

How dare this cowboy tell him how to run his business! Bristling, Cameron snapped, "And just who are you? This is between me and Miss Gallagher."

"From now on, any accounting business is between you and me," Matt growled.

Lark relaxed within Matt's grip, feeling protected. Cameron's face turned a dull red and he took a step back from them.

"Who the hell are you, cowboy?" he repeated.

Matt smiled slowly. "I'm Miss Gallagher's ranch manager, Matt Kincaid."

Lark blinked up at Matt. That was a lie, of course, but she was thrilled when Cameron's face drained of all color.

"Ranch manager?" he ground out, giving Matt a head-to-toe inspection. "Somehow I doubt that."

Matt held Cameron's insolent gaze. "You can believe anything you want, Cameron, but understand this. You won't be making any more mistakes on the Gallagher Ranch accounts. I'll be there to make sure Lark's money is correctly deposited and her mortgage payments correctly recorded. Understand?"

His voice was far too cultured for a gunslinger, Jud decided, holding on to his thinning patience. He glanced around to see a number of the other customers watching the scene intently. Gripping the book, he snarled, "Wait here. I'll get the payment slip and the cash."

Lark gripped Matt's hand, squeezing it in her excitement. "I can't believe this! He's going to do it!"

For a split second, looking down at Lark, Matt allowed the harsh mask he wore to melt away. Her expression was radiant with hope, her eyes lustrous with disbelief. How he wanted to lean over and kiss those breathless, parted lips! "It's because you're wearing a dress," he said solemnly.

"Oh!" Then she realized he was teasing her and smiled shyly.

"I keep telling you, women in dresses are respected by men."

Lark's mouth quirked. Perhaps Matt was right after all . . .

After Cameron had given her the payment slip, Matt led her onto the wooden sidewalk and halted her a few paces from the bank's doors. "Next we're going to go see the sheriff."

"No, Matt." Lark pulled from his grasp. "It won't do any good."

"Maybe. We'll see."

Adamantly, Lark shook her head. "I don't want to see the sheriff or even talk to him."

"Why don't you walk over to the dry goods store, then? Paco's over there getting the buckboard loaded with supplies. I'll meet you there in a few minutes."

Relieved that he understood, Lark walked quickly down the street, acutely aware of the way the people were staring at her. But this time several women smiled tentatively at her, and two men respectfully tipped their hats. Still, Lark felt naked and defenseless without her knife. Matt had talked her into leaving it in the buckboard, beneath the seat. Ladies, he'd told her, carried a parasol or gloves, not an eighteen-inch bowie knife.

Abe Harris greeted her enthusiastically and his women customers continued to shop after Lark swept into the busy store.

Abe gripped her hands, squeezing them warmly. "How

are you? We heard about that terrible attack you suffered leaving Prescott last time. Are you all right?''

She managed a slight smile. ''Yes, I'm fine, now. Thank you.''

''You look wonderful. And that dress . . . Why, young lady, you're the prettiest woman in Prescott!''

''Oh, Abe . . .''

''No, no, I mean it.'' He raised his voice. ''Millie! Come and look at Lark.''

Millie, his rotund wife, came waddling out of the rear of the store, her apple cheeks bright red as she came over and hugged Lark. ''Sweet mercy! Lark Gallagher, you look scrumptious! Why, all you need is a pretty little parasol and a hat to make you the envy of every single lady here in Prescott. I do declare, ain't she purty, Abe?''

Lark felt overwhelmed by their compliments. Shyly she thanked Millie and Abe, her voice barely above a whisper. When she saw three other white women standing by the bolts of dress material, watching with interest, she blushed even more.

''My dear,'' Millie went on, taking her by the hand and coaxing her across the wooden floor, ''you simply *must* have a hat to set off that lovely dress you're wearing.'' She showed Lark a display of hats on a far counter. ''Look! Abe just got these in from New Orleans. Can you imagine wearing a hat from there? Why, these bonnets are the latest rage.'' She touched Lark's flaming cheeks. ''And with that purty face of yours, a hat will just set you off.''

''Set me off?'' Lark imagined being bucked off a horse and sailing through the air.

Millie chose a straw bonnet decorated with a blue velvet ribbon and a cluster of purple flowers. ''Of course, my dear! A hat sets off a young lady's face to a decided advantage. The right bonnet can make your eyes look larger, and emphasize your cheekbones.'' Millie squinted and peered up at Lark. ''My spectacles are in the back,'' she explained, her nose inches from Lark's face. ''Why, yes! This bonnet will bring out your beauty, Lark. Here, try it on!''

"But, Millie—"

"Pshaw! Now, come sit over here in front of the mirror."

Uncomfortable at all the attention, Lark did as she was told. Millie settled the bonnet on her head and tied the velvet ribbon into a bow near her right cheek.

"There," Millie crowed. "Oh, my, my. Abe, come and look at Lark! Doesn't she just look scrumptious enough to eat? I declare, if Madam Bouchard saw you, she'd never let you go. Such a perfect figure you have! And your face . . ." Millie sighed rapturously and stepped back.

Lark forced herself to look in the mirror. Gone was her familiar and comfortable Apache look. What stared back at her was a stranger. And yet, as she probed her face, Lark saw her familiar eyes, mouth, and nose. And the bonnet was beautiful. She caressed the velvet ribbon longingly. It did match her dress.

"Really, Millie, Abe, I can't buy this." Lark quickly untied the bow and gently set the bonnet down on the counter. "It's beautiful, but—"

"Oh, dearie, you can't afford not to have it with your dress," Millie chided gently. "No lady walks around in this awful sunlight without a bonnet or a parasol to properly protect her face."

"Oh?"

"Of course! Sunlight ruins a lady's skin."

"Millie, my love," Abe began awkwardly.

Lark knew Millie meant well. She rose, rubbing her hands against her skirt. "The bonnet costs too much. I'm sorry. I was robbed of three hundred dollars and I just can't afford it. At least not right now."

Abe patted Lark's cool, damp hand. "Don't pay any attention to Millie. She's like a team of runaway horses when she gets excited about something. We want you to take the bonnet as a gift. You've had so much sadness befall you of late, Millie and I were searching for a way to make you smile again.''

Lark heard sudden gasps behind her and felt a flurry of movement. She turned, perplexed. Her eyes widened. Her stomach knotted. Bo Shanks was standing by the open doorway, his hands on his narrow hips, watching her. A cheroot dangled from his lips, the smoke making his eyes squint as he studied her. The three women hurried out of the store, fear written clearly on their features.

Millie croaked out a sound and moved behind her husband's slender frame. Abe scowled.

Lark's attention turned to Paco, who was lifting the last box of supplies at the rear of the store and was still unaware of the gunslinger's presence. She remembered Paco's swearing to even the score with Shanks if he ever got a chance. Shanks was now watching her foreman with interest. Terror sizzled through her, and she walked to the center of the store, placing herself between the two men.

"What do you want?'' she demanded.

Shanks smiled lazily. ''Word gets around in a hurry, honey. I was at the Silver Spur Saloon when they said the breed was in town wearing a dress.'' He sucked deeply on the cheroot before dropping the butt to the floor. His wolfish grin lingered as he held her angry stare. ''Ya think a dress is gonna change how these town folks treat ya?''

Her nostrils flared and Lark clenched her fists. ''I don't have to stand here talking to you, Shanks.'' She turned to Paco, who was now glaring at the gunslinger. ''Paco, take that last load out to the buckboard and stay there.''

''Don't move,'' Shanks warned the Mexican foreman, his hand dropping lazily to the gun placed low on his hip.

''Get out of here!'' Lark cried at Shanks. ''You have no right to do this!''

''Sure I do, breed.'' He looked her up and down, nice and slow. ''And damned if ya don't look better in a dress. Kinda shows off yore good points. Makes ya look like a woman.''

Coloring fiercely, Lark took a step toward Shanks. "You foul dog's belly!"

He grabbed her wrist and jerked her toward him. A cry was torn from Lark and pain raced up her arm. She stumbled, tripping over the hem of the dress. She heard Paco drop the box of supplies. Before she could do anything, Shanks pushed her savagely aside.

As she fell to the floor, she saw Shanks's lightning draw. Paco shouted a warning just as the shattering explosion of two guns going off sent her reeling. The reek of cordite gunpowder stung her nostrils as she crawled to her knees. Shanks stood there, grinning. With a cry, Lark lurched to her feet. Paco was lying on the floor groaning, blood splattered everywhere.

Falling to Paco's side, Lark bit back a cry. Shanks had shot him in the shoulder and blood was pumping from the gaping wound. Torn between the need to care for Paco and an overwhelming urge to grab the first weapon she could find and use it on Shanks, Lark begged, "Lie still, Paco, lie still." She pressed the clean towel Abe handed her against the wound.

"I'll get the doc," Abe said hurriedly.

"Ya ain't gonna do anything," Shanks snarled, opening the chamber on his gun and dropping out the spent cartridge.

"My God," Abe exploded, "he'll bleed to death!"

"One more greaser dead. Stay where ya are unless ya want a belly full of lead, too."

Lark struggled to her feet, all her hatred and anger exploding deep within her. No matter what it took, she was going to get Paco to the doctor. Then she saw Matt Kincaid standing in the doorway. Shanks was putting his gun back in the holster when Matt clamped a hand on the gunslinger's thin shoulder. In one motion, he picked Shanks up and threw him off his feet. Shanks threw his arms over his head before he slammed into a bin filled with fabric.

Matt stood there, surveying the carnage. He saw Lark

totter to her feet, her hands stained with blood, her skirt crimson. "Get a doctor and bring the sheriff," he told the storekeeper quietly. "Lark, stay with Paco."

Abe nodded and hurried past Matt. Shanks shook his head, crawling to his hands and knees. He glowered at the cowboy. "You'll regret this, mister," he snarled.

"No, you're the one who's going to be sorry." Matt walked toward the gunslinger.

"He's dangerous, Matt!" Lark cried in warning. "A killer!"

"He's a yellow-bellied snake. Get on your feet, Shanks."

Damn! Shanks thought. This must be the man the breed had hired to protect her. Cameron had ordered him to find him earlier. He sized up the man, a frisson of anger moving through him. He couldn't have lasted four years as top gun here in Prescott without being good, but just the way this cowboy wore the Peacekeeper, he knew he was in for trouble.

Slowly, he got to his knees. "Keep yore nose out of business that don't concern ya," he warned.

Matt stared down at him, leaving less than four feet separating them. "You're a weasel, Shanks. One of those greasy little gunslingers who makes his reputation by plugging people in the back."

Shanks slowly got to his feet, hunched over, ready to go for his gun. "What's yore name? I want to know it 'fore I kill ya."

"Kincaid. And I hope like hell you go for your gun."

Shanks hesitated. Something in the voice warned him not to draw. He grinned, showing his yellowed teeth. "Kincaid . . . can't say I've heard the name."

"I'm the new manager for the Gallagher Ranch."

"I see . . ."

"You'd better, scum."

Hatred leaped into Shank's feral eyes. "No one calls me scum . . ."

"Go on, Shanks, give me a reason to draw on you.

Any reason . . .'' he taunted softly. "I want to make this all real legal. That's the last time you'll touch Lark or draw against one of her ranch hands.''

Lark continued to press the towel against Paco's shoulder, her throat aching with tension, aware that Paco was going into shock and needed help badly. The Mexican groaned loudly.

Shanks used the unexpected distraction to his advantage. His palm slapped against the pearl handle of his gun.

With a curse, and before Shanks could get the weapon out of the holster, Matt struck him hard in the jaw. The gunslinger slammed into the fabric bin. The satisfying sound of teeth breaking beneath his fist made Matt feel slightly better. He heard Lark cry out his name but ignored her, limping over to where Shanks lay dazed on the floor.

"Get up,'' he snarled, jerking Shanks to his feet.

Lark hovered over Paco, her hand pressed against her mouth. As Matt dragged Shanks upward, she saw the gunslinger pull a knife from his belt.

"Matt!'' she screamed.

In a flash he caught Shanks's right wrist and squeezed the thin blade from his clawlike fingers. Shanks let out a shriek of pain as his wrist was bent back. He fell to his knees, and Matt pressed his weight down into the gunslinger. His breath came in ragged gasps.

"You've gone too far this time, Shanks. The sheriff will catch up with you. No one shoots a man without provocation and gets away with it. Get the hell out of here before I decide to put my gun to your filthy head.'' He shoved Shanks away, watching the gunslinger leap to his feet.

Lark turned back to Paco as Shanks left the store. The Mexican was pale and still. She pressed her hand against his neck. There was still a faint pulse. Shaken, she didn't realize Matt had knelt opposite her until she looked up.

"How is he?''

"I—I think the bleeding's stopped."

Matt pushed the hat off his wrinkled brow. "Good. Here comes the doc."

The doctor, an older man than Abe Harris, placed his black bag down beside the foreman and rapidly examined him. "Abe, I'm going to need help," he said. "This man's got to be taken over to my office."

Lark stood with her back against the wall, feeling numb and exhausted. She stared mutely as Matt and Abe carried Paco out the door. Silence settled around her. She looked down at the puddle of blood, and a chill ran through her. With another towel she tried to blot it up. Millie peeked out of the back storeroom and promptly swooned. Lark managed to get her to a chair and found some smelling salts, which she held under the woman's nose.

Assured that Millie would survive the shocking event, Lark ignored the large crowd of curious onlookers who had gathered in the doorway and pressed to get through them. Finally she broke clear and, picking up her skirt, ran across the dusty street. Gasping, she bounded up the wooden walkway and entered the doctor's office.

Matt turned. "Lark?"

She closed the door and leaned heavily against it, out of breath. "Is he going to live?"

"I don't know. Doc Friar's got him under ether right now to take out the bullet." He took her arm. "Come on, sit down. You look like you're going to faint."

Just the touch of his hand brought all her feelings to the surface. Valiantly she fought the deluge of emotions. "I—I'm all right. Really . . ."

"I know you are," he soothed, watching her closely. "You were very brave in a very bad situation."

Lark couldn't force herself to sit down. She craved his closeness, his protection. She searched his dark gray eyes. "Matt?"

"Yes?"

"Hold me? Just for a little while. If you—"

With a groan he swept his arms around her, crushing her against him. A sob escaped Lark and he held her tighter, caressing her black, silky hair. "It's all right, my golden cougar. Everything's going to be fine."

# Chapter 9

Cameron rose from his desk as Shanks shuffled into his office. "What the hell happened to you?"

He sat down, holding his swelling jaw. "Goddammit, boss, don't holler at me. I gotta get to Doc Friar. That bastard Kincaid busted up my teeth."

Cameron sat back down, his mouth thinning. "I thought I told you to go over there and chase that breed out of town."

Shanks flashed him an irritated look. "Ya forgot to mention he was a hired gun, not just another drover, goddammit."

Cameron pretended indifference. "Oh? Kincaid said something about being her ranch manager. How could I know? He did that to you, didn't he?"

"I'm in a lotta pain!"

Snorting violently, Cameron gestured savagely toward the door. "Get the hell out of here. I don't need no snotnose dribbling blood all over my new carpet. Now get going!"

Shanks rose slowly. If he didn't like the money Cameron paid him so much, he wouldn't take this shit from the bastard. "Look, that bastard's meaner than a rattler that's been riled. That breed bitch done got her a tough *hombre*. I'll get him, I just gotta have time!"

Giving Shanks a withering stare, Cameron muttered, "All right. Get your ass back over here when the doc's fixed that mouth of yours. And make it fast."

161

As Shanks jerked open the office door, he saw Sheriff Cole walking down the carpeted hall. Cole came to a stop and poked his head inside Cameron's door. "Gotta take Shanks in, Jud."

Cameron scowled. "For godsakes, why? What the hell's going on?"

"He shot Paco Hernandez in broad daylight and there are witnesses. That Mex foreman of the breed's is over at the doc's office right now getting patched up." Cole lifted his hand toward the gunslinger. "Let's go."

Cursing roundly, Cameron leaped to his feet, his eyes blazing. "You shot a greaser in broad daylight?"

Shanks winced. "He got in the way of me pushin' the breed around."

"You stupid louse!" He turned to Cole. "Put him in jail for now. I'll fix things to spring this idiot after the breed and that gun leave."

"But, boss, my jaw. I gotta get over to Doc Friar."

Cameron clenched his teeth. The urge to strike Shanks was very strong, but he didn't want to get blood on his good clothes or bruise his knuckles. "Cole, get this silly bastard out of my office and out of my sight! Now! He can damned well cool his heels over in the jail for a couple of days."

Glaring at Cameron, Shanks tenderly held his aching jaw. "Aw, boss—"

"Sit in jail and think about what you've done, Shanks," Cameron snarled, stalking across the office to confront the gunslinger. He jabbed his finger into Shanks's chest. "The people of Prescott won't put up with flagrant disregard of the law. The only reason I get away with some things is because we do things quietly and behind the scenes. You've disobeyed my orders. Shooting a man in broad daylight is the stupidest thing you've ever done. Cole, get him out of here before I puke. And then get back over here. Morgan's due any time now. We've got some planning to do."

Cole nodded. "Yes, sir."

Cameron sat for a long time in silence after Shanks and Cole left. Sonofabitch! Lark Gallagher knew she had him by the balls. And who was that drifter? He'd never seen his face before. He clenched his manicured fingers, the nails biting deep into his palms. He hadn't expected the breed to hire a gun, he'd expected her to run. Dammit!

Cameron paced his office, thinking long and hard. Sheriff Cole returned with Colonel Parker Morgan. Good, the northern end of the Tucson Indian Ring was convened. Cameron sat down behind his desk, steepled his fingers, and looked gravely at each man.

"I've got trouble," he began heavily. "Originally, I thought that with Roarke Gallagher out of the way, I could get his ranch and water rights real easy. I was wrong. That breed daughter of his has hired a gunman by the name of Kincaid."

"Matt Kincaid," Cole clarified.

Cameron's black brows rose. "How do you know?"

"The gent was over in my office earlier filing charges against Bo and pressuring the hell out of me about Gallagher's death. He questioned that report you had me file on it."

Cameron ran a finger around his tight collar. "Is Kincaid wanted for any crimes?"

"Nope," Cole answered. "Not as far as I can tell."

Parker Morgan shifted, frowning. "Is he a government agent, do you think? You know, with all our activity between Prescott and Tucson last year, I was afraid they'd send some undercover agents in to investigate."

"Parker," Cameron warned, "stop running like a scared coyote. This Kincaid isn't a damned agent. I told you before, Ga'n's been doing our dirty laundry. The Apaches are gettin' blamed for everything. No one suspects we're behind it."

"I don't know, Jud," Cole countered, twisting one end

of his handlebar mustache in thought. ''That Kincaid fella's smart. He ain't no ordinary cowpoke. The man uses his words well.''

''I know one thing,'' Cameron added bitterly, ''he sure as hell caught me red-handed trying to cheat the breed out of a mortgage payment.''

''I say he's an agent,'' Morgan reiterated. ''I warned the southern branch of the Ring that there were too many raids being pulled down there by whites posing as Apaches. The ranchers and homesteaders are up in arms. They're writing to the federal government for help.''

Cameron rolled his eyes, shutting out the rest of Morgan's litany. If he didn't need some help inside the U.S. Army, he'd have gotten rid of the pompous, aging Morgan a long time ago.

''I wonder if that bastard Captain Frank Herter has anything to do with this,'' Morgan muttered aloud. ''He's real sweet on that breed.''

Cameron considered the possibility. ''Herter's due to retire shortly, isn't he?''

''Yes, and none too soon. I don't like him looking over my shoulder. The last time I sent my patrol in the opposite direction from where we knew Ga'n was going to attack some settlers, Herter asked questions. He's been making a lot of noise about my tactics and strategy during the last four months. The captain smells something, I know he does.''

''He'll be out soon,'' Cameron soothed. ''And once he retires and becomes a civilian, he'll be harmless to your command. Relax.''

Dan Cole hitched a boot up on one of the office chairs, frowning. ''Let's get back to this Kincaid fella. If yore gonna try and get the water rights, he'll be in the way.''

''He'll be one man against all our forces,'' Cameron said. ''Once I get the Gallagher land, the Ring's power here in the north will increase considerably. I don't think Saunders, who owns the Circle S Ranch down near Tucson, is going to protest my decision. Nor will Colonel

Williams, commander of Fort Apache. They want to see us strengthen our position here in Prescott. Bringing down Lark Gallagher will be a good way to do it.''

Morgan nodded reluctantly. "I think it's time we contacted Ga'n again. Let him take care of the breed for us.''

Cole snorted. "You know that red devil ain't gonna touch the Gallagher Ranch. He respected the breed's father, and she's half Apache. No way will Ga'n do anything to hurt her or the ranch.''

"We'll see," Cameron snapped. "Once Bo is found innocent of plugging that greaser, I want him to ride to Ga'n's hideout and tell the renegade I want to meet him at our usual spot near the cliffs." He rubbed his hands together. "If anyone can persuade him to get Lark Gallagher, I can.''

Cole nodded. "Word's out that the breed and her gunslinger are stayin' here in Prescott overnight.''

Cameron shrugged, then smiled. "Maybe I can reconnoiter over at the hotel and find out more about this Kincaid fella. The more we know about him, the better. And while I'm at it, I'll give the breed my final offer for the water rights to her ranch. She needs the money too badly to say no.''

Lark had never before taken a hot bath in a copper tub. At the ranch, she always washed in the cold mountain stream behind the house or swam in one of the shallow lakes during the summer. Now, as she languished in the tub in the middle of the afternoon, the hot water miraculously dissolved the soreness from her back and shoulders.

Matt had taken care of everything, she thought drowsily, resting her head against the rim. Where had he gotten the money to pay for two rooms at the hotel? And later he was going to take her out to eat.

Worriedly, Lark forced open her eyes. Matt had given a young boy over at the livery stable fifty cents to ride

out to the ranch and tell Maria, Paco's wife, of his injury.
A sigh escaped her lips. Paco was going to be all right,
the doctor had assured her. The bullet had been removed
and the Mexican was resting comfortably over at the
office. But he couldn't be moved for at least two days,
so they'd have to stay in Prescott until he was better.

Restless, Lark sat up and scrubbed herself clean with
the French milled soap. She inhaled the lavender scent,
finding it delightful. Her hair was next. Afterward, feeling
exhausted by the day's turn of events, she wrapped a
thick towel around her body and lay down in the big bed,
falling immediately into a much-needed sleep.

Matt knocked softly on Lark's hotel room door. He
waited patiently. No one answered. He frowned. Shifting
his parcel to the other arm, he knocked more firmly. It
was nearly six o'clock and Lark had said she wouldn't
leave her room. Why wasn't she answering? A tremor of
fear ran through him.

He couldn't wait any longer. He twisted the knob. The
door opened, yet he'd instructed Lark to lock it. Heart
pounding heavily in his chest, he pushed the door wide
and scanned the silent room, missing nothing. He released
his held breath and stepped inside, quietly closing the
door behind him, remaining motionless until his heart
slowed down.

Matt gazed at Lark's sleeping form. A towel covered
her from her breasts to halfway down her long, firm
thighs. He shouldn't be here, staring at her. He should
get the hell out before she discovered his presence.

Taking careful steps, he quietly placed the large parcel
on the dresser. Lark stirred and he froze until he was sure
she was still asleep. He'd never forget the feel of the
thick, clean strands of her hair between his fingers when
he'd held her earlier over at the doctor's office.

Closing the door, Matt left the room, shaken in a way
he couldn't explain.

* * *

Lark awoke an hour later. She fumbled to light the kerosene lamps in the cozy room. Still groggy, she noticed the large parcel on the dresser. How did it get here? Heat settled in her cheeks. Matt must have come into the room and left it while she slept.

She brought the package to the bed and carefully unwrapped it. Her drowsiness vanished as she stared down at a carefully folded dress. Tentatively, as if half afraid to touch it, she ran her fingers across the soft golden material.

Matt had known she would be too embarrassed to dine in the hotel's public dining room wearing the violet dress that had been stained with Paco's blood. Stroking the soft material, knowing that it wasn't the cotton she was used to wearing, Lark eagerly slipped into the ivory chemise and numerous petticoats that had also been provided.

She fumbled with the violet ribbon, trying to arrange her hair as Maria had done so deftly earlier. In the flickering lamplight she stared at herself in the mirror. The boat neck of the gold dress was edged with dainty lace, displaying her prominent collarbones and emphasizing her slender neck. Lark felt embarrassed by the low cut of the gown, but she loved the white lace that edged each sleeve at the wrist. Lace also ran in rows down the front of the dress and the waist was tied with a gold velvet ribbon. Slowly she ran her fingers down the dress, glorying in the rich texture of the fabric and the rustle of the full skirt. She felt beautiful.

As she walked down the carpeted hall to the wide staircase that led to the lobby, Lark's heart began to pound in earnest. Would Matt be waiting for her in the dining room?

There were a number of people in the lobby, mostly men but also a few well-dressed women. Lark couldn't ignore the looks of interest on their faces. She felt a tap on the shoulder and turned around. An elegantly dressed man with a young woman on his arm smiled down at her. He tipped his hat to Lark.

"Excuse me, Miss Gallagher. My name is Cyrus McDonald. This is my wife, Melinda. We knew your father, Roarke Gallagher. We heard about the awful tragedy concerning him, and we just wanted to say how sorry we are that it happened."

Stunned, Lark could only stare at the couple. Their eyes were filled with genuine regret.

Melinda McDonald reached out her gloved hand, briefly touching Lark's arm. "Father Mulcahy told us what happened last Sunday at church. We've been meaning to drive out and see you, to pay our respects to your father, Lark. Perhaps this coming Saturday? The ladies from the church want to bring you some clothing that was being collected for the families that live on your ranch. Roarke had told us the children could use them. May we come to call on you?"

Overwhelmed, Lark barely nodded. "I—well, yes . . ."

Melinda smiled warmly and patted Lark's arm again. "Wonderful. We'll come calling this Saturday then."

It took Lark several moments to recover from the unexpected encounter. They were whites, but they had been sincerely sorry for her father's death. Shaken, Lark sought out the desk clerk and asked where the dining room was located. The clerk smiled and gave her directions.

The wine-colored drapes fringed in silver that hung in the arched entrance to the dining room fascinated Lark. The hotel was lavish compared to the spareness of her ranch. She hesitated in the doorway. Heat fled up her neck and face as a few patrons turned to look at her.

Relief flowed through Lark as she saw Matt rise from a corner table and make his way through the crowded room. His gray gaze was warm with welcome and with . . . what? She tilted her head, trying to decipher the smoldering flame in his eyes that made her go hot and shaky.

"Lark?" Matt held his hand out.

She placed her fingers in it. "Why are those men staring at me?" she whispered as he came to her side.

He smiled gently, cupping her elbow. "Because you're the most beautiful woman they've ever seen."

And she was, he realized. The dark gold of the dress accentuated her clean, classic features. Her black hair shone in the lamplight, an ebony cape against her back and shoulders. Her skin glowed. He led her toward their table. She was fidgety and nervous, her eyes dark and darting, like those of a trapped animal.

Once seated at Matt's left, Lark leaned toward him, keeping her voice low. "Apaches would never stare at me like some of these people are doing!"

Matt smiled. "Even Apaches would if they saw you in that dress."

Not sure how to respond, she stared down at the fine china plates and silverware. Everything about this hotel shouted of wealth. "I—I should thank you for buying this dress for me."

"The other one was dirty. I didn't think you'd want to wear it."

She toyed with the lace at her wrist. "This one is so pretty. I mean—it's expensive."

"Consider it a gift."

"A gift?"

"Yes."

"Oh . . ."

"Why?"

"Well, Apaches give gifts to one another all the time."

"So do white people. Especially on holidays like a birthday or Christmas. I told you before, Lark, these are your people, too. They aren't all murderers like Shanks or cheats like Cameron. Has anyone else given you a hard time on this trip?"

"No," she said eagerly, and launched into a description of her encounter with Cyrus and Melinda McDonald in the lobby. She saw approval in Matt's features as she finished.

"Give us a chance, Lark. Believe me, there are more people like the McDonalds than you know. I get the impression that your father was highly respected here in Prescott. And even though the townspeople have had little contact with you, they still want to reach out and help you at a time like this."

"I think you're right," Lark admitted faintly. "I've committed a terrible error, haven't I?"

Matt shook his head. "If you hadn't accepted the McDonalds' help and friendship, then you would have made a mistake. Right now, you're learning just how many people loved your father, Lark."

"Do you think they will accept me, then?"

"I think they already have."

Contrite for the way she had thought of whites for so long, Lark hung her head and said softly, "Yes . . ."

Matt saw the regret written all over her face. "They've forgiven you. Forgive yourself, Lark. No permanent damage has been done. Come on, give me a smile."

Rallying beneath his coaxing tone, she lifted her head and managed a small smile.

"Good. Ah, here's our waitress. I don't know about you, but I'm hungry as a bear."

Lark's smile grew over their shared joke.

The waitress, a buxom blond dressed in a gaudy red and white outfit, sauntered over to them and smiled winningly at Matt. "The name's Ezzie, short for Esmerelda. What'll it be, mister?"

Matt glanced over at Lark, who was staring like a child at Ezzie's low-cut, tight-fitting dress. "We'll each have a proper steak with all the fixings, Ezzie."

She smiled, batting her eyelashes in Matt's direction. "Anything else? You're a strapping man, mister. Maybe you want a little more?"

Matt caught the innuendo. Lark did not. She was like a child in a new world. "That'll be all, thanks."

Pouting playfully, Ezzie turned and wriggled away.

"What are those things on her eyes?" Lark whispered fiercely under her breath.

He grinned. "The ladies of the night sometimes snip off a bit of their hair, hand knot it into some silk thread, and glue it to their lashes."

Lark blinked. "But . . . why?"

He shrugged. "I guess they think it makes them look prettier."

"They looked like yellow caterpillars!"

He grinned. "They did, didn't they?"

Lark stared at Ezzie as she flounced dramatically around a corner. "And did you see how low-cut her dress was?"

"Yes."

"Why, you could see—I mean, you could almost see . . ." Matt's gray eyes had filled with amusement, but she knew he wasn't laughing at her. She glanced circumspectly around the room. There were a number of well-heeled women sitting with men, all of them dressed beautifully. She leaned over, cupping her hand to her mouth so that no one else could hear her. "The other women don't wear their dresses so low. Why did Ezzie?"

"It's her way of catching a man's attention," Matt drawled, enjoying Lark's discoveries.

She frowned, thinking about that answer for a long moment. "Then these other women don't want to catch a man?"

For her sake he held on to his laughter. Lark's expression was so serious and naive. "There are many ways to get a man's attention. Ezzie's is one way, but there are others."

"But their clothes are like mine. Why do the men sit with them, then?"

"Why am I sitting with you?"

Lark frowned, meeting his smiling eyes. "Because you have to."

"Because I *want* to," Matt amended gently.

"Then, what a woman wears doesn't catch a man anyway?" She was completely confused.

"Clothes can help," Matt explained, getting serious, "but what's in the woman's heart and head counts most."

"Oh . . . that makes sense. Apaches feel the same way about the women they take as wives. It helps if she can grind corn well and cook, but that isn't everything."

Matt drolly agreed. "White men like to know that their woman can cook also."

Pleased with what she was learning about the white world, Lark relaxed in the upholstered chair and smiled up at Matt. Lark drowned in the dove-gray depths of his eyes.

A few minutes later, Ezzie returned carrying a huge tray piled high with food. Lark watched her intently, mesmerized by the "caterpillars" on her eyelashes.

Lark wiped her mouth with a napkin when she was finished eating. Her eyes narrowed.

"Cameron," she warned Matt.

Scowling, he looked up. Jud Cameron was making his way directly to their table. He smiled at them, his hat in a gloved hand.

"Evening, Miss Gallagher, Kincaid."

"What do you want?" Lark demanded in a fierce, low tone.

He smiled genially. "Just came to see how you're doing, Miss Gallagher. After that unfortunate shootout in Abe Harris's store, I thought you might be feeling a bit peaked."

She didn't understand the word *peaked*. "I felt fine until you came in."

Matt placed a hand on Lark's arm. "Let the man tell us why he's here," he counseled her. "What do you want, Cameron?"

Tension vibrated. Cameron kept smiling. "I see I'm too late to buy you dinner, but I'd like to buy you a drink."

Lark fumed, glaring up at the banker. He was an oily

snake, from his slicked-down black hair to his bear-grease-polished boots.

"You're not too late to buy us dinner, Cameron," Matt said with a smile. "Ezzie hasn't brought the bill yet."

Cameron hid his annoyance and sat down between Matt and Lark. "I'd be happy to." He knew Kincaid was laughing at him. It was in his eyes. A gunslinger's eyes: sharply focused, narrowed, and icy. Yes, the breed had hired herself a gun. "My pleasure," he said smoothly, setting his hat on the table.

Ezzie came flouncing into the room, picked up all the dirty dishes, and left cups of coffee. Cameron ignored Lark, who sat glaring at him, her eyes hard with hatred, and focused instead on Kincaid, who was leaning back, relaxed.

"So, I hear you're the new foreman for the Gallagher Ranch."

"Business manager," Matt corrected. "Paco Hernandez is foreman."

"Yes. Unfortunate accident Paco had. I understand from the doctor that Paco will be all right. But his accident's going to leave you a bit shorthanded at the ranch, isn't it, Miss Gallagher?"

Lark opened her mouth to tell him it wasn't any of his business, but Matt interrupted her. "I'll be filling that capacity until Paco can handle his duties again, Mr. Cameron."

Lark jerked her head around, openmouthed. Would he? She had the wisdom to remain silent, understanding that Matt was somehow playing a game with the banker. She sat back, arms folded across her breasts.

"I see. Then you're going to be in the area for quite a while."

"Until things quiet down."

"Tell me, Kincaid, where did you come from originally?"

"I don't think a man's past is important, Cameron. What counts is what he's doing now."

Cameron toyed with his coffee cup and grinned. "You strike me as a man who was in the war."

"Who wasn't?"

"North or South, Kincaid?"

"I always make a point of being on the winning side."

"I see . . ."

Matt sat up, resting both elbows on the table, nailing Cameron with a black look. "I think you do see. Where I come from, Cameron, men aren't shot in public and defenseless women aren't attacked in broad daylight. Next time Shanks comes prowling around, you'll have to bury him six feet under. Understand?"

Shifting uncomfortably, Cameron held Matt's frigid stare. "I don't know what you're talking about, Kincaid. Shanks is a free agent."

"He's dead next time he tries to harm Lark or any of her ranch hands."

Turning his attention to Lark, Cameron said soothingly, "Let's talk of more pleasant things, shall we? Miss Gallagher, I have a check here in my vest pocket that could set you up for the rest of your life."

Perplexed, Lark asked, "What are you talking about?"

Cameron placed a check in front of Lark. "Five thousand dollars for your ranch, Miss Gallagher." He tapped the check smartly with his index finger. "With that kind of money, you could live like a queen in the east. In return, you agree to sell your ranch to me, and I'll have the necessary water and grass for my growing herds of cattle."

Lark grew rigid. She shoved the check back toward the banker. "I don't want your money."

Cameron felt some of his patience slip away. "No woman can run a ranch by herself! That's unheard of. Further, I've got a bumper crop of calves this spring and I've got to have extra water or my entire herd will die."

"Your cattle will die? My father's been *murdered!*" Lark leaped to her feet, nearly upsetting the table. Her voice grew dangerously low, wobbling with anger. "As far as I'm concerned, Cameron, you're responsible for my father's death. He wouldn't give you water rights and neither will I.''

Cameron itched to slap Lark Gallagher's impertinent face. "Why, you little hellcat," he rasped, snatching up the check and jamming it in his vest pocket. "You can't run a ranch—"

Matt stood and took Lark firmly by the elbow. "Miss Gallagher has me to help run her ranch, Cameron. I'm taking over her father's duties, and I don't see any problem with her being able to maintain the integrity of the ranch. Do you?"

A gasp of surprise escaped Lark. Did Matt mean it? Was he going to take a more active role in her life? She searched his eyes, suddenly weak with relief. Not until that moment had she realized how much she worried about the ranch's survival under her inexperienced hand.

"This is your last chance," Cameron gritted out, glaring down at her stubbornly set face.

New strength and confidence filled Lark. Matt's hand on her arm felt comforting, supportive. "Matt Kincaid's giving me the chance I want to take, Cameron. Keep your money."

Matt's voice broke the look of hatred that burned between Lark and the banker. "Come on, it's time we turned in," he told her.

Lark stood in the doorway to her room as Matt investigated the shadowy depths. He stepped back out in the hall.

"You can go in now."

"You don't trust anyone, do you?"

He smiled. "I don't trust Cameron. Right now, we're on his territory."

"Shanks is in jail."

"Men like Cameron often have more than one hired gun around, Lark."

She agreed. "Did you mean it down there, Matt? That you would help me run the ranch?"

He warmed to the hopeful look in her eyes. The need to place his arms around her, to draw her against him, weakened his resolve. She looked too pretty, her blue eyes shining. Matt fought with himself not to take advantage of her. "I meant it. With Paco severely wounded, he won't be able to carry out his duties for at least another three months. Though my leg is healing fast, I won't be able to ride for at least two of those months. But I can fill in where you need me, Lark. That is, if you want me to."

She nodded, unable to hold his intense gaze. "Then you'll leave when Paco resumes his duties?" It hurt to think that Matt would eventually leave.

With a sigh, he lightly touched her cheek. "Yes. But until then, I'll help you in any way you want me to, Lark."

She managed a strained smile, holding his gaze. "You've answered so many of my prayers, Matt. I don't know how to thank you."

"You've earned the help through your own actions. Do you realize that?"

Lark shook her head. "I don't understand."

"People need people, no matter what their color or race, Lark. You saved my life and put up with a hell of a lot from me at first. If I try to repay all that you've done for me in the next two months, it still won't be enough."

"I won't have much money to pay you," she reminded him.

"You didn't take me in because I could pay you money, did you?"

"No. It's the Apache way to help those less fortunate than themselves."

"Debts to another person can be paid in many ways."

"Apaches do that," she said softly, with a growing

awareness of the similarities between her Indian ways and the ways of her father's people.

"Now you're getting the idea," Matt said. "Get some sleep. You have a ranch to run."

"So now you protect me as a dog would its master?"

"You could say that."

Lark nodded, sobering. She reached out, sliding her hand down his arm. "Matt, I have so much to thank you for."

"Shh, let's get some sleep."

"But—"

"Let's save any more serious conversation for the trip back to the ranch."

She acquiesced, not understanding his sudden reluctance to let her thank him for all he'd done. "All right."

With an inward groan Matt moved away from her provocative figure. "I'm right next door to you, Lark. If you need anything, just bang on the wall."

Disappointed by his sudden distance from her, she nodded halfheartedly. ".I will. Good night."

# Chapter 10

A few days later, to Lark's surprise, Melinda McDonald met her downstairs in the hotel lobby, just as they were preparing to leave for the ranch. Paco was resting comfortably at Doc Friar's, who had urged Lark to allow the foreman to remain in Prescott for another week. After introducing Matt, Melinda gripped Lark's hand, excitement dancing in her green eyes.

"Come outside. I'm just dying to show you what the ladies of the church were able to gather for the families on your ranch."

Lark couldn't hide her surprise. There, standing proudly on the wooden sidewalk near a wagon, were five other women. They wore neat dresses, with hats and gloves in abundance. Lark felt out of place without such trappings, but swallowed her pride as Melinda introduced her.

"I went to Father Mulcahy and told him that you were unexpectedly in town. He asked all of these ladies to come and help sort through the clothes we had been gathering for your father."

Matt stood back, resting against an oak support beam in front of the hotel, watching Lark's shy expression change to one of open gratitude. Melinda, dressed in a green silk skirt with a white blouse and matching green jacket, was the epitome of fashion. She took Lark to the wagon and talked at length about the clothes, then pointed to a small sack of toys.

"I don't know how to thank you, Mrs. McDonald," Lark began. "Father never said anything about this—"

"Of course he didn't! Roarke had been planning a huge surprise for everyone. Two months ago he came to speak to Father Mulcahy about the poverty of some of the families. We've known of Roarke's generosity to the poor and aged for a long time." She smiled gently. "The ladies of the church decided to do something about it."

Lark looked over the neatly bundled packages. "My father never turned down anyone who asked for a meal and a place to sleep," she said softly, stunned by such generosity.

Patting her arm, Melinda nodded. "Abe's son, Hastings, will drive this wagon out to your ranch for you and then return the same day."

"You've done so much, I don't know how to thank you. I know the families will be—"

"Don't thank us, Lark," Melinda chided. "It's about time this town showed their thanks to Roarke Gallagher. Your father was a man of honor and integrity. We can't tell him that now, but we *can* help his daughter."

She looked at Melinda for a long moment, then at the other women who had surrounded her. "I—I owe all of you an apology," she began. "For so long, I thought only the Apache could be unselfishly giving to those less fortunate than themselves." Her voice grew strained. "I was wrong. So wrong . . ."

Millie Harris came forward and slipped an arm around Lark's waist. "No tears, dearie, or we'll all stand here weeping on the sidewalk with you!"

Laughter replaced the tears among the women. Lark took each of the women's hands in turn, squeezing hard, trying to convey her heartfelt thanks. Hastings came over from the dry goods store and took his place on the wagon seat.

At fifteen years old, he was a strapping youngster, and he sat with the traces in his hands, waiting for Lark to give the signal to proceed.

Matt stepped over to Lark and gave her a gentle smile. There were so many things he admired about her. She had grit and determination, and a courage that Katie had lacked. It left him in awe. "Ready to head back to the ranch?" he asked huskily.

Nodding, unable to trust her voice, Lark allowed him to guide her toward their own buckboard.

The moment Lark got back to the ranch, there were problems to resolve. Maria came flying out of the house, wanting to know how Paco was coming along. And then Primo came riding up.

"*Patrona!*" he shouted, pulling his horse to a halt.

Lark had her arm around Maria, trying to assuage the woman's tears. "Yes, Primo?" she asked, irritated because the Mexican wrangler wouldn't wait his turn. Couldn't he see how upset Maria was?

"Paco must be avenged!" He pulled out his gun, waving it recklessly. "This has gone too far! I've already talked to the other men, and we've agreed that this must stop."

"You'll do no such thing!" Lark ordered. "There's no justice in Prescott, Primo. Sheriff Cole's as crooked as Cameron, and Shanks won't be prosecuted. But if you try to do anything, Cole will dump all of you in jail and throw away the key."

The young wrangler's thin brown face wrinkled with concern. "*Sí*, we know that. That's why we're going to ride into Prescott, find Shanks, and string his filthy hide up on the nearest tree!"

Matt came around the side of the wagon after handing over the mule team to Ramone. He saw the desperation in Lark's face and heard it in her voice. Primo was angry and it was obvious Lark wasn't going to make the wrangler obey her orders. He stepped up on the porch beside Lark.

She shot him a desperate look. "Matt—"

"Hold it, Primo."

Primo scowled. "What is it, *señor?*"

"Miss Gallagher has hired me to take over Paco's job while he's recovering. I'm foreman now and what I say goes. If she doesn't want you or the men going into Prescott, you stay here."

Primo's sorrel danced nervously, picking up on the tension between the two men. The wrangler's brown eyes grew as dark as a thundercloud. "Patrón Gallagher would not let you or Paco be harmed," he declared.

"My father never once resorted to bloodshed, Primo," Lark said. "And I won't either. What Mr. Kincaid says, goes. Do you understand?"

Primo's hand clenched into a fist on his chaps. His angry gaze went from Lark to Matt. "I will think about it, *patrona.*"

Matt stepped off the porch and stood directly in front of the wrangler. "There's no thinking to be done, Primo. You either obey the lady's order or you can pack up your gear and leave right now."

Glaring down at Kincaid, the Mexican cursed. He yanked his gelding around and galloped off toward the corrals, where the rest of the men were branding newly captured mustangs.

Maria blotted her eyes with a kerchief. "I'll be fine now, *patrona.* I'm sorry for so many tears."

Distracted by what Matt had told Primo, Lark patted the woman's shoulder absently. "Paco's going to be fine. In another week, we can send a wagon to bring him home. If you want, I'll have Hastings take you back into town to be with him. Would you like that?"

*"Sí . . ."*

The day passed swiftly. Lark didn't even have time to take off her dress, so involved was she in taking care of the many small but important details that concerned her people. Toward evening, she ran into Matt once again. He was limping heavily from the barn to the house. She picked up her skirts and ran to meet him halfway.

"You look so tired," she told him, slowing her steps to match his.

"You're tired, too." He gazed hungrily down at her. All day he had watched her deal patiently and skillfully with each problem that was presented to her. Now Maria was bound to Prescott with Hastings Harris, the new clothes for the ranch families had been distributed to everyone's satisfaction, and the petty squabbles that had arisen in her absence had been settled. He was so proud of her.

"Did the men accept you as the new foreman?" Lark asked.

Matt took the wooden steps one at a time. His leg was hurting like hell. "I think they have."

"Primo was very angry. I've never seen him so upset."

"He was letting off steam, that's all." Matt gave Lark a faint nod as she opened the door for him. "Let's go to the office. We've got some things to discuss."

Lark followed him. Matt sat down carefully in the chair, propping his wounded leg on a stool. She stood in front of the desk, hands clasped.

"What's wrong?" she asked fearfully.

He took off his hat and set it aside. "Nothing's really wrong," he corrected, trying to get Lark to relax. "This last herd the wranglers brought in are confined to too small a pen, that's all. Another, larger pen needs to be built immediately, otherwise those mares are going to injure themselves. They're wild and jumpy. We need to get them settled down if we're going to breed them to those two studs of yours."

Tiredness overwhelmed Lark. Outside the window, she could see dusk rapidly settling over the fertile valley. "My father had a number of plans for the herds we would capture."

"Did he discuss any of them with you, Lark?"

"No." She sighed and rested wearily against the chair. "Now I wish I'd taken a greater interest in the ranch. My first love was the horses. That's all I know about."

Matt wanted to say: It doesn't matter, Lark. She looked
so excruciatingly feminine in the dress, which in no way
diminished the spirit and courage she'd displayed all day.
"You know about more than horses," he began quietly.
"I saw you dealing with the women and children." With
a slight smile he added, "You'd make a great mother.
Did you know that?"

Heat stole into her cheeks and she bowed her head.
"No . . . I didn't."

"You dried the tears of the women, kissed the hurts of
the children, and got the ranch back on its feet. Your
ability to deal with both animals and people is special,
Lark. Very special."

Warming to his compliment, she raised her chin. "But
without your help, this ranch won't survive. What else
needs to be done?"

"We need another barn."

She sat up. "What?"

Matt nodded, noting her shock. "You need more room
for hay this coming winter. There's no place else to store
it. All the room has been taken up with young foals and
weanlings."

"Oh, no . . ." The burden on the already strained
financial resources would be too much. Where would she
get the kind of money needed to buy the necessary
lumber? And diverting the wranglers from horse hunting
to building a barn would completely destroy her plans to
provide the army with a goodly number of horses in the
next few months.

Getting slowly to his feet, Matt came around the end
of the desk. Lark's shoulders were hunched and he knew
she was close to tears. "Come here," he ordered gruffly,
pulling her to her feet and into his arms.

Blindly, Lark sought Matt's embrace. "W-we can't
afford it, Matt. Do you know how much it would cost?
And the men—they don't have time to—to—"

Matt felt Lark tremble. It struck him that, despite the
shocking events of the last few weeks, he'd never seen

her cry. Rubbing her back in slow, circular motions, he whispered, "We'll think of something, Lark. Come on, now, let it out. Cry for everything that's happened . . ."

The roughness of Matt's voice triggered the deluge. Lark buried her face against his massive chest, quickly soaking his cotton shirt with her tears. Terrible sobs were wrenched from deep within her. Lark was lost in the blackness of all her losses, clinging to the only person who had given her sanctuary from all the pain she'd carried for so long by herself.

Rocking her gently in his arms, Matt felt new tendrils of distress grow around his own aching heart. He fought against the wonderful perfume that lingered in her hair, fought against the pull of her enveloping softness. "Easy, my beautiful cougar. It'll pass, I promise you."

He closed his eyes. But when Lark unconsciously nuzzled her cheek against his jaw, the last of his straining control disintegrated. He pressed a kiss to her hair and found the strands clean and sweet beneath his mouth. Heat throbbed through him and he groaned, gripping her hard against him. The firmness of her small breasts, the flatness of her stomach, and the curve of her slender hips all sent a molten ache through his loins.

Lark sobbed, seeking Matt's protection. He had offered his strength when she had none left herself. Burrowing against him, she felt her senses fill with the masculine scent of him, a scent that made her dizzy with new, unexpected needs.

She heard Matt groan and felt him press against her, and out of some feminine instinct, she lifted her lips to him. His mouth covered hers with fiery urgency, shattering her, triggering a burning sensation between her thighs that spiraled up to her breasts, making them taut and aching against his chest. With hungry abandon, Matt parted her tear-bathed lips and drank deeply, heating her very blood. Lark's knees gave way beneath his powerful assault and she sagged against him. Her fingers clenched and unclenched against his chest. Moistness collected between her thighs, and a sharp, throbbing yearning centered there as his lips continued to explore the sweet, warm cavern of her mouth.

With another groan, Matt tore his lips from Lark's, his breath coming in ragged gasps, like hers. Her breasts were rising and falling beneath the dress she wore, and her lips were wet and swollen from the branding kiss. He was suddenly contrite. Trying to gather his own scattered emotions, he gripped her arms.

"I—I'm sorry, Lark," he rasped. "I didn't mean to kiss you . . ."

Stunned by wave after wave of heat flowing through her, Lark stared uncomprehendingly up at him. Dizzied by the assault, she gripped his arms, swaying.

"Here, sit down," he ordered thickly, leading her to the wing chair.

Lark avoided his turbulent, stormy eyes as she sat down. A kaleidoscope of sensations whirled through her. A gnawing hunger begged to be satiated. "W-what happened?" she asked, her voice wispy, unsteady.

Angry with himself, Matt said, "Something that shouldn't have happened. I'm sorry, Lark. I got carried away with the situation." He turned away to avoid the luminous, dreamy expression in her eyes. "Too much has happened to both of us recently. We're vulnerable in ways we wouldn't ordinarily be."

Confused by the anger in his voice, thinking he was angry at her because she had responded to his kiss, Lark nodded. She clenched her hands in her lap. "I—I'm sorry, too. When you told me we needed a new barn, I just started to unravel." She felt tears dribbling down her cheeks again and tried without success to wipe them away.

"It's all right, Lark. You've been through a lot. You needed a good cry." Matt winced, torn in two by the anguish pouring out of her. Damn his rampant emotions. Damn his lust. No woman had ever triggered those feelings like Lark had. Every time he was near her, he could feel himself unwinding like a ball of yarn. Even now, he longed to put his hands on her shoulders and comfort her. My God, he wanted to take her down on the floor and love her until she cried out in ecstasy. He'd seen the fires of desire burning deep in her eyes, had felt her banked passion stir as he'd kissed her. Every inch of her soft, firm body had responded to him.

Matt was unable to stand Lark's nearness. He was blind to everything except his raw, aching heart and her desire for his closeness and strength. He limped back behind the desk and sat down, scowling.

Sniffing, Lark got her emotions back under control. She lifted her head to see Matt's disapproving frown. Humiliated by her actions, she lowered her lashes. She strove to break the unbearable tension swirling wildly between them. "The barn," she began, searching desperately for a neutral subject to cover her embarrassment over the unexpected kiss. "I know we don't have the money. How—"

"The ranchers down in Tucson hold a barn raising whenever one needs to be built," Matt answered, relieved to get on a safe topic. "It usually takes a weekend, but the barn gets built without any money passing hands." Matt berated himself: he sounded like a snarling dog and he was making Lark shrink back into some far corner of herself. Angry over his loss of control, he waged a silent inner battle before continuing. "Usually a letter is sent out to the neighbors. The people who are having the barn built feed those who come to help build it. Judging from the welcome you got in Prescott, I'm sure we could get a number of parishioners from your father's church to supply the manpower. They seem to want to help you through this difficult period, Lark. Why not let them?"

"What about lumber?"

"I noticed two mills in Prescott. Why not trade a couple of your good horses for the needed lumber?"

She sat there considering Matt's ideas. Shaking her

head, she whispered, "I'd never have thought of those things by myself."

Matt rubbed his face savagely, unable to stand being near Lark after kissing her. He had to get a solid hold on himself. "Yes, in time you would have. There are other things we have to discuss," he said heavily.

Alarmed by the tone in his voice, Lark jerked her head up. "What?"

"I can't stay in this house any longer, Lark." He saw the pain and embarrassment in her too-vulnerable features. Cursing himself, he tried to keep his voice gentle for her sake. "I'm well enough to bunk over in the single wranglers' quarters now. People would start talking if I stayed here. I can't—won't—make you the target of gossip." Lark felt as if a knife had slashed through her heart. Reflexively, she pressed a hand to her breast. "Yes . . . that would be best," she murmured, but every fiber of her being screamed just the opposite. Matt was her strength and her mainstay. She'd come to anticipate seeing him at night when she finished the day's duties, hearing his laughter and enjoying his nearness.

"I'll miss you . . ."

Matt grimaced. "I know." He got to his feet and made his way slowly toward the office door, fighting the urge to touch her shoulder, if only briefly.

One kiss. Matt saw the damage it had done to Lark. God, how could he have let it happen? How? Placing his hand over the brass doorknob, he said, "I'll be here during the day, though."

She couldn't bear to look at him. She nodded. "I—I'll see you tomorrow morning."

"Tomorrow," he agreed.

The month of June came and plans for the new barn solidified. Since their kiss, Matt had avoided Lark with great success. Often he was in Prescott, arranging for the supplies necessary to build the barn or contacting people who would come and help. One of the few times Lark saw Matt was when she changed the dressing on his rapidly healing wound. But because of her responsibilities with the foaling mares, Maria usually ended up attending to Matt.

On June fifteenth, ten wagons made their way to the ranch, arriving just as the sun came up. Lark stood on the porch, in awe of the numbers of men who had come. There were at least twenty-five. Matt emerged from the bunkhouse, clean-shaven and looking excruciatingly handsome. He gave her a smile as he climbed the steps and stood watching with her.

"It's quite something, isn't it?" he said.

Lark was wearing a dress she had recently purchased at Melinda McDonald's urging. It was delicate pink with a ribbon woven into the scooped neckline and around the daintily puffed sleeves. The color brought out the flush in Lark's cheeks.

Matt shoved all his feelings down a little deeper. A day didn't go by when he didn't miss her. Each night, whether he wanted to or not, he hotly recalled their only kiss. When Lark had lifted her chin, her blue eyes upon him, he had known it was an equal agony for her, too.

"Yes. It's wonderful," she said.

Matt tried to lighten the tension that always ran taut and raw between them. "Maybe now we might qualify to be Apaches?" he teased.

Lark's smile was warm. "All of you."

Rufus, the grub cook, came walking over, a big grin on his round face. "Missy Lark, I done got those two steers on the open fire pits." He waved a long, thin arm toward the approaching wagons. "Looks like there's a heap o' people comin'."

"Do we have enough food for them, Rufus?"

The cook nodded his curly black head. He was dressed in a new pair of Levi's and a bright blue shirt with a bright red bandanna tied around his throat. His skin shone like polished ebony. "Jus' enuf, missy. Jus' enuf. Made a good sauce that oughta make them smack thar lips, too." He cackled. "Yep, these good folks are gonna talk loud and long about mah cookin, thar ain't no doubt!"

"Don't burn their tongues off, Rufus!" Lark said in alarm. The cook was known to like his food hot and spicy. And, of course, the Mexicans only encouraged Rufus in that regard. Eating his chili was a test of nerves as far as Lark was concerned.

"Oh, no, ma'am!" Rufus held up both hands. "I was real kerful with the hot sauce, I promise you."

With a laugh Lark said, "What else have you got cooking over those fires?"

He widened his eyes. "Why, I got the best batch of rum beans you ever laid eyes on, missy." He winked at Kincaid. "Must be two bottles of rum in them."

"Rufus! You can't go around getting these folks drunk, either! What will they think of us?"

He chuckled, a devilish twinkle in his eyes. "Why, I'd say thar gonna feel *real* good when thar buildin' that barn, missy."

Lark failed to suppress her smile. Rufus could always make her laugh. Already he'd dispelled most of her nervousness over meeting so many new people. "I'm coming back there to taste those rum beans, Rufus," she warned him.

"Fair enuf, Missy Lark. You can taste mah huge skillet of pan fries, sourdough bread, and apple pan dowdy, too."

"He's making me hungry already," Matt said.

Rufus waved to them as he took off at a lanky trot toward the spits at the rear of the ranch house. "You better watch it, missy," he called. "You're liable to find more men sniffin' around mah food than workin' on that barn!"

"Well," Matt said, "are you ready to meet them all?"

Lark glanced up at him. "As long as you're at my side, yes."

Cupping her elbow, he led her down the porch steps. "There's no other place I'd rather be," he told her.

As he guided Lark out to the group of wagons pulling to a halt, Matt looked closely at Lark. In the past month, he'd almost come to think of her ranch as his. The wounds from the past were healing, he discovered. When he took a walk down to the horse barns, he no longer thought of his barn back near Tucson. And when Lark was out planting the garden, he saw her, not Katie. Gradually, he was putting the past behind him.

He squeezed Lark's arm gently to reassure her. There was so much he wanted to discuss with her. She was so easy to confide in. Once he got his own emotions toward her under control, he'd like to share his thoughts and feelings with her. He realized he needed her more than any other woman in his life, and the deep ache in his chest never went away; it only got more intense.

"Well, what do you think?" Matt asked Lark as they toured the newly finished barn late that same day. The wagonloads of people had left an hour earlier. It was evening, and the sun was dipping below the mountains, sending shadows across the pastures.

Lark gazed in awe at the just-erected building, breathing in the sharp scent of pine. "It's beautiful," she whispered.

The barn was two stories high, with a cavernous hay-mow. She turned to Matt, who was walking slowly at her side. "I could never have done it without you." Fighting her emotions, she reached out and touched his arm. His muscles were hard and tense beneath her fingertips. She gazed earnestly up at him, confused by the darkness entering his gray eyes.

"You've done so much," she began softly. "Ever since you rode into my life, everything's changed."

Her touch was as light as a butterfly on his arm. Dragging in a deep breath, Matt tried to ignore it. "For better or worse?" he asked.

Lark removed her hand, content just to be close to him.

"Better." She licked her lips, unsure how to proceed. "Have you felt better since being here?"

Matt removed his felt cowboy hat, and wiped the sweat on his brow with the back of his hand. He settled the hat back on his head. "I was thinking the other day," he admitted as he took her arm so they could continue their inspection, "how much you've changed my life."

Lark stole a look up at him. Suddenly the new stalls seemed unimportant in comparison to this unexpected turn in their conversation. "I have?"

"Yes."

"In good ways?" She held her breath.

"Always good, Lark." Matt pulled her to a stop at the other end of the opened doors. From here, they could look out over the mountains that encircled the valley. "I don't miss Katie or Susan as much. The grief's not there like it used to be." Matt managed a gentle smile, holding Lark's gaze. "The ranch has been good to me and so have you."

Lark nodded jerkily, filled with a flood of emotions. How she had craved this kind of closeness with Matt. Finally, he was sharing with her! Breathless, she said, "I don't think about my father as much either. I mean, when I do think of him, which is often, the hurt isn't as strong here, in my heart."

"We're like two wolves, you know that?" Matt said.

"What do you mean?"

"They mate for life. If one's hurt, the other will lick the injured mate's wounds and care for it. We were like that, Lark. Both wounded and hurting deeply. We each, in our own way, have healed the other's wound."

A tremor of yearning moved through her. "I don't understand how it's happened, but it has."

Matt studied her in the gentle silence that surrounded them. Lark was strong and unafraid to face an uncertain future. He admired and respected that about her.

She was there in his mind, like sunshine glinting off a still lake surface. Not an hour went by in which he didn't wish Lark was at his side. So many times he'd stopped himself from going over to the main house and sharing a small but important moment with her.

One day he'd found a baby robin that had fallen out of its nest. The bird was young and naked, with a huge yellow beak open and begging for food. He had called Ramone over to climb the tree and put the chick back. But before he had, Matt had wanted Lark to see the baby. Why had he been afraid to include her in his life?

Lark sensed the power of his emotions and fought the need to walk into his arms and be held once more. She agonized over the fact that time was flying by. He would leave in August at the latest to continue to hunt down Ga'n. Time . . . there was so little left.

The late July weather was hot and dry. Lark sat on her medicine-hat mare, Four Winds, on a hill overlooking the ranch. Sweat trickled down her temple, and she wiped it away with the back of her hand. Beside her, Boa Juan motioned toward the holding pens.

"Holos dries up everything."

"Yes. Even our creeks are gone." The drought had set in with a vengeance.

Boa Juan, half Apache and half Mexican, glanced over at her. "Ny-Oden must sing to the sky spirits and bring rain our way."

Absently, Lark agreed. Her mind and, if she was honest with herself, her heart were elsewhere. Paco was healing rapidly, thanks to the old shaman's medicine, but he was still unable to resume all his responsibilities. Duties still plagued Lark. Not only did she have brood-mares to care for, but no one knew how to track down mustangs better than Paco. Only her own tracking abilities, coupled with Boa Juan's natural talent with horses, had yielded them enough mustangs for the rest of the breeding season.

The boughs of the pine trees shielded them from the hot sun overhead. Boa Juan spoke again, gesturing toward the ranch. "Will the water from those ponds near the pens last through the season?"

She nodded. "Yes, they're spring fed, from what my father said. We'll be able to get through this time safely, Boa Juan."

"Others won't."

She grimaced, knowing he was referring to Cameron's ranch and livestock. "No." Tonight she wanted to discuss the problem with Matt.

Matt . . . Lark tried to suppress the pain in her heart. Why had he distanced himself from her? He was always polite, but he never encouraged the kind of intimacy they had shared in the barn that one June evening. Unconsciously she touched her lips. Was he angry at her? Disappointed in her unladylike behavior in that one sweet moment? She *had* acted shamelessly, she knew, and that could be the only reason why Matt had grown remote.

"How long do you think Kincaid will be with us?" Boa Juan asked.

Lark stirred in the saddle. "His leg is nearly healed. I don't know." Her heart tore open a little more.

"He's strong and fair."

"Yes, he's a good man," Lark admitted in a whisper.

"At first, I thought he'd be like other *pindahs*." Boa Juan grinned, his dark face crinkling. "But he is more like us."

She nodded. Matt had many Apache traits. He treated everyone fairly and without prejudice. The children, whether Mexican or Indian, followed him shamelessly, begging him to tell them stories. Sometimes when Lark rode into the yard with her wranglers at the end of a long, exhausting day, she would find twelve or more children clustered on the porch, listening to one of Matt's many yarns. He called them fairy tales. She'd never heard of such a thing, but she saw the rapt expression on each tiny face, and it sent happiness tremoring through her.

Rubbing her aching head, she murmured, "Let's get

down to the ranch. We've done all we can up here today."

Matt was in the office working on the ledgers when he heard Lark's familiar footsteps. As always, he had to stop himself from getting up and going to her. He frowned and laid down the pencil. Every day was torture. And every night hell. He lay in the bunkhouse, heatedly recalling Lark's special warmth and responsiveness, the yielding softness of her lips beneath his hungry, starving mouth. Time, Matt reminded himself. He had to give himself time to get over Katie's and Susie's deaths. It wouldn't be fair to Lark to lead her on and then be unable to give her anything in return. He had to hunt down Ga'n first. Only if he survived that could he come back to the ranch and pursue a genuine relationship with her.

When he lifted his head, he saw her standing tiredly in the doorway. As always, she wore her Apache garb. Her blue shirt, black trousers, and boots were covered with dust. Exhaustion shadowed her eyes. Automatically he rose, concerned.

"Lark?"

She made a gesture toward the ledgers. "I'm sorry to interrupt, but I need to speak with you about some things."

"Of course." She looked hauntingly fragile to him. Matt saw the hurt and confusion in her eyes and mentally kicked himself. She was suffering badly because of his rejection. Damm it, anyway.

"Are you all right?"

Lark nodded. "Finding the mustangs is getting tougher. They're fleeing up to the high canyons now that the snow has melted. It's just harder."

"How about if we eat dinner together tonight? I'll have Maria bring it to the office. There are some things I have to discuss with you, anyway."

Lark knew what Matt was going to tell her—that those

fifteen two-year-old colts needed to be broken. The money situation was critical now. She rubbed her brow, feeling grit beneath her fingertips. "Let me get cleaned up."

"Fine." He watched Lark turn away. Normally her shoulders were thrown back, her chin held at a proud angle. Not anymore. Sitting back down, Matt cursed softly. In one way his being there was putting an additional burden on Lark. But considering the drought that had struck the entire northern Arizona Territory, with disastrous results, he knew she still needed his help. Ranches all around the Prescott area were losing hundreds, if not thousands, of head of cattle. Water sources were drying up everywhere. Although the Gallagher Ranch was doing all right so far, he didn't want to leave until he could be assured it would weather the drought successfully.

Lark had no appetite that night. She picked at the food on her plate. The silence between them was shredding her carefully hidden emotions. At last Maria took the plates away, leaving them alone.

Earlier, Lark had bathed in the stream, washed her hair, and changed her clothes. Ever since Maria had arranged her hair with a colorful ribbon, Lark wore it that way every evening. Tonight, she also wore the freshly laundered violet calico dress, which looked enchanting. The faint lavender scent of the soap that she had used clung to her skin. Sitting next to her, Matt was incredibly aware of her.

As she rose, her hands clasped in front of her, he spoke. "We're getting to the point where that three hundred dollars is absolutely necessary, Lark. Someone needs to start breaking those colts."

"I know." She turned, frustration in her voice. "But I can't spare a single wrangler right now! With the hot weather, the snows have melted and the mustangs have gone into the mountains to get water. Each day it becomes harder to find them. I've got to breed at least thirty more mares in order to produce a big enough group of foals next year.''

Matt nodded sympathetically, appreciating the problem. ''Our water reserves seem stable.''

She paced. ''We've got enough for our own stock, that's all. The three ponds out back are spring fed.''

''And the creek near your border with Cameron?''

''Dried up. Everything's dried up.'' Dejected, she bit her lower lip. ''It's all so hopeless . . .''

Matt didn't dare respond to the pain in her voice. This time, he might not stop at just a kiss. This time, he might love her until she cried out in pleasure.

''I talked to Paco the other day,'' she went on, her voice low and halting, ''and he said you're going to leave soon. Do you have any idea when?''

He shrugged. ''Maybe in another couple of weeks. I don't know exactly yet.''

*I want you to stay.* It was on her lips, in her heart. She fought her emotions. ''Is there anything else you wanted to talk about?''

''No. You?''

''No . . .'' And then, ''Excuse me. I have to check on Ny-Oden. He's not been feeling well lately.''

Matt nodded. ''I'll see you tomorrow morning, I guess.''

Blindly, Lark opened the door, her throat tight with words and emotions that wanted to boil up and spill out of her. She flew across a yard bathed in the rose color of the sunset. Trying to push the chaos deep within her, Lark climbed the steps of the bunkhouse.

''Daughter?''

She halted. Ny-Oden was walking with mincing steps from around the corner of the log structure, leaning heavily on his oak cane. ''Grandfather. What are you doing up?''

His ebony eyes glinted with laughter. ''Now you chide me.''

She retraced her steps and walked out to meet the old

man, slipping her hand beneath his elbow. He reminded Lark of a gnarled tree weathered by too many storms. "I did not mean to sound sharp, grandfather. I'm sorry."

With a smile, he motioned to the yard. "Come, I need exercise. You can be my support."

"Being around you always makes my troubles seem small, grandfather."

"And what small troubles do you have?"

She sighed. "I don't want to bother you. I know this heat has kept you in bed most of the time."

"I'm never too old or too bedridden to listen to your heart. Now, what troubles you?"

Lark walked slowly at his side. They reached the far end of the yard and stood beneath the long, reaching boughs of a fragrant pine tree. They turned to watch the setting of the sun in the west; it was one of the holiest times of the day for the Apache. Lark ran the long pine needles through her fingers. "I don't know what's wrong with me, grandfather."

"You've lost weight. Maria said you're not eating well." He cocked his head, studying her in the silence. "If your ailment came from your body, I could give you an herb or sing a chant to send it away. But I have nothing for the wounding of a heart."

"What do you mean?"

"A heart torn by unhappiness can only be healed with love."

"Love?" Lark's voice went off-key.

Ny-Oden nodded, pursing his thin lips. "Matt Kincaid has awakened your heart, daughter."

Lark held the shaman's arthritic hand gently. "Oh, grandfather, what am I going to do?" she whispered tightly. "What I feel toward Matt is so new . . . so different."

"Yes?"

"He kissed me," she blurted out. "In the office shortly after we came back from Prescott. It was so sudden, so unexpected."

"For both of you?"

"I—I think so. Ever since then, Matt's been avoiding me. I think he's ashamed of me and of my actions."

"Oh?"

Helplessly, Lark shrugged. "When he touched my lips, I was shocked. And then my shock turned to a fire that grew inside me. I—I didn't know what to do. All I remember is responding to him. And when I did, he tore away from me as if I'd burned him. I've shamed myself in front of him, grandfather. He avoids me. He hardly smiles at me anymore and it's rare if I see him even once a day."

Ny-Oden sat down on the soft, dry pine needles and patted the ground beside him. "Come," he invited, "sit here."

Miserably, Lark joined him. "Soon he'll leave, grandfather, and I don't know what I'll do. I've come to rely on him. Matt knows so much about money and ranching."

"You will miss him, the man," the shaman corrected.

"Yes." She toyed with a dried pine needle. "May I ask you something?"

"Of course."

"Is what I'm feeling in my heart what my mother told me about? Is this love?"

Ny-Oden's face crinkled into a gentle smile. "I think you can answer that yourself."

"Mother said love binds two people. I swear I can feel him. I feel his moods, his changes." Her voice faltered. "Sometimes, I feel his hunger for me. Is that silly? Am I *heyoke*, crazy?"

"The heart never lies, daughter. And it's not unusual for people in love to be attuned to one another."

Hope filled her. "It isn't?"

"No."

"Then—it is love?"

"That is a part of love."

"Part? You mean there's more?"

"Yes."

"Such as?"

He held her distraught gaze. "This is something you must discover on your own." He gestured toward the sunset that had faded to pale colors of lavender, violet, and dark pink. "Love is like Holos striking those clouds above us, changing the colors in Father Sky. Love is not just one thing or another."

She tried to grasp his meaning. "Then, love touches two people and changes them?" she said.

"Yes."

She tugged at a long strand of her hair, thinking. "I'm the one who is changing, grandfather. I feel like a flower opening for the first time. I'm aware of my body as never before. So many changes are happening within me. But . . ."

"Yes?"

"I don't see any changes in Matt. All he does is avoid me. He can share stories with the children and tease Maria and the other women, but he avoids me."

"That is a change, is it not?"

Frowning, Lark threw the bent and twisted pine needle aside. "Not a good one."

"Patience, daughter."

"There is so little time left. He's going to be leaving soon."

"Patience," Ny-Oden repeated gently. "Love takes many forms. Your heart is full and cannot see everything. Right now, you're like muddy water. Time will allow the mud to settle to the bottom, leaving clear water above it. Then your heart's eyes will see."

"See what, grandfather?"

"The truth, daughter of my heart. And your destiny."

# Chapter 11

"I want that breed bitch kidnapped," Jud Cameron growled, standing at the window of his ranch office. He barely turned his head, buttonholing Bo Shanks, who lounged lazily against the doorjamb.

"Somethin's gotta be done or yore gonna lose part of yore herd, boss."

Cameron snorted, settling his hands on his hips. It was Saturday. During the weekdays, he lived in Prescott and managed his bank. On weekends, he drove out to his ranch, the Bar T, located fifteen miles outside of town. He saw the foreman who ran the ranch in his absence, Tom Huffman, ride by, his leathery face grim. "My cattle are starting to die," he muttered. "I'm not going to lose them just because that breed thinks she can stand her ground with me."

Shanks drew deeply on his cheroot and remained silent. He'd just been released from jail, after spending almost two months there for shooting Paco Hernandez. For a while, Shanks had wondered if Cameron was going to spring him or not. The townspeople were upset over the shooting. If Cameron hadn't paid off the judge, he'd still be locked behind bars. What bothered him even more, was that Cameron had hired another gun. A Bart Devlin was coming up from Tucson. He worked for Saunders over on the Circle S and was frequently employed by the Ring. Devlin would arrive in Prescott in another three weeks. Was Cameron going to oust him? Damn, but he liked the money he was making. Shanks tried to figure out a way to get back into Cameron's good graces.

"What can I do to help ya, boss?"

Cameron stared darkly at the gunslinger. "Ride over to Ga'n's hideout and tell him to meet me at Cottonwood Forks two days from now."

"Right away, boss."

With disgust, Cameron watched Shanks quickly leave. Minutes later, he saw the gunslinger ride by on his buckskin gelding. Anger ate at him. It was late July and his water sources would no longer support the additional cattle. Something had to be done! Already the milk was drying up on the cows who were trying to suckle their young. Next his calves would start dying.

Cameron smiled savagely. Soon, very soon, the Gallagher Ranch would be his—one way or another. And Ga'n was going to help him get it.

"I will not kill Lark Who Sings," Ga'n said angrily. He shifted position on his mustang pony, holding Jud Cameron's glare. Next to him his companion Alchise shifted uneasily in the saddle. "Roarke Gallagher saved my life many seasons ago." Ga'n made a slicing motion through the morning air. "She is his daughter. I will not do as you wish."

Cameron's fury simmered. "I said kidnap her, not kill her, for godsakes! Hold her until she agrees to sign over the water rights to her ranch."

A sly smile shadowed Ga'n's hard mouth. "Kidnap Lark Who Sings?"

"Yes. Take her over to Devil's Canyon. There's a series of caves over there. Tie her up and tell her she's not going to be released until she agrees to give me what I want." Cameron fingered his sleek black mustache. "Well? Can you do that much without upsetting your sensitive Apache conscience?"

Ga'n straightened up in the cottonwood saddle. "How much?" The *pindah*'s green-skinned paper would purchase more bottles of firewater. His first taste of liquor over at the Gallagher Ranch long ago had eased his pain and the memory of his family's death. Since then, a need to drink had shaped the rest of his life. And the only way he could get the firewater was to work for *pindahs* who paid him the paper needed to purchase the bottles from the traders.

Cameron smiled. Now he was back at what he knew best: buying something for little or nothing from these savages. "Five dollars," he said.

"Five!" Alchise, who was six feet tall and had a broad copper face, sneered. "This is worth more than that to you."

Ga'n nodded, glancing over at his war partner.

"Six, then."

"That won't buy many bottles of firewater!" Ga'n muttered.

"It will keep you good and drunk for a long time!" Cameron snapped back.

Alchise gave Ga'n a dark look.

"All you have to do is slip in under cover of night and take Lark from the ranch house. There are no sentries or guards. Probably a dog, but you know how to get rid of it. This will be easy, Ga'n."

Cameron decided not to mention that the gunslinger, Matt Kincaid, was at the ranch. He'd be sleeping in the bunkhouse and would be conveniently out of the way. "All right, seven dollars and that's my last offer. Take it or leave it."

Ga'n grunted. "We take it." He held out his hand. "Pay now."

"You get paid afterwards, Ga'n. I don't want you drunk on the job. That's how you and I work with each other."

Ga'n scowled. "I will take her to Devil's Canyon."

"Fine. When she's ready to sign, send Alchise to my ranch. I'll ride out to where you're holding her and let her sign the papers."

"You want this done tonight?"

"Yes. The sooner, the better."

Matt left the barn when he saw Lark appear at the door to the ranch house, wearing the calico dress. He'd seen her ride in an hour earlier, just before sunset. Apparently she'd bathed and changed out of her Apache clothes since then. He walked across the yard to her. No longer did he limp on his wounded leg. He'd fully recovered from the gunshot wound.

Holding Lark's gaze as he approached, Matt tried to gird himself for their meeting. There was surprise in her eyes and he knew why. Rarely did they see one another during the day.

"Matt?"

He took off his hat and mounted the steps, standing a few feet from her. "Evening, Lark. I need to talk with you. Can we go to the office?"

"Of course." She turned and led the way.

Matt shut the office door quietly. Lark stood uncertainly near the desk. He took a deep breath. "I'm going to be leaving in another week, Lark. It's time."

Pain squeezed her heart as she remained standing, stunned by his announcement. Finally she found her voice, but even she could hear the strain in it. "You've been restless." More than once, Boa Juan had told her how Matt would get up and leave the bunkhouse to pace the yard late at night. He was obsessed with finding Ga'n. She met his gray eyes, seeing the anguish and despair in them. Gathering all her strength, she forced out the words she didn't believe herself. "You're right, it is time."

Matt searched her tension-lined face, feeling Lark's agony. "I don't want to, but I have to," he said thickly.

"I know."

He saw her sway and then catch herself. She threw her shoulders back and thrust her chin at a defiant angle, telling him that she was fighting to look strong and confident for his sake. He managed a slight smile. "You've learned the sums well. I don't think you'll have any more problems with bookkeeping.''

"No, I won't. You taught me well, Matt." *And I've lost my heart to you.* The words were on her lips, screaming to be said, but Lark fought the need. There could be no life, no happiness, for Matt until he put the ghost of his family to rest. And finding Ga'n was the only way for him.

Fumbling for the right words, he held her luminous blue gaze. "There's no future for me, Lark. Not until I get Ga'n."

Matt wanted to stay. Over the last months, Lark and her ranch had come to mean everything to him. He couldn't imagine life without her vibrant presence or the pleasant demands of the horse ranch. Lark had given him back life, given him back his dreams that he'd thought were destroyed with Katie's and Susan's deaths. Instead of pain when he remembered his family, there was only a warm, good feeling in his heart. Whether Lark knew it or not, she had healed him.

"When you're finished avenging your family's death, what will you do?" Lark asked faintly, gripping the edge of the desk for support.

Matt dared not tell her how he felt about her, how much he needed her—forever. "I don't know."

Swallowing against her tight throat, Lark risked everything. "W-will you come back here? Back to the ranch?"

He stared at her, the silence becoming excruciating. "Is that what you want?" he asked hoarsely.

Giving a jerky nod of her head, Lark whispered, "The ranch needs you. I need you . . .''

Drawing in a deep breath, Matt gently held her fearful gaze. "All right, I'll be back, Lark." Trying to break the tension, he opened the door to the office. He could promise her nothing yet. If Ga'n killed him, it would be less painful for her if she didn't know he'd fallen in love with her. "Good night."

"Good night." Lark stood there, watching him disappear down the hall. The front door opened and closed. Then, suddenly, all her strength fled and she leaned weakly against the desk, overcome by emotion.

She knew Ga'n's abilities as a warrior. He'd survived years of being chased by the cavalry, bounty hunters, and lawmen. Matt had nearly died once at his hands. This time . . .

She shut her eyes, willing away her fears, then rose and headed toward her bedroom, seeking the oblivion of sleep.


Ga'n waited with the patience of his ancestors. He and Alchise had arrived shortly after dark. Alchise had already dispensed with the only dog, slitting its throat and dragging it under some brush near the yard. Now Ga'n sat back on his haunches, watching. Much earlier, he'd seen one of the wranglers leave the house. Lark was alone.

Alchise, growing impatient, spat to the left.

The last light had been extinguished two hours ago. Ga'n noted by the position of the stars that it was close to midnight.

"The full moon will be up soon," Alchise muttered.

"It cannot be helped."

"This smells of a trap."

Ga'n studied the war partner who had been with him for nearly twenty years. Though they weren't true brothers, they were bound in many other ways. Ga'n respected Alchise, and could count the many times he'd saved his life.

"How is it a trap?" Ga'n demanded.

With a shrug, Alchise said, "I feel something is wrong."

"Lark Who Sings is alone. We saw no one else enter after that *pindah* left."

"I will send prayers to Us'an to protect us," Alchise returned.

"She is only a girl," Ga'n soothed. And then he

smiled. "Wild like a mustang but still a girl. Perhaps we will endure a few scratches and curses, but that is all."

Alchise nodded, rubbing his square jaw. Whatever else he was thinking was hidden by the curtain of ebony hair as he bent forward, studying the curled toes of his well-worn kabun boots.

Lark tossed restlessly in bed and threw off the blankets. Weak moonlight filtered through the curtains and she sighed. She had to get to sleep!

She tried to shut out the raw pain in her heart. Seven days . . . that's all that was left to her. How had Matt become so important to her? Resolutely she shut her eyes. Exhausted from ten hours in the saddle chasing mustangs, she felt sleep finally conquer her roiling emotions.

A hand clamped cruelly against Lark's mouth and nose, effectively cutting off her breathing. Her eyes flew open and she jerked backward, moaning. Ga'n!

Ga'n grunted, one hand on Lark's chest to pin her to the bed and the other across her mouth.

Lark saw Alchise standing nervously at the door, his rifle held in readiness. Again she fought Ga'n, striking out at him with her small fists.

"Don't fight," he snarled harshly, "and I will not harm you. We intend only to kidnap you."

Terror convulsed through Lark. She saw the blade of Ga'n's knife as he pulled it from the scabbard. He was going to kill her! The thought gave her more strength and she tried to jerk away from the warrior, the floor-length nightgown hampering her efforts. The material slid above her knees, and she lashed out, bringing up one leg.

Ga'n groaned, and his hand loosened over Lark's mouth.

Biting as hard as she could, she clamped down on Ga'n's groping fingers. He snatched his hand back, screaming. Now! She scrambled up on all fours in the center of the bed. Ga'n rolled away from her, cursing. Alchise remained ominously at the doorway, blocking it.

"Matt!" she screamed, slipping off the bed. "Matt! Help!" Her shriek echoed through the darkened house.

Having given up on sleep, Matt was fully dressed and sitting on the porch of the bunkhouse when he heard Lark's scream. Automatically he reached for the Colt strapped to his leg and leaped off the porch, racing across the yard. Just as he pounded up the porch steps, he heard a scuffle in the hall. Cocking the gun, he jerked open the front door.

An Indian warrior stepped out into the hall, his rifle poised. Lark screamed again. The Apache aimed the rifle in Matt's direction. Matt threw himself to the floor, firing the Colt twice as he dived. The gunshots reverberated loudly.

Ga'n hissed and jerked Lark along by her hair. He pulled the gun from his holster, using her as a shield. To his horror, he saw his friend Alchise fall and lie in an ever-widening pool of blood. His eyes narrowed. There, at the other end of the hall, blocking his escape route, crouched Matt Kincaid. Terror turned to hatred as he saw the man who had hunted him for a month rise to his feet. The barrel of the Colt was steady and aimed directly at him. His lips lifted away from his teeth.

"Shoot and you kill her!" Ga'n cried out, jerking Lark roughly in front of him.

She gasped, stumbling against Ga'n. He held his left arm tightly across her throat, cutting off her breathing. Her breath came in ragged gasps.

"Let her go, Ga'n!" Kincaid roared.

Ga'n stared down at Alchise. His partner was dead! But he was smart enough to realize that he couldn't kidnap Lark now. Already he could hear sounds of activity coming from the bunkhouse. In a matter of seconds, the ranch would be swarming with wranglers and he'd be dead. Jerking his attention back to the cowboy, he snarled, "You've killed my war partner! You will be next! Count your days, *pindah!* I'll slit your throat and scalp you!" With a growl, he gave Lark a savage shove and leaped for the window.

Lark cried out as she tripped across her nightgown, throwing out both her hands to break her fall.

Matt moved quickly, but not quickly enough. Ga'n escaped like a shadow into the night, dissolving into the darkness. In three strides Matt was at Lark's side. He heard several of the wranglers shouting and racing toward the house. Gripping her shoulder, he gasped, "This isn't over yet. Stay here until I get back."

Nodding, she crawled to her knees as Matt ran past her. She heard him giving orders to the wranglers out on the porch. Within moments, the men had spread out across the yard to try and locate Ga'n.

She staggered to her feet and leaned weakly against the wall. Alchise lay in a pool of blood. Lark had seen only two other people shot—her father and Paco. Now, all of the grief and terror she associated with those shootings surged through her. She uttered a small cry and slid downward, her arms wrapped around her drawn-up legs, her brow pressed against her knees.

That's the way Matt found her thirty minutes later when he returned to the house. Ga'n had escaped. After posting a guard to be changed every three hours, Matt ordered everyone except Boa Juan and Primo back to bed. As he stepped over Alchise to reach Lark, he gave orders to the two wranglers to take the body outside. Burial would have to wait until tomorrow morning.

The Colt dangled in Matt's hand as he crouched wearily next to Lark, his heart wrenched with violent emotions. She could have been killed. She wasn't safe here. Ga'n was after her now. His fingers trembling, Matt touched her tense shoulder.

"Lark, can you walk? Let me get you to the bed." His voice was shaky, his senses screamingly acute. He felt her shudder.

With a soft curse, Matt rose. He holstered the Colt, jerked a quilt off the bed, and threw it around Lark's shoulders, then lifted her into his arms.

Lark clung mutely to Matt, her eyes tightly shut. She was wildly aware of his strong, warm body, his familiar scent. When he placed her on the bed, she huddled against the headboard, knees locked tightly against her body.

Matt shut the bedroom door and grimly returned to her. She was in shock. Wouldn't any woman be after such an ordeal? He moved across the bed and brought Lark, quilt and all, into his arms. She clung to him, her head buried beneath his jaw, her fingers flat against his chest.

"It's going to be all right," he soothed softly, stroking her unbound hair. "Just relax, Lark. It's over . . . it's over . . ."

"N-no," she cried, her voice thin and wobbly. "It isn't over! Ga'n said he was going to kidnap me."

Matt's eyes burned in the darkness. "What are you talking about? And how does Ga'n know you? Why would he attack you?"

The gentle stroke of his hand on her hair and shoulders began to dissolve her shock and terror. She tried to talk, but she wasn't coherent, the words tumbling out in fragments. "M-my father saved Ga'n from death when I was five years old, Matt. Ga'n swore never to hurt us from that time on. Even though he went on to become a renegade, Ga'n always left us and our ranch alone. Oh, Matt, he came here a few hours before you first arrived at our ranch. He was hunting you! I didn't know what he'd done to your family then, or I'd have shot him myself! I'm sorry . . . so sorry . . ."

Matt held her, rocked her, and soothed her with his deep voice. "It's all right, Lark. I'm not angry with you. Hush, honey, everything's going to be all right."

"You don't understand, Matt. Ga'n pledged never to hurt me. Why would he suddenly try to kidnap me? It doesn't make sense!"

Grimly, Matt held her tear-filled gaze. "Maybe he knows I'm here."

She sniffed and choked back the rest of the tears. "Then why didn't he go to the bunkhouse? He knows I live alone in the main house."

Matt nodded. "You're right," he muttered. He was becoming excruciatingly aware of other feelings, feelings he'd tried to deny since coming to the Gallagher Ranch. Lark was in his arms, soft and vulnerable. He felt the richness of her hair, smelled her fragrant scent, and took a deep, ragged breath. Burying his face against the lush thickness of her hair, he whispered hoarsely, "My God, you're not safe here with Ga'n stalking you now, Lark." He gripped her tightly to him, the words torn from him. "I need you. I can't let anything happen to you."

Lark slowly pushed away from his chest. She lifted her chin to look into his face. Her eyes widened as she realized he was suffering as much as she was. "Y-you need me?" The words came out faintly.

He nodded. "God help me, but I do," and he caressed her cheek, choking on his words.

Lark sat there, trembling. The trauma of the gunfight and now Matt's admission staggered her. His face looked ravaged, the eyes red-rimmed and filled with anguish. Matt needed her. Warmth, like the light of Holos, flowed through Lark.

Matt saw hope gather in her eyes and realized she was coming out of the shock. Gently he framed her face with his hands. "I don't know what it is," he admitted heavily, "but ever since I woke up here, you've been in my blood, Lark."

Not understanding, she shook her head, aware of the callused warmth of his hands against her face. "But you're leaving to chase down Ga'n."

Groaning, Matt rested his brow against hers. "Not right now. I can't leave you when I know he's stalking you, too. He's killed my family, and I'll be damned if he's going to take you, Lark. You're a part of me. God help us both, but I can't let you go.'' Matt couldn't stop the torrent of words. "I don't know how it happened. Seeing Ga'n here in your bedroom and you his prisoner made me realize just how much you mean to me.''

Lark listened with her heart. Matt had not said he loved her, only that he needed her. But that was enough. Perhaps that's what Ny-Oden had meant when he'd said love comes in many guises. Even need was a form of love, she thought. Reaching out, her fingers resting lightly on his arms, she asked, "Then you'll stay here? With us?''

Matt drowned in the luster of her eyes, eyes filled with such incredible happiness that the sight stole the breath from him. Swallowing hard, he managed a shaky nod. "I'll stay. I can catch him here as well as elsewhere.'' He caressed Lark's cheek. "Your life's more important to me than Ga'n right now.'' He smiled shakily. "It damned near took losing you to get that through my thick head.''

Lark had been kissed only once in her life, but she knew that a kiss expressed what lay in one's heart. She leaned up and inexpertly pressed her lips against the tortured line of Matt's mouth.

He groaned and swept his arms around her, crushing her hard against him. She became like a willow in his embrace.

Matt tore his mouth away from her shy, questing lips. "God, no . . .'' he groaned.

Her lips tingled from the brief contact. Already her nipples were growing taut beneath her cotton gown. She gently touched his cheek. "Did I hurt you? Was it wrong to share the feelings in my heart with you in that way?''

Matt gripped her arms. Lark knew nothing of the raging passions that were about to explode through his hard, aching body. She had almost been kidnapped earlier. Her innocent overture toward him was a result of the shock, he tried to tell himself. His voice was a harsh whisper. "No, you didn't hurt me, Lark.''

She sat helplessly in his grip, staring at him, the planes of his face shadowed and harsh. Her heart was fluttering wildly in her chest and her breasts were taut with a peculiar ache. "I only wanted to show you how I feel," she said lamely.

Fierce longing swept through Matt. Lark sat guilelessly before him, her black hair in sharp contrast to the pristine white of the cotton nightgown, the shapeless garment unable to hide the nipples that thrust against the fabric, taunting him. Her lips were parted, begging to be kissed. And her eyes . . . They were shining with unspoken invitation. Did she realize what she was doing to him? No, she couldn't possibly know . . .

"Listen, golden cougar, I'm not in control of all my feelings right now. Your touch drives me to the edge. You're so beautiful, and I don't want to hurt you."

Frowning, Lark tilted her head. "I don't understand, Matt." She touched the region of her heart. "Why is it wrong to share with you how I feel here? Even Apaches, when they tell their parents that they love one another, are allowed to hold hands or steal kisses. I don't have parents anymore, or I would tell them of my desire to share my life with you."

Words. Soft, pleading words from a child-woman. Matt stared long and hard at Lark's upturned face, absorbing the yearning and commitment he read in her eyes. "Do you know what you're asking?" he demanded harshly.

"I want us to share our hearts."

"There's more to it than holding hands or stealing a kiss, Lark."

"I've listened to my heart, Matt. You are the only man for me. Unless you turn me away, I am yours. That is the Apache way. A woman is allowed to choose her warrior, unless he doesn't want her as his mate for life. I—I know I don't touch your mouth with much skill, but my heart is behind my actions—"

"Dear God in heaven," he muttered.

"Your god won't get you out of this. And neither will mine."

A smile tipped the corners of his mouth. Matt gently cradled Lark's face in his hands, drawing her lips to within inches of his own. "You're a little wildcat, do you know that?"

She pouted, refusing to be drawn into the sudden warmth he bestowed upon her.

"I could end up hurting your forever, Lark."

"Hurting me?" Her voice wobbled. "To be around you yet denied your smile, to be refused your touch, hurts me much more deeply. When you kissed me, I ached inside. I went around feeling tied in knots. And since that kiss, you've ignored me, and my heart cries daily. Don't you understand? I'd rather risk hurt than live with the unending pain I carry now."

Matt shut his eyes tightly, unprepared for her honesty. Her love. And that was what it was. He opened his eyes. "Listen carefully, Lark," he began, shaken. "Sharing hearts means sharing other things, too."

"All right."

He gave a slight groan. "It means sharing this bed together, sharing ourselves with one another. Are you prepared to do that?"

She nodded, lost in his burning gray eyes. "I have chosen you. I want no other man for the rest of my life. If you will have me?"

He saw so much in Lark's expression. "I can't give you an answer right now, Lark. A woman's affections ought to be tied to a commitment, and I can't give you one until I get Ga'n. I may be killed—"

"Then let us share the time we do have. Together."

"I won't marry you, Lark, and then leave you a widow a day, a week, or a month later. I stole Katie's innocence and made her live a life that she considered hell. I won't ruin your life that way, too."

"By taking me to your bed, you will bind me to you forever in the eyes of The People. If I was widowed, I would not be considered spoiled goods. I want that day, week, or month with you. I pray to Us'an that you'll be the victor so that I can share as many years as he will grant to us.''

Matt winced, holding her face gently in his hands. ''Your Apache world is simple in the ways of love, Lark. The white world is more complicated.'' He leaned down and kissed her lips lightly, chastely. ''I want you to sleep on it, Lark. The decision you're making will hurt you the most. People will talk. They'll say you're a fallen woman.''

''Only in the eyes of some. The Apache will understand.''

''I know that,'' he said softly, gathering her into his arms one last time before he had to leave. ''Come on, I want you to lie down and try to sleep. Some time tomorrow you will tell me what you've decided.''

Lark savored his embrace and then reluctantly slipped beneath the coverlet. With a sigh, she closed her eyes. ''I will tell you tomorrow,'' she whispered, her words slurred from exhaustion.

Matt pressed a kiss against her brow. Sweet God in heaven, what had he agreed to? He stood unmoving, stirred by Lark's womanliness into painful wakefulness. Very soon, her breathing deepened. Forcing himself to leave her side, Matt knew sleep would evade him.

Questions plagued him. Why had Ga'n suddenly turned on Lark? Had someone ordered him to kidnap her, or was he acting for his own selfish purposes? He had to find the answers.

Lark awoke slowly, feeling as if she'd never slept so well in all her life. Rolling onto her back, she stared at the ceiling, remembering her conversation with Matt and the near kidnapping of the night before.

The fear that Matt might have changed his mind and left the ranch spurred her into action. Lark found Maria in the kitchen, preparing tortillas.

"Ah, *patrona*. You are well this morning?"

"Yes. Have you seen Matt?"

Maria gestured toward the stockyards. "*Sí, patrona*. He ate a hearty breakfast with the wranglers and then he left."

Terror shot through Lark. "Left?"

"*Sí*, he and Paco are over at the two-year-old colts' pen. Señor Matt said he was going to begin breaking them out today."

Lark stood openmouthed. "But—"

"He said to tell you not to worry. Come, eat breakfast."

"He'll reinjure his leg," Lark said, ignoring Maria's entreaty and hurrying down the hallway.


"Let him go." Matt braced himself in the saddle as Paco released the blindfold around the eyes of the black colt Matt was riding.

Just as the colt squealed and humped his back, Matt caught sight of Lark running toward the corral. He concentrated on staying on the back of the enraged colt, which crow-hopped around the arena on stiff, unbending legs. One thing he'd found out a long time ago: two-year-olds were a hell of a lot easier to break than crafty four- or five-year-olds. Each time the colt came out of his buck, landing with all four feet on the ground, Matt felt the horse losing energy. Finally, after a few more halfhearted attempts to throw him, the colt allowed himself to be guided around the circular corral by the hackamore and reins.

Lark climbed up on the fence and hung over the edge, watching as Matt expertly worked with the black colt. Her fear and anger gave way to admiration. Matt had a skillful touch with the young horse. Paco came over, smiling broadly, his teeth stark white against his dark flesh.

"*Patrona,* I think Señor Matt and I have found a way to be useful to the ranch even though we're both injured."

Lark frowned down at her foreman, whose left arm was in a sling. "I'm not so sure, Paco."

"Eh? Already we've broke four colts this morning."

"You have?" Lark's eyebrows shot up.

"*Sí.* I help Señor Matt saddle them, then I put a blindfold across their eyes and twist an ear while he gets in the saddle. It's easy."

"His leg won't stand up to that kind of punishment, Paco."

Paco leaned against the logs, watching Kincaid. "He knows what he's doing, *patrona.* We need these colts broke, eh?"

Lark bit down on her lower lip. She saw no evidence of blood on Matt's thigh. Perhaps Paco was right. Maybe the wound wouldn't bother him. Maybe she was being overprotective.

Matt brought the colt to a halt in the middle of the corral and dismounted, then led the sweaty, hard-breathing animal over to where Lark and Paco waited. Pushing the hat up on his perspiring brow, he noted the concern in Lark's gaze. Smiling, he handed Paco the reins. "Walk him out a little, Paco. Then put him in that holding pen."

"*Sí, señor.*" Paco patted the colt heartily, smiling.

Matt took off his hat and wiped his brow with the back of his sleeve. "Four down and eleven to go."

"Why didn't you tell me you were going to break the colts?"

"Because you would have squawked like an old broody hen."

Lark climbed off the fence and joined him. "And your leg?"

"A little tender, that's all. Walk with me to the barn? I want to get a drink of water at the trough."

Lark fell into step beside him, wildly aware of him as a man. Had Matt forgotten their conversation of last night? He seemed so casual this morning, as if nothing had happened. They entered the shadow of the barn and halted at the huge wooden watering trough. Matt took off his thin deerskin gloves and tucked them in the belt of his shotgun chaps. Leaning down, he cupped the cold water and sipped several handfuls, then sluiced water over his sweaty face. Wiping his mouth, he sat down on the edge of the trough, studying Lark. "How are you feeling this morning?"

"The truth?"

"Between us? Always."

Her heart beat painfully in her breast. Matt was wearing a dark red shirt and red bandanna around his throat. Sweat emphasized his rugged features. She stared at the fistful of black hair peeking over the top button of his shirt. He was so masculine, so beautiful in a haunting way that made her go weak and hot inside. "I awoke this morning and Maria said you had left."

"And?"

"Well . . . I thought . . ."

Matt heard the tremor in her voice. "Forever?" he guessed.

She nodded once, unable to speak for several moments. "I was afraid our conversation, the things we shared last night, had frightened you away."

Matt held her hands gently. "We're both people of our word, Lark," he told her quietly. "Look at me."

She lifted her lashes, dying a little bit inside because she had no experience of relationships and didn't know what to expect from him. But the instant she met his dark gaze, her heart burst with joy. "What?"

"I haven't forgotten a word of what we talked about last night, golden cougar. And judging from the look on your face, you haven't either."

"No, I haven't."

"Well?"

"I still want to share my heart with you."

Matt looked away. The sky was a bright blue, the mountains surrounding the ranch a deep green. The sunlight held promise, warming everything it touched. "You know," he began softly, "you're like that sunlight out there beyond the shade. Everything you come in contact with, you make better. You're a healer in many ways, Lark.''

"Ny-Oden has said that the greatest healer is love,'' she ventured in a whisper.

"He's right, I think.'' Matt rose, releasing her cool fingers. "Come on, let's walk into the sunlight.''

She walked slowly at his side, waiting, wondering.

"Have you given thought to how this arrangement might influence the opinion of the people who live and work here at the ranch?''

She hadn't. Lark shook her head, her heart sinking.

"Do you think the people will treat you differently if we share the same bed?''

"The Apache way is to share a bed to let others know we're bound to each other for life.''

"The Apaches who live here will accept your decision. But your Mexican wranglers and their families? What will they think?''

Lark knew all about the Catholic religion that her Mexican hands embraced. Her parents had been married by Father Mulcahy.

Matt saw Lark's brows draw downward. He read the confusion in her eyes. "Until I can hunt down Ga'n, Lark, I won't expose you to that kind of talk or hurt. I can wait.'' *Liar,* he berated himself. "Different people embrace different rules to live by.''

"And you're saying that because I live in two worlds, I must adhere to both sets of rules?'' she challenged.

He paused at the corral. Paco had brought in another colt, a sorrel this time. "Sometimes, Lark, people have to make decisions based not on what they want, but on what is best for everyone.''

She bristled, not wanting to admit the truth of his words. Unexpectedly, she felt the caress of his fingers against her cheek.

"Listen, I don't mean to be a devil's advocate about this. I just want you to think clearly about it first, Lark.''

"But you need me."

"I'll always need you, golden cougar. Whether it's today, tomorrow, or years from now, that'll never change."

She considered Matt's words as he climbed the rails and went about the business of breaking another colt. Frustrated, she headed back to the barn to saddle one of the mares. She would ride the arroyos high above the ranch and check on her men, who were hunting for mustangs. Perhaps by then she would have the answers she sought.

"Paco!" she called a few minutes later, mounted and riding up to the corral.

"*Sí, patrona?*"

"Where are Boa Juan and his men?"

Paco's eyes widened. "*Patrona*, Señor Matt doesn't want you to ride anywhere without him. He says Ga'n will be around and it's not safe for you to go out alone."

Snorting, Lark snapped, "He's not the boss here, Paco, I am. Now, tell me the direction Boa Juan rode this morning."

Smarting beneath her anger, he pointed to the west. "They were going up into Devil's Canyon for the next week, *patrona.*"

"Very well. I'll be up there for the day, Paco. And tell Matt to stay here. I'll have the protection of eight wranglers and will be safe enough." She sank her heels into her horse before Paco could voice his protest. The mare grunted, startled, and leaped forward into a gallop.

"You didn't kidnap her?" Cameron demanded.

Ga'n sat tensely on his mustang, his eyes hard with anger as he studied the rancher.

"You lied to me, Cameron," Ga'n accused, placing his hand over the butt of his gun. "You said Lark Who Sings would be easy to kidnap. She wasn't. Matt Kincaid was there and he killed Alchise!" His nostrils flared as anger shook his voice. "I should kill you for the death of my friend!"

Cameron's hand went to his gun. Like a fool, he'd told Shanks to stay behind, fully expecting Ga'n to tell him that the half-breed had been kidnapped. Now he was in danger of being shot by the renegade.

"How in the hell was I supposed to know Kincaid was around?" Cameron demanded.

Ga'n studied the *pindah*. "You speak with many tongues, Cameron. Even a snake is honest compared to you!" He spat into the dust and thrust out his hand. "Give me the money!"

Cameron was going to argue, but quickly decided against it. He knew Ga'n would gun him down if he refused. He jerked the dollar bills from his vest pocket and threw them at the Apache. "Get the hell out of here. Go get drunk like you always do. I won't need you or the other renegades for at least a month. We're planning another attack near Phoenix then, and I want you to lead it."

Ga'n slid off his pony and picked up the money. "Kincaid is nearby. Until I kill him, I'll go nowhere."

"Fine, you do that." Cameron didn't care. If Ga'n got rid of the gunslinger gratis, that would be unexpected luck. Cameron spurred his horse into a gallop. There was work to do. As soon as he got back to Prescott, he was going to put Shanks to work.

Being out in Devil's Canyon chasing wily mustangs up and down the vast, rocky canyon gave Lark no time to think or feel. It was nearly two in the afternoon and she had already changed horses three times. The running, scrambling, and climbing it took to catch the mustangs quickly wore out the hardy ranch horses. At the moment she was mounted on Four Winds, her fleetest mare.

Boa Juan, Carlos, and Lark rode toward another section of the canyon, Devil's Mouth, an area riddled with large caves. The other wranglers had gone in another direction to hunt down five mustangs they had seen earlier that morning.

Lark's crew was stalking One Eye, a man-hating stud who had made her life miserable. An albino stallion with one glassy blue eye in his hammer head, he stole Gallagher Ranch mares every season.

This year, One Eye had boldly jumped over a corral fence and slashed and cut at the mares, sending them crashing through the rails to freedom. Now Lark and her men were rounding up those mares, who had already been bred to Kentucky.

Lark wiped the sweat off her face. Boa Juan rode at her side on his small black mustang. He pointed toward the end of the canyon. "There he is!"

Lark saw One Eye surrounded by at least six of their mares. "I see him."

"The bastard's going to make those mares climb out of the canyon and escape along the rim," Carlos warned, getting out his lasso and lengthening the loop on it.

Lark saw that Carlos was right. The steeply angled hill behind them, nearly four hundred feet high, was the only avenue of escape out of the canyon. One Eye knew this country well. Lark saw that he'd spotted them. With a squeal, the stallion began slashing at the mares rumps and running doggedly back and forth, aiming them toward the steep hill strewn with boulders, brush, and cactus.

"Some of those mares might lose their foals," Boa Juan muttered, taking the rope off the saddle horn and quickly running a large loop into it in his gloved hands.

"Not if we get there first," Lark said, automatically reaching for her lasso. "Boa Juan, Carlos, you ride around the canyon and come down that incline. If One Eye sees you up there, he's going to be forced to turn back."

"Back toward you," Boa Juan guessed. "You know One Eye. He attacks riders in a group or alone. You won't be safe, *patrona*."

"Yes, I will." Lark's eyes glinted. "If I get a clear shot at him, I intend to kill him with the rifle."

"Good!" Carlos exclaimed. "And if we can draw a bead on him, we'll kill him first."

Lark nodded. She didn't like killing animals unless it was necessary, but for years her father had tried to track One Eye down and destroy him. If he had been like other mustang studs, who left the ranch and the mares alone, Lark wouldn't take such an extreme measure. And right now, this was the first opportunity they'd had to get close enough to kill the animal.

*"Darse prisa!"* Carlos called, spurring his horse forward.

Lark held Four Winds back. The mare danced nervously, wanting to join the galloping riders disappearing around the rim of the rocky canyon. "Four Winds, I'm going to need all your courage," she crooned to her mare. "We're going to have to face One Eye. Be brave, my heart. Stand quietly beneath me when I draw my rifle . . ."

Lark cantered down the floor of the canyon, all the while warily watching the stallion who stood less than half a mile away from her. One Eye shrieked in a high, angry bugle when he saw the two wranglers appear at the top of the steep hill. Immediately the mares turned, skidding wildly back down the grade, raising a cloud of choking dust. The stallion turned, and Lark knew he realized he couldn't drive the mares upward. Ordinarily a good stallion would stay at the rear of his herd to make sure no mares escaped. This time Lark saw him take the lead and head directly at her. She was the only rider preventing his escape from the canyon.

Lark watched the albino plunge ahead of the scattering band of frightened mares. She saw a bay mare go down, rolling end over end. When she finally got to her feet, her left front leg dangled, broken. Crying out in anger, Lark pulled the rifle out of the case beneath her leg. One

Eye leaped to the canyon floor at a gallop, his screams caroming off the ocher walls.

Pulling Four Winds to a halt, Lark had only seconds to lift the rifle, pump a round into the chamber, and aim at the charging stallion. She saw One Eye's mouth open, his yellow teeth exposed in a vicious snarl. His tiny ears were pinned against his thick neck, his nostrils flared and bloodred in color.

"Steady, steady," she crooned to Four Winds, who heaved for breath between her clamped legs, all four feet planted firmly. The cross hairs of Lark's gun wavered on the approaching stallion. Sweat trickled down her wrinkled brow. Taking a breath, she prepared to fire.

Before she could pull the trigger, shots rang out behind her. Shaken, Lark saw Boa Juan and Carlos scatter away from the rim, disappearing in a cloud of dust. Who had fired those shots? She jerked her attention back to One Eye, but it was too late.

The stallion, a battle-hardened veteran of many fights, lunged toward the mare's head, his teeth ripping into the flesh of her neck. He threw all his weight into the staggering mare, using his shoulder to send her crashing to the earth.

Lark was thrown upon impact, the rifle flying out of her hand. One Eye skidded to a halt and wheeled around, the ground thundering beneath his hooves. Lark scrambled to her hands and knees, but just as her fingers closed over the rifle, the stallion lashed out at her. Her head exploded with bright light and pain. Darkness engulfed her.

# Chapter 12

Nearly three hours had passed since Shanks had captured Lark Gallagher. He'd bound her hands in front of her so she couldn't reach out and claw him like she had two years ago. The yellow cotton shirt she wore had been torn, exposing the subtle shadow of her cleavage. He itched to put his hand on those small, firm breasts. But he'd wait. He'd wait until she was awake, when he would enjoy forcing her to sign the papers. He wasn't going to disappoint Cameron this time. He didn't want to lose his job to that new gun from down South.

"Come on, Lark, wake up!" he growled, prodding her shoulder. Her hair was a blue-black sheet around her head. He leaned over, fingering the dusty strands while keeping an eye on her. Her lashes fluttered. He grinned, waiting . . .

Pain throbbed between her eyebrows and fanned upward, through her brow. Lark ached all over. Groaning, she opened her eyes to mere slits. It took her several moments to digest the fact that Bo Shanks was crouched over her. Her throat closed in terror. No! It couldn't be! Her mind whirled with questions. He was grinning like a wolf prepared to eat his prey, his yellow teeth glistening with saliva. She looked around and found herself in a cave.

"Welcome back, Lark. That stud got to ya before I could." Shanks leaned over, barely touching her left temple. "Clipped ya, he did. That's all right, I got the bastard. Shot him through the heart after he run ya down. Ol' One Eye has gone to horse hell by now.''

Lark's first thought was that her hands were tied, her second the realization that Shanks had shot her wranglers. Her blood chilled and she fought a sudden nausea and dizziness. ''What happened to Boa Juan and Carlos?'' she croaked out.

She cringed as Shanks picked up some of her hair, sifting it gently through his long fingers. ''Oh, them . . .'' He laughed, a high giggle. ''Well, it was like this: I wanted ya and not them. So I got rid of 'em by firin' a couple of shots over their heads. By the time they circled around to get into the canyon, I'd thrown ya over my horse and hid in this cave. They musta spent a good hour tryin' to find ya, but I'd wiped out my tracks. They finally gave up and left. That horse of yores lit outa here, too.'' He chuckled, pleased with himself. ''So ya see, no one knows where yore at. Purty smart, huh?'' He rested easily on his haunches, grinning at her.

Lark shut her eyes, desperately trying to think. Her head throbbed where One Eye had grazed it with his hoof. She was lucky to be alive. Finally she settled her gaze on Shanks. ''Why have you done this?''

He pulled out a paper and dangled it in front of her face. ''Sign this, breed, and I'll let ya go.''

She scowled, ''What are you talking about?''

''Sez here that yore to sign over the water rights of yore ranch to Mr. Cameron.'' He pointed to the bottom line. ''Ya sign this now, and I let ya go. Pure and simple. Or you and I can enjoy this cave until ya sign it. Take yore pick.'' His eyes glittered. ''Personally, I'd like to spend a lot of time here with ya.'' His gaze settled hotly on her breasts.

A frisson of fear cleared away her lingering grogginess. Shanks was capable of anything, including killing her. ''So Cameron's behind all this,'' she snapped. ''Did he pay Ga'n to try the same thing?''

"Yeah, that red renegade botched the job." Shanks threw the paper down in her lap. "But I ain't gonna."

Licking her dry lips, Lark looked nervously up at her captor. "Don't you realize what Cameron's doing? If you don't let me go, you'll go to jail."

"Girl, yore plumb outa yore head." He slapped his knee gleefully. "Ol' Dan Cole ain't gonna arrest me. Prescott's owned by Cameron, in case ya haven't figured that out yet. The law listens to him."

"What if I don't sign this paper?"

Shanks slid his hand along her denim-covered thigh. "Cameron said to persuade ya. He didn't say how."

"You bastard!" Lark cried, and spat into his face.

Shanks reared backward, unprepared for such an attack. He rubbed his eyes furiously.

Scrambling to her feet, Lark propelled herself toward the opening of the cave. Devil's Mouth! She knew the series of caves well. Running hard, her breath torn from her lungs, she slipped through the opening.

"Stop or I'll drill ya!" Shanks shrieked.

To her left was a sheer rock wall. Trying to jerk the bonds free, she ran to the right and down a narrow, pebble-strewn path. She heard Shanks hard on her heels, his angry yelps growing closer and closer. Desperately she ran, slipping and sliding, and spotted Shanks's buckskin gelding at the bottom. He wasn't saddled, but that didn't matter.

A shot rang out. The slug bit into the dirt near her feet. Sobbing for breath, Lark leaped off the path and tumbled down the steep incline to where the horse was tied. Another shot ricocheted off boulders inches from her head.

The buckskin shied as Lark rolled to a stop near his dancing hooves. "Whoa!" she ordered. The buckskin froze, too well trained to think of moving when that command was given.

Lark jerked a look over her shoulder. Shanks appeared at the top of the hill. She fumbled with the straps to the hobbles. There! Grabbing a chunk of the horse's black mane, she vaulted onto his back. "Giddyap!" she shrilled. The buckskin's eyes rolled when she sunk both heels into his flanks. Leaping forward, he galloped out of the area, heading down another, narrower path.

Wind stung Lark's eyes as she clamped her thighs around the hurtling animal. The buckskin obviously hadn't been trained to respond to light touches and subtle shifts of weight. The only thing he knew was a spade bit in his mouth. Now Lark was careening down the canyon path on a frightened, runaway horse over which she had no control. She heard a gun being fired once, twice, three times. Three bullets stung the air nearby, raising puffs of dust on the rocky canyon wall above her head. Clinging to the buckskin with her tied hands wrapped in the mane, Lark urged the animal on at a terrific pace. No matter where the horse ran, it would be away from Shanks. He'd be on foot, unable to follow her. Home! She had to get home!

The buckskin charged out of Devil's Canyon and onto a dry, dusty flat. Lark tried to steer the gelding by yanking his mane right and left, but the horse wouldn't respond. She tried to slow him down, but to no avail. Sobbing for breath, Lark studied the land ahead. The flat ended in a thick forest grove. Beyond that, the land became rocky and treacherous. If she couldn't slow the buckskin down, she could well be thrown from the wild-eyed animal.

A shout drew her attention. At first Lark couldn't tell who it was, only that it was a wrangler on a gunmetal-gray horse riding rapidly toward her from the edge of the forest. Hope rose in her. It must be one of her ranch hands. She began tugging and jerking on the buckskin's heavy neck, trying to get him to slow down. Her only hope was the man riding toward her.

Lark's spirits soared. It was Matt! She recognized his set features as he spurred the gray ever closer. Sobbing his name, she clung to the buckskin, praying Matt could swing alongside and rescue her. The drowning hoofbeats reverberated as Matt circled slow and wide, so as not to terrorize her animal even further.

Matt edged his gray closer and closer to the fleeing buckskin. He saw that Lark's hands were tied and her shirt torn open. What the hell had happened? Grimly he caught and held her wide, frightened gaze.

"Steady!" Matt shouted to her. Just a few more feet . . . a few more . . . Reaching out, he hooked his arm around Lark's waist. At that instant, the buckskin shied, moving away at a right angle from them. Unprepared for the unexpected action, Matt nearly dropped Lark. He jerked hard on the reins and the gray settled on his hind legs into a long, skidding stop.

Lark hung perilously. She gasped, feeling Matt's arm slipping . . . slipping . . .

The long slide cost the gray dearly. Pebbles tore at his hindquarters and produced bloody scratches on his rear legs. Matt leaned perilously to one side in the saddle as the horse sat down.

"Roll!" he commanded her, and then let go, almost falling out of the saddle himself.

Instinctively Lark curled as the ground rushed up to meet her. Her shoulder hit the hard ground and she rolled away from the tottering horse and rider.

Dismounting quickly, Matt ran over to where Lark lay. She was slowly getting to her knees when he arrived. He gripped her shoulder.

"Lark? What the hell happened?" he asked between ragged gasps.

"Shanks," she cried. "He tried to kidnap me!"

Matt raised his head, searching the direction from which she had ridden. "What are you talking about?"

Shaken, Lark sat still while Matt untied her wrists.

"Cameron hired Ga'n to kidnap me. When that didn't work, he sent Shanks to do it. That bastard had orders to make me sign a paper giving my water rights to Cameron! I managed to escape and grab Shanks's horse."

"Hold on," Matt growled, "I'm going to carry you over to my horse."

She was about to protest, but he lifted her into his arms before she could. Clinging mutely to him, Lark whispered, "Paco was right. I shouldn't have come out here without you."

"Hush, Lark." Matt placed her in the saddle, picked up the reins, and mounted behind her. He put his arm around her when she swayed in the saddle. "Lean back," he ordered. "We're going to get you home." Though he desperately wanted to go back and search the canyon for Shanks, he knew Lark needed his attention more. She'd suffered cuts and scratches from her escape.

"How did you find me?"

"Boa Juan and Carlos rode back to the ranch. They told me someone had shot at them, that they had become worried about you and had gone back to the canyon but couldn't find you anywhere. I organized the wranglers and sent them in three different groups to search for you along the rim. I was going into the canyon to try and pick up your tracks."

"Maybe they'll catch Shanks walking out of there."

"I doubt it. The search pattern we laid out was taking them away from the canyon."

As they rode in silence through the forest, Lark's tense muscles began to relax. Matt's arms were strong around her, protective. She lay against his powerful chest, knowing he would keep her safe from any further harm. Although still in shock, she was also aware of Matt's vigilant lookout for bushwackers. There was a constant tension in his body, and his eyes were constantly alert. Lark trembled.

"When is this all going to stop?" she asked hoarsely. "Shanks said Sheriff Cole is in cahoots with Cameron. What can we do?"

"Plenty," he promised grimly. "I'm going to ride into Prescott tomorrow morning and wire Phoenix. I'll request that they send a marshal up here to investigate."

Anguish wound through Lark, numbing the pain of her physical injuries. "I—I can't understand how anyone can do what Cameron's done and get away with it. What's wrong with him?"

"Cameron operates without any kind of moral code, honey. He's worse than an animal," Matt said. He pulled the gray to a halt and dropped the reins across the horse's neck. "Come here," he said roughly, pulling Lark around so that she sat sidesaddle across his lap. Taking her into his arms, he held her tightly. "We'll fight Cameron together. I'll be there for you . . ."

Her fingers digging into the leather vest he wore, Lark pressed her cheek against his dark blue cotton shirt. "I was so afraid on that buckskin," she blurted out. "All I could think was that I didn't want to die without having given you my heart. I felt such loss, so alone . . ."

"Shh, honey, you've got my heart. It's going to be all right," he soothed thickly, caressing her hair.

"Don't leave me alone tonight, Matt. I can't take it. I'm so afraid. Every shadow will remind me of Ga'n or Shanks."

Any reservations Matt had about making Lark his woman dissolved. There was real terror in her voice, something he'd never heard before. He pressed a kiss to her cheek, and his voice was rough with emotion. "You'll sleep with me every night, Lark. I won't let you be hurt again. I promise."

"But the men and their families—what will they think? I don't want them to lose respect for me."

Matt smiled faintly. "Like a good leader, you'll be careful to keep up appearances for their sake, Lark. I'll join you after everyone in the bunkhouse has gone to sleep. And I'll go back before dawn. No one will know. How does that sound?"

"Wonderful."

"You were angry when you left this morning."

She nodded, finding solace in his arms. "I didn't want to hear the truth of your counsel. After I rode out to the canyon and thought about what you'd said, I knew you were right, Matt. I may not feel comfortable walking between two worlds, but the ranch has to come before my own needs.''

"You're growing in your role as *patrona*, honey," he congratulated her. He squeezed her gently, realizing she must be sore and tender from the fall from the buckskin. "I'm proud of you. Proud as hell."

Lark ignored her discomfort once they arrived at the ranch. She helped Matt organize the rest of the returning wranglers. A sentry would be posted and changed every three hours, around the clock, to guard the main buildings of the ranch.

Near dark, another group of wranglers arrived from the rim of the canyon. Their hard, worried expressions melted into smiles of welcome when they saw Lark standing on the porch. A day of near disaster had turned to one of relief and happiness.

It was dusk when Lark washed herself in the stream and dressed in the cotton nightgown. Usually she stayed up until midnight, but the day's harrowing events had sapped her reserves of strength and she was going to bed early.

The kerosene lamp sputtered on the dresser as she pulled back the sheet and quilt on the brass bed. Exhausted, all she wanted to do was sleep. Within seconds, she spiraled into darkness, escaping the grief of the day.

Matt waited until the wranglers' snores told him they were all asleep. Throughout the evening and into the night, he hadn't forgotten his promise to Lark: to remain at her side and protect her. The events of the day had wiped away all his self-doubt. The thought that Lark might have been found dead somewhere in the canyon still hovered in the shadowy recesses of his mind. In that galvanizing moment, he knew he loved her more than any other woman.

After quietly dressing, he made his way across the deserted yard, careful to avoid detection by the sentry on horseback. He slipped inside the silent ranch house and trod lightly down the hall. Pushing the door open, he saw Lark curled up in the bed like a lost kitten, looking excruciatingly feminine. She was beautiful, a woman, and she deserved to be treated as such, not like a child.

After undressing and allowing his clothes to fall in a heap near the bed, Matt blew out the kerosene lamp. Blackness engulfed the room, and he waited for his eyes to adjust.

The moon was just rising, sending slender streamers across the sky, vaguely outlining Lark's sleeping form. Matt slid carefully into bed, not wanting to awaken her. Now was not the time to love her; they were both too exhausted. Instead, he moved to her side, fitting her against the curve of his body. Contentment eddied with simmering desire, but he checked it. Just the softness of her form in his arms and the fragrant scent of her newly washed hair were enough for him. A miracle had occurred today, he realized groggily. The miracle of life being handed back to him when he had thought everything he had ever loved had been destroyed—forever. Lark was his miracle of the heart.

Lark shifted, unconsciously nuzzling into the warmth. Vaguely she realized that something was different, and abruptly she awakened. It was still dark, although something told her dawn would come in another hour or so. Moonlight filtered into the room, softening the hard surfaces and providing a dim light by which she could see Matt, who was holding her in his arms. With growing dismay she realized that the length of her body was pressed against him. Her dismay turned to alarm. Matt was naked, and her nipples were already hardening, pressing insistently against his firm, warm flesh.

Her alarm dissolved in a matter of heartbeats as Lark studied Matt's sleeping features. A strand of dark hair had drifted across his brow. A thin, almost unnoticeable white scar marred the corner of his left eye. Had he gotten that scar as a small boy? Without thinking, she caressed the area with her fingertips.

Matt stirred and slowly opened his eyes. He saw Lark's guileless features, the concern in her dark, fathomless blue eyes. He felt her hip pressing against his loins. Heat uncurled through his body, and he felt himself hardening. She felt so good. It felt so right to be with her. Managing a smile, he lifted his hand and caressed her hair.

"Aren't you supposed to be asleep?" he asked hoarsely.

Lark trembled as he continued to stroke her unbound hair. "I awoke for no reason."

"You're like a cat," he murmured, "arching into my hand every time I stroke you."

His words were dark and held much promise. Lark sighed, responding to his tone, unconsciously moving against him. She felt rather than heard his groan. Thrilled that such a feather-light touch could evoke in him a reaction of such magnitude, she leaned upward.

Matt felt Lark's lips graze his, lips that were warm and filled with invitation. Sitting up in bed, his back against the headboard, he slowly undressed her, letting the cotton nightgown fall to the floor.

"Come here," he told her gravely, positioning her across from him so that he could see her drowsy features. He studied her in the silence, drowning in the smoldering fire in her wide, vulnerable eyes and her parted, waiting lips. The moonlight softly caressed her naked form and he stared in awe of her lithe body. "We're going to take this slow," he told her, holding her gaze. "As slow as you want it to be. If you become afraid, tell me."

Lark tilted her head, lost in the roughness of his voice and the warmth of his dove-gray eyes. "Is speaking allowed?"

He smiled faintly, caressing her smooth cheek. Her flesh had always reminded him of a ripe, golden peach. "I want my woman to talk to me in many ways. You can use your voice, your hands, and your body to speak to me."

Her voice was breathy, expectant. "I see."

Matt nodded, studying her intently. He pulled the covers off his lower body, exposing his total nakedness.

Mesmerized by the tightly coiled power of his body, Lark felt heat rush to her cheeks. He was dark with hair, and his muscles were well accentuated and radiated a heat that made her feel weak with need.

"Do I frighten you?" He waited patiently, seeing many conflicting emotions cross her face. Time, they had time. But could he fight his own inner need of her? Dear God, he was hard and ready for her right now.

Lark stared at his thick shaft, unable to tear her gaze away from it. A strange new sensation twisted through her lower body, the ache sharp, exquisite. "I'm not afraid."

"Sure?"

"Well, maybe a little."

Matt slowly rose to a kneeling position in the center of the bed. He spread his thighs wide and brought Lark between his legs. She knelt before him, her lashes against her cheeks, and gently he cradled her face, forcing her chin upward.

"Look at me," he commanded quietly. She opened her eyes and he saw that the smoky blueness now flashed with golden flecks of fire. "You're my woman," he promised her thickly, running his fingers through her black hair. He began gently kneading her scalp, watching her eyes close from the unexpected pleasure. "Touching one another like this is good, my golden cougar. We should give one another pleasure, not pain. Yes, enjoy it . . ." And he captured her mouth, fire singing through him.

Lark moaned, the sound drowning within his mouth as his large hands cupped her breasts. The sensation was surprising, molten. Automatically she lifted her arms, her fingers gripping his upper arms for support. A small cry of delight was torn from her as his thumbs encircled the buds of her breasts. Pulling her mouth from his, she breathed in ragged gasps of air.

"Easy, easy, my woman, my own . . . let the feelings race through you. Feel, just feel . . .".

Stunned, whirling in a cauldron of spiraling fire, Lark released a whimper as he continued his slow assault upon her ripened senses.

Her cry rippled through Matt in waves and he broke out into a sweat. His own body was screaming at him, hammering at him to take her now, to make her his. His lips settled over the peak of her breast, and pulled it into the moistness of his mouth. Her fingers dug into his chest and she twisted and writhed against him, uncontrolled. Joy swept through him as he sampled her other nipple. Her cries continued and he marveled at her responsiveness.

"Sweet," he told her raggedly, "my God, but you're sweet . . ." He slid his hand downward across her belly, slowly circling the silky ebony mound with the palm of his hand. At first Lark tensed, but as he slipped his finger between her thighs, a shudder wracked her. "It's going to be fine, my woman . . . Relax, let me help you," he crooned, claiming her lips and moving his tongue into her warm, waiting depths.

Lark arched, moaning, at the same moment that she felt him sparking new fire to burning life by pressing his fingers gently between her thighs.

"Lark," he breathed against her, "let me touch you, let me ease your ache, my woman."

Mindless, sobbing, she opened her thighs, feeling his fingers slip closer, closer, until . . .

"My God," he rasped, "you're so wet." And he began to massage her molten feminine core.

A cry of pleasure lodged in Lark's throat. Fire expanded and leaped from deep within her. She pressed wildly against his palm, moving, moving to reduce the ache that was scalding her, burning her. The ache was too deep, the demand to be satiated too powerful, and she twisted her hips against his hand, lost in a building crescendo.

Matt suddenly felt Lark stiffen, her fingers digging into his tightly bunched shoulders. Perspiration made her entire body gleam like gold in the predawn light as she arched deeply into his arms, a scream tearing from within her.

Suddenly exhausted, dazed by the unexpected sensation, Lark fell back into Matt's arms. She stared up at him, wide-eyed, satiated. Weakness stole through every part of her, making her feel like a child in his arms. He was smiling down at her, pride reflected in his eyes as he gently stroked her hips and thighs.

"You're so fiery, so sensitive," he whispered, laying her back on the bed. He caressed her damp cheek, stroking her hair to soothe her, to bring her back from her dreamy state.

Lark tried to gather her thoughts. She reached out, her fingers touching his arm. "What . . . happened?"

He leaned down, worshipping her kiss-swollen lips. Smiling lazily, he slid his hand down to her mound of ebony hair and started to massage her once again, watching as her eyes became heavy-lidded with desire. "You gave me the gift of yourself," he explained hoarsely. "A man can go a lifetime without his woman ever giving herself to him like you just did to me."

Lark smiled weakly, thinking that he was like Holos, the light of her world. She slid her arms around his neck. "I want to make you feel like me. How can I do it? Teach me . . ."

Sweat stood out on his brow and upper lip. Matt rested his head against hers, his breath quickening as he felt her respond to his touch. "It will hurt," he rasped, warning her.

"No . . . nothing you could do would hurt me. I know you'd never do it intentionally," she whispered, kissing his brow and nose, then seeking out his mouth, wanting the powerful, commanding feel of his tongue against her seeking lips.

Groaning, Matt slowly covered her body. He broke her wild, sweet kiss, drowning in her lustrous gaze. "I'll be as gentle as I can, sweet woman of mine. Trust me, just trust me . . ."

His words soothed the edges of her momentary panic. She felt his massive shaft begin to massage her as his fingers had done earlier. She sighed, surrendering to the sensations, and became lost in so many new, wonderful explosions that she began to move unconsciously against him.

"That's it," he gritted out hoarsely, "rub against me. Enjoy it, golden cougar. Come to me . . . come to me . . ." He clutched the bed sheet and quilt in one massive fist, sucking air between his clenched teeth as she followed his coaxing. How long could he hold back? My God, but she was so wet and felt so tight against him. Sweat beaded his furrowed brow, and each breath became an agony as her sweet, guileless body twisted and moved beneath his.

Lark felt another explosion building within her heated body. She was trembling now, clutching at Matt's shoulders as she increased the tempo of her hips against his shaft. This time the ache went deeper and, yearning to soothe it, she angled her hips higher.

She was so small and tight! Matt felt the walls of her femininity pressing against his shaft. He gasped for breath, wanting to beg her to stop, to give him time to control his overwhelming need. But when she lifted her hips and pulled him barely within her, his control snapped. The need to claim her, to brand her, to make her his own, overrode all else. He crushed Lark to him and thrust deeply into her, smothering her mouth with his own, stifling her cry of painful discovery of a new, unexplored world.

The momentary pain made Lark stiffen. She felt Matt

tense, as if he was holding himself in tight check. Her eyes flew open and she met his turbulent gray gaze as he broke the kiss.

"Just lie here," he told her raggedly. "The pain will go away in a minute, I promise you." He kissed her brow, nose, eyes, and finally her mouth.

Trembling, Lark slid her arms around his sweat-slick shoulders. Her heart swelled with such emotions that all she could do was kiss him and bury her head beside his. She felt stretched tight, so full, but the sensation wasn't unpleasant. Seeing the anguish in his face and hearing it in his voice, she sought to erase it and moved her hips slightly.

Matt groaned. "God . . . don't!"

The pain in his face was replaced by something else, something primal and savage. Spurred on by these revelations, sensing her power as a woman, Lark tested her newly found discovery and moved her hips gently but insistently.

Gritting his teeth, Matt buried his head beside Lark's. Every sweet movement of her inexperienced hips sent a burst of fire through him. He tried to pull out of her, but she clung to him, silently asking him to stay. Gulping for breath, he raised his head, dazed. He wanted her so badly. All of her.

She looked into his anguished eyes and framed his face with her hands. "Make me your woman. I've given you my heart, now give me yours . . ."

He nodded, unable to speak. As carefully as he could, he moved experimentally within her. She was so damned small and he was so large. Yet, to his amazement, he heard a familiar husky purr coming from deep within her, telling him that his tentative thrusts felt good to her. He slid his hand beneath her hips, showing her how to rock in motion with him. Her cries of pleasure increased and he abandoned himself to her wild, hungry body that was sucking him deeper and deeper into her. Each thrust of his hips burned him more, took him higher. She was damp with perspiration, their bodies fused. She was liquid and molten as he slipped back and forth within her loving sheath. And then he groaned, tensing.

Lark felt Matt grow stiff, like a bowstring pulled taut. His face went rigid, yet her newly awakened female senses told her to hold him, to twist her hips and prolong this feeling for him. She did so, and in moments he fell weakly upon her, gulping in sobs of breath. She smiled as a new warmth and contentment settled over her. She gloried in Matt's weight upon her, in his utter maleness. Lark realized that her life had changed forever, and her heart felt free and joyous.

# Chapter 13

"No . . . stay . . ."

Matt remained motionless when he heard Lark's husky voice. Thinking he was too heavy for her slender form, he'd started to withdraw from her velvet depths, but she had wound her arms around him, holding him close. He shifted some of his weight off her, his other hand protectively wrapped around her hip.

"I don't want to hurt you, honey," he said, resting his mouth against her damp cheek. Inhaling her special scent, Matt caressed her skin with his own cheek.

"You're not hurting me. You would if you left." Lark lifted her lashes, wrapped in a cocoon of warmth within his arms, his body like a blanket over her.

She reveled in her new discoveries. *So this is what it means to be a woman.* Smiling softly, she closed her eyes, her fingers tracing the outline of his powerful shoulders. "You're so strong and sleek. Like the bear I first thought you were."

He nuzzled her neck, taking small nips from it, smiling. "A bear and a cougar are usually a mean combination."

"Yes."

"But we aren't," he said, sifting his fingers lazily through her hair, marveling at its texture and color.

Lark shook her head, continuing to explore his naked form. "I never realized these feelings existed," she confided, holding his gaze. "My heart shines like Holos."

He understood what Lark meant. He never wanted her to change. "I like the way you think. More importantly, the way you feel."

A hint of urgency crept into her low voice and Lark paused in exploring his back. "Was I . . . I mean . . ."

Matt caressed her lips with a feather-light kiss. "You were perfect," he assured her, wanting to erase the doubt in her luminous eyes. "No man could have asked for a more responsive woman." Concerned, he gently withdrew from her and brought the sheet over them, then held her against him. "You're a very special woman, Lark," he said. "I don't know whether it's the hot Apache blood in your veins or your wild Irish ancestry. Whatever it is, you're like a thoroughbred."

Lark traced patterns on his chest with her fingertips. In another hour, dawn would awaken the world, but for now she languished in the wonderful feelings that made her glow. "My mother, Mourning Dove, said that when a warrior claimed my heart, I would fly like an eagle toward Holos. I think I know now what she meant."

Matt closed his eyes, never wanting to let Lark out of his embrace. "Honey, you made me fly higher and farther than any eagle ever could."

"I felt like sunlight on water."

"You were the earth, Lark—fertile, rich, and giving. Very few women know how to give so fully."

Lark struggled to sit up on one elbow, holding Matt's gaze. She saw happiness for the first time in the depths of his intelligent gray eyes. It made her want to press herself to him and somehow convey that she felt the same. "Giving back to you is natural," she murmured.

Despite his effort not to, Matt remembered Katie and how she had lain on her back in bed that first night after their wedding, tense and unmoving. When he had touched her, she had not responded. Matt still couldn't understand it. "Some women, a lot of women, don't enjoy what we shared."

Fascinated, Lark sat up, no longer shy about her nakedness. She reveled beneath his inspection, feeling as if she were truly a part of him now. "How could they not?" She gestured toward the eastern window where the first rays of the morning sun stole through the lace curtains. "You gave me sunlight! I felt as if warm waves were flowing through me, like a raging river out of control. How could any woman not enjoy that?"

"I've often asked myself that, Lark. I don't have an answer."

She frowned, resting her chin in her folded hands. "Mother often said that among the Apache, this closeness was necessary. When Ria, a woman on the ranch, married last year, I wondered why she was so happy the morning after." A glow came to Lark's animated features. "Now I know what she was smiling about!"

"Come here, golden cougar." Matt pulled her on top of him as he rolled onto his back. In her shining eyes he saw her surprise and then the pleasure that throbbed palpably between them. His flesh burned hotly wherever she came in contact with him. Her breasts became more firm, the nipples hard. Roving his hand across her rounded hip, he murmured, "You're mine and I always want you to smile like that after we make love." His voice caught as her hair pooled across his chest. "I want to always make you happy, Lark."

She laid her head on Matt's chest, feeling the thunderous beat of his heart beneath her ear. "I'm so happy, I'm afraid I'll fly apart, my bear." Savoring his firm body and feeling his shaft begin to grow beneath her hip, Lark leaned upward, kissing his mouth. This time, she tried to duplicate the motion she remembered that he'd used on her. Startled when Matt gripped her hard, his mouth claiming her hotly in return, she relaxed, sinking against him. Her blood sang and Lark felt like so much molten sunlight as he worshipped her lips. And when he caressed the corners with his tongue, she shivered.

Groaning, Matt gently broke the torrid kiss and moved Lark to his side. "You're a wild-blooded cat and if we don't stop now, I won't be able to say no later." Seeing the disappointment in her shining eyes, he added, "Listen to me, Lark. You're going to be very sore from what we've done this morning. As much as I want to bed you again, I don't think it's wise."

She pouted for only a moment, drowning in his burning gaze. To be cherished was such an overwhelming feeling that she acquiesced with a nod of her head.

A fiercely protective feeling smothered Matt, and it took every ounce of his remaining control to get out of bed. "I've got to leave whether I want to or not." In an effort to ease their parting, he discussed another subject as he dressed. "Paco and I finished breaking all those colts. In a day or two we can herd them into Prescott and pick up the money from the U.S. Army. We'll probably be gone a few days."

"A few days?" At that moment she couldn't bear to think of their being separated for so long. At that moment, all she wanted was to throw her arms around Matt and hold him as he had held her: with all her heart. Sliding off the bed, she collected her nightgown and slipped back into it, retying the bows.

After dressing, Matt drew Lark into his arms. "I don't want to leave you for that long, honey, but we've got to let ranch matters take precedence."

Burying her head against his chest, Lark closed her eyes. "The ranch and the people come first," she agreed faintly, savoring the last precious minutes within his arms.

Within half an hour, the wranglers would awake. "I've got to go," Matt whispered, placing his mouth against her lips.

Reluctantly, she agreed.

Lark swallowed her surprise when Captain Frank Herter

arrived late that afternoon. This time he was wearing the garb of an ordinary wrangler and not his U.S. Army uniform. Lark recalled that he had talked about retiring.

"Afternoon, Miss Lark," he said, tipping the edge of his hat to her. "I heard that Paco was shot by Shanks. I thought I would come out and lend you a hand."

"Thanks for the offer. Paco's going to be fine, but we are running shorthanded, captain—"

"I'm retired now, Lark, so just call me Frank." He gestured to the left. "Who's that? Another new wrangler?"

Lark turned. "That's Matt Kincaid."

"The man Ga'n wounded?" Frank asked, recalling their conversation the last time he was out at her ranch.

Lark avoided Herter's penetrating gaze. "Yes. He's helped me—all of us—so much."

"Sounds like you're a little sweet on him," Frank teased gently.

Lark chewed her lower lip, heat prickling her cheeks. Frank Herter had always had startling insight into her, which kept Lark forever off balance, but she also sensed the approval in his eyes and in his amused voice. "Uh, yes, a little sweet," she admitted.

"You never could fib well, Lark," Frank said. "Come on, introduce me to this man of yours. He sounds like someone made of good mettle."

Lark was eager to introduce the two men. Frank had always said he was sweet on her. Now he seemed to realize at once that she was Matt's woman. How could he? Was it written all over her face? Stepping back so the two men could shake hands, she moved to Matt's side.

Frank held the cowboy's assessing gaze. "To be honest, Mr. Kincaid, I've just retired from the army and am looking for a job as a wrangler. Miss Lark knows I'm good with horses, and I know you're running short-handed. How about it?"

Lark's mouth fell open and she quickly shut it. "Frank,

are you sure? I mean, we can't pay you that much—at least not yet.''

"Don't worry, I've got my army pension to supplement me. What do you say, Lark? Do we have a deal?'' He thrust out his gloved hand toward her.

Lark looked to Matt.

"Once we get those colts to Prescott, we can afford him,'' Matt told her, reading the question in her eyes.

"The budget can stand it?''

He smiled down at Lark, wanting to sweep her into his arms. Her cheeks were flushed, her eyes filled with love for him alone. "It can.''

Lark gripped Frank Herter's hand. "Thanks, Frank. You're going to be an awful good replacement.''

"I've got a job for you,'' Matt said, motioning to the corral. "Tomorrow morning, we're taking those colts to town.''

"Sounds good to me,'' Frank said, smiling at both of them. "I can hardly wait to see the look on Cameron's face when we come riding in with them. Talk around Prescott is that the Gallagher Ranch is dying.''

With a snort, Lark placed her hands on her hips. She told him of the two attempted kidnappings, and Cameron's attempt to swindle the water rights out of her.

Rubbing his lean jaw, Frank pursed his lips and exchanged a look with Kincaid. "Well, I heard tell Cameron's going to get your water at any cost. Just watch your backside, that's all.''

"We've already had a taste of Cameron's methods,'' Matt muttered. "Tomorrow, when we go into Prescott, I'm going to telegraph Phoenix and ask for a marshal to intervene up here and investigate Cameron.''

Shrugging, Frank rested his right hand on his pistol. "Won't do any good. Prescott's Cameron's territory, and he backs up his brand of law with guns like Shanks. I'm sure Lark's already told you that.''

"If we can get outside law enforcement to come in, it will help.''

"Still might be a showdown," Frank warned.

Matt smiled grimly. "That's fine with me. Cameron's going to pay for all he's done or else."

Jud Cameron paced the length of his office, his fists clenched behind the expensive black coat he wore. Shanks lay sprawled on the floor, nursing the bloody nose his boss had just given him. Cameron's knuckles ached, but it had given him great pleasure to punish the stupid bastard.

"Of all things," he shouted, "you let her escape! First that goddamned Injun gets his war partner killed by Kincaid, then you lose her out of pure idiocy!"

Shank's feet were blistered and bloodied from the long trek back from Devil's Canyon. It had taken him nearly twenty-four hours to reach the road to Prescott. From there, he'd hitched a ride on a passing stagecoach.

"I told you, boss, she fought like a wildcat! I had to let her go!"

Breathing hard, Cameron hunkered over the gunslinger on the floor.

"You're worthless, Shanks. Worthless. Get up!"

Eyeing Cameron warily, Shanks got slowly to his feet. He hobbled over to the chair and sat down.

Cameron glared at him. "I'm giving you one last chance to square things between us, or I'm firing you. And I'll make damned sure no one hires you as a gun in the Tucson Indian Ring. You understand?"

Shanks nodded, burning beneath Cameron's black gaze. "What do you want me to do?"

"Get Ga'n sobered up, then take the boys on a little ride to Bottleneck Valley. The Gallagher Ranch sits at the narrow end, and there's a thousand acres of dry grass surrounding them." He jabbed his finger at Shanks. "I want you to start a fire at the western end of the valley. The wind blows from west to east. The ranch sits downwind of that thousand acres and it'll go up in smoke, just like the rest of that goddamned valley. All that will be left are the wells, and that's all I want. That breed will sign then. She'll have no buildings, her hay crop for the winter will be gone, and there will be no reason for her to stay.''

The plan seemed simple enough to Shanks. Most important, it would allow him to avoid Kincaid's deadly gun. ''That's a good idea, boss.''

''While they're fighting that fire, I want you to steal that Kentucky Stud the breed owns,'' Cameron went on. ''Take the horse south to Tucson. You and Ga'n will be responsible for his arrival there in good health. Deliver him to Robert McCray over at the Double Deuce Ranch. I've made a deal with McCray: he keeps the stud, but I get half his offspring for the next two years. That way I can improve my horse herd and get better money from the army.''

His eyes bulging, Shanks struggled to speak. ''You want me to cross that infernal desert with that stud?''

''You'll have Ga'n as your guide. That Injun knows how to make juice leak out of rock, if he has to. Tell him I'll pay twenty dollars if he'll take the job. I'll telegraph ahead and have McCray waiting with another job for Ga'n once he arrives. Money talks and Ga'n will listen.''

Rubbing his aching jaw, Shanks asked, ''What if Kincaid gets wind that we stole the stud? He's crazy enough to follow us.''

''He's not an Injun. There's no way in hell he's going to try and ride across that desert in pursuit.'' Cameron smiled. ''Besides, he's going to be too busy rebuilding a burned-out ranch, unless I miss my guess. Anyway, by that time Lark Gallagher will be happy to sell what's left of her father's holdings to me. She won't have the gumption to start over again. It would take too much money and she hasn't got it.''

Shanks warmed to the idea. ''When do you want it done?''

''As soon as possible. Get the boys from my ranch, all

ten of them. Then ride east and find Ga'n. You know where he usually stays. He'll be nursing his hatred of Kincaid for killing his war partner. I know he'll want revenge and will like the idea of stealing a horse. That's what the Apache are best at—murdering and thieving.''

Lark rode the magnificent Kentucky Stud back toward the ranch. Her mind wasn't on the stallion's playful antics, but on Matt. He'd left for Prescott four days ago with the colts, taking Frank Herter with him. Why weren't they back yet? Had something happened to them? She tried to curb her worry. Ever since Matt had made love to her, her heart had opened like a flower struck by Holos, and she felt invisibly bound to him—forever.

As she rode the last three miles to the ranch, she agonized over the devastating drought. Holos had sucked every last bead of moisture from the earth; the grass stood nearly two feet high but it was withered and dry, rustling in the infrequent wind. The three ponds on Lark's land were drying up at an alarming rate, and she wondered whether they could survive this, the worst drought in her memory. In the deep blue sky, there wasn't a cloud to be seen over the green-caped mountains that surrounded the valley.

When she slipped off Kentucky's bare back, Paco greeted her. She patted the tall, sleekly muscled stallion and handed the reins to her foreman.

"Anything, Paco?"

The Mexican shook his head sadly. "Nothing, *patrona,* but they will return soon. I know they will."

Anguished, Lark wondered. Would Matt and Frank come home in the back of a buckboard drawn by Father Mulcahy, bullets in their backs? She shivered, though the temperature was well into the nineties, the noontime heat bearing down upon the thirsty land. Touching her aching heart, she headed back to the broodmare barn to check on the latest foals, trying to escape her terrifying thoughts. She loved Matt with her whole being. She could still taste his wonderful male mouth on hers, still sense his masculine scent teasing her nostrils.

Near midnight, as she sat in the office with the kerosene lamps brightly lit, Lark fought off tiredness. Everyone on the ranch was sleeping, except for the posted guard making his rounds. Matt and Frank still weren't back. Something had happened. Something terrible. She gripped the fountain pen between her fingers, the numbers blurring before her bloodshot eyes. Since Matt had left, she'd slept poorly, tossing and turning, missing his warmth, missing him. Sudden neighing of horses in the corral alerted Lark instantly. She was on her feet, running out of the office and down the hall toward the front door. She halted on the wooden porch, her heart pounding. There! Two riders bathed in the light of the full moon were coming down the hill toward the ranch. Matt! Her lips parted and she waved breathlessly.

Matt's exhaustion was ripped away when he saw Lark's slender form standing on the porch. When she waved her hand, he straightened up, a powerful infusion of emotions sweeping through him. Four of the most godawful days had passed without her sleek, loving body beside him. He missed her laughter, her voice. Most of all, he missed her.

From his slouched position on his own horse, Frank Herter glanced over at Kincaid. "Looks like you're a sight for sore eyes, Kincaid."

Matt grinned, urging his fatigued gelding into a ground-eating trot. "I think I am. She is, too."

"Go ahead. I'll be heading to the bunkhouse as soon as I take care of my horse," Frank called.

Kincaid urged his gray into a canter down the hill and into the front yard.

"Matt!"

He pulled his animal to a halt and instantly dismounted. Lark flew off the porch, her arms wide. Dusty and tired, Matt dropped the reins. "Come here!" he called to her huskily. She was wearing the gold dress, her hair loose and flowing like a black mane across her shoulders. Her eyes were wide with joy, her full lips parted. Matt braced himself as she threw herself into his arms. He crushed her to him, burying his face in her hair.

"God, I've missed you," he muttered thickly, whirling her around.

"Oh, Matt!" Lark cried, and began to kiss him with wet, puppy-dog kisses.

He laughed, kissing her in return, seeking, finding her soft, smiling lips. "Come here," he growled, covering her mouth with his own. Her heart was beating hard against his chest, her body pressed tightly to his. He smelled the lavender soap on her skin, and the fresh fragrance of pine in her hair. Drowning in her sweetness and the liquid warmth of her mouth, he groaned.

Reluctantly Matt set Lark down on her feet, keeping an arm around her as she swayed unsteadily. He laughed shakily, realizing she was just as swept away by the kiss as he had been.

Frank entered the yard and dismounted. He tipped his hat to Lark, who was flushed and breathless. "Evening, Miss Lark." He untied a parcel from the back of the gray's saddle and handed it over to Kincaid, who thanked him. "Here, Matt, I'll take that cayuse to the corral for you."

"Thanks, Frank. Next time it'll be my turn."

Lark smiled over at Frank, her lips tingling wildly. "I'm so glad to see you both back safe and sound."

"We had some business to take care of first," Frank said, "but I'm sure this man of yours will fill you in on all the details. G'night."

"Good night," Lark called softly, her arm wrapped around Matt's waist.

"Good night, Frank." Matt turned, absorbing Lark's rapt expression. "You look delicious," he confided in a low tone that only she could hear.

Happily she waited until Frank Herter had left. "The bunkhouse wranglers are asleep," she said, then added, "all except Frank." There was a question in her voice. Would Matt go to the bunkhouse and wait until Frank went to sleep before coming over to the house?

He gazed down at Lark, a slight smile tugging at his mouth. "Frank already knows about us, Lark."

Her brows flew upward. "What? But how?"

Taking her by the elbow, Matt led her toward the house. "I like the man, Lark. He's sharp." He lightly touched her cheek. "He saw your love for me in your eyes before we left for Prescott."

Climbing the steps, she shook her head. "Frank's always been like that with me."

"He's a keen judge of character. In a roundabout way, he let me know that he approved of us, saying that under the circumstances it must be tough for us to find ways to be alone together."

Lark shut the door and they stood just inside the foyer. "He amazes me."

"He thinks an awful lot of you," Matt offered, "and he's a good friend to both of us."

Mutely, Lark agreed. Drowning in Matt's heated gaze, she followed him into the bedroom and sat down on the rocker, watching as he shut the door. Matt walked over to her.

"Here, this is for you." He handed her the large parcel and then sat on the bed, tugging off his dusty boots and tossing them to one side.

"A gift?" Lark exclaimed, pulling off the brown string.

"Something I saw at Madam Bouchard's shop that I think you might look good in," he said, rising. He unbuttoned his shirt and let it drop to the floor, watching her animated features. Once again, Lark was his child-woman, so uninhibited that her happiness radiated like sunlight, touching everyone with her joy.

"Madam Bouchard's?" she whispered, her hands stilling over the parcel. "Oh, Matt . . ."

He unbelted his trousers and climbed out of them. "What?"

Her excitement deepened as she drank in the sight of him, his body taking on a silvery cast in the moonlight. "You're so beautiful," she breathed softly.

He chuckled and leaned down, kissing her lips. "Open the package, golden cougar."

Her hands trembling, Lark could barely concentrate on the package. He was naked, standing before her like a god of Apache legend, but a flesh and blood man who made her body tingle and aroused an oh-so-familiar ache between her thighs.

Her hand flew to her mouth as the crinkly brown paper fell aside. There, in her lap, lay the most beautiful dress she had ever seen. "It's beautiful!" she whispered in awe, hardly daring to touch the soft turquoise material edged with white lace.

Matt smiled and crouched down in front of her, resting his hands on her knees. "The color of the dress reminded me of the color your eyes turn when I make love to you."

"It's so expensive. Oh, Matt, how could you afford such an extravagance?"

He framed her face. "My golden cougar, who's so easily touched," he whispered, and slid his mouth against her lips.

A moan caught in Lark's throat and she hungrily pressed her mouth to Matt's. His hands caressed her breasts, gently kneading the hardened nipples that were begging to be touched.

Matt caught himself and slowly drew away from Lark's velvet lips, staring hungrily at her. His hands remained on her waist. "I need to wash up first. I smell . . ."

She laughed lightly. "You smell wonderful to me, Matt Kincaid."

He rubbed his jaw. "I need to shave, too. Wait here for me?"

"I'll wait forever."

Grinning, Matt got up. "I won't make you wait that long. I'll bathe in the creek in back of the ranch house. Get undressed and I'll come to you in bed."

After hanging the lovely dress in the closet, Lark moved to the bed and slipped beneath the covers. Wide-awake now, she pulled at the thin quilt as she waited for Matt. To her, it was a long fifteen minutes before he padded back into the bedroom, his hair damp against his skull, his jaw scraped free of that four-day-old beard. As he approached the bed, she smiled and held out her hand to him.

"I missed you so much."

Matt slipped beside Lark and took her into his arms. She was like a wriggly puppy, and he smiled. "You were never out of my thoughts," he said, and pressed his mouth to her smiling lips, drinking in her sweetness. With a groan, he broke the kiss.

"We've got some things to discuss."

Lark felt immediate fear. "You telegraphed Phoenix for a marshal?"

"Yes."

"And?"

"We won't know anything for at least two weeks. Dealing with government services is always slow, Lark," he said, seeing the disappointment in her features.

"What about the horses?"

He propped himself up on one elbow. The shadowy light emphasized Lark's proud Indian heritage, but it was her wide eyes that burned into his soul until he burst into a bright, hungry flame. Caressing her hair, he said, "We got three hundred for the colts, like I figured we would." He grinned. "Afterward, Frank and I went over to the Silver Spur Saloon to play a little poker."

"You did? Both of you?"

"Frank's a damned good card player. You should have seen the card shark we met. Oliver Preston was his name. The gent had just blown in from Flagstaff and was ready to line his pockets with our money. We raked in four hundred dollars off him instead. Preston thought he was going to fleece two cowboys, but we turned the tables on him."

Lark sat up, her eyes large. "You won money?"

The satisfied smile lingered on Matt's face. "Frank won a hundred and fifty and I won the rest." He touched her chin. "That two fifty went into your new account."

"What new account?"

"I transferred all your money to a different bank. And I've applied for a new loan on the ranch at a lower interest rate. As soon as that comes through, we'll pay off Cameron's mortgage and be free of him forever."

Lark clapped her hands, delighted. "So you bought the dress with some of the poker money?"

"Sure did."

"And you used the colt money as grubstake in the game?"

Matt shook his head, seeing the worry in her eyes. "I'd never do that, Lark. I wouldn't risk your money. No, I had some money of my own. Frank had some with him, too, so we decided to sit down and fleece a wolf." He grinned. "We sure did. Preston was madder than a wet hen," he added, chuckling.

Relieved, Lark was able to laugh with him.

Absently he ran his hand across her gowned thigh, feeling the softness and warmth that were uniquely hers. He sat up and maneuvered her around so that she lay in his arms. "Enough of business. For the last three nights I've been dreaming of being with you again."

Lark waited impatiently, hungering for his touch. The gray of his eyes grew turbulent and intent as he slowly pulled each bow free, exposing the shadowed cleft between her breasts. With a tremulous sigh, Lark caressed his cheek. "I feel like a starving cougar for you," she admitted.

"And I'm a hungry bear."

Laughing softly, she closed her eyes as his hands slipped beneath the material. The instant he pulled aside her nightgown, exposing her shoulders and breasts, she tensed, waiting. As his teeth grazed the hardened nipple, a new, exquisite sensation bolted through her lower body.

Lowering Lark to the bed, Matt pulled the nightgown off her. Her eyes were dark and smoldered with lupine fire, and her golden, dusky skin gleamed with a thin film of perspiration. "You're so responsive," he said, sliding his hand across her flat belly.

His weight was welcoming and Lark smiled tremulously, sliding her arms around his shoulders and drawing him down upon her. "Love me," she coaxed huskily, opening her thighs to receive his thick shaft. This time, there was no pain, only the wonderful joy of having him fill her. She was a vessel for him, able to hold him gently in her embrace. A sound of utter pleasure stole up her slender throat as he moved his hips experimentally, and her heart soared with the knowledge that she could give him equally intense pleasure in return. Again, she slowly moved her hips, first one way, then the other.

Matt groaned. "Sweet God in heaven, Lark . . ." Fighting for air, he eased himself forward. Lark was so small, yet he felt her heated, liquid depths give way to his thrust. Unable to stop himself, or the explosion building steadily within him, he began to move more urgently, with each stroke losing himself more completely. He heard Lark sobbing his name. She was his woman, wild, hot, and yielding beneath him. Their flesh moved slickly against each other, their breath came in ragged gasps, and their fingers gripped desperately.

The instant Matt placed his hand beneath Lark's hips, lifting her to another angle, a heat rolled through her, catching her breathless, stunning her in its wake. She cried out, clutching him as her body turned to molten heat beneath his mighty thrusts. As she spun into a shower of rainbow light, directionless, she heard him groan like a bear claiming his territory. He gripped her hard, his body taut beneath her hands. A weak smile fled across her mouth as she sank beneath him, fulfilled as never before.

Kentucky's shrill scream brought Lark out of a deep

sleep. She jerked into a sitting position. Matt stirred beside her, his hand finding hers.

"What's wrong?" he muttered, barely opening his eyes. Hours earlier, they had fallen exhausted into each other's arms.

Lark twisted her head. "I don't know. I thought I heard Kentucky." She rubbed her face, trying to clear her groggy mind.

Matt lay back down on the pillow. "Probably just a dream. Come back here . . ."

But the stallion screamed again, and Lark knew it wasn't her imagination or a dream. She slipped quickly out of bed and pulled her nightgown over her head. "Let me go check at the office window," she said, her voice husky with sleep. "It's not like him to awake at this time of night and make such a fuss."

"Go ahead," Matt agreed.

Lark hurried down the hall to the office, which would afford her an excellent view of the barn area. Her hands pressed against the window, she gasped. Beneath the light of the full moon, she saw Ga'n and Bo Shanks leading Kentucky out of the barn. Then terror rooted her. To the west, all along the horizon, she saw fire.

"Matt!" she cried, racing back to the bedroom. He met her at the door. "Ga'n, Shanks! They're stealing Kentucky! And there's a prairie fire coming toward the ranch!"

He gripped her arm. "Get ahold of yourself," he ordered. "Get dressed. Those bastards probably set the fire." His eyes blazed in the darkness. "I'll try and stop them."

"No!"

Matt pulled Lark back into the bedroom. He grabbed his Levi's and threw on his shirt and boots. "Wake the men in the bunkhouse," he ordered. "I'll try and stop Shanks and Ga'n." Racing down the hall, he cinched the gun and holster around his hips and bolted out the door. His boots sounded hollowly on the porch as he ran to the

end and leaped into the yard. At least a half-mile away
he saw two shadowy riders heading for the safety of the
mountains, the stud in tow. "Sonofabitch!" He was too
far away to make a clear, safe shot. At this distance, any
bullet he fired might hit the valuable stallion instead. Matt
saw the guard lying near the barn, either dead or unconscious. He turned, his eyes widening. The entire horizon
was a red-orange color, turning darkness into day.
Retrieving the horse would have to wait. Right now,
every man jack of them would have to work to save the
ranch from the oncoming prairie fire.

Lark stood near Matt and the knot of men, women, and
children. They had watched the fire growing nearer and
nearer by the hour. Half the horizon was now an ugly
orange color, and licking yellow flames flared into the
sky. For two hours, Matt and the wranglers had worked
without rest to build a firebreak around the large ranch.
Lark gripped his hot, sweaty arm and shot him a
questioning look.

Breathing hard, Matt wiped his glistening face with the
back of his arm. "There's only one way to save the
ranch," he said.

She trembled, remembering their earlier conversation.
Matt had wanted to start a backfire that would burn
toward the oncoming inferno. The backfire would burn
the grass close to the ranch before the main wall of flames
arrived. It would be the lesser of two evils, Matt had told
all of them. The backfire wouldn't have the height or
intensity of the original fire stalking them. The backfire
might mean that the ranch buildings would sustain some
damage, or that the restless, panicked horses might injure
themselves, but at least they might be able to save the
ranch and animals. The fire in the distance was at least
six to eight feet high, twisting in shadowy shapes as it
bore down upon them.

"Lark?"

She swallowed hard, frightened. "Yes . . . do it."

He nodded. "Paco, get the torches," he ordered.

Paco nodded grimly. *"Sí, señor. Hombres! Pronto!"* They headed toward the firebreak with lighted torches.

Maria clung to Lark, watching the men. "Aiyee, *patrona*, will this work?"

"I don't know."

"If not, our ranch will burn. Oh, the horses! The foals! What are we to do?"

Lark absently patted the head of a child who was clinging to her trousered leg. "I don't know, Maria, I don't know." Her throat ached with smoke and tension. Never in her life had she seen a fire of this magnitude. Matt was right: Cameron must be behind it. Kentucky was gone, stolen, and Ga'n and Shanks had done it. Anger simmered in her. If they could save the ranch from this terrible inferno, she swore to Us'an she'd go after her enemies. Cameron wanted to destroy her, but she would never submit to the bastard. Never!

Buckets of water moved down a human chain of children, women, and elderly Apaches to the buildings closest to the backfire. The dry grass caught quickly. Within minutes, the wall of fire leaped to six feet in height and, like a hungry monster, headed toward the other wall that was now only a mile away. Sweat trickled down Lark's temples as she threw another bucket on the sides of the barn, trying to keep the wood soaked and therefore less vulnerable to the heat of the fire. Shouts and orders among the men were drowned out as the backfire roared with violent life, reminding Lark of an angry thunderstorm bearing down upon them.

They worked unceasingly for another hour, continuing to drench the buildings. Smoke curled and twisted above the barns, and everyone wore handkerchiefs over their faces to protect them from it. A shower of cinders began falling all across the ranch and Lark grew alarmed. Here and there, where those red-hot cinders floated down to earth, they started smaller fires. She worked with Frank Herter and a number of children, running to each spot and putting out the potential blazes. Sweaty faces blackened by ashes gleamed in the light of the inferno.

Choking and coughing, Lark turned away from the barn when she heard a roar grow louder behind her. The backfire was half a mile from the ranch, about to meet the original fire. The ranch hands suspended their activities, watching in awe and terror as the fiery mating took place.

Matt draped an arm around Lark's sagging shoulders, holding her hard against him. She was trembling from exhaustion. Everyone was, he thought grimly, blinking sweat from his eyes. The ranch people formed a semicircle around them, watching, waiting.

It was almost dawn, and the sky was lightening above them. Lark watched the rolling white and gray smoke tower hundreds of feet into the air, twisting at the whim of the capricious wind. The roar intensified and she gripped Matt, terrified.

"It'll be over soon," he whispered in her ear. "I think we're saved."

The walls of fire met and the combustion of air between them made the flames leap higher, wilder. Lark had never seen anything like it in her life. Then, suddenly, an awesome silence descended. She blinked, watching as the eight-feet-high flames dwindled to nothing but a few tiny fires spotting the valley here and there. A hoarse, jubilant cheer went up. She blinked her smoke-filled eyes, her throat too raw to allow her to join in.

Matt embraced her hard, once, then abruptly released her. "Frank, Paco, get us horses," he shouted over the crowd. "We're going after Ga'n and Shanks."

Stunned, Lark cried, "No!" She whirled on Matt, her voice raspy. "*I'm* going after them!"

"Like hell you are. You'll stay here, at the ranch, where it's safe."

Anger raged through Lark as she met and held his glare. "None of you can track like I can. I'm Apache. I know how to live and hunt off the land." She punched her chest with her thumb. "No, Matt, I'm going. And there's nothing you can say or do to stop me. You'll need a guide. You need me."

# Chapter 14

"Now, look," Matt said in a low voice once he got Lark inside the ranch office, "there's no way in hell I'm letting you go, Lark!" He wasn't going to argue the point with her in public.

Breathing hard, hands on hips, Lark held his tortured gaze. They were all exhausted from the hours spent fighting the fire, and her temper was short. "I'm not some white woman you can boss around, Matt Kincaid!"

"I'm not bossing you around because you're white, pink, or purple!" he roared back, pacing the office. What the hell was the matter with Lark? Didn't she realize how dangerous it would be to track Ga'n and Shanks? He shoved his fingers through his damp, dirty hair.

"You forget, I'm half Apache. I've been trained to track!"

"I wouldn't care if you were *all* Apache, I still wouldn't let you go." He turned to her, his hands open, his face pleading. "Dammit, I don't want you to get hurt."

Her eyes flashing, Lark muttered, "The only people to get hurt will be Ga'n and Shanks! I need Kentucky back! Without him, our entire breeding program is destroyed. Cameron knows that, too, the bastard!"

Matt was used to white women who meekly did as their husbands ordered. But not Lark. And not now. The defiant angle of her chin guaranteed that. Part of him loved her fiercely for her courage, but another part cowered in abject terror of losing her. Damn her bravery. Damn her Apache blood! ''I'll take Paco,'' Matt growled, daring her to challenge his decision.

Lark stared at him. All she could hear was their heavy, chaotic breathing in the room. They sounded like a bear and a cougar in a fight to the death. ''Paco's still injured. He'd never maintain the pace you're going to set. I know Ga'n. He'll push his horse until it dies and then he'll find another one and push it until it dies. If he has to, he'll go on foot. Believe me,'' she added, ''no one can match an Apache on foot. We can travel almost as many miles in a day on foot as on horseback and you know it! Paco will never be able to stand the bumping around that wound will take.''

''Then I'll take Herter.''

''I need him here to help fill in for Paco. He knows horses, Matt. He knows where to find them. We've got to breed twenty more mares to the second stallion, Hulega, before this season is over. Frank's the only one who can oversee all of those things. None of my other wranglers are trained in all aspects of the operation.''

He glared at her, his hands on his hips. ''Then I'll go alone. I will *not* take you, Lark. I won't lose you.''

She heard the iron will in his voice, but this was one time she would not stand idly by, no matter what Matt thought or felt. She would let him think she was staying behind and track him later. ''All right, go,'' she declared.

''You'll stay here with Paco and Herter?''

Lark ignored his question. ''You'll need an Apache mustang for a mount,'' she said, opening the door. ''He'll know how to forage for food in any kind of situation when a *pindah* horse would not. If you go to the desert, he'll be able to survive on cactus. No *pindah* horse can cross that desert without water. Let me get Maria to make you enough food to fill your saddlebags. I'll meet you in the stud barn.''

Matt stood there, scowling. Exhaustion pulled at him. Time was of the essence if he was going to find fresh tracks on Ga'n and Shanks. Kentucky was shod, so the trail would be easier to pick up.

In the bunkhouse, he packed a set of fresh clothes. A savage pleasure worked through him as he picked up his Winchester rifle. Already his mind was turning toward the hunt, knowing that Lark would be safe here at the ranch.

A murky dawn had arrived on the horizon just as Matt left. Paco stood on Lark's right, Herter on the left, watching him gallop across the now blackened valley.

Wearily, Lark turned to Paco. "I want a cottonwood saddle put on Four Winds."

Paco stared at her. "But, *patrona* . . . are you going after Señor Matt?"

"Yes." She looked up at Herter. "Frank, will you see that Maria packs my saddlebags with Apache food?"

Frank gave her a measuring look. Like everyone's, his face was darkened with smoke and grime. A slight smile hovered below his mustache. "You're going to follow him, aren't you?"

"Yes."

"I'll see to the provisions and your horse."

Relieved that at least Frank understood, Lark hurried to the broodmare barn, where she found Ny-Oden. Throughout the fire, he had been with the animals, talking soothingly to ease their panic. The shaman patted the bay mare's nose affectionately and watched Lark approach.

"You leave now, daughter?"

Lark halted and smiled wearily. "I'll never understand how you know certain things, grandfather."

He walked slowly toward a small room. "Us'an tells me what I need to know. If you follow Ga'n and Shanks, you will need powerful protection." He opened the creaky door and reached inside the shadowed depths.

"I have to go, grandfather. I know Matt won't be able to survive without my help."

"I understand." Ny-Oden held a five-foot cedar bow and a quiver filled with two-foot-long arrows between his gnarled hands. The ivory-colored flint tips on each arrow gleamed in the dim light. "Here, you will need these. To use a rifle will tell your enemy your position. Any food you kill must be done silently."

Reverently Lark took the bow and arrow. When she was a child, Ny-Oden had taught her how to use the weapon with deadly accuracy. The cedar of the bow was strong and smooth beneath her hand. Just knowing she had Ny-Oden's blessing gave Lark the confidence she needed. "Is there anything else I will need?" she asked in a husky voice.

The old shaman cocked his head, studying her in the silence of the barn. A mare snorted in the background. "Like a medicine person, you walk between two worlds, my daughter."

With a grimace, Lark muttered, "I'm finding out."

"The blood in your veins is both white and Apache. Men such as Matt Kincaid and Frank Herter have taught you that white blood is no different from The People's."

"You speak the truth, grandfather," Lark admitted softly. "Matt has changed my life in many ways."

"And you are comfortable with yourself?"

"As never before." She clasped his clawlike hand. "You knew all along, didn't you?"

His eyes sparkled. "Remember, I told you that if you decided to save Kincaid's life, many changes would occur within you?"

"I've found out what love is, grandfather. My heart is breaking because I'm not with him."

"Then, go. Us'an is with you. You will need his strength and endurance, which only he can bestow upon you in times of need."

Heartened, Lark leaned down and embraced the shaman. "Pray for both of us," she whispered, and then walked quickly out of the gloom.

Giving last-minute instructions to Paco and Frank, Lark knew the ranch would be in good hands while she was absent. Herter knew of Cameron's plan to get the water rights signed over to him and would make sure it didn't happen. As she mounted Four Winds, Lark lifted her hand to the gathered people, her extended family. Outside the group, Ny-Oden stood hunched over, watching her intently. Without a word, she nudged the mare into a ground-eating trot.

Lark knew that if Matt was aware of her presence too soon, he'd try to send her back to the ranch. It was easy to track his horse's hoofprints through the charred grass. At first the tracks headed north, then they swung east, and finally due south. Once on the slopes of the tree-clad mountains, where pine needles hid the evidence of hoofprints, Lark had to resort to more subtle signs such as broken branches on brush or disturbed pine needles.

By the time Holos was at his zenith, Lark had crested the last ridge. Below her, she could see the beginning of the great desert that spread like a vast red carpet in all directions. Her eyesight was sharp, and she could barely make out Matt, who had reached the edge of the desert. Taking a sip of precious water from one of her two canteens, Lark washed the liquid around in her mouth before swallowing it. She searched for signs of Ga'n and Shanks without success. Worry nagged at her: Kentucky was not a mustang who knew how to survive in the reaches of the vast desert. He hadn't been taught as a young horse to eat the bitter pulp of cactus for water and food. And even Ga'n could not force a horse to eat it if he didn't want to. How close was she to Ga'n? He'd sold his honor in her eyes by breaking his word to always protect her. He'd betrayed one of the most sacred trusts between two Apache people. Now Lark considered him an enemy, too.

Starting down the gentle incline, weaving through the pine trees, Lark remained alert, her thoughts always circling back to Ga'n. Like all Apaches, he was afraid to travel after dark, when it was said ghosts walked the land. But she knew Shanks wouldn't accept Ga'n's superstition. Traveling at night was cooler and less water was lost from the body. She herself felt uneasy about traveling at night, though her father had often traveled then without ever seeing a ghost. Wishing Ny-Oden had given her a small bag of ash to throw at any ghosts who approached to chase them away, Lark wrestled with her own fears.

When darkness fell, Lark found herself well into the desert. As long as the wind didn't blow too hard, the sand retained the hoofprints. Proud of Matt's ability to track, Lark contented herself with making a small camp. She hobbled her horse and shot a jackrabbit with her bow and arrow. After digging a hole in which to build the fire so it would not be seen, Lark skinned and placed the rabbit on a skewer. The food in her saddlebags was emergency rations only. All Apaches were taught to eat off the land and to conserve the food they carried. There might come a place or time during the trip when there was no food available, and the rations would save her life. Lark went in search of cactus, a source of liquid and food for her horse.

Night had almost completely fallen, and cicadas and crickets were chirping and singing. Lark located a small barrel cactus. The long, heavy spines had hooked ends. With her bowie knife, she deftly peeled away the protective covering of spines, then sliced up the cactus and carried huge chunks of the plant back to camp. Four Winds nickered, her ears pricked forward with interest. Lark carved out the pulpy interior and gave the mare her fill. Wanting to conserve her two canteens of water, she sucked on the astringent and bitter liquid of the cactus.

As she sought refuge from the chill of the encroaching night, Lark wrapped herself up in her wool saddle blanket. The cottonwood saddle became her pillow, and she slept lightly.

Matt squinted against the overhead sun. Shimmering waves of heat, reminding him of curtains blowing gently in the breeze, surrounded him. Under his guidance the hardy mustang pushed on at a steady trot. For the second day in a row, there had been little wind. That was good, because the tracks of the three horses were still clear. Judging from them, he guessed Ga'n and Shanks were at least half a day ahead of him. He wiped the sweat from his mouth with the back of his hand.

A rider appeared in the distance like a dancing mirage—an Apache on a spotted chestnut and white mustang. Frowning, Matt drew his Colt. Was it Ga'n? Was it a trap? Had Ga'n joined up with the Yavapai, whose territory this was?

His fear turned to surprise, then fury. It was Lark! She was sitting on her mustang at the base of a small, sandy hill peppered with yucca, waiting for him. Placing the loop back on the Colt .45, Matt reined his horse to a stop a few feet away from her.

"What the hell are you doing out here?"

"Waiting for you." Lark held his angry gray gaze. Motioning to his horse, she said, "He's thirsty. Have you cut open a cactus and given him water yet?"

Disgruntled, and realizing Lark had a much better knowledge of the terrain than he did, Matt smarted. "Not yet. You disobeyed me, Lark."

Her jaw went rigid, her eyes flashing with fire. "That is *my* horse that was stolen! I have every right to track him down!"

Yanking his mount next to hers, Matt reached out and grabbed her shoulder. "I ought to shake that fool head off your shoulders." His voice rose a notch, vibrating with irritation. "There isn't a woman alive who can go up against two thieves like Ga'n and Shanks." He glanced at the bow and arrow she carried. "Those weapons are child's toys against them."

Lark jerked away from him. "Stop shouting at me! If I can track and find you without your knowledge, don't you think I can find Ga'n and Shanks the same way? Arrows are silent. Guns will give away our position." Her nostrils flared with indignation. "You might as well get used to me being with you on this hunt. I'm not leaving, Matt Kincaid!"

Matt stared at her proud, tense form. She sat straight in the saddle, a warrior now, not just a woman. "I don't give a damn what you say, Lark, you're a woman. You don't have a man's strength—"

"I don't need a man's muscle!" she flared. "Apaches use their brains and skill instead. You may not realize it, but many Apache wives ride with their husbands into battle. They are equally dangerous and courageous. My mother was a chief, and I have her blood in me. To stay at home and let someone else try to get back my horse would bring shame on her and me. I won't do that." Dismounting, Lark drew her knife and went over to another barrel cactus, quickly slicing it open. When Matt dismounted and joined her, she prepared herself for his anger. Her hands shook as she gave the black mustang one handful after another of the pulp. Matt towered over her, his hands on his hips, anger radiating from him like the rays from Holos.

"I knew you'd need my help," she began defensively, risking a look into his dark face.

"I ought to—"

She lifted her chin defiantly. "What? Paddle me like a child?"

He took off his hat and scratched his damp scalp. "You're too old to paddle." Despite her Apache garb, she was beautiful in Matt's eyes. Settling the hat back on his head, his eyes shaded by the brim, he muttered, "Feed the damned horse and then let's get going." He jabbed a finger toward her. "The minute you can't keep up, I swear I'll hogtie you, ride to the nearest town, and make you stay there until this business is taken care of. Understand?"

She fed the last of the pulp to the mustang and wiped her hands on her trousers, then rose, holding Matt's intense gaze. Pride in her ability would not allow her to cower at his demands and threats. "I can outride or outwalk any *pindah*," she said. "Apaches are known for their stamina and endurance. I'll keep up with you."

Matt wasn't ready to relent. "It will only take once, Lark. Just once."

Relieved that he wasn't going to send her back to the ranch, Lark nodded. The noonday heat was stifling; the clothes they wore stuck damply to their skin.

Lark took up another subject, hoping to deflect his anger into something more constructive. "I'm worried about Kentucky."

"Why?"

She motioned for him to follow her to the hoofprints visible in the sand and crouched down next to them. "He's tiring badly," she said, showing how his hoofprints were distorted in the sand. "I don't think he's eating cactus to stay alive. Horses that aren't raised on it usually won't eat it. I found where Ga'n and Shanks spent the night and there were a number of uneaten pieces of cactus pulp lying around. I think Ga'n tried to get Kentucky to eat it for liquid, but he refused."

Matt knelt opposite her. "If Kentucky doesn't get water soon, he may die."

"Either that or they'll slow down and we can catch up with them.

"They didn't travel last night. That's good."

"Ga'n's afraid of the darkness," Lark said.

He held her gaze. "Are you?"

"My Apache side is."

A crooked smile softened his set features. "Maybe it's time to switch to your white side so we can travel at night and catch up with them."

She knew he was correct and reluctantly nodded. "I'll try."

Matt rose, helping her to her feet. Squeezing her work-worn hand, he murmured, "I'll keep you safe, Lark," but inside, abject fear ate at him. *Could* he keep her safe? She was so unlike most women, unafraid to face danger. Mounting, he watched her leap with graceful ease into the simply made cottonwood saddle. With the quiver filled with arrows on her back, the cedar bow in her left hand, she looked like an Apache warrior.

They kept up a steady walk-trot during the rest of the afternoon. Near evening, Lark stood up in the stirrups and pointed excitedly at a gnarled mesquite tree.

"Water!" she cried, and pushed her mustang into a fast trot.

To Matt, it was impossible to believe that water existed anywhere on this arid land dotted with cactus, mesquite, and yucca plants. He watched Lark slip from the saddle and move beneath the sparse shade provided by the forty-foot-high mesquite, kneeling down beneath it. Dismounting, he saw her digging rapidly, the darkened sand flying beneath her hands.

"Look," she told him excitedly, recognizing Kentucky's distinctive hoofprint nearby. "They've watered the horses here." She pointed to the churned up sand around where she was digging. "His prints are everywhere around this hole. Kentucky must have gotten a drink. He'll be good for another day, at least."

Matt looked around the immediate area. Lark was right. The animals had been eager to get to the small source of water. He scratched his head. "How did you spot water?"

Lark made a pleased sound as the hole she had dug at least two feet deep beneath the roots of the mesquite began to fill slowly with water. "This mesquite is larger than the rest, which means it has found a way to trap water and keep it longer than most of the others. Twisting a look up at Matt, she motioned for him to join her. "Come, drink your fill."

The water was brackish and gritty, but it was water, just as Lark had promised. Matt drank only two cupped handfuls before motioning for her to drink as well. Their thirst slaked, they brought over their eager mounts, one at a time, and allowed them to sip noisily from the hole.

Matt noticed the salmon-colored dusk and gold-tinted clouds high above them. They weren't rain clouds, but they signaled the possibility of wind. The prints would be hard to follow if the wind picked up and erased them.

Matt watched as Lark patted her favorite mare and checked the girth on the saddle. There was an economy to her motions, almost a delicacy. She was achingly feminine, and he found himself wanting her more powerfully than ever. Perhaps it was the constant danger that spurred his hunger to claim her as his own. Each minute was precious to him, because in the next he might lose her to a bullet or an arrow.

"Let's rest here and eat," he told her.

Surprised, Lark nodded and smiled. There was a pale pink wash to the bone-colored desert now; the land lay flushed and radiant. "It's good to let the horses rest after that big drink of water. Are you hungry?"

Matt nodded and began to strip the saddle off his gelding. "Yes." The word came out clipped and hard. He was still upset with her.

Lark shared her Apache food with Matt for dinner—ash cakes made of juniper ashes, cornmeal, salt, and in this case a bit of animal fat and pinyon nuts, to give it a nutty flavor.

"The Apache can live on one ash cake for many days," she said, watching Matt slowly chew.

"They aren't very appetizing," he muttered.

His face was deeply shadowed, emphasizing the chiseled strength of his features. A wellspring of warmth made her heart swell with such fierce love that Lark thought she might die of the unexpected feelings rushing through her. Despite Matt's anger over her appearance, she was glad to be with him.

He glanced over at her. He was still simmering with irritation, but there was no sense holding on to his anger, he decided. He loved her too damned much.

He filled the canteens, set them near their saddles, and sat down close to where Lark was crouched. "Ga'n is moving in a southeasterly direction, away from the Hassayampa River," he said. "I don't think he wants to risk being seen by the Yavapai, who have many rancherias along that stretch of water.''

Lark agreed. The Yavapai were the enemy of the Apache. "He'll avoid them at all costs.''

"So you think he'll stick to open desert, avoiding all white and Yavapai trails?'' Matt guessed.

Lark nodded. "Ga'n runs a greater risk of being discovered by the Yavapai than by the cavalry or a wagon train.''

Matt frowned, mulling over the possibilities in his head. "Where do you think he's heading?''

"I would think he'd want the safety of Apache territory.''

"That means San Carlos or the White Mountain region.''

"Yes.''

It would be dark in about three hours. With a grimace Matt finished off the last ash cake; they tasted terrible. "I want to travel tonight,'' he said, knowing Lark would balk.

Her heart pounded, but she knew Matt would send her back if she refused to ride with him. "All right. We'll take an hour's rest and then saddle up.''

# Chapter 15

The moon had risen near midnight. Lark tried to concentrate on using the silvery light to follow the hoofprints. Anxiety stalked the edges of her mind. Ny-Oden had filled her head full of stories about ghosts that walked the land at night. She feared seeing an owl, knowing it was a dire warning of danger.

Near two in the morning, Matt called a halt. Wearily Lark slid off Four Winds, giving the sturdy mustang mare a well-deserved pat. The animals were thirsty and hungry. She spent another half hour finding and cutting up barrel cactus pulp for them, her senses constantly on guard, an uneasy feeling hovering around her.

When she made her way back to their camp beneath the shelter of a small mesquite tree, she saw worry etched in Matt's exhausted features. Sinking down beside him on a blanket, she sat tensely, listening to the night sounds. Not far away, she heard the ominous hoot of an owl.

"Lark? What's wrong?"

"An owl. It's a warning," she said softly, trying to penetrate the deep gloom of the night.

Matt stared up at her, holding the Winchester rifle across her lap. "Did you hear a movement?" Maybe they were closer to Ga'n and Shanks than he'd originally thought.

"No." Lark gnawed her lower lip. "Owls are a warning by the spirit people, Matt. They come to you only if there is danger nearby."

He slid an arm around her tense shoulders. "What kind of warning?"

"I don't know," she admitted, trembling. Her fingers tightened around the rifle. "One of us should keep watch while the other sleeps."

"Good idea."

"I'll take first watch. I'm too frightened to sleep."

He kissed her cheek, inhaling her musky fragrance. "Okay. Wake me in two hours?"

"Yes."

Matt jerked awake. Had it been a noise that had shaken him out of sleep? A nightmare? He sat up, searching for and finding Lark standing three hundred feet away where the first threads of a gray dawn were visible, silhouetting her tall, willowy figure. He was about to speak to her when she suddenly crouched. What the hell?

Automatically his hand went for the gun at his side. He heard a sound. Was it some kind of animal? Just as he got into a kneeling position, Lark turned in one graceful motion and sprinted toward him.

Her eyes were wide, her breath harsh. Relief washed through her when she saw that Matt was awake with his gun drawn. She knelt beside him.

"Yavapai!" she exclaimed, pumping a round into the chamber.

Matt gripped her arm. "How many?"

"Five. It's a war party. They're half a mile away, coming west on foot, toward us."

"Take it easy," he soothed. "Let's saddle up and ride hard. I don't want to confront them. If we fire these rifles, we're liable to attract Shanks's attention. We can't risk it."

Lark was more than willing to evade the war party. In no time, they had saddled the mustangs. As she leaped into the saddle, Lark could see them more clearly, gray ghosts coming out of the darkness. Sinking her booted heels into Four Winds, she leaned low on the mustang so as not to be a possible target.

Matt gestured for Lark to ride well ahead of him. He didn't want her to be endangered by a stray bullet in case they were discovered. The mustangs wove in and around sagebrush, yucca, and cactus, galloping for almost an hour before slowing down. To the east, the sky had turned a glorious shade of pink and red, flooding the surrounding land with vibrant color. Matt rode up alongside Lark.

"All right?"

She nodded. "I was so afraid. I kept hearing things out there in the night. I thought it was ghosts."

He gripped her hand and squeezed it hard. "No, flesh-and-blood men, honey. You did a good job."

Weariness tugged at Lark. She hadn't slept in twenty-four hours and another long, hot day stretched ahead of them. Riding in a large circle around the Yavapai warriors, they finally picked up Kentucky's trail once again.

Holos was beating down, sapping Lark of what little strength she had left. For the last six hours, they had pushed on without rest.

"Look," Matt said, pointing to the left. "If I don't miss my guess, that's the Agua Fria River."

Lark shaded her eyes. There, in the shimmering waves of heat, she saw what looked like a small river. Her mouth was dry, and she longed to wash the grit and sweat from her skin. "I wonder if Shanks and Ga'n are there."

"Could be," Matt agreed. He studied her intently for a moment. "If they aren't, let's rest awhile there. We can get washed up and you can sleep."

Praying that the river was free of Yavapai rancherias, Lark gave Matt a brave smile. She had endured the torturous ride just as she had promised him.

"Most women couldn't have gone half the distance you have," he admitted, riding close to her, their legs occasionally touching.

Lark rallied beneath his praise. Very soon, the shimmering heat waves disappeared and she gazed hungrily at the green mesquite that lined either shore. A number of birds, among them woodpeckers that made their homes in the saguaro cactus, flitted nearby. Matt rode ahead, his rifle resting across his thighs.

When Lark arrived at the sandy bank scattered with lamb's-quarter, curly dock, and sedge grasses, Matt lifted her from the saddle. "Go get a bath and then sleep," he told her. "I'll take care of the horses."

Grateful, Lark turned and embraced him briefly. "Thank you."

The river was little more than a shallow stream, barely knee-deep. Seeing no evidence of human beings, Lark quickly stripped off her clothes, knelt in the cooling water, and scrubbed her skin with a handful of grass she had retrieved from the bank. As the cooling liquid sluiced across her hot, sweaty body, she uttered a soft moan of relief. Next she rinsed her hair free of grit and sand.

Matt had spread out a blanket beneath a towering mesquite. He divided his attention between watching Lark bathe and staying alert for unwelcomed visitors. Lark was like a sleek golden cougar, the water gleaming off her tall, proud figure. Her hair, heavy with water, was plastered like a second skin against her young, uptilted breasts and long back. He smiled, thinking how beautiful she truly was. Her flesh was a dusky gold, and he vividly remembered touching her, kissing her. The look of utter enjoyment on her face made him ache; the soft smile tilting the corners of her lips enticed him.

Lark turned toward the bank, leaning over and squeezing the excess water from her hip-length hair. She smiled over at Matt. "I feel alive again!"

He handed her a fresh red cotton shirt. "You look beautiful."

Looking up, Lark heard the tremor in Matt's tone. Heat collected between her thighs as she stood before him. His eyes burned with desire, telling her of his need for her.

Lark barely grazed his stubbled cheek with her fingers. "Let me dress and then I'll lie down and sleep."

Matt knew she was right not to encourage his lust. It would be far too dangerous to make love now. Sunlight made her black hair dance with sapphire highlights as it outlined her glorious young form. He swallowed hard and nodded. "Go ahead. I'll keep watch this time."

Lark awoke slowly in the late afternoon heat, sprawled across the blanket on her belly. The whirring of a katydid caught her groggy attention as she lifted her lashes to see Matt standing naked in the river washing himself. He was beautiful . . . .

Matt left the river and pulled on a set of fresh clothes. His face, once lined with fatigue and tension, looked more relaxed. Lark's gaze settled hotly on his mouth.

So, this is what love is, she thought. A wonderful, euphoric sensation, like an eagle soaring through the sky. No wonder her mother had been so happy with her father. No wonder she'd often had a soft, shy smile on her mouth. No wonder her father's eyes had danced with undisguised warmth. Lark felt closer to her parents because of her new understanding. Simultaneously she understood her father's raw grief when Mourning Dove had died.

The thought that Matt might be killed by either Shanks or Ga'n sent such an unexpected pang through her heart that she sat up. Her unbound hair slid across her shoulders as she drew her legs up to her chest.

"Feel any better?" Matt asked, sitting down on a log to pull on his boots.

Lark's eyes were fraught with darkness. "No . . . yes."

He knelt in front of her. "What's this I see?" he teased, lightly smoothing her wrinkled brow with his thumb. "Did you have bad dreams?"

With a muffled sound, Lark threw herself into his arms, and clung to him, burying her head beneath his chin. The moment his strong arms closed around her, she took a deep, ragged breath.

Stroking her hair, Matt held her tightly, sensing her anguish. "What is it, my golden cougar?"

His deep, calm voice soothed her terror. "I—I now understand my father's grief after my mother died," she began haltingly. "Four seasons ago, Mourning Dove died of the white man's sickness. I couldn't understand then why my father never smiled or laughed afterward, why he became like a ghost."

Matt gently eased her from him, forcing her to look up at him. "Your father loved your mother very much, Lark."

She nodded, feeling the heat of tears pricking her eyes. "And I love you with that same fierce feeling. I never understood their love, Matt. Until now . . ."

He leaned over, kissing her cheek. "We've got a love like that, yes. It's so rare, Lark, that sometimes it scares me."

Nuzzling Matt's cleanly shaved cheek, Lark stole her hands around his massive neck. "I'm afraid of losing you," she quavered.

"I carry the same fear of losing you, Lark."

"Now I understand why you didn't want me along." She rubbed the cleft between her breasts, trying to will away the fear in her heart.

With a faint smile, Matt tilted her stubborn chin upward. "We're going to live to be very old and very happy together, my woman. That's a promise."

"How do you know? Only medicine men and women can see future events."

"I feel it here, in my heart."

Leaning her head against his chest, Lark closed her eyes. "My heart is too frightened to feel anything else, right now."

"Then trust mine," Matt teased huskily.

It would be so easy to bring Lark into his arms and love her. He wanted to take away the pain in her eyes and kiss away the hurt on her tight lips. He wanted to hear her cry out in passion and satisfaction, not out of fear of their unknown future.

Breaking the warmth that bound them to each other, Matt murmured, "We've got to get going. While you were asleep, I did a little tracking, and it looks like Shanks is continuing to follow the river south."

Reluctantly Lark sat up, forcing her thoughts back to the present situation. "Ga'n's being forced to stay near rivers or creeks in order to provide Kentucky with water," she observed.

"That will save us the problem of finding water for our own animals," Matt said, getting to his feet. He held out his hand. Her grip was firm, her fingers slender.

"I'd like to know whether Ga'n's going to take Kentucky to an Apache chief or sell him to the whites," Lark said.

"With Shanks along, my guess is he's taking the stud to a white man."

"Is it possible Shanks is taking Kentucky to someone in the Tucson Indian Ring?"

Matt walked with her toward the hobbled horses. "That's what I was thinking. It would make sense to assume Cameron's behind all this, and that Shanks is acting on his behalf. If that's true, they're probably heading to either Phoenix or Tucson."

Lark saddled Four Winds. "Why?"

"Frank said the members of the Ring are probably located in the major cities of Arizona, where they have access to a telegraph and can keep in touch with one another." Matt threw the heavy leather saddle over his bay gelding. "A buyer for Kentucky may have already been found."

Lark nodded. "Cameron knows how important Kentucky is to our ranch. If I lose the stallion, I've lost everything."

Matt mounted up. "There are a lot of rich land barons

around either city who would pay good money for your stallion.''

Lark leaped gracefully into the saddle and gave Matt a disgruntled look as they began to follow the river southward. "If Ga'n sells him to the Apaches, we'll have a good chance of getting him back. Once a chief found out he was stolen from me, he'd give him to us. That's the Apache way.''

Matt pulled his hat a little lower to shade his eyes from the glaring sun. "We'll have an idea where they're heading once the Agua Fria meets up with the Gila River,'' he told her. "If they go east, they'll be heading toward Phoenix. If they go southeast, Tucson.''

Near dusk, they spotted a wagon train consisting of five schooners camped near the river. Matt gave Lark a worried glance. "Better let me do the talking. These people are from back east and might panic when they see you.''

Lark understood and dropped behind Matt's horse. Spotted oxen and a few horses were foraging near the river. A knot of white people were standing together outside the wagon train itself. Lark's hand tightened around the Winchester balanced across her lap.

As Matt drew closer, he saw why the fifteen people were gathered in a tight circle: someone had recently died and a cross had just been erected over a freshly dug grave. Those fifteen faces were now trained on him and Lark.

He could feel their distrust. The children hid behind their mothers' skirts. The men held their rifles in readiness. Matt's heart started a slow, hard pound. They didn't look at all friendly. How would they react to Lark? He didn't want to lose her to a bullet from one of these bearded men dressed in somber black trousers and wrinkled cotton shirts. The apparent leader, a man with a flaming red beard, wearing a flat-brimmed black hat, stepped out of the group, his rifle pointed at Matt.

"Best stop there, mister," he warned in a gravelly voice.

Matt glanced back at Lark. There wasn't time to instruct her on what he wanted her to do. He sat easily in the saddle, purposely keeping his hand away from his own gun.

"We're just passing through," he called. "Was wondering if you might have seen a drover and an Apache with a big sorrel stud in tow."

"We saw 'em all right." The man's round face grew scarlet and he jerked a thumb over his shoulder. "That Apache savage just killed our wagon master."

Lark gasped.

Matt held up his hand. "The name's Matt Kincaid. The woman with me, Lark Gallagher, is tracking for me. We're hunting those two down. They stole the horse they've got with them."

The leader eyed them angrily, his green gaze settling on Lark. "That's a white name yore puttin' on that squaw."

*Squaw.* The word hit Lark squarely, it had been spoken like a vile insult.

"My blood's just as red as yours, mister! You have no right to call me anything except by my given name."

The leader's thick brows rose in surprise at her clear, flawless English. He raised the rifle a little higher, keeping it trained on them.

"Lark," Matt warned darkly.

She glared at the red-haired leader and then over at Matt.

"Kincaid, you and that squaw better move on. We're in deep enough trouble now without having you two around. When that drover and Injun rode in asking for supplies, we were generous with them. Then that Injun turned around and killed Mr. Gerard. Nothing says you two ain't up to no good, either."

Hostility was evident in every face. Keeping his voice low and calm, Matt said to the leader, "We come in peace and we'll leave in peace. If you can tell us which direction they went, we'd be obliged."

"I overheard the drover, Shanks, say that they were headin' for Tucson."

"How long ago did they ride through?"

"Six hours ago."

Lark couldn't contain herself any longer. "Please, can you tell me about the sorrel stallion? Was he all right?"

"I've answered all the questions I'm gonna. Now, both o' ya, git! We're without a wagon master now and need help ourselves."

Matt held out his hand, cautioning Lark to say nothing further. "Maybe we can help. Which way were you headed?"

"We're goin' to California. The wagon master was takin' us as far as Fort Yuma."

Matt pointed west. "Turn your wagons around and follow this river until it intersects with another one. You'll be on the Gila River. Follow it west. Fort Yuma sits right on it. The only thing you'll have to watch for are Yavapai raiding parties. They make their home along the Gila."

Eyeing him warily, the leader gradually lowered his rifle. "How do we know you ain't lyin' to us, Kincaid?"

Matt held on to his temper. "You don't. But if you keep following this river, you're going to end up in the middle of a desert and you'll never survive." He glanced over at Lark. "Let's go."

They steered a wide circle around the group. Lark smarted beneath the glares of the women. When one child, a boy of seven, came racing over, throwing stones in her direction, Lark ignored the attack. Matt gave her an apologetic look. They were a mile from the wagon train before he spoke.

"I'm sorry, honey."

She set her lips, staring straight ahead. "I don't blame them for their anger, Matt. Ga'n killed their leader." She rubbed her brow. "How could he? Why? Those people were generous to them and he repaid them with murder."

He gripped Lark's hand. "He's a renegade, honey. Don't take on Ga'n's guilt because you share the same blood."

"How can I not? Did you see their hate? With Ga'n murdering whites, it's no wonder they hate all Indians!"

There was no way Matt could assuage Lark's pain. He released her hand and tried to get her to focus on more important matters. "We repaid those people by giving them good directions."

Miserably, Lark nodded.

"Now that we know they're heading for Tucson, we can skirt Phoenix and cut across the desert. If we're lucky, we might arrive there ahead of Shanks."

"You aren't going to try and catch them on the desert?"

"No, not now." He didn't want to tell Lark that she'd be safer in Tucson. Already a plan was forming in his head. He forced a smile he didn't feel and was glad to see Lark rally. "Feel like riding hard for the next couple of days?"

She nodded. "What are you going to do?"

Urging the gelding into a fast trot, Matt said, "Set a trap for two foxes."

For three days, they pushed their mounts to the limit, riding at night and sleeping during the heat of the day. It was in the rocky Sacton Mountains, south of Phoenix, that a group of Apaches swooped down upon them.

Lark saw the four warriors, mounted on sturdy, thin mustangs, appear out of a canyon. She gave Matt a quick look.

"Don't go for your gun," she told him, pulling her mare to a halt. "Let me talk to them."

Matt watched as the warriors galloped toward them in a cloud of dust. They were dressed in colorful, long-sleeved cotton shirts and dark trousers with bandoliers of ammunition slung across their chests. One wore a turquoise and silver necklace. They were darkly browned

by the sun and kept their long black hair out of their eyes
with cotton headbands wrapped about their foreheads.
Lark's eyes widened. Could it be? She glanced over at
Matt.

"Goyathlay," she whispered.

Matt scowled. The Apache name for Geronimo.

Matt had never met the savage leader, who had refused
to live on a reservation, but he'd heard stories of his
many raids between the border of Arizona and Mexico.
What would Geronimo do with Lark? Would he respect
her? As the group drew nearer, he saw that one of the
warriors was a tall, proud woman. Matt had heard of
Apache women riding with their men to make war, but
he'd never seen one. She was a striking woman with hair
as long as Lark's and golden eyes.

Matt tensed as Geronimo drew to a halt in front of
Lark.

"*Shis-inday*"—hail to the chief—Lark greeted.

Geronimo's piercing black eyes stared out of his square
face at Lark for a long moment. "You speak The
People's tongue, yet you are not like us," he finally said,
gesturing at Lark's eyes.

"I greet you through my mother, Mourning Dove, of
the Chiricahua. I am Lark Gallagher."

Geronimo's eyes glinted with an unreadable emotion.
Twisting in his cottonwood saddle, he gestured for the
woman to come forward. "Shanaei, is this the message
the eagle brought to us earlier this morning?"

Lark watched as the Apache woman drew alongside
Geronimo. She was young, perhaps Lark's age, but her
youth didn't detract from her dignity. Lark had heard of
the famous medicine woman who possessed eyes the color
of the cougar.

"Great chief, the eagle we saw wheeled from the north,
flying south. It was a message from Us'an telling us of
an important passage." She gestured toward the two
people. "An eagle is fitting. I remember Mourning Dove.
Her wisdom and bravery as a leader beneath Cochise's

command are well known." Shanaei focused on Lark. "I greet you, daughter of the great woman chief."

Drawing a sigh of relief, Lark knew that Geronimo's medicine woman may have saved their lives by openly acknowledging her birthright and place in the world of the Apache. One of the warriors gave Shanaei a disgruntled look, but he didn't challenge her greeting.

"I greet you, Shanaei," Lark returned. "I've heard of your power as a medicine woman."

"She is more than that," Geronimo informed Lark testily. "She is my chief. Five days ago, she battled four enemy Comancheros, killing their chief, who had been abducting our women and children for slaves." He looked upon Shanaei with obvious admiration.

Lark saw the medicine woman grow uncomfortable at such praise and wondered why. Surely she was a fine example of an Apache woman in every sense. "Goyathlay, we come in peace to your land and ask permission to cross it." Lark said. "Matt Kincaid and I are tracking down two men who stole a horse from my father's ranch up north."

Geronimo relaxed, eyeing Kincaid. "What does this horse look like?"

"He is a red stallion, great chief. Without him, our ranch will perish. Perhaps you have seen the two men who have stolen him? One is a gunslinger, a *pindah*. The other is . . ." She hesitated, glancing at Shanaei for support. "Ga'n."

"Ga'n!" the Apache chief exploded. "That miserable bastard of a renegade is no longer a member of my rancheria! He has disgraced me! He has dishonored The People!"

"My chief," Shanaei interceded in her husky voice, "the daughter of Mourning Dove does not blame you. Rather, she acknowledges your shame of this warrior and tries not to upset you."

Lark closed her eyes for a second. Thank Us'an the medicine woman understood. She reminded Lark of Ny-

Oden, for both possessed wisdom far beyond their years. Shanaei's understanding would help bridge any misunderstandings between Lark and the volatile Apache leader.

Yawning, Geronimo shrugged. "Ga'n is a ghost. He no longer exists."

"I understand that," Lark murmured, "but he lives to murder innocent people. Apache or *pindah*, it does not matter to him."

"This I know," he muttered with a wave of his hand. "So what do you want of me?"

"The honor of finally meeting you is enough," Lark answered diplomatically, watching Geronimo preen beneath the compliment. Such power emanated from the chief that she felt frightened. But she musn't show her fear, because no Apache honored weakness. "We know Ga'n is heading to Tucson and we wonder if you've seen him or this red horse."

"No, we've not seen them." Geronimo's eyes glittered with animosity. "But hear me, Mourning Dove's daughter. Ga'n is dead. Shortly, I will send Shanaei and a band of warriors with her to hunt down and kill Ga'n. I will not tolerate his killing of The People. He has no heart. I don't care if he lifts the scalps of *pindah* or greaser, but not those of his own blood. If you find and kill him, I ask that you bring me the amulet he wears around his neck. Shanaei's mother, the great medicine woman Nadina, made it for him many seasons ago. It is a powerful amulet that protects him from our arrows. So if you stalk him, do so with your rifle or knife. To those, he is vulnerable."

"I will remember that, great chief."

Yawning again, Geronimo looked over at his medicine woman. "And what of this *pindah* who rides with you? Should I spare him from a deserving death by my hand?"

Lark stiffened. "Great chief, this man shares my heart." She waited, realizing that the Apache disapproved of The People marrying outside their own kind.

Shanaei leaned forward. "The eagle we saw this

morning was followed by a hawk, my chief. Us'an tells me that we should allow both of them to go in peace. After all, they seek your enemy and mine.''

Since they were speaking in Apache, Matt had no idea what was being said, but when he saw Lark go rigid, he slowly moved his hand to the butt of his Colt, slipping off the loop that held it in the holster.

Geronimo glared at Lark. "You give your heart to this *pindah?*" he snapped.

"My mother married a white man," Lark retorted just as sharply, "and I am the result of their heart's mating. If you disdain this man at my side, you also dishonor me, and my great mother's name.''

"You'll be lucky not to be turned into a braying donkey in your next lifetime," he said ominously.

"I'll let Us'an judge me at the end of this life and decide whether I deserve such a curse."

Geronimo's face crinkled with the bare hint of a smile as he looked at Shanaei. "I remember Mourning Dove. She had a sharp tongue. Obviously her daughter is no different." He trained his glittering eyes on Lark. "You will need that courage if you stay with this *pindah*. His people will no more respect you than the dirt they walk upon.''

"I'm getting equal respect from you, right now," Lark parried tightly. "I thought The People were less judgmental, but I can see I was wrong."

"The People see the wisdom of marrying with their own kind." He shrugged. "You must follow your path, whatever it is." He dug in a pouch he carried on his belt and tossed Lark a small leather bag. "Here," he said. "Other Apaches may not be as lenient and understanding as I. The contents of that pouch will give you safe passage through our land." He kicked his black gelding and moved past them.

The other two warriors followed, but Shanaei reined alongside Lark and motioned to the pouch. "Our chief is generous with you. There is a sacred arrowhead made of red pipestone in that bag. It is great protection." She regarded Lark somberly. "He honors your courage. I honor you. *Ya lan.* Goodbye."

"*Ya lan,*" Lark answered softly, nodding in deference to Shanaei.

Matt watched the foursome disappear down the cactus-strewn hill before turning to Lark. "What did he give you?"

"Safe passage among the Apache." She tucked the worn pouch into the sash at her waist. "No one except Ga'n, of course, would dare stop us now. Everyone honors Geronimo. We'll be safe."

Matt nudged his horse and they continued their trek over the series of rugged mountains that rose like sharp, jagged points out of the desert floor. "Sounds like the conversation got a little heated there for a while. What happened?"

Lark launched into the story, leaving out no details. Despite Geronimo's seeming disapproval, she knew he would never have given her a gift such as the sacred arrowhead if he didn't respect her. Lark's heart lifted. Despite her half-breed status, The People had accepted her. More important, they'd also accepted Matt.

Coming out of the mountains, they followed the Santa Cruz River that would take them into Tucson. By sunrise the next morning the town stood before them, a cluster of buildings, shacks, and tents that bustled with human activity. Matt guided Lark to a grove of mesquite on the bank of the river just outside of town and told her, "I want you to stay here until I get back."

Tired from riding all night, Lark frowned. "Where are you going?"

He smiled. "Into Tucson to buy you a dress." He pointed to her attire. "Honey, you can't ride in looking like an Apache or, believe me, word would get around in a hurry. We don't need that kind of attention. I'll get us a hotel room, then come back out and get you. In the meantime, rest."

Would Matt try to tackle Ga'n and Shanks by himself? Lark wondered. She tried to read his expression but to no avail. Reluctantly she dismounted. "How long will it take you?"

"Probably three hours. It'll take an hour to ride in."

"Matt, you're not going in by yourself to find them, are you?"

"No."

Lark rested a hand on Matt's thigh and held his weary gaze. "Promise?" she asked softly.

Leaning over, he kissed her lips, tasting the salt of her sweat and the sweetness of her mouth. "I promise," he whispered. "I'll be back as soon as I can."

# Chapter 16

Lark waited impatiently at the river, hiding in the brush, feeling vulnerable because of the clothes she wore. Several buckboards and wagons passed nearby loaded with goods bound for Tucson. A small herd of cattle pushed past with three drovers in tow. Keeping her hand over Four Wind's nose so she couldn't whicker in greeting to the passing horses, Lark stayed well hidden in the grove. Holos was at its zenith before she spotted Matt returning, a large bundle under his arm.

Dismounting, his face glistening with sweat from the ride, he offered Lark the package. Ignoring it, she threw her arms around his neck. "I was so afraid you wouldn't come back."

Caught off guard, Matt took a step or two backward. He laughed softly and wrapped one arm around Lark, squeezing tightly. "A promise is a promise," he muttered, kissing her offered lips longingly. She tasted warm and willing, and Matt groaned.

Trembling in the aftermath of their powerful kiss, Lark smiled shyly as she eased from his arms. "I was afraid you had been shot . . . or killed. So many terrible thoughts ran through my head . . ."

He understood. "I also had a terrible feeling that someone had discovered you here and shot you," he admitted, handing her the package.

Her eyes widened. "You did?"

"Love makes you worry more than necessary," he

confessed, grinning slightly. "Come on, open up this parcel. I want to know what you think of the dress."

Lark knelt in the shade, Matt crouched opposite her. Her hands trembling, she eased off the string and pushed aside the paper. There, beneath her stilled hands, lay a maroon wraparound skirt and a tight-fitting basque, or jacket, of the same color. The jacket was edged with lustrous shell buttons from the high lace collar to the braid-trimmed hem. A pink ribbon ran the length of the skirt, and shell buttons were sewn down the center of it.

Reverently Lark ran her fingers over the sleek, smooth fabric, awed by its beauty and simplicity.

"Like it?" Matt could see the pleasure dancing in her eyes as she lifted her chin. He smiled and picked up a long pink grosgrain ribbon. "This is for your hair. As I recall, you like to wear them."

Lark accepted the ribbon. "Everything is so beautiful . . ."

"There's more," he said, motioning for her to remove the skirt. "The seamstress said no fashionable young lady would be caught withot the proper number of petticoats and a chemise."

Lark examined the lace work on the ivory-colored chemise and fingered the soft cotton material of the three petticoats before setting them aside. "I have to clean up, first. I can't wear these beautiful clothes feeling gritty."

Matt nodded. "Go ahead. I'll keep watch."

"On who?" she baited.

"None of your business, young lady. Now go on, we've got a room reserved for us at the Star Hotel."

Excitement replaced Lark's previous dread. The Santa Cruz River was much larger and deeper than the Agua Fria had been. She waded out into knee-deep water and quickly washed. Matt sat on the bank, chewing a piece of grass, watching her beneath half-closed eyes. Instead of feeling embarrassed by his undivided attention, Lark gloried beneath his glittering gray gaze.

"Do you think Shanks and Ga'n are in Tucson yet?" she called.

"I don't think so. After we get our room, I'll check each livery stable."

Lark picked her way daintily to shore, and Matt handed her a towel. "I want to go with you." She wriggled into the chemise and carefully fastened each of the twenty buttons.

"No."

She frowned, pulling on the three layers of petticoats. Why did women wear such inhibiting material? Already she was perspiring from so many clothes. "Why not?" she asked. "Do you think for one minute that I'll be content pacing that room, wondering if they've found you or not?"

Matt watched as she fastened the skirt around her slim waist. She certainly didn't need the corset the seamstress had tried to sell him. Her breasts rose high and proud against the chemise, the nipples outlined, as if begging to be touched.

"Yes, I expect you to stay in the room and pace."

Lark gave him a dark look and slipped on the jacket. Just putting on such an expensive and beautiful article of clothing made her feel feminine. "I won't."

Matt rose and began to shed his clothes, dropping them on the blanket. "You will."

Pouting, Lark stared mutinously up at him. Her pulse bounded as he shrugged out of his shirt, his chest looking brazenly male. She wanted to run her fingers through that curly, dark hair but stopped herself.

Reading the desire in her eyes, Matt smiled. "You can touch me if you want to."

She colored prettily as he stood naked before her. Her gaze dropped circumspectly to his manhood, which stood hard and ready. Her unsettled, molten sensations grew into an ache deep within her. "If I do, I might not stop," she admitted, her voice strained.

He caressed her flaming cheek. "Tonight I'm going to love you . . ." he promised thickly, then left her side and waded into the river.

Lark's knees grew weak as wave after wave of heat flowed through her. Trying to shake the magical euphoria, she brushed her hair and tied it with the ribbon. Since she had no mirror, she went upstream a few yards to a quiet pool of water and knelt on the grass. The reflection that stared back at her was of a different person—a woman fulfilled, happy. Had love transformed her to such a degree? Lark wondered in awe. The face staring back at her was soft, beckoning, not defensive or scowling as she had once been.

"You look ravishing," Matt called to her, stepping out of the river, flinging drops of water off his arms.

Lark picked up her skirts and walked back to where he was getting dressed. "I look . . ." She struggled to find the words. "Different."

Matt hungrily drank in her vulnerable, upturned face. "Yes," he answered softly, "you're a woman now, Lark. No longer a little girl."

She touched her cheek, aware of its inordinate warmth. "I never realized love could change me so much."

"Do you like what you're becoming?"

"Becoming? You mean, there's more?"

"Much, much more," he answered, pulling her into his arms.

Tucson was much like Prescott in some ways, Lark thought, as they rode down the hard-packed dirt of the main street. It was just bigger. She saw many more saloons, dance halls, and mining supply stores, all filled with soiled doves, miners, and drovers.

This was silver country, Matt had informed her. Indeed, there were so many canvas tents and wooden shanties that Lark lost count. This was a mining boom town. To the southeast, in Cochise County, was Tombstone, another silver center. Lark had heard many colorful stories of Tombstone and the gunslingers who inhabited it.

The Star Hotel was located near the center of the bustling city. Matt dismounted and helped Lark off her mustang, since she had had to suffer the indignity of riding sidesaddle. She straightened her skirt and slipped her hand around his proffered arm. The clatter of wagons passing, the cries of children playing tag along the wooden walk, and the bark of dogs filled the afternoon air. Lark was able to spot at least three livery stables. Was Kentucky in one of them?

The clerk behind the registration desk was a small, stooped man with spectacles perched on the end of his thin nose. He bobbed his head and smiled.

"Ah, this is your young bride, Mr. Butler."

*Butler?* Lark felt Matt give her elbow a warning squeeze. Of course, she realized, they wouldn't register under their real names; that would be folly.

"Yes, this is Mrs. Matt Butler. Darling, this is Mr. Samuel Peekins."

Lark smiled shyly. "How do you do, Mr. Peekins."

"A pleasure, ma'am, a pleasure. You were right, Mr. Butler. Your bride is, indeed, beautiful." He turned the register book so that Matt could sign it with a fountain pen. "And how long will you be staying?"

"I want to give my bride some time to rest up from our long journey, Mr. Peekins. We'll probably be here two, perhaps three, days at the most."

"Fine and dandy. Pay for two nights now and if you're staying a third, you can pay that morning." Peekins smiled, revealing a nearly toothless mouth beneath his white mustache.

Lark paused hesitantly, not sure of what to say or do. In Prescott, she'd seen women curtsy to men. They lifted their skirts with both hands and bobbed up and down like a blue heron dipping for fish in a pond. Did Mr. Peekins expect her to do that too? It looked so silly.

She was relieved when Matt paid for the two nights and

took her by the elbow, guiding her down the red-carpeted hallway to a wide staircase. The Star Hotel was garishly decorated. Relatively quiet and clean, it was too expensive for the partying drovers or miners and catered to a more refined clientele. Lark would be safe here, Matt hoped. Upstairs, he stopped at Room 22 and opened the door for her.

Lark entered. Pink lace curtains framed double windows. A large feather bed with brass head- and footboards dominated the room. There was also a cherry dresser with a vase of fresh summer flowers on top. Compared to the spareness of the Gallagher Ranch, this room was opulent.

"It's beautiful," she breathed, turning around, admiring all the expensive appointments. A huge floor mirror stood in one corner. Lark walked over to it, getting the first, full impact of herself in the dress.

Matt walked up behind her, watching various expressions flit across her face. He placed his hands on her shoulders, and drew her back against him. "You like it, eh?"

"Yes." Lark stared at herself. The maroon and pink outfit enhanced her blue eyes and black hair. She looked up at Matt. "This dress makes me look so—"

"Beautiful. And you are. Stay here, I'm going to get our gear."

She whirled around as he left her side. "Are you going to the livery stables?"

"I will a little later." Matt saw the fear in her eyes and tried to alleviate it. "First things first. After I get the gear up here, I'll take our horses to the livery." He left, closing the door quietly behind him.

Lark stood in the middle of the room, clasping her hands. What if Matt ran into Shanks or Ga'n? She doubted that Ga'n would show his face in a *pindah* community, but he might stay outside the town with the stallion while Shanks made contact with whomever he was supposed to meet.

When Matt returned, placing their riding gear in one corner, he startled Lark out of her deep thought. He came over and kissed her cheek.

"I'll take the horses down to the livery now. Then I'll go over to the telegraph office and send a telegram to Frank Herter. I want him to know where we are and what's going on."

She saw the wisdom of Matt's idea. "And then?"

"Then I'll make the rounds of the liveries. After that, I intend to take you to an early dinner."

"But what if you see Shanks?"

"*If* I see Shanks or Ga'n, I'm not going to call them out on the street for a gunfight, honey. Our first order of business is to find Kentucky. After I know he's safe, then I'll try to track down each man individually."

"What about the sheriff here in Tucson? Can't you ask for his help?"

Matt hesitated. "What if he's part of the Ring? We can't be sure he isn't. If I went to the sheriff for help, Lark, I could find a slug in my back. No, it's too risky."

Everything was risky. "Why can't I help look in the liveries?"

"Because I love you and I don't want you in danger, that's why." He saw Lark's jaw tighten and braced himself.

"And what if Shanks or Ga'n finds you first?" She asked. "I'll be here, sitting in a hotel room when I could be helping you!"

"You can't go around carrying that bowie knife on you, Lark," he teased gently. "Don't you think it would look out of place with the dress you're wearing?" Before she could reply, he added more seriously, "I know they're not here yet. I'm just taking the precaution. Don't worry, I'll be back very soon." He kissed her hard, then turned, closing the door quietly behind him.

Lark stood for a moment, fuming. She glared at the white door decorated with gold paint and stamped her foot, muttering one of the few Apache curses she knew.

Going to the windows, Lark pushed aside the filmy curtains. Below her was the main street of Tucson, criss-crossed with evening shadows. She saw Matt walk down the opposite side of the street and disappear into the nearest livery stable with their horses. Ten minutes later, he reappeared. To her chagrin, he then went into the Glass Slipper Saloon next door. So he was going to check more thoroughly than he had told her!

Fearing for Matt's safety, Lark sought a way to help him. An idea sparked and fanned to life. Turning, she flung open the door and hurried down the hall, looking for one of the uniformed bellboys.

Shanks chose the Jenkins Livery, located at the north end of Tucson, to stable the sorrel stallion. Ordering Ga'n to hide in the mesquite along the hill behind the livery, he led the stud into the building. A young boy of ten came out of the stall he'd been cleaning, his eyes lighting when he saw the magnificent stallion.

"Yes, sir?"

"Need a couple of stalls, boy," Shanks told him, dismounting.

"Yes, sir! That's a right nice horse you have, mister." The lad patted Kentucky's dust-coated hide.

"Keep yore hands off him, boy. He's mean and he bites. Which stall can I put him in?"

Quickly stepping back, the lad said, "The name's Jethro, mister, and you can bring your horse back here. This ought to hold him."

Shanks made sure the stall was well built. The damned red stud had been nothing but trouble since he'd stolen him. There had been times when he'd wanted to lay a thick leather strap to the beast's hide, but the new owner, Robert McCray, would probably lay one to him if he did. Shanks threw the kid a nickel.

"I'll be back with this other horse around midnight. In the meantime, water that red devil and give him grain a good two hours afterward."

Jethro bobbed his sandy-colored head. "Yes, sir."

"If you need me, I'll be at the Glass Slipper Saloon."

"Yes, sir!"

Lark settled the wide-brimmed black hat on her head and regarded herself critically in the mirror. She'd gathered her hair up into a knot and fit it inside the crown of the cowboy hat. Thanks to an innocent bellboy who had loaned her a set of men's clothes, her disguise was complete. She made sure that the black trousers fit over her kabun boots so that no one could identify her as Apache. The green cotton shirt hung loosely on her slight frame, but it adequately hid her curves. The leather sheath that held her bowie knife was belted around her slender waist. She looked like a young boy.

Opening the door a crack, Lark saw that no one was in the carpeted hall and slipped out, running silently down the corridor to the back exit. In moments she found herself at the rear of the hotel in a narrow alley between the hotel and a dry goods store that led to the main street.

Her heart beating hard in her throat, she quickly descended the rickety wooden stairs and, pulling the broad-brimmed hat low over her face, edged out of the alley onto the wooden walkway.

She looked both ways before crossing the busy street, dodging a buckboard going one way and a couple of men on horseback coming the other. She kept her head down, the brim of the hat providing protection against prying eyes.

Nervously she approached the swinging walnut doors of the saloon. She had never before entered such an establishment. The stench of cigar smoke and the noise of men talking loudly assaulted her as she carefully pushed one door aside.

The Glass Slipper Saloon took her breath away. Her mouth dropped open. Inside was a huge, intricately carved mahogany bar, the wood highly polished and glowing a deep red in the light of kerosene lamps suspended from the ceiling. Behind the bar hung a painting of a nude woman lying on a sumptuous velvet couch. Lark swallowed hard and eased inside, hugging the wall.

The bar was packed with miners standing elbow to elbow. The sour smell of sweat permeated the stale air, and the haze of smoke was like a thick fog. Lark began to search for Matt among the patrons. The smell of whiskey stung her sensitive nostrils. How could any man enjoy a place like this? It was awful! Then she spied a woman who was scantily dressed in the most shocking costume she'd ever seen. The woman affected an exaggerated walk, swinging her ample hips beneath the thin material of the purple and gold robe she wore. Her red hair clashed with her attire, which revealed a generous portion of her ample breasts. Several times she stopped at different tables filled with men, leaned over, and smiled through painted red lips, deliberately flaunting herself.

Lark held her breath, watching the woman go from table to table, teasing, joking, and laughing with the men she seemed to know so well. A couple of them patted her well-rounded rear. How could she allow men to touch her like that? Lark wondered, confounded. Tearing her attention from the soiled dove, she craned her neck, trying to pierce the layer of smoke and haze to find Matt.

Suddenly her breath jammed in her throat. Shanks! She automatically pressed her back against the wall, frozen. He was lounging lazily at the other end of the magnificent bar, swilling down a shot of whiskey. Where was Matt? Had he seen Shanks? Anxiously Lark continued her search, praying that Shanks wouldn't spot her.

Matt must have already left the saloon. Her heart pounding triple-time, Lark sidled toward the swinging doors, hoping to make her exit as quickly and unobtrusively as possible. Ducking beneath the doors, she scrambled out onto the sidewalk, gasping for breath, and moved down the street. Where was Matt? Had he gone to the next livery? Was he checking out another saloon? She hurried down the sidewalk, deciding to search the liveries first.

An hour later, it was dark except for the kerosene lamplight of the saloons and dance halls, and the streets were almost deserted. There were only a few cowboys on foot or horseback heading for their favorite saloons. Gradually Lark's footsteps slowed. She'd been to almost every livery in town, but Matt was nowhere to be found. Had Ga'n somehow taken him prisoner? Apprehensive, she rubbed her arms and headed toward the last livery on the northern end of town, all her senses keenly alert. Kentucky had to be here since Shanks was in town.

The Jenkins Livery was cloaked in the shadows of the cactus-strewn hill behind it. The wooden walkway stopped at a mining supply store, and Lark leaped to the dry earth, padding quietly toward the building. Listening carefully, she picked up the soft snort of a horse. She rested her palm over the butt of her bowie knife, needing the security it gave her.

A small kerosene lamp hung outside the door beneath the name of the stable. Gently she removed the lamp and entered the straw-littered aisle, holding the light high. She stopped at each occupied stall. A slight breeze stirred the opened doors of the barn, as she crossed the aisle.

"Kentucky!" The cry was out of her mouth before she could stop it.

The red stallion had been lying down but quickly rose to his feet. He whickered and thrust his head and neck over the door, his ears pricked forward.

"Oh, Kentucky!" Lark set the lamp aside and lifted the latch. She threw her arms around the stallion's neck, pressing her face against his long, sleek neck. "I was so worried about you!" she said, her voice muffled.

The stallion nuzzled her shoulder, standing very still while she hugged him. He whickered again and thrust his velvet nose against her cheek.

Lark released her hold and turned, petting his nose. "You rascal, I was worried to death about you. Are you all right?'' She began a thorough inspection of him, carefully checking each of his long, slender legs, then patted him affectionately. ''You've lost some weight, but you're fine. Oh, I've missed you!''

''You were a fool to follow us.''

Gasping, Lark spun around, her eyes widening. Ga'n stood just outside the door, scowling at her. His long face was hard and uncompromising, his eyes black as midnight, his darkly clothed form blending into the gloom. He wore two bandoliers of ammunition across his chest.

''Ga'n!'' Lark pressed her back against the stallion. Kentucky snorted, his ears flicking restively.

''Get out of here, Lark Who Sings. Your life is worthless if that *pindah* Shanks returns before you can escape.''

Gathering her wits, Lark eased away from the stallion. ''You broke your word to me!'' she said fiercely.

He scowled. ''How? I've sworn never to harm you.''

''You tried to kidnap me! And now you've stolen my horse!''

Ga'n shrugged, his eyes warming with amusement. ''Have I *harmed* you?''

Lark caught the emphasis. A growl rose in her throat. ''I see! Your oath was to cause me no bodily harm, is that it? Kidnapping and horse stealing do not violate your pledge!''

''Now you understand. That is the promise I gave to Voice of Thunder. And I will carry out that sacred trust until my last breath.''

''Stealing other people's property isn't right, Ga'n,'' Lark sputtered furiously.

''I stole fire spirits from your father and he didn't mind.'' The hard line of his mouth softened just enough to show a hint of a smile. ''As I recall, you did my bidding and got the bottles for me.''

Lark marched out to the center of the aisle. ''I was only five years old then. And I felt sorry for you because you were in such pain from your wound. How could I know it was wrong to take my father's whiskey and give it to you?''

Ga'n relaxed slightly, his eyes glittering. "That is why I swore allegiance to you, Lark Who Sings. You trusted without question. You felt my pain and tended me, as did your fine mother. Remember how you sang to me? Songs your mother taught you that would make me heal faster.''

She swallowed some of her anger. "Yes, I remember.''

"I've never forgotten your kindness. You could have gone out and played with the other children, but you didn't. You stayed with me.''

Scowling, Lark muttered, "Because I knew you were lonely and grieving for the loss of your family.''

"The fire spirits kept away their ghosts,'' he said sadly, scowling once again. "The *pindahs* are good for one thing only—their bottled fire spirits. When I drink them, no memories can haunt me.''

"Ga'n,'' Lark pleaded softly, "you've killed so many innocent people.''

His eyes flashed with instant hatred. "*Pindahs* pay me green skins so that I can drink and forget. Do I care if they direct me to scalp a greaser or another *pindah?* It makes no difference to me. Even if they send me to raid my own kind, it does not bother me. Not after the women of Goyathlay's rancheria cold-bloodedly killed my sister.'' He snorted and made a violent gesture. "The *pindah* who killed my war partner will be next!''

Lark stared up into Ga'n's tense, sweaty features. "You murdered that man's family!''

"I was paid to do it.''

Breathing hard, Lark tried to keep her voice steady. "My father always said one reaped what one sowed, Ga'n. Matt Kincaid has pledged the rest of his life to finding and killing you.''

A twisted smile crossed the Apache's face. "Let him try. He means nothing to me. He's only one more *pindah.*''

Lark could no longer control her fury. "I saved his life

after you almost killed him, Ga'n. That's right, he was at my ranch."

With a curse, Ga'n stalked over to her. "You lied to me, then!"

"You stole my horse, and I didn't lie to you. I found him after you'd left. Even if he had been there, I wouldn't have let you finish him off—*pindah* or not!"

Ga'n balled his right fist slowly into a knot. "So you've become a *pindah?*" he spat at her.

Lark held her ground. "I've always carried the blood of Apache and *pindah* in me, Ga'n. I love Matt Kincaid! And I'll do anything to keep him alive." She lifted her chin, holding his glare, her knees trembling with fear. Ga'n had changed so much from the man she remembered of long ago. "He will be my husband one day, Ga'n. I've waited all my life for the warrior who could hold my heart."

With a snort, Ga'n turned and paced the aisle in front of her. "Your mother married a *pindah.* Why shouldn't you?"

"Would you deny me the man I love?" she whispered harshly, halting Ga'n's pacing. "You've sworn never to hurt me, Ga'n. Matt killed Alchise in self-defense when you tried to kidnap me. If you try to avenge his death by taking Matt from me, you will kill me, too."

"No!" he roared, whirling around and grabbing her shoulders.

His fingers sunk deeply into her flesh and he shook her hard. "You dare to plead for his life?" he rasped, inches from her face.

His breath was hot against her, but Lark held his burning gaze. Her fear turned to rage, and then became her strength. "Yes, I dare! My father saved your life. Now you can save the life of someone I love." She felt his grip easing and her voice dropped into an anguished tone. "Is there no honor left in you, Ga'n? Will you destroy my future as well as your own? Will you murder me as you have so many others? The path of blood must haunt you. Can you not find it within you to leave Matt alive?''

Ga'n was breathing hard, his chest rising and falling sharply. Abruptly he released Lark. ''I have *no* honor left in me!''

''Yes, you do,'' she insisted. ''I know you do, Ga'n.''

''No!'' he said harshly. ''Nothing bothers me anymore! I feel nothing!''

Lark reached out and gently touched his tense arm. ''You feel,'' she whispered in an aching voice. ''I saw your eyes change and your voice grow strong with emotion earlier when we talked of your stay at our ranch so long ago.''

With a curse, he stepped back, as if scalded by Lark's hand. ''You are blinded by love of that *pindah!* You saw nothing in my eyes or voice, Lark Who Sings. Nothing!''

She stood trembling before the Apache warrior. Ga'n was suffering greatly from his terrifying past, but she could not seem to help him. Woodenly she picked up the stallion's lead rope.

''This is *my* horse, Ga'n. And I intend to return him to the ranch.''

''I will not harm you, but I will not let you take the horse either.''

Lark tensed at the guttural warning in Ga'n's voice. She had to take the stallion out of the livery now, or Matt might find them. ''I'm leaving,'' she said, and went back into the stall, placing the lead on the horse.

''No!'' Ga'n's mouth thinned as he jerked open the stall door. ''Get out! You fool, if Shanks finds you here, he'll gladly take your life.''

Lark kept several feet between them, her hand resting tensely on her knife. ''I am Apache. I will do whatever is necessary to take what belongs to me.''

At that instant, Lark saw the barn door suddenly swing open. Shanks! His gun was drawn, his eyes narrowed as he leaped inside. Before she could scream, Ga'n had heard the intruder and turned, stepping directly into the path of the aimed gun.

Shanks squeezed the trigger, and the gun roared. He saw a man drop. And the other? Shanks dived for the floor and rolled behind another stall door. "Whoever's in there, drop yore gun and move out into the aisle," he shouted.

Lark gave a small cry as the stall door swung wide, leaving her standing in full view for Shanks to see. "D-don't shoot! I'm not armed!" she pleaded.

Cursing, Shanks was on his feet in an instant. He'd recognize that voice anywhere. Then who was the *hombre* with Lark? Kincaid, maybe? Cocking the trigger on the Colt, he yelled, "Who else is with ya? Git out of there, Lark!"

She shuddered, watching as blood spread across Ga'n's chest. "N-no."

"Come out with yore hands up. Now!"

She walked out into the middle of the aisle, her hands raised. Shanks melted out of the dark shadows of the barn. "You killed Ga'n," she cried.

"What?" He stepped cautiously forward. First he checked the stud's stall, then he squinted over to where Ga'n lay unmoving. Well, one Injun was either dead or close to it, that's all. Cameron wouldn't be very upset. "Looks like I'll deliver that stud to McCray by myself." He leaned down. The Apache's eyes were closed, and Shanks couldn't detect any breath coming out of him. He stood and turned to Lark. "My only problem now is you," he said. "If I let ya go, you'll go to the law." A slow smile spread across his glistening features. "Yore comin' with me, breed. I'll truss ya up and ya can ride with me. Once we get out of town, I'll take my pleasure with ya and then kill ya. I'll dump ya somewhere on the desert. Once they find ya, there won't be no evidence of who killed ya." He grinned wider, watching her blanch. "Maybe I'll scalp ya, just to make it look like yore own kind did it to ya." He snickered, pleased with the plan.

Shanks glanced back at the Apache. There was a bullet hole through his upper chest. "I didn't like the red-skinned bastard anyway," he said, walking toward Lark.

With a cry of terror, Lark tried to escape.

"No, ya don't!" Shanks warned her. He grabbed a handful of her hair, yanking her backward off her feet. Pain exploded in her head as she was hurled to the barn floor and Shanks's fingers sank into her shoulders. Sobbing with anger, Lark struck out with her boots into his laughing face.

Dodging her first blow, Shanks laughed softly. "No, ya don't, honey. I know yore a wildcat when ya get riled." He stepped back, aiming the barrel of the gun at her heaving chest.

Lark went rigid, staring up into his wolflike eyes.

"That's better," he crooned. "Now, be a good girl and sit up. Cross yore hands together so I can tie 'em. You and I are leavin' *pronto.*"

She bit back a sob, trying to think. Where was Matt? Surely someone must have heard the gunshot! And, judging by Shank's sudden nervousness, he wanted to leave town for just that reason.

"Sit up," Shanks ordered. "Ya try kickin', bitin', or screamin', and I'll blow yore head off here and now. Understand?"

Lark believed him. She crossed her wrists and he quickly bound them with a piece of twine rope. "Where are you taking me?" she demanded.

"Gonna go east, honey. Got a rancher who wants to buy that stud of yores." He gave the triple knot a jerk, watching pain cross her face. Grinning, he said, "A little pain's good for ya. I'm gonna give ya a hell of a lot more before we're finished with each other." He gestured to his scarred cheek. "Since ya was stupid enough to follow us here, I might as well make ya pay in full for every-thin' else while I'm at it." He jerked her to her feet. "Now look," he snarled, wrapping his hand in her hair, and twisting her against him, "settle down or you'll be sorry. Who'd ya come with? Ya didn't come alone."

Sobbing for breath, trying to move away from Shank's lean, hard body, Lark rasped, "I came alone."

"Bullshit! Ain't no woman alive can track that good." He rubbed his hand across her dirt-stained cheek. "Now be sensible and tell me the truth."

Clenching her teeth in an effort to withstand his revolting touch and clammy hand on her skin, Lark cried, "I came alone!"

Just then Shanks heard the faint sound of voices coming from down the street. He shoved Lark into a heap at his feet. "Stay there. Ya get up, I'll shoot ya."

Dazed, she watched as he led the stud out into the aisleway. He brought his saddled gelding over and jerked her to her feet. "Mount," he growled, shoving her toward the bay.

She climbed shakily into the saddle, bracing herself as he mounted behind her. Tying Kentucky's lead to the horn, he clamped one arm around her waist and picked up the reins. Spurring the gelding, they galloped out of the barn and into the darkness.

The road out of Tucson was hard and smooth. Lark clung to the horn all too aware of Shanks's lean form pressing against her as he spurred on his mount like a madman. Why they didn't stumble or fall, Lark didn't know. She tried to swallow the bitter taste in her mouth as memories of Shanks's last attack of her returned to haunt her. He'd nearly raped her on Denton Road. This time, he would.

*Matt!* she screamed in her head. *I love you! I'm sorry I disobeyed you . . . so sorry!* There was no hope. None. Shanks had got away clean. Matt would have no lead, no clue as to her whereabouts. Miserably, Lark knew what her ultimate fate would be—repeated rape, and then death.

Matt was the first to arrive at the Jenkins Livery after the gunshot. His Colt drawn, he eased inside the shadowy depths of the stable area, his hand tightening on the Peacemaker when he heard a distinct grunting. Cocking the gun, he moved forward.

"Hold it," he ordered, aiming at the dark figure leaning against the door at the other end of the livery.

Ga'n had managed to drag himself upright and stagger the few steps to the rear of the barn, toward escape and freedom. He was holding a gun. Pain sharpened his already keen senses. With a snarl, he recognized Kincaid crouched tensely, his Colt aimed at him.

"You . . ." Ga'n growled.

The hair stood up on the back of Matt's neck. Ga'n! Hatred roared through him.

"That's right, it's me," he rasped. "And you're going to die, you bastard. You killed my family, and now you're going to pay."

A harsh laugh broke from the Apache. "Before you pull the trigger, *pindah*, I will pull mine." The gun wavered in his hand. "We will go to the Big Sleep together."

Matt saw the gleam of blood across the Apache's chest. "Looks like someone already tried to get you. Where's the red stud?"

As he breathed laboriously, Ga'n's mouth drew into a sneer. "There isn't much time, *pindah*. Lark Who Sings has been captured by Shanks." He paused, pain ripping through him. When he spoke again, his voice was little more than a harsh rasp. "He will kill her. I swore . . . I swore an oath to always protect her but I cannot." He waved the gun slightly. "Shanks rides east with her toward the Double Deuce Ranch. The stud is with them."

Stunned, Matt stared at the Apache warrior. How had Lark been captured? Damn, he should have known she wouldn't stay in the hotel room, the little fool. His mind spun with questions. Ga'n's ragged breathing sounded loud in the tense silence. Matt saw the gun waver and fall slowly to the Apache's side.

"What are you waiting for?" Ga'n snarled, his eyes

mere slits. "Do you hate me enough to stand here, wasting what little time is left, and throw away your future? Or will you ride east to save Lark Who Sings? She said you loved her. She begged me to spare your life." He shut his eyes, leaning weakly against the door. "If you cannot go after her, then you are no better than I am . . ."

The Peacemaker wavered in Matt's hand. His mouth tasted bitter with hatred of the Apache. Violent emotions tore through him; grisly pictures of Katie and Susan lying dead in the ranch yard wavered in front of him. And then came images of Lark's upturned face, of her eyes lustrous with love. An animal cry wedged in Matt's throat. Somewhere in that murderous bastard Ga'n, there was still a shred of honor. The Apache's words haunted him.

"All right," Matt whispered unsteadily, lowering the gun, "I'll ride east."

Relief flowed through Ga'n. The gun slipped from his bloody fingers, falling to the floor. "Hurry. Shanks will have his way with her, and then he will kill her."

Shoving the Peacemaker into his holster, Matt turned to see three people running toward the livery. They would discover Ga'n and get him the medical help he needed. Taking one last look at the Apache, Matt said harshly, "We're even."

Ga'n nodded, his eyes glittering with some unknown emotion. "Yes."

Spinning on his heel, Matt hurried outside. As he headed back toward the Star Hotel livery, he told the group of approaching men that Ga'n was in the stable and needed the sheriff and a doctor. The image of Lark's smiling features stayed before him, sending dread and terror washing through him. There was only one road out of Tucson heading east. He'd have to ride like hell to catch up. *God*, he prayed, *please don't let me be too late.*

Hours passed. Every bone in Lark's body felt tender and sore from the long, hard ride. A gray light ribboned the horizon, silhouetting the proud saguaro cactus that stretched their mighty arms skyward. Dawn would come in another hour. Shanks pulled his lathered horse to a halt in a wide, dry creek bed. The bank was only two feet high and mesquite lined the rim of the wash, providing adequate cover.

"Well, pretty filly, I'm going to take my pleasure with ya first before I drill ya." Shanks eased his grip on Lark's waist, splaying his fingers and running them up across her breasts. She gasped and jammed her left elbow into his gut with all her might. Unprepared for her savage reaction, Shanks let out a loud "oomph" and jerked both arms back to protect his belly from further assault.

Lark saw her chance. She threw her leg over the saddle and leaped to the sand. Many hours of riding had made her knees weak, and they gave way beneath her. Scrambling wildly, Lark forced her legs to work, gasping for breath.

Shanks hissed a curse and jumped from the saddle. "Why, ya little wildcat," he cried, reeling after Lark. Damn her to hell! In six strides, he was within striking distance. He launched himself through the air and caught Lark's legs, gripping them hard. Both of them fell, rolling to the ground.

"No!" Lark screamed, trying to jerk her legs free. Her wrists were tied together, but she clasped her fingers and showered Shanks with blow after blow. He released one foot. With a sob, she smashed the heel of her boot into his angry face. Boot met bone with an awful crunch. Shanks screamed and grabbed his nose. He released her. She was free!

Lurching to her feet, Lark sped on down the creek bed, never looking back. Her breath came in ragged sobs as she leaped to the bank, scrambling like a wild horse up and over the top. Shanks was still screaming at her, his voice muted as she escaped from the wash. Everywhere she looked, the world was ebony tinged with a hint of gray. She had to hide! If Shanks found her, he'd kill her outright. Had she broken his nose with that blow to his face? Was he coming after her yet?

Scrambling up a small, rocky hill, Lark slipped several times. She was shaking badly, her fingers torn and bleeding from falling over rocks and cactus. There would be no way to escape Shanks once he mounted his horse and followed her. There had to be someplace to hide! Sliding down the hill, Lark tripped. She fell and automatically rolled to prevent further injury. At the bottom, she landed with a thud and came to rest against a felled fifty-foot saguaro cactus. Sitting up, trying to control her fear, she looked around. She found a sharp, narrow rock, clamped it between her knees, and rapidly rubbed the twine that bound her wrists against it.

Anxiously Lark kept looking back toward the creek to see if Shanks was coming yet. It was quiet except for her harsh breathing. *I have to steady myself. I have to think!* The twine broke. With a soft cry of victory, Lark quickly tore the rest of the restrictive bonds off her wrists. In Shank's hurry to leave, he hadn't disarmed her. She still had her bowie knife. New courage infused her as she got to her feet, her knees shaky. She knew a knife against a gun was no match. Still, with a knife she could survive in the desert long enough to get rescued.

"Where are ya, bitch?"

Lark froze, whirling around, the black hair settling across her hunched shoulders. Shanks released a piercing, crazed cry. Terror worked its way up her spine. To the left, she saw him on horseback, heading in her general direction. What should she do? Stay and hide behind the saguaro or run? Either way, he would eventually spot her as soon as the sun rose.

Lark's blood pounded urgently through her veins. She crouched and turned, beginning to run with long, even strides. Her lungs took in great draughts of air. There was enough light now to see where she was placing her feet. She remembered her mother telling her that an Apache on foot could outtravel a horse. Well, she was going to put that claim to the test. She could expect no help. It was Shanks, his horse, and his gun against herself and the bowie. Ny-Oden would say they were evenly matched, Lark thought in a flash of wry humor.

Each stride took her further and further away. She prayed that she blended into the gray landscape, her black hair and dark clothes acting as camouflage. The fear that had eaten at her was miraculously being transformed into a tenacious determination to outwit her enemy.

The kabuns were perfect for a test such as this. Already the flat plain of cactus and mesquite had begun to undulate into small hills. Breathing evenly, Lark turned her mind to other details. She would have to circle back to Tucson. Matt would be worried sick. And Kentucky? She slowed her pace, frowning.

Holos would bridge the horizon in another half hour at the most. Lark had a keen sense of direction, and she knew she had run perpendicular to the creek. What if Shanks had left the immediate vicinity of the creek trying to find her? Kentucky hadn't been in tow when Shanks had crossed the creek bank to look for her. Chances were Shanks had tied the stud up to some mesquite and hobbled him. Wiping her face with the back of her hand, Lark crouched and scanned the horizon. Squinting, she could barely make out a lone rider far to the west of her. It had to be Shanks.

# Chapter 17

Where was that breed bitch? Shanks jerked his horse to a halt and glared at the quiet desert landscape. The hundreds of stately saguaros made it difficult to distinguish between a person and the cactus. Anger that Lark could escape boiled up through him. His nose was busted and ached without reprieve. Then his eyes widened as he spotted her no more than a quarter of a mile away, crouched low and running in a shallow wash.

"Giddyap!" he said sharply to his horse, sinking his spurs into the animal's flanks. Shanks's nostrils flared as he thundered toward the dry stream bed, whipping his horse mercilessly. Just as the horse leaped into the sandy bottom of the creek bed, Shanks saw Lark glance over her shoulder, her face etched with shock.

"Hey!" he yelled at her, his voice echoing sharply. He yanked the Colt .45 out of his holster, preparing to fire.

Lark saw Shanks careening down the wash like a madman, his gun drawn. He meant to kill her. Coming to a sudden halt, she spun around and moved to the center of the wash, her legs slightly spread for better balance.

The horse bore down on her, foam streaming from his opened, bleeding mouth, the thundering reverberation carrying through the earth to where she stood. Lark pulled the eighteen-inch bowie knife from the sheath at her side.

Shanks cocked the pistol, aiming at Lark. The gun roared. Damn! The first bullet strayed to the left, kicking up a geyser of sand. Taking better aim, he steadied himself, standing up in the stirrups. Again the gun fired.

Lark flinched as the second bullet dug angrily into the sand inches from her booted feet. There was only one way to get out of this alive, and that was to stand her ground. The horse bore down. She knew Shanks's third shot would tear through her. He was too good a marksman to miss three times in a row—even from the back of a fast-moving horse.

Lark clenched her teeth and focused all her strength and awareness into the act of throwing the bowie.

The blade whipped through the chilled morning air. Shanks tried to swerve to miss the glittering blade. A scream jammed in Lark's throat as it missed Shanks's heart but struck his right shoulder. The Colt flew out of his hand. Shanks let out a cry and tumbled from the saddle. As he slammed into the ground, the bowie dislodged from his shoulder, flipping through the air behind him.

Now! Lark dodged the wild-eyed gelding and dug her toes into the sand. Shanks lay groaning in the middle of the wash, the gun behind him, no more than thirty feet from where her knife was dug into the ground. She had to get both weapons or he could still kill her.

The gunslinger writhed in the sand, gripping his wounded arm, cursing. Compressing her lips, Lark approached him and at the last possible second, leaped across him.

"You little bitch!" he screamed, lunging upward and catching Lark's booted foot. She fell hard to the ground just ahead of him. Twisting onto his belly, he saw her stretching—stretching toward the bowie that lay inches away from her grasping fingertips. No! Cursing again, he jerked her backward, but she flipped over on her back and her second boot came slamming into his jaw. Blackness struck Shanks.

Sobbing for breath, Lark slithered on her belly toward the bowie. Her fingers closed over the hilt. Scrambling to her knees, Lark jerked around to face Shanks. The gunfighter was on his feet, lunging toward her.

"No!" she screamed, leaping to her feet. She held up the bowie, standing between him the gun. "Don't try it, Shanks, or I'll gut you."

He stood weaving on his feet, blood and saliva running out of the corner of his mouth. "Ya would, wouldn't ya?"

"Yes!"

He eyed his gun, a good ten feet behind Lark. "This ain't over," he rasped softly, and yanked his own hunting knife from the sheath on his belt. His right arm hung uselessly at his side, but like any good gunfighter, he'd taught himself to fight equally well with either hand. He waved the tip of his knife toward her in a lazy motion.

"Okay, breed, I'll finish ya off this way. Makes no never mind to me." He licked his lips and slowly approached her. Shanks knew that Lark couldn't circle; to do so would leave a clear path to the gun. "After I pin ya, I'm gonna strip those clothes off ya. Then I'm gonna take ya like I said I would. After I get done pleasurin' myself with ya, I'll slit that breed throat of yours. How does that sound?"

Lark ached to turn and run for the gun, but Shanks would throw his knife into her back if she attempted such folly. No, she'd have to make her stand. The wash was barely five feet wide, not enough room to maneuver well. The sand sucked at her already tired and trembling legs. She lunged forward, throwing him off balance, her blade arcing outward.

With a shout of surprise, Shanks leaped back. The bowie sliced through his vest and shirt, leaving a livid red cut across his heaving chest. "Why, you little polecat!" he hissed, backing off another few feet. He wanted to wrap his fingers around her throat and kill her. "I've changed my mind. Once I corner ya and take that blade outa yore hand, I'm gonna skin you alive. Ya hear me?

I'm gonna start by scalping ya, and then I'm gonna peel off yore goddamned Injun hide one strip at a time.''

He was rattled, Lark realized with soaring pleasure. She advanced cautiously, keeping her left hand in front of her, the knife close to her hip. "I want to know one thing before you die, Shanks. Tell me about the Tucson Indian Ring.''

Grinning, he moved his blade in lazy circles. "The Ring? It's gonna wipe out all yore kind, breed, that's what it is. Who do ya think killed yore pa?''

Jolted, Lark froze momentarily.

Shanks laughed his high, silly laugh, gripping his knife a little tighter. He'd diverted her attention by provoking her anger and outrage. "I killed him, breed. Shot him in the back, pure and simple.''

White-hot anger exploded through Lark. "You shot my father?'' Her voice was low and wobbly.

"Sure.''

Rage and hurt blotted out the rest of her whirling thoughts. Lark fastened her glare on Shanks, who was grinning at her. His arm was bleeding heavily and he must be feeling faint from the loss of blood.

"I'm glad I'm half Apache, Shanks,'' she whispered fiercely, advancing upon him. "Apache law gives me the right to avenge my father's death. You killed him, you no good yellow belly.''

With a laugh, Shanks held his ground, his eyes feral. "Come on, breed, come an' get me. If yore wantin' to go by the law, ya gotta get me first and then a whole passel of others comes next. It was the others who ordered yore pa shot. All I did was pull the trigger for 'em.''

Blood roared through her head, destroying all Lark's caution. With a scream of fury, she attacked Shanks.

He turned deftly aside. He hadn't been a gunslinger all these years for nothing. With one well-aimed kick, Shanks struck her wrist with the toe of his boot. Lark screamed out in pain and the bowie went flying harmlessly into the air. With a grunt of satisfaction, Shanks leaned forward, catching her as she tried to escape.

They landed in the wash. Lark rolled over and over again, fighting Shanks. With her nails she raked his sweating face, provoking a scream of pure outrage. She saw his knife come up. Her hair swirled around and between them, hampering her efforts to protect herself. Shanks got one leg across her, straddling her effectively.

"Now," he declared, holding the blade near her scalp, "yore mine—"

Lark threw up her hands to protect herself. She heard the bark of gunfire. Shanks gurgled once and jerked involuntarily. His eyes bulged. His mouth opened in a scream he never released. The knife in his hand dropped to the ground beside them. Lark's eyes widened as the gunslinger crumpled forward on top of her. With a cry, she scrambled out from beneath him.

Crawling away, she saw Matt pull his lathered horse to a halt in the wash and dismount. He held the Winchester rifle ready as he ran to where she knelt in the sand. He hauled her to her feet, pulling her away from Shanks.

"Lark?" he rasped.

She threw her arms around him. "Oh, Matt!"

"Shh, it's okay, honey. Everything's going to be all right. Shh . . ."

"How did you know where I'd be?"

"Stay here," he ordered her.

Lark's knees buckled, and she sat down unceremoniously in the wash, shaking badly. Matt turned the gunslinger over. There was a bullet between his shoulder blades. He was dead, but Lark didn't feel any satisfaction, only a terrible grief. The fact that she had come so close to death herself shook her deeply. When Matt returned and knelt at her side, she moved blindly into his arms.

The sun had risen, sending long, thin streamers of light across the cool desert. Matt held Lark for a long, long time. Awkwardly he brushed sand from her cheeks with his gloved hands. Her eyes were dark with pain, her lips soft and parted with grief. Leaning over, he molded her mouth to his, seeking to draw the agony from her eyes.

Lark drank of Matt's strong, clean mouth, tasting his maleness, his gentleness, all that he gave so effortlessly to her. Her arms slipped across his shoulders, her fingers nestling in the dampness of the hair at the nape of his neck. His beard was rough against her skin. Each pressing motion, each caress took a little more of the hurt out of her heart, out of her soul. Finally Matt eased away, breathing raggedly.

"I almost lost you," he said hoarsely, framing her face, looking deep into her wounded blue eyes.

Lark swallowed hard. "I—I'm sorry, Matt. I was afraid you'd investigate without me. And then I saw Shanks in the Glass Slipper Saloon where you had been earlier. I was so afraid that you wouldn't see him and he'd kill you . . ."

"I didn't see him, Lark. I'd gone out the rear of the saloon earlier to check out another livery down the street. You couldn't have seen me leave." He kissed her eyes, nose, and finally her trembling mouth. "My God, I was so scared I'd lost you."

"How did you find me?"

"I and some other people heard the gunshot over at the Jenkins Livery. I got there first. I caught Ga'n trying to escape out the back door. He was hurt bad. He told me Shanks had taken you and was heading east toward McCray's ranch with the red stud. He could have shot me, but he didn't. In his own twisted way, he had honor."

Lark sank against him, stunned. "Ga'n saved my life. Shanks fired first, not realizing it was him. He stepped in front of me and took the bullet meant for me."

"It's the only decent thing that renegade has ever done, then," Matt muttered, holding her tight in his arms.

Lark squeezed her eyes shut. "He didn't break his promise to protect me, then."

Some of the terror was draining from Matt. Lark was alive. It was over. "I'm not sure Ga'n's going to live," he said.

Lark's heart squeezed with pain. Ga'n's pain. He hated himself, the world, and yet there was a shred of decency still alive within him. "Did he get medical help?" she asked.

Gently, Matt lifted her to her feet. She swayed against him. "I'm sure he did. I told the men heading for the livery to get the sheriff and the doc. Come on, let's get you back to Tucson."

Mr. Peekins met them at the desk when they walked into the Star Hotel. "I've got a telegram here for you, Mr. Butler. Sez urgent."

Lark stumbled to a halt beside Matt. Mr. Peekins's white eyebrows shot up at her disheveled appearance and men's clothing. Despite her weariness, she felt Matt tense.

"Matt? What is it?"

Taking Lark's arm, he guided her toward the stairs that led to their room. Once out of earshot of the hotel clerk, he said, "It's from Frank Herter. He says trouble's brewing with Cameron and that we're to get back to the ranch as fast as we can." He looked deeply into Lark's shadowed eyes. "I can ride out within the hour and you can stay here and rest—"

"No!" Lark halted at the top of the landing, gripping the banister. She hadn't meant to sound so angry, and lowered her voice. "That's my father's ranch, Matt. If Cameron thinks he can take it from us while we're gone, let him try. He'll have to face both of us, not just you."

Sliding his arm around Lark, Matt brought her against him. "Come on, my fierce cougar. We'll get a bath, put on a fresh set of clothes, and then ride like hell."

Cameron swore softly while reading the telegram from Robert McCray one more time. According to the rancher, a loyal Ring member, Bo Shanks's body had been brought into Tucson by a sheriff's deputy. He slowly crumpled the paper.

"What's goin' on?" Bart Devlin asked from one of the wing chairs in his bank office.

Barely turning his head, Cameron snarled, "Shanks fouled up the transfer of that breed's stud to McCray. He went and got himself killed."

Devlin, a tall, well-muscled gunslinger of twenty-five, shrugged his shoulders. "You said that Injun Ga'n was with him. He dead, too?"

With a snort, Jud threw the paper into the waste basket. "He's been badly wounded and is in jail, pending a trial for horse stealing."

"Can the sheriff spring him?" Devlin asked, thinking that the lawman, Porter Sanderson, was getting well paid to look the other way on certain occasions.

"I'm going to wire McCray and see what can be done. Ga'n's the leader of the renegades. We can't let him hang. That isn't the worst of my problems, though. I've got to have water for my cattle. Now."

He paced the length of the office. It was hot, murderously hot, and the frustration he felt was as high as the hundred-degree weather, which had been burning up Prescott for the last two weeks. Shanks was gone, but Cameron had had the foresight to replace him with an even more competent gunslinger. Bart Devlin had worked for McCray for the last two years and was very capable. One look into those blue eyes that glittered like those of a wolverine ready to attack, and Cameron felt a surge of power. Yes, Devlin was the right man for this job.

Devlin chewed on the toothpick, most of his upper lip hidden beneath a long, blond mustache. "Your cattle are starting to drop like gnats in a sandstorm, boss. If they don't get water in the next couple of days, you're gonna lose the entire herd."

Stinging beneath Devlin's slow Texan drawl, Cameron snapped, "I've run a ranch for the last fifteen years.

Don't you think I know the crisis I've got on my hands?"
He paced some more.

"McCray didn't say anything about where Kincaid and
Lark Gallagher were staying after the shooting," he
muttered more to himself than Devlin. "Chances are,
they're going to take it easy coming back to Prescott."

"When I rode over to the Gallagher Ranch last week,"
Devlin said, "there was a gent there by the name of
Herter who was running it in the breed's absence. He said
the boss lady was going to be gone for a spell."

"Herter!" Cameron ground out. "I figured the bastard
would head west to California after he retired. Instead he
hires on with that outfit! He's acting foreman?"

"Yeah."

Frank Herter wasn't one to be underestimated and
Cameron knew that. "Did the wranglers respect him?"

"Looked like it." Devlin had ridden over at Cameron's request to check out the ranch and water situation.
Since Devlin was new to the Prescott area, Herter had had
no inkling that he worked for Cameron. "They were busy
building stout fences around each of those three artesian
wells. They're rationing the water to their own stock and
didn't want any of them drinking too much at one time."

Folding his hands behind his back, Cameron set his
jaw. "This is the perfect time to let my cattle get a drink
of water, then."

"What are you saying, boss?"

Jud smiled tightly. "If we drive a thousand head to the
Gallagher Ranch to drink their fill, those stupid greasers,
niggers, and Injuns won't know what to do. When they
see that herd stampeding hellbent-for-leather down on
them, they'll scatter like the yellow bellies they are."

Devlin frowned. "What about that *hombre* Herter? He
ain't no coward."

"One man can't get all those wranglers organized." He
paused. "We'll attack them at dawn tomorrow."

"What will you do after that breed and her gunslinger
return?"

Cameron eyed Devlin. "That's what you were hired to do—kill the both of them."

Lark pulled Kentucky to a halt at the crown of the ridge that overlooked the ranch. Matt drew up alongside her, and they both looked down at the quiet homestead that stood shadowed against the forthcoming dawn.

Wearily Lark wiped the sweat from her cheek and brow with the back of her sleeve. They'd had only a few hours of rest for the horses or themselves for the last three days. Taking a mountain route from Tucson, Lark had been lucky to find water along the way for Kentucky, since he still refused to eat cactus.

"Everything looks quiet," Matt observed. He pointed to the south where a lone sentry rode at a slow walk around the corrals. "Looks like Primo's in the saddle."

"Yes." Lark absently patted the stallion's damp neck. Exhaustion stalked all of them. Her heart sank as she gazed out across the blackened valley. No tree had been spared in the march of that monstrous fire, and the once fertile land looked like a wasteland. "There's so much to do, Matt," she whispered.

He found her hand and gave it a gentle squeeze. "We'll do it together, Lark."

Rallying at his husky words, Lark drowned in his dark gray gaze. There had been no time to hold him, much less to show her love. "Together sounds so—"

"Jesus Christ," Matt breathed, gripping Lark's hand hard.

She looked in the direction he pointed. "No!" she cried angrily. From their vantage point on the ridge, they could barely see the outline of a herd of cattle making its way from Cameron's land onto her property. The cattle were crossing the last series of small hills that would funnel into the end of the valley, and to the ranch. Lark's heart pounded wildly in her breast as she swung her gaze back to Matt. His face was drawn in fury.

"That bastard Cameron's going to try and water his cattle with or without your permission."

Lark gripped the reins, making Kentucky rear nervously. "We've got to stop them!"

"Ride for the family homes, Lark. Get the women, children, and old ones to the main house. I'll roust the wranglers out of their bunks and get them organized."

Sinking her heels into the stallion, Lark flew down the tree-clad slope. The stallion was tired, but he had heart, and as if sensing Lark's urgency as she leaned low over his neck, calling to him, he gave every last ounce of strength he possessed. There was so little time!

Lark was the first to ride into the yard, Matt not far behind her. He hauled his horse to a sliding halt in front of the bunkhouse. "Herter! Wake up! We've got trouble!"

Primo came galloping in from the opposite direction. *"Señor!"* he screamed. "Cattle are coming! There's a herd of at least a thousand no more than three miles away!"

"Primo, get over to the main house and get fifteen rifles and boxes of ammunition. Come back here and hand them out to everyone."

*"Sí, sí, señor!"* Primo whirled his horse around. Frank Herter stumbled onto the porch, still pulling up his pants. Two more wranglers followed in quick succession.

"Frank," Matt roared, "get the men saddled up! Cameron's got a herd of cattle heading straight for the ranch. Make it *pronto!*"

Herter spun around, issuing a series of curt orders to the sleepy-eyed men.

The mustang Matt rode whinnied plaintively as ten wranglers stumbled off the porch and raced toward the corral. Men shouted, horses neighed nervously, and clouds of dust rose as the wranglers slipped through the logs of the corral fence and grabbed the first horses they could catch.

Matt's eyes narrowed toward the hill where the cattle

would come. In the gray dawn light, there was nothing to indicate that Cameron's herd would be upon them in less than thirty minutes.

After awakening the residents of each house, Lark ordered the sleepy children and wide-eyed mothers to run for the homestead. Their husbands grabbed Levi's and shoved their arms through shirt sleeves as they ran across the yard to join the armed resistance. Then Lark rode back to the center of the busy yard.

"Matt!" she cried, bringing Kentucky to a halt in front of him. "I've got a plan!" She pointed to the southeast. "If we can turn the herd in time, there's a deep ravine we can drive them into. Cameron won't want to risk losing his herd to broken legs and necks. That might force him to turn back."

"If we can turn them," Matt agreed. "Does Cameron realize how close that ravine is or how deep?"

She shook her head. "No, it's covered with heavy underbrush. Only the people on the ranch know its location."

He nodded. "I'll ride out to meet the herd with Herter and the wranglers. I want you to stay with the women and children," he told her. He held her eyes, which were dark with fear and anxiety. "This time, you'll do as I say. And no argument, Lark."

She opened her mouth to protest, then shut it. The stormy look on Matt's face and the threat in his tone were very real. "All right. But we're not going to sit here at the ranch without any protection."

"There's plenty of ammo left. Give the women and Apaches who know how to shoot a gun or rifle and position them at every window. The only safe place will be the house. If that herd gets past us, it'll destroy everything in its path, but that house is strong enough to withstand their charge."

Nodding, Lark saw the wranglers mounting up. Suddenly she was more afraid than ever before. She gripped Matt's arm. "Please, be careful. I know Shanks is dead, but Cameron's hands are all dangerous."

Matt slid his gloved hand around Lark's slender neck and drew her against him. "I love you," he whispered hoarsely against her lips before covering them with a burning kiss.

Abruptly Matt released her and laid the spurs to his gelding, leaving Lark dazed in the saddle. The fifteen wranglers that worked at Gallagher Ranch rode by at a gallop, leaving her behind.

Dismounting, Lark led the stallion to the barn. She had no time to strip the saddle or bridle from him. Too much had to be done, and he'd be safe enough in the barn. Making a run for the house, she saw Maria waiting on the porch for her, wringing her hands.

"Get the rest of the rifles from the cabinet," Lark ordered. "And get the children into the bedrooms. Tell them to hide under the beds where they'll be safe."

"*Sí, patrona.*"

The Old Ones were waiting for Lark in the main room. Their serenity infused Lark with new confidence as she handed Ny-Oden a rifle and a box of ammunition.

"The Thunder Beings are with you, daughter," he told her.

The Thunder Beings were the forces that shaped and moved thunderstorms across Father Sky. For a long time, Lark had suspected that the shaman received his power from the Sky People. To tell her that the mighty warriors of the sky were with her meant powerful luck.

"Matt will need their power more than I will," she said, quickly dispensing rifles and bullets to the other Old Ones.

Ny-Oden gripped the rifle. "No, daughter. Before this is over, you will need their strength. This day, you will become a warrior, like your mother."

Shaken by the dire warning in the shaman's voice, Lark halted momentarily. "I don't understand . . ."

The shaman patted the rifle he held. "I will keep this loaded for you. You'll need it soon."

Lark had no more time to question the Apache. Whether Ny-Oden spoke in mysterious riddles to force her to be on guard, or if that's all his power had told him, Lark wasn't sure. Maria was calling to her, but as Lark walked swiftly down the hall, her thoughts turned to Matt. *Us'an,* she prayed fervently, *protect him.*

As they crested the ridge, Matt saw the cattle no more than two miles away, spread out across two hills. Frank Herter pulled up at his side. "I count twenty men," he shouted.

Matt nodded and threw up his hand to signal a halt. The wranglers drew to a stop around him, dust billowing in thick, choking clouds. Matt glanced over at Herter. "Let's stretch a line of men to match the length of the herd. I want you to watch for my signal. When I raise my hand, I want everyone to fire their rifles into the air. That ought to scare that herd back toward Cameron. Then we'll try and swing them south, toward the ravine."

Paco Hernandez pushed through the group. "What if those *hombres* fire at us, *señor?*"

"Then you fire back," Matt ordered.

He looked grimly at the Mexican, Negro, and Apache men sitting on nervous horses, their set faces mirroring their determination to win despite the odds against them. "Under no circumstances are you to let the herd break through our line. If we have to, we'll start shooting the cattle to stop them. If they get within half a mile of the ranch, they'll smell water and then no one will be able to halt them. They'll go crazy, and the women and children will be in danger. Understand?"

Every man nodded his head.

Matt twisted in the saddle. "Boa Juan?"

The Apache lifted his gaze. "Yes?"

"You've got the eyes of an eagle. Can you spot Cameron? Is he with his men?"

Boa Juan stood in the stirrups, peering intently toward the herd. "The *pindah* is there," he snarled. "There's a yellow-haired man riding next to him on a paint horse."

"Yellow hair, huh?" Herter snorted. He looked over at Matt. "That might be the gent who came to the ranch last week and prompted me to send that wire to you. I had a bad feeling about him. He's probably Shanks's replacement as top gun for Cameron's outfit."

"You're probably right, Frank." Matt held the ex-cavalryman's gaze. "You take the northern end and I'll stay here in the middle of the line. Paco, you take the south. Ready, men?"

Shouts went up and horses danced nervously beneath the reverberating cry. Matt raised his voice. "This is for Roarke Gallagher, men, and for his wife, Mourning Dove. Their dream built this place, but you've helped it become a reality. Defend it. Defend your families."

The wranglers gave hoarse shouts in three different languages. Matt ordered them to disperse and take their places along the line. As he spun his gelding around to face the herd, he wondered what Cameron was going to do now.

"Sonofabitch!" Cameron yelled, smashing his fist against his chap-covered thigh. He rode at the northern flank of the herd, staying clear of the dust raised by the cattle. "How in the hell did they find out we were coming?" he demanded of Devlin.

Devlin shrugged, checking the position of the holster on his right leg. "Doesn't matter, we got 'em outnumbered."

Fuming, Cameron clenched his teeth. "You see that cowboy on the black horse in the middle of their line?"

"Yeah."

"That's Kincaid." Cameron counted the Gallagher

ranch hands. "That's all of their hands, too. I don't see the breed. She's probably back at the ranch with the families. If all the men are here, that means that place is undefended."

"Which one you want me to finish off first? Or does it matter?"

"My boys will handle Kincaid. He'll be a moving target once we get close enough. You know where the ranch is. Ride there and find that bitch. Kill her. Then come back here and start picking off the vermin that's riding with her outfit."

Grinning, Devlin nodded. "Be right back, boss." He spurred his paint horse into an immediate gallop.

Cameron turned to his foreman. "Stampede them, Tom," he snarled. "Drive them right down the throat of that valley."

"Yes, sir!" The foreman pulled the gun from his holster, aiming the barrel skyward.

The Colt roared into the dawn, sending a rippling shock wave through the herd. Almost immediately, every hand followed the foreman's signal and fired his gun. Within moments, the cattle became a thundering herd that shook the hills. Excitement poured into Cameron's blood. He urged his horse into a gallop, unable to resist the awesome spectacle, wanting to be there to watch the herd destroy that pitiful line of wranglers waiting for them in the distance. And all the time, he kept his gaze fixed on Kincaid. "Finally, you bastard, I'm going to get you!"

A chill gripped Matt. The cattle were like a mighty engine bearing down on them. He remembered the times he and his men had had to charge enemy lines during the war. This was no different, he thought. Raising his gun, he fired it and then spurred his horse forward, into the melee.

The gelding took ground-eating strides, his neck stretched, his nostrils flared. Matt leaned low, looking right and left. His men were moving with him from the various points, heading straight into the flying hooves of the runaway herd.

Each pounding stride took him closer. Checking his men, Matt urged them forward at a faster pace. If the cattle smelled the water, everything would be lost. Each second counted. At last he could see the crazed eyes of the steers, their tongues hanging out the sides of their mouths, foam flecking their damp coats.

It was now or never. Matt began to fire his gun. The others did, too. The cattle began to slow their momentum toward the onrushing line of riders, caught between guns roaring in front of them and behind them. One old steer, a spotted longhorn, veered to the south to escape. Soon the rest of the herd blindly followed.

"No!" Cameron shrieked, riding into the laboring herd. "Turn them! Turn them!" he screamed to his men. Taking out his gun, he fired at the Gallagher hands. "Kill them!"

Cameron's bay grunted when a steer bolted in front of him. Shrieking above the plaintive mooing of the cattle, the gunfire, and the whinnying horses, Cameron tried to get his men to turn the herd back to the east, back toward Gallagher Ranch.

Matt saw Cameron gallop into the herd in an effort to get it to change direction. The cattle were frenzied and confused, caught between two walls of gunfire.

Cameron's lips peeled back in a snarl. Savagely kicking the bay, he forced the horse to gallop against the tide of moving cattle. He'd kill Kincaid himself! He raised his Colt, less than four hundred feet from his target. But just as he aimed, the gelding was hit broadside by a careening, wild-eyed steer. The gun flew out of Cameron's hand as the horse lost his footing.

Cameron's eyes bulged. He felt the horse going down . . . down beneath hundreds of cattle hooves. With a scream, he jerked back on the reins, hoping to pull the animal's head up so that he could regain his balance. No! The horse grunted and slammed into the ground. Cameron lifted his legs clear of the stirrups and somersaulted over the animal's head. Landing on his back, Cameron waited five seconds before the first steer plowed headlong into him.

# Chapter 18

"Teresa, no!"

The shriek from Consuelo in the foyer made Lark whirl around. She saw the woman try to grab her escaping ten-year-old daughter before she slipped out the front door of the house. Too late! The child ran toward the barn.

Consuelo sobbed and turned to Lark. "*Patrona,* she's frightened! I told her to stay here! Every time Teresa is scared, she runs to the barn to hide. Oh, *patrona,* what am I to do? The gunshots, they're so close!" The woman picked up her skirts, preparing to go after her daughter.

"No," Lark said, gripping Consuelo's arm. "I'll go. I know where she hides. Dry your tears, it will be all right."

Would it? Lark had heard gunshots echoing over the hill for the last fifteen minutes. Ny-Oden stood at the front door, holding out a rifle to her.

"Take this, daughter."

Lark eyed him warily. Unnerved by the gunfire and worry over Matt's safety, she didn't question his command and accepted the weapon, slipping out the front door.

The yard was deserted. Even the chickens seemed to have realized the danger coming their way and had hidden under the porch. The horses in the corral were restive, nickering nervously to one another.

Loping across the yard, Lark gripped the rifle in her left hand. Just as she neared the barn, a rifle shot shattered the tense stillness, exploding a geyser of dirt at her booted feet. Lark's eyes widened at the sight of a blond man dressed in wrangler's clothes mounted on a pinto. He was holding a Winchester aimed directly at her.

Lark threw herself to the ground and brought up her own rifle, firing off three shots. The bullets went wild, but they were enough to startle her assailant. The pinto leaped backward as the third shot landed very close to his hooves. The gunman had to concentrate on controlling his startled mount, lowering the rifle momentarily. Lark leaped to her feet and sprinted for the safety of the water trough. Two more shots were fired at her. The first bullet struck the water trough. The second dug savagely into the ground directly behind her.

Lark rolled to her belly behind the huge trough. Who was that, and why was he shooting at her? He had to be one of Cameron's men. Fear turned to rage. Just as Lark peeked above the trough to aim the rifle, gunfire erupted from the main house toward the horseman.

She watched as the gunman whirled his mount around and galloped out of the yard, heading deep into the woods for safety. With a hiss, Lark scrambled to her feet and raced into the barn. She found Teresa hiding in the haymow, only her huge brown eyes, tiny nose, and trembling mouth visible.

"Stay there!" Lark shouted to her, jerking open Kentucky's stall and leading him out. What if the man was a scout for Cameron? If Lark allowed him to return alive to tell Cameron that the ranch was practically defenseless, everyone's life would be in jeopardy.

Grimly she leaped into the saddle and dug her heels into the stallion. The animal leaped forward. Lark guided the stallion out of the barn and galloped across the yard. Once inside the tree line, she wove the horse rapidly among trees, sometimes so close that the bark brushed against her trousers and boots. Ahead, she spotted the white and sorrel pinto galloping in and around the towering pines.

"Run!" she urged the stallion. "Run like the wind that bore you!"

The horse strained, his long legs eating up the distance between Lark and the escaping rider. Lark leaned low, not wanting to become a target herself. She watched the pinto. The animal was tiring, the distance between them closing.

Just as Lark prepared to use the rifle, they broke out of the woods and onto the hill above the ranch. Lark called to the valiant stallion, urging him to produce every ounce of strength he possessed. She was barely cognizant of the herd of cattle or the gunfire to the south of her. The gunman changed direction, riding directly for the cattle in the distance. Lark dropped the reins on the stallion's neck and, guiding him with leg commands, steadied the weapon against her shoulder. She fired twice, but both bullets went wide.

The rider suddenly slowed. To Lark's surprise, he skidded his horse to a halt and spun around to face her, aiming his rifle at her. Without thinking, Lark fired off three shots in quick succession to cover her escape, then veered the stallion to the right. When she looked back, she saw the man topple off the horse and hit the ground. Pulling Kentucky to a trot, Lark circled back, her rifle ready.

Wary of a trick, she dismounted and approached the blond-haired man lying on the churned-up earth. To her shock, the man appeared dead. One of the bullets had caught him in the center of the chest. She stood, trembling. The bright crimson blood glinted in the sun's strengthening rays. With a cry of disgust, Lark sank to her knees, gagging.

Matt was the first to recognize the red stallion up on the hill. The cattle had been successfully turned back north and were heading for Cameron's property once again. He shouted at Herter to take over, then rode across the barren earth toward Lark.

Lark had dropped the rifle and was bent over, holding her stomach. Bile stung her mouth and tears filled her eyes.

"Lark?" Matt dismounted and ran to her side. "Are you wounded? Talk to me. Are you all right?" Pulling the curtain of black hair away from her face, he noticed how pale she was, then saw the dead drover ten feet away. Anger that she had disobeyed him warred with concern as he pulled Lark to her feet.

"I—I'm all right," she said, seeking and finding his arms.

"What the hell happened?"

Fighting her revulsion, Lark pulled away and looked up into Matt's drawn features, covered with sweat and dust. "I—I killed a man. He came to the ranch and tried to kill me. I was running to the barn to catch Teresa, she'd been frightened by the gunfire. I thought he was a scout for Cameron. I thought he was going back to tell him we were unprotected. I had to stop him. I had to . . ."

Matt's anger melted. Lark was safe. Taking her into his arms, he held her tightly against him. "You didn't have a choice under the circumstances," he whispered hoarsely. "I understand."

"Take me away from here, Matt. Please," she begged. "I'm so tired of all the bloodshed and fighting."

"I know," he whispered gruffly. "Come on, let's get back to Herter and the men." He set her behind his own saddle and then mounted in front of her, pulling the red stallion behind them.

With a sigh, Lark rested against Matt's strong back, her arms slipping around his waist. "You got the cattle turned?"

Matt rested his hand on her right thigh, wanting to make sure she didn't fall off in her shock and exhaustion. His eyes burned with anger. "Yes."

"How many went into the ravine?"

"Not many. Maybe fifty. Cameron's foreman saw what

was happening and had his men turn the rest of the herd north."

"And our men? Is anyone hurt?"

"I saw Primo fall."

Lark moaned. "No!"

Patting her leg reassuringly, he added, "We're still gathering everyone, honey. Let's not speculate. Hold on, I'm going to gallop."

To her right, Lark saw the fleeing cattle herd and the wranglers taking them back to Cameron's property. The wounded were being helped along by other hands. She wondered bitterly if Cameron was waiting back at his ranch to find out what had happened.

Matt pulled his horse to a halt in front of the assembled wranglers, who were waiting for them near the ravine. Frank Herter took off his hat, wiping his sweaty brow. "We're all accounted for, Miss Lark. Primo here got a flesh wound in the neck." He grinned, his teeth white against his dark mustache. "Knocked him out of the saddle, but he'll recover."

"We done shooed them off, Miss Lark," Rufus said. "Every last one of them sidewinders ran."

"You did well," Lark commended all of them. Primo held a bandanna over the bloody neck injury. Boa Juan had sustained a more serious wound to his thigh. Lark met and held the Apache's pain-filled eyes. "Can you make it back to the ranch?" she asked quietly.

"Yes."

"Have Maria help you until I can get there."

Boa Juan nodded and turned his horse away, walking the animal toward the ranch.

"Hey!" Paco called, "did you see Cameron get it?"

Lark looked up at Matt. "He was out here?"

Matt gestured to the hill behind them. "Yes. He was trying to get close enough to take a shot at me and rode his horse into the stampeding herd. The horse went down and Cameron was trampled."

Shutting her eyes, Lark swayed against Matt. "Is he dead?"

Herter laughed sourly. "If he ain't, he oughta be."

"I don't think so," Rufus spoke up loudly. "I saw them boys of his pickin' up what was left of his carcass and puttin' him on a horse."

Lark's stomach churned. She felt Matt's comforting hand upon her leg. "What was it father said," she asked Matt softly. "That a man reaps what he sows?"

Matt held her gaze, worry clearly etched in his eyes. "Cameron had it coming."

"Has it ended?" Lark asked him.

"I think it has. Cameron knows he can't run over us, law or no law. Shanks is dead."

"So is that fancy gunslinger with the blond hair," Frank pointed out.

"A hired gun?" Lark whispered, feeling even more ill than before. She hadn't gone up against an ordinary drover but a skilled killer.

Matt looked over at the grime-covered wranglers. "Let's go home men. The fighting is over."

It was early afternoon when the Gallagher sentry spotted Sheriff Cole coming and rode in to alert Matt. Matt left the bunkhouse, where he was checking on the injured wranglers. Boa Juan was asleep in his bunk. Primo had a headache from the fall he'd taken and was wearing a white bandage around his throat. Matt thanked the sentry and walked across the yard. The ranch was still in turmoil from the morning's attack. Matt could see the fear in the darting eyes of the children, who remained close to their mothers' skirts.

Stepping up on the porch, he took off his hat and entered the house. He found Lark sitting in the office talking to Maria and Consuelo. Both Mexican women excused themselves when he appeared in the doorway. Lark looked up, her eyes shadowed.

"The sheriff's coming," he told her quietly. "I think we ought to go out and meet him."

Lark rose wearily to her feet. She'd had no rest since returning to the ranch. All she wanted was to bathe and sleep, but right now that was impossible. She followed Matt out onto the porch.

"I wonder what Cole wants," she said.

Matt placed an arm around her stooped shoulders in an effort to give her some of his strength. "Cameron's probably filed some trumped-up charges against us for this morning's fiasco," he guessed.

Anger replaced Lark's exhaustion and she straightened up, throwing her shoulders back as Cole halted in front of them, his watery blue eyes fixed on her.

"I've been sent out here to call a halt to the range war between you and Mr. Cameron."

Lark stiffened. Range war? How ridiculous! She was about to speak up when Matt put a cautioning hand on her arm.

"Just what exactly does that mean, sheriff?" he demanded.

Cole spat to the left and leaned an elbow on the horn of his saddle. "Let's put it this way, Kincaid: Cameron damned near got killed this morning. He's gonna be laid up for a long time with a busted leg, a punctured lung, and half his face stoved in. He wants no more to do with you." Cole's eyes shifted to Lark. "Ya murdered one of his men."

"It was self-defense," Lark said.

"Cameron wants to make you a deal, Miss Gallagher. If you don't press charges against him, he won't press charges against you for killing his ranch hand, Bart Devlin."

Lark exchanged glances with Matt. Cameron wanted peace. She could vindicate herself of the murder charge Cole was threatening her with. She also realized this was Cameron's way of getting out of an embarrassing situation with his pride intact.

Matt placed an arm around Lark's shoulders. "We'll dispute Cameron's accusation. Lark killed that hired gun in self-defense. And just for your information, sheriff, you ought to know that I've requested a marshall from Phoenix who will investigate Cameron's entire campaign against the Gallagher Ranch. Further, we're going to tell him everything we know about the Ring."

Cole sat up straighter. "You *what?*"

Matt gave a twist of a smile. "You heard me. I think you'd better drop the murder charges against Lark, don't you?"

Clearing his throat, Cole nodded. "Er, yes, under the circumstances, I think yore right."

"And we won't bother Cameron so long as he leaves the Gallagher Ranch alone. Is that understood?"

Shifting uncomfortably in the saddle, Cole pulled the brim of the hat a little lower across his face. "I don't think Mr. Cameron will bother you again, Miss Gallagher. I think he'll see the wisdom of droppin' the charges. Good day."

Lark watched the sheriff turn his mount and take off at a swift trot. "It's really over now, isn't it?" she said softly.

Matt allowed her to sway against him and pressed a kiss to her hair. "Almost."

With a muffled protest, Lark lifted her chin. "Almost?"

He smiled gently, brushing her pale cheek. "Say you'll marry me tomorrow morning in Prescott. I think Father Mulcahy would like to do the honors."

Lark's eyes flew wide as she gazed up into his smiling features, into gray eyes that smoldered with promise, with love. Suddenly, all her weariness melted away. "What of your vow to hunt down Ga'n?" she asked in a hushed voice.

"We settled that score between us the night he told me Shanks had kidnapped you. Ga'n didn't have to tell me where you were, but he did. I had one family I loved taken from me, and I didn't want to lose you, too. I think he knew that. Will you be my wife, Lark?"

She closed her eyes, leaning heavily against Matt, hearing the ragged beat of his heart beneath her ear. His proposal was overwhelming to her, and it took several seconds to find her voice. "Yes, I'll marry you. I would become like a ghost without you at my side, Matt."

"You made me want to live again, honey. You made living in the present more important than dying for the past." He slid his arms around her, holding her tightly. "I'm convinced Ga'n will hang for horse stealing if he survives that gunshot wound."

Momentary sadness filled Lark. "Ga'n died the day his family was killed. When his sister was tortured to death by his own people, something snapped inside him and he went on a killing rampage that has lasted all these years. Perhaps death will be a welcome relief to him."

"He's a part of our past. We're going to look toward the future from now on, honey."

Matt's husky voice brought tremors through Lark and she embraced him with all her strength, suffused with joy.

He ran his fingers through her hair. "I'm letting the past go," he told her huskily. "Right now, all I'm concerned about is our present"—he brought her mouth to his—"and our future."

Dizzy with need, Lark rested her lips against his mouth. "Tomorrow morning," Matt whispered hoarsely, holding her shimmering eyes, "we'll be husband and wife. I want you at my side, Lark. I love your strength and your courage." He cradled her face. "But most of all, I love you." He pressed a series of kisses to her hairline. "I like the way you think . . ." He moved down to her mouth, finding it sweet and pliant for him. "And I like the way you speak to me. I want you to be mine. Forever."

With a cry of joy, Lark threw her arms around his massive shoulders. "Oh . . . Matt!" She stood on tiptoe, kissing his sensual mouth, happiness bursting in her breast. "You were special to me from the moment you came to the ranch." Her voice lowered with emotion. "Just as I pulled you from your grief, you also lifted me out of mine."

He smoothed her brow, outlined her nose, and caressed her soft lips. "We were both hostages to our past, Lark. But our hearts knew better and allowed us to love each other, regardless."

"We've freed each other, beloved heart. I never knew what life really was until you came into mine. Ny-Oden was right: you are my destiny."

Matt smiled gently, holding her close. "And you're my heart, golden cougar. Forever."

# EILEEN NAUMAN

These days, EILEEN NAUMAN divides her time between doing research for her novels, writing, and being with her family. Married fourteen years to her husband, David, the author confesses that life gets happier each year. On weekends, they become "rock hounds," panning for gold, finding semiprecious stones, or just simply enjoying the wilderness. Of course her mother, Ruth, comes along, and sometimes even her brother Brent and his expanding family join in the fun. The author explains that getting back to nature renews her and that by Monday morning she's eager to return to her word processor, because, more than anything else, Eileen loves to spin tales for her fans. She says, "I like to make my readers laugh, think, feel, and sometimes cry. After surviving forty years, I've found that love has sustained me through every kind of crisis. Maybe that's why I like to write about it so much."

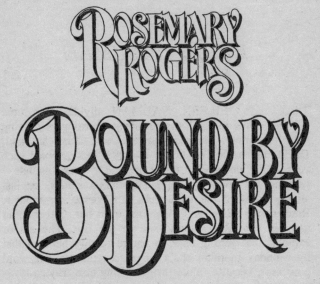